# THE STRANGER YOU KNOW

# ANDREA KANE

# THE STRANGER YOU KNOW

HARLEQUIN® MIRA®

ISBN-13: 978-0-7783-1501-8

THE STRANGER YOU KNOW

® HARLEQUIN®
™ www.Harlequin.com

**Printed in U.S.A.**

To Mom and Dad—
always in our hearts, forever our nucleus, and forever connected.
I love you and miss you both more than words can say.

# CHAPTER
## ONE

*April*
*Offices of Forensic Instincts, LLC*
*Tribeca, Manhattan, New York*

*Just one more body.*

*But this one had a name. And a grieving father who needed answers before he died.*

Casey Woods shoved the dozens of newspaper clippings that she'd collected into the thick file and slapped it shut. Then she leaned back in her chair, pressing her fingers to her closed eyelids.

It was Sunday, just after dawn. The streets were sleepy, occupied only by ambitious joggers and early morning coffee drinkers headed for the nearest Starbucks.

The brownstone that housed the private investigative firm Forensic Instincts was quiet.

Casey—the company president—was alone in the building, other than her bloodhound, Hero, who was stretched out by her feet, resting but alert. Casey had been up and working all night. Sleep wasn't on her agenda. Work was.

As usual, she sat at the large second-floor conference room table, her notes sprawled in front of her. There were plenty of smaller offices to choose from in the four-story brownstone. She could even have worked in bed, since the fourth floor was her apartment. But the main conference room infused her with a sense of discipline and productivity she didn't get anywhere else.

She needed to be productive now.

She wasn't doing a hell of a good job.

Purposefully, she picked up the notes she'd printed out last night after her client meeting and reread them. She was unnerved, not by the meeting but by the entire case. That didn't make her happy. She liked being in control. She almost always was.

This time was different. It wasn't because this new assignment had come from the NYPD rather than from the client himself, but because it established a connection that was both unexpected and shocking. Not in the eyes of the police, who would have no reason to spot the common thread. But in Casey's eyes? Instant recognition. A major punch in the gut, and a throwback to a time of her life that had been traumatic.

The tragedy remained unbearably painful, even after fifteen years.

And now? A different case. A different victim. But the same university. The same year. The same basic physical descriptions. One victim was murdered. One was missing—possibly murdered.

How could all that be a coincidence?

The murder, which was branded in Casey's memory, had

been tagged a cold case. Still, for her, it had never gone away. Now, out of the blue, it was back, albeit from an entirely different angle, centered on an entirely different girl. The enormity of it had hit her hard.

The first case—*her* case, the one involving *her* friend—had been the driving force that ultimately led her to form Forensic Instincts. She'd never forgotten, never gotten over it. And now, after talking to Mr. Olson last night, seeing how gaunt he was, reading the anguish in his hollow eyes, she found her own memories crashing back....

Casey nearly leaped from her chair as a firm hand was planted on her shoulder.

Instinctively, she whirled around to defend herself. Hero leaped up and began to bark at her abrupt reaction.

"Hey, both of you, take it easy. It's me." Patrick Lynch, one of her valued FI team members, walked around the conference table and lowered himself into a chair. Hero followed, and Patrick leaned down to scratch his ears. The human-scent evidence dog—the sole canine FI team member—sat down to enjoy the attention.

Simultaneously, a wall of floor-to-ceiling video screens began to glow, and a long green line formed across each panel, pulsing from left to right. "Good morning, Patrick," a computerized voice greeted him. The voice emanated from everywhere in the room, bending each line into the contours of the voice panel. "Casey, I apologize for not alerting you to Patrick's arrival before you became alarmed. But you did put me in sleep mode. I responded the instant I sensed activity." A pause. "Your heart rate has accelerated. There is no need."

"I can see that now, Yoda," Casey responded dryly. "A minute ago I thought I was being attacked." She'd long since ceased questioning the artificial intelligence system built by team member Ryan McKay. She just accepted that Ryan was a genius and Yoda was omniscient.

Patrick did the same. "Not to worry, Yoda," he said, addressing the voice. "I have a feeling Casey wasn't in a good place even before I walked in."

"Correct," Yoda confirmed. "She is under duress."

Casey didn't deny it. "You should be home with Adele," she told Patrick. "Your wife will have my head if she thinks I've got you slaving away on a Sunday morning without a damned good reason."

"Adele knows where I am, and she's fine with it." Patrick studied Casey's expression. "Besides, I couldn't sleep."

"So you drove in from New Jersey to visit, since you don't already spend enough hours at work?"

"No. I followed a hunch and made a phone call to Marc."

Marc Devereaux was Casey's first hire for Forensic Instincts, and her right hand. He was a former navy SEAL, former FBI agent and former member of the FBI's Behavioral Analysis Unit in Quantico, Virginia. He was the total package, and he'd been with Casey from the beginning.

"You haven't been yourself in days," Patrick continued. "Not since I introduced this case. Now I realize why. Marc was reluctant, but he finally filled me in on what he thought I should know. So here I am. I'm sorry, Casey. I never would have brought this case to the table if I had a clue what it meant to you personally, or what it would do to you."

"How could you have? Talk about a bizarre coincidence. What are the chances of that happening? And now that it has, my personal feelings shouldn't factor into it. The case is important. It has to be investigated."

Patrick arched a brow. "This is *me* you're talking to. Who's more apt to understand your internal conflict and ambivalence?"

Casey tucked a strand of shoulder-length red hair behind her ear. Patrick was right. He'd understand better than anyone. He'd lived through it firsthand.

He'd been an FBI agent for over thirty years before coming on board at Forensic Instincts. His joining the team had been the direct result of a child kidnapping case that had haunted him since early in his career and had resurfaced in a new form that was investigated by FI. The emotional reverberations had eaten away at him.

"This situation is different," Casey said. "You had no idea you were treading on my Achilles' heel. There's no need to feel guilty."

"I don't feel guilty. I feel responsible."

"You shouldn't. Captain Sharp is your friend."

Patrick nodded. He'd spent a chunk of his FBI time working the Joint Robbery Task Force with NYPD Captain Horace Sharp. They'd become tight. So when Horace had been approached by a dying neighbor, Daniel Olson, begging him for closure, convinced that his long-missing daughter had been murdered and pleading with him to find her body, Horace had agreed to try—*if* Forensic Instincts agreed to work the case jointly with his detectives. FI had the money and the manpower to give to this case-that-wasn't-a-case. The NYPD didn't. As a result, the retainer was an IOU—a favor to be redeemed sometime in the future. And the stipulation was that Forensic Instincts would work *with* the police detectives, not alone.

So, yes, Patrick had brought the case to the FI team. But from the minute they'd sat around the table discussing it, he'd picked up on some weird vibes. He'd waited patiently for someone to fill him in. No one did. Not in three days. So he'd finally taken the bull by the horns and called Marc. And now he got it. This was close to home for Casey—maybe *too* close.

Watching her now, seeing how conflicted she was, only substantiated his concerns.

"Should I tell Horace we can't help Mr. Olson?"

"No." Casey gave a hard shake of her head. "You shouldn't. Our team has the skills. I have the insight. My reaction is my problem. Not yours." She paused for a moment. "But at least now you know the reason for my crazy behavior. I should have told you myself. I just wasn't ready."

Casey rose, walking over to the windows and folding her arms across her chest. "I'm not handling this well. It pisses me off that, after all this time, I'm still so emotionally affected."

"Stop beating yourself up. It is what it is. Delving back into the past is both a blessing and a curse. It reopens old wounds. It makes them bleed. But sometimes it also helps them heal."

A hint of a smile. "When did you become so philosophical?"

"It's called the voice of experience."

"Yes, well, your experience held you emotionally hostage for thirty-two years."

"You're right. It did. Which is precisely why I'm the person you should be talking to."

Casey couldn't dispute that. "In your case, you found closure. I thought I'd found some level of closure with my case, too—when they located Holly's body. But I was wrong. I guess I'll never get closure. Because the bastard who raped and killed Holly when we were in college was never caught. And that's what I'd need to find peace."

"I know." Patrick, as always, was blunt. "I also know that might never happen."

"Unless it turns out that Jan Olson was murdered and that her killer is the same offender who raped and killed Holly," Casey said quietly. "It's possible, Patrick. The facts are closely related.

Maybe our investigation into Jan Olson's disappearance will lead us to Holly's killer."

Patrick didn't look surprised by Casey's theory. He'd obviously expected her mind to veer in that direction. It was natural, given the circumstances. "I hear you," he responded. "And I'm not arguing that the parallels are strong. But identifying the murderer after fifteen years? It's a long shot. And we were hired to find a body, not an offender."

"You don't need to remind me." Casey's jaw tightened. "Our job is to find the body of Daniel Olson's daughter. To help him find peace. Stage four pancreatic cancer is a death sentence. He's only got weeks or months to live."

"By giving him what he needs, we'll be paying tribute to your friend Holly," Patrick said. "You could look at it that way."

"My head knows that's true. But I'm having problems separating my head from my heart. I need objectivity in order to run this investigation." She turned to frown at Patrick. "And if you suggest that I take a backseat and let you head up this case—or worse, Marc, Ryan or Claire—I'll punch you first and call you a hypocrite second."

"Then lucky for me I wasn't going to do that. You've got a mean right hook." Patrick gave a wry smile—one that rapidly faded. "But, Casey, you're thrown by this. Badly. You've got to work through that. Why don't you tell me the details about your friend Holly? Marc was his usual tight-lipped self. He gave me just the need-to-know basics. You've discussed the details with him, and maybe even Ryan and Claire, but I think, in this situation, I'm the one who can help you focus."

"Marc knows more than anyone, except Hutch. Hutch is the only one I've totally broken down to."

Marc had introduced her to Hutch—Supervisory Special Agent

Kyle Hutchinson—who was currently with the FBI's Behavioral Analysis Unit, and who'd become the man in Casey's life.

"Okay, so Hutch and Marc know," Patrick acknowledged. "Now it's time you talked to a kindred spirit—me."

"You could have researched the case yourself," Casey pointed out. "You certainly have the contacts."

"You're right. I do. But they could only supply me with facts. They couldn't offer me your perspective. Only you can. So I'm listening."

Casey nodded, walking over to make two cups of black coffee from their Keurig, then returning to the conference room table.

She handed a cup to Patrick, then took her own cup and sat down.

"I was a freshman at Columbia. My friend Holly Stevens lived off campus. She was a loner, very shy and reserved. She had a few close friends. I was one of them. We met in Psych 101 and hit it off. One day, she told me she sensed she was being followed, even stalked. I urged her to go to the police. She did. They had nothing solid to work with, so they arranged for a few patrol cars to keep an eye on her apartment. It wasn't enough."

Casey drew a slow, unsteady breath, staring into her coffee as she spoke. "Holly's body was found wrapped in a canvas tarp and tossed in a Dumpster a few weeks later. She'd been raped and murdered. It was a nightmare—one that could have been avoided with the proper resources."

"You weren't those resources, Casey. Not back then."

"But I was the one Holly confided in. Irrational as it might seem, I always felt that maybe I missed an opportunity to prevent what happened."

"That irrationality is what's getting in your way now. Lose it. You may not have had the right resources to do what should've been done then, but you have the right tools for what you need to do *now*. You have Forensic Instincts."

"Which is why I can't let this case slip through my fingers. Not that I blame the police for what happened to Holly. I don't. They did all they could. But a private investigative firm with our expertise could have done more. We could have focused our manpower and our skills on her predicament, dug deeper, put enough security on her to keep her safe. But, as you said, we didn't exist, not then. Now we do. And now I've been approached to help a dying man find his daughter's body—a man whose daughter could very well have been killed by the same psycho pervert who killed Holly. The time frame fits. The location fits. The victimology fits. If I'm right, that would make this bastard a repeat offender, maybe a serial killer. Which paints an even more gruesome story. He was never caught. Jan Olson's body was never found. How many others were there?"

"That's a question we might or might not be able to answer." Patrick took a deep swallow of coffee, continuing to share his thoughts with Casey in a calm, straightforward manner. "I know you want to go back and solve it all—catch the killer, assign names to all his victims and provide closure for all the families involved. Maybe we can make that happen. I don't know. What I do know is that the best way to increase our odds is to fulfill our obligation."

*Follow the case that's been handed to us. Find Jan Olson's body.*

"That's how it was with me, remember? Start with the present, step back into the past. This process is going to take you down some dark alleys. You're going to lose a lot of sleep and relive some painful memories. But you need this. Otherwise, you would have squashed the case the minute I brought it to the team. You knew it was too close to home, that you probably should refer it out. But you didn't. You're the president of Fo-

rensic Instincts. You made the call for us to take on the case—
and you made it without missing a beat."

"You're right," Casey conceded. "I couldn't have lived with
myself if I didn't see this through. For many reasons. Daniel Olson is dying. And if his theory is correct, if his daughter
really did suffer the same fate as Holly, then she was raped, killed
and dumped…somewhere. No father should have to die with
those kinds of unanswered questions, and without his daughter's body being found. Plus, if the offender really was the same
bastard who did that to Holly, then I have twice the motiva-
tion to solve this."

"Agreed." Patrick reached over and scooped up Casey's notes.
"So let's review your interview with Daniel Olson. Then we'll
go over all the newspaper articles you compiled. I got a glimpse
of them. You dug up everything, not only about Jan's disappearance, but about the disappearances of all young women who
lived in Manhattan during a five-year time span."

"I'm going to give the whole pile of them to Ryan and have
him set up a database. But I know it's a stretch. Most of those
young women probably just packed up and moved."

"Well, it's up to us to figure that out. So let's go. If anything
rings a bell or recalls a memory that in any way relates to Holly,
we'll zero in on it. Go with your gut. No one has better instincts than you do."

Casey smiled. "You'd make a great life coach."

"Not really. I've just been where you are. It took me thirty-
two years to get my answers. Maybe we can come up with yours
in half that time. Let's figure out what happened to Jan Olson.
And let's find her."

# CHAPTER
## TWO

Glen Fisher lay on his cot in the cell of Auburn State Correctional Facility, a maximum security prison in upstate New York.

He folded his hands behind his head and stared up at the concrete ceiling. First, six weeks in Downstate Correctional Facility undergoing all those ridiculous evaluations and test. And now? Seven months, two weeks and four days in here. More than half a year of his life shot to hell. Thanks to that firecrotch.

One day blended into the next. A meal. His job in the mail room. Another meal. Exercise. Mail again. Back to his cell. A gloomy little six-by-eight hole with a sink, a toilet, a cot, a shelf and bars that separated him from a dark hall equipped with a centrally controlled tear gas system.

Mundane. Boring. A waste of his life.

His lawyer had been a wimp. He should've driven home the coercion plea and gotten him off. Instead, the judge had thrown out the defendant's plea, the evidence had been ruled admissible and here he was, facing a life sentence.

His lawyer was long gone. Good riddance. Representing himself was the smartest thing he could do. He continually found new loopholes. He'd filed another appeal last week. Eventually, maybe those idiots on the parole board would listen to him. All they kept reiterating over and over like some stupid litany was the list of rapes and homicides he'd been convicted of. They couldn't see that he'd done the world a favor.

Considering law enforcement's one-dimensional stupidity, he should have kept his fucking mouth shut when he'd been cornered. Even if that Neanderthal from Forensic Instincts had started the ball rolling by practically killing him in the alley. Uncharacteristically, Glen had been caught off guard.

Never again.

They'd found the bodies just where he said they'd be. And the jury—not one of whom had an ounce of brains—had labeled him scum. They'd focused only on the words *rape* and *murder.* Couldn't see past them. Couldn't know what he knew about those whores. Who they were. What they were. What they did to their victims.

The entire system was useless. It was up to him to bypass it and finish what he'd started.

He pulled out his drawing tablet and crayons and began another detailed sketch. It slowly came alive. Even the outline excited him. Especially when he made sweeping crimson strokes across the page.

A smug smile twisted his lips. Funny thing about life. It had a way of evening out.

He might have lost his freedom.

But Casey Woods was about to lose a whole lot more.

*Columbia University*
*John Jay Hall*

Cramming for exams sucked ass.

Nick Anderson opened his dorm room door, gazing sympathetically at the regular crowd—a half dozen of his bleary-eyed dorm mates. They all traipsed in and stuffed five-dollar bills into his empty beer stein to chip in for the pizza that was about to be delivered. The head count had been taken at around ten o'clock. Now it was almost midnight. They'd studied enough. Their brains were fried. It was time to stuff their faces, drink some beer and unwind.

"Did you get pepperoni?" Donna Altwood asked. She'd just come out of the shower. She was wearing damp sweats, with a wet mane of long blond hair hanging down her back. She looked scrubbed clean, stressed and cranky. Then again, she was pre-med, and studied more hours than there were in a day.

"Yup," Nick assured her. "One deluxe, one half pepperoni, half sausage and one plain. You can tip me later."

"Nice," Charlie Green muttered. "The sausage and the pepperoni will give me heartburn. That'll keep me awake. And if I'm awake, I'll study." He set down the case of Miller Lite he'd brought, since it was his turn to contribute the beer.

"No, you won't," Dominick Peretti said. "You'll get wasted and sleep through your classes." He grinned. Dom didn't have a mean bone in his body. He was just Dom—direct, comfortable in his own skin. So no one was offended by his comments.

"Getting wasted sounds good." Amy Sheehan wasn't smiling. Then again, she didn't need to. She was one of those girls every other girl wanted to look like—great body, long, thick black hair, huge blue eyes. Worse, she wasn't even arrogant about it.

That made it really hard to hate her. "My brain's not taking in anything tonight. It's done. So I might as well be, too, right?"

Kenny Bishop didn't say anything. He rarely did. He didn't hang out with this crowd, except to eat pizza and drink beer. He didn't really hang out with anyone. He was a loner. Brilliant. Weird. And in his own world. Maybe he was high half the time. No one knew. Or asked. He just sat on the floor, his head against the bed frame, his curly hair a dark mop. His dark eyes were hooded but somehow intense as he watched the rest of the group talk and complain. Whatever he was thinking, he kept it to himself. But he didn't bother anyone, and he always paid promptly, so no one objected to him being there.

"My bio professor is a tool," Nick complained. "The only one he makes sense to is him."

"Serves you right," Donna retorted. "You satisfied your science requirements two semesters ago. Who the hell takes advanced bio when they don't have to?"

"Spoken like a dedicated future doctor," Dom said, rising to get himself a beer.

Donna raised her brows. "I *have* to take those courses," she reminded Dom. "Nick's a history major. He doesn't have to suffer."

"True."

"Have you ever studied ancient Greece?" Nick asked. "Trust me, that's suffering."

A knock interrupted the conversation. "Ah, finally. Provisions." Nick headed over and opened the door. "Hey, Robbie." He greeted the solid guy in the striped Pizza King T-shirt who was standing on the threshold with three steaming boxes. "You got here just in time. We were either going to starve or eat one another."

"That's pretty harsh." Robbie grinned. "I'm glad I got here

before any of that happened." He looked a little like the Cheshire cat, stripes and all. Only he couldn't perform magic, so he was paying his way through grad school by working late-night pizza delivery shifts.

"Hi, guys," he said, glancing into the room and waving.

They all waved back. They liked Robbie, and they knew the feeling was mutual. And why not? They called three times a week to order pizza or hot sandwiches, and they always gave him a good tip. Nice frequency, nice amount of cash. And with the price of grad school credits skyrocketing, every little bit helped.

Robbie passed the boxes to Nick, along with a white bag. "Almost closing time means leftover garlic bread," he explained. "I figured you'd want it."

"Want it?" Dom piped up. "Pass it this way. I'll make it disappear before we even settle up."

Robbie chuckled. "Now why did I know you'd be the first voice I heard?"

"Because you know me. Garlic bread and I are like this." Dom held up two crossed fingers.

"I wish I could say eat it all, there'll be more pizza for us," Donna said. "But you're a bottomless pit. You'll swallow all the garlic bread and half a pizza before I can finish my first slice." She sighed. "It sucks that guys can eat like that and never gain a pound."

"It also sucks that we chip in as much cash as they do, and eat a fraction of the amount," Amy noted.

"True. I vote that we revisit the contribution breakdown," Donna said.

"Forget it. I'm broke." Nick placed the pizza boxes on his desk and tossed the bag of garlic bread to Dom. "Save some for the rest of us. And don't expect us to wait. We're eating all these pizzas, including your share, if you don't hurry up."

There was a tentative knock on the open door, and Josh Lochman poked his head around the corner. He was the star linebacker for the Columbia Lions and was built like a young Arnold Schwarzenegger, but with a thick head of dark hair and equally dark eyes. Josh wasn't a frequent participant in these late-night pizza breaks, but he did drop by once in a while. And he never came empty-handed.

"Hey, guys," he greeted them. He held up an extrawide pizza box, simultaneously clapping Robbie on the shoulder. "These calzones were delivered by the man himself a few minutes ago. Four extralarge. After a two-hour workout, I could eat them all myself. But I won't. Am I welcome?"

"By all means." Nick beckoned him in. "Join the party. Anyone bearing food is welcome."

While Josh settled on the floor, Nick picked up the contributions container. He already knew how much the bill was; the cheery voice at the other end of the phone had told him when he ordered. He counted out the cash, then added twenty percent for Robbie.

"Here you go, my friend." He handed it to him. "Although I could tell you a dozen things more worthwhile to spend it on than school."

Robbie took the cash gratefully. He stuffed the bills in his money pouch and the rest in his pocket. "I'm sure you could. But I'm hell-bent on that degree." He waved. "Thanks, guys. You have a good night."

That wasn't an issue. The minute the door shut, they attacked the pizzas, calzones and garlic bread as if they hadn't eaten in days.

"Hey," Amy complained. "Give Donna and me a head start next time. We can't chew as fast as you male animals."

"No chance." Dom grinned. "Be happy I shared the garlic bread. I could have eaten the whole thing."

Charlie glanced up, swallowing his mouthful of sausage pie. "Where's Kendra?" he asked. "She said she'd be coming by on her way back from the library."

Donna shrugged. "You know Kendra. She probably got involved in a philosophy book and lost track of time. But we'll save her some pizza, right, guys?"

The guys exchanged reluctant glances. "We'll give her fifteen more minutes. Then all bets are off," Dom decided for them.

"Fine." Donna rolled her eyes. "It's touching how far you're willing to go for a friend."

Ten minutes later, Kendra opened the door and hurried in. She looked the way she always looked—rumpled and rushed. Her curly auburn hair was tousled, and her eyes were glazed from too much reading. She yanked off her coat, tossed it somewhere and grabbed the closest pizza box.

"What's left—one slice or two?" she asked dryly.

"We fought for you," Donna told her. "So there might be some hope of leftovers. What kept you—Plato?"

Kendra shook her head. "In this case, no. I was actually in the parking lot. Some sedan blocked in Robbie's pizza delivery truck and he was having trouble getting out. I couldn't see the driver because the windows were tinted. But whoever it was, he or she was in no hurry to move, and didn't catch on until Robbie tapped on the window. The sketchbag only shifted over enough for Robbie to inch his way out and then went back to whatever he was doing."

"Probably texting someone," Amy said in disgust. "I feel sorry for delivery people. Same with maintenance workers. People treat them like they're invisible. The hired help. It sucks."

Kendra nodded. "I was half tempted to go over and rip the

driver a new one. But Robbie waved me away, like it was no big deal. He's too sweet for his own good. Anyway, he just drove off and probably chalked it up to another crappy aspect of the job."

"Probably."

They dropped the subject and returned to the important issue at hand—eating.

But outside, the dark sedan continued to sit there, motor running, the driver intently staring at their window.

# CHAPTER
## THREE

The entire Forensic Instincts team gathered around the conference room table, ready to begin their day and their morning briefing.

As of now, the team consisted of five members, six counting Hero. Marc and Ryan had been with Casey from the onset. Patrick and Claire had come on board last year, around the same time that Hero had been retired from the FBI Canine Unit and Casey had adopted him. Each team member was extraordinary in his or her own way. Casey was the behaviorist, whose sharp mind and keen instincts about people, their body language, their responses and reactions, was the cornerstone of Forensic Instincts. Marc was a true right hand—brilliant at everything from his mental to his psychological to his physical capabilities. Ryan was both a strategic and a technical genius. Claire was a gifted intuitive, a psychic in the eyes of most, although she hated that term, and preferred to refer to herself as a claircognizant.

Patrick was a lifelong trained investigator. And Hero had an ol-
factory sense that was incomparable.

They were a very tight group, a real professional family. Any
one of them would risk it all for the others. And that was a loyalty to which no dollar amount could be ascribed.

Now, Casey sat at the head of the table, fingers linked in front
of her, and began the morning catch-up session.

"As you all know, I had my second meeting with Daniel Olson
last evening. He's convinced that something ugly happened to
his daughter. And I'm apt to agree. He gave me every scrap of
information he had on Jan's life at the time of her disappearance.
There's nothing there to suggest that she'd just take off without ever contacting her family again. So I took it another step."

She indicated the file on the table in front of her. "I put this
together. It's an assortment of newspaper articles relating to
crimes—and potential crimes—against college-age girls in the
New York City area during the five-year period surrounding
the time when Jan vanished. Ryan, I'd like you to assimilate all
this and set up a database we can follow."

Ryan leaned back in his chair and eyed Casey for a second,
then spoke up in his usual blunt manner. "Okay. But before
we get into details, can we address the elephant in the room?"

Claire Hedgleigh winced. Ryan's oblivion to sensitive subjects never ceased to astound her. He might be brilliant, but he
was about as tactful as a freight train.

"I think we should stick to the facts of the case," she said,
shooting Ryan a hard stare. "We have an investigation to conduct."

"Stick to the facts?" Ryan looked more amused than put off.
"That's a joke coming from you, Claire-voyant. You get inside
people's heads and play touchy-feely with inanimate objects.
Now you're suddenly the scientist of the group?"

"She's just being sensitive to my feelings." Casey broke up the argument before it could begin. She took a deep breath, then continued. "Look. You all know varying amounts about my personal connection to this case. I'll lay out the whole thing for you in a short summary, and then we'll all be on the same page. But, as Patrick so astutely pointed out to me, the only way I'll find any level of peace or closure in my own situation is to throw myself into this investigation. So once I've spoken my piece, let's leave it and get to what matters—finding out what happened to Jan Olson."

Quietly and succinctly, she retold the story she'd told Patrick last night.

"So the man who raped and killed your friend and whoever's responsible for Jan Olson's disappearance—you *do* think it's the same person," Ryan responded the instant she'd finished. He'd known enough about Casey's past to have skimmed the surface of Holly Stevens's tragic murder.

"I don't *know* anything," Casey replied. "Other than the fact that the victimology is the same, as is the time frame. I don't see any overlaps in the two girls' lives. So I can't allow myself to assume anything."

"Yeah, but it's a very real possibility." Ryan studied Casey with those probing blue eyes. "The bottom line is, you're never going to be objective about this case. Do you think you should turn over the reins to one of us?"

"Probably. But I'm not going to." Casey spoke as bluntly as Ryan, meeting his stare head-on. She wasn't offended by his directness; that was Ryan. He spoke his mind, but he didn't have a mean or disloyal bone in his body. "I won't lie and say that solving Holly's murder wouldn't be cathartic for me. But my main goal is finding out what happened to Jan Olson. My skill set makes me best qualified to run the show. Plus, I'm the boss." A glint of humor glittered in her eyes. "That means the final decision is mine. And I've made it."

Ryan nodded. This was one of those times when arguing would be futile. This wasn't going to be put to a vote. Casey was making that infinitely clear.

"Don't look so dubious." Casey responded to the expression on Ryan's face. "You're welcome to call me on the carpet if I get off track." A quick glance around the room. "You all are." She opened the file. "I've scanned the notes from my two interviews with Daniel Olson, plus all the documents in this file. Yoda?"

"Everything is stored on the Forensic Instincts server dedicated to current investigations," Yoda replied. "Including several photos of Jan Olson at age nineteen. All the pertinent material is indexed and readily available to the entire team."

"Good." Casey nodded. "I've divvied up initial assignments." She looked from Ryan to Marc. "Jan was a typical college kid. She didn't exactly confide in her father. So he's not the best source of information. But he did give me the name of Jan's best friend. It's Brenda Miller. I don't know where she is, if she's married or single or if she still goes by that name. Ryan, you find out. Marc, you go and talk to her. Get the full picture on Jan Olson. Boyfriends, friends, roommates, favorite hangouts, state of mind—anything Brenda can remember. Including enemies."

"Done," Marc responded.

"Once Marc has *that* info, I'll track down all those people," Ryan said.

Casey's gaze flickered to Patrick. "After that, you and Marc split the list and interview each and every person on it. We need to build a real profile on Jan Olson."

"And fast," Patrick said. "So, at the same time, Ryan can build a real timeline on her activities."

"No problem." Ryan scribbled down some notes. "Besides

setting up that database, I'll start poking into Jan's college schedules. Her transcripts will be on file. That'll give me her course-
work and her professors. It's a good start."

Casey nodded again. "Claire, you, Hero and I are meeting
with Daniel Olson early this evening at his home in Brooklyn.
Jan grew up there. Her bedroom is still relatively unchanged.
Mr. Olson has agreed to let you explore her room and handle
any personal articles you're drawn to. He's also agreed to let Hero
sniff out the area. We'll make some scent pads. I know it's been
fifteen years. But they still might come in handy."

"Hell, yes," Ryan agreed. "Hero can isolate her scent in a
dorm or apartment where hundreds of people have lived since.
Right, boy?"

The bloodhound gazed at Ryan and let out a quiet woof. He
recognized his name. He knew he was being discussed. And he
sensed the serious atmosphere in the room. Thanks to his training in the FBI Canine Unit, he'd be as disciplined about performing his job as any other FI team member.

"Casey, did you request your friend Holly's file?" Marc asked.

"Yes. The precinct is going through their fifteen-year-old cold
case files to hunt it down. I should have it sometime today. I
doubt there's anything substantive in it. It's probably a one-page
complaint and a one-page police report. But definitely review it
once we have it in our hands. Maybe you'll see a fact or a cor-
relation there that I missed or have forgotten."

No one said it aloud, but they all knew that Casey hadn't forgotten a damned thing about Holly's murder. She had a steel-
trap mind even when it applied to cases she wasn't personally
vested in. And in this situation? She'd recall every minute detail.

"We'll all review it as soon as it comes in," Marc replied, tact-
fully sidestepping the obvious. "We'll also dig more deeply into
Holly's life. There might be things about her you didn't know,

things that match up with Jan Olson's life—incidents, activities, people. Ryan's database will be key in determining that. But, in the interim, if one of us spots a clue or a connection, you'll hear about it. Also, while we wait, I'm going to review the details of your second interview with Daniel Olson. Maybe I can find another starting point we haven't considered."

"And I'm going to do an in-depth search on Holly Stevens." Ryan stated his intentions up front. "I want to have a workup to go along with your memories and that skinny police report. The more we know about her before the file even reaches us, the faster we can act."

If Ryan expected Casey to be upset, he was wrong.

"I agree with you," she told Ryan. "Find out whatever you can. Patrick and I pored over Jan Olson's file last night, and nothing jumped out at me. You're right. Holly and I were friends. But she could have been involved in any number of things with any number of people I knew nothing about. So dig hard. If there's even the slightest parallel between Holly's and Jan's lives, I want to pounce on it."

Tim Grant was a prison guard at Auburn Correctional Facility. He didn't make a hell of a lot of money, and he had two daughters in high school whom he wanted to put through college. Lacy was an All-State soccer player and Sarah's grades were sky-high. But in today's world, neither was enough to ensure a scholarship to a good school. So he worked a second job for a private security company. One of the guys he worked with, Bob Farrell, was a retired NYPD detective from the Twenty-sixth Precinct, the precinct in which Columbia University fell. Bob had a beautiful vacation house in the Thousand Islands, and a new young wife who spent money faster than his retirement checks could pay the credit card companies. Not to mention his whopping alimony checks and four grandkids he liked to spoil. So he needed extra cash—lots of it.

Bob had kept up his ties to the precinct and nurtured relationships with others, more than enough so that he could gain information about current cases—especially ones that precinct captains were way too busy to care about. The Jan Olson case fell into that category, particularly since it had been farmed out to Forensic Instincts. So when Tim asked him to dig into the investigation and find out what was going on, it was an easy assignment to fulfill. And it came as no surprise that the information was being requested, given that part of his job was to keep tabs on whatever Forensic Instincts was doing.

Passing along whatever he learned to Tim was a welcome task, considering the generous payment he got in return. He knew that Tim made a bundle from the arrangement, and that was just fine with him. After all, Tim was the one who took the risk and delivered the information. Bob didn't know the name of the prisoner who received it. And he didn't want to know. He had a creepy feeling that the guy pulling the strings was one scary felon.

Tim was thinking much the same thing as he approached Glen Fisher's cell that afternoon. He glanced inside, caught a glimpse of Fisher lying on his cot and found his gaze drawn to the sketch the inmate was working on. The minute he saw it, he flinched, wishing he'd never looked. The perverse drawing was like all the others. It depicted the figure of a woman sprawled on the ground, covered by more slashing strokes of bright red than his stomach could take. The guy was a psycho. Tim didn't doubt it for a minute. He not only saw it in his drawings, he felt it every time Fisher stared him down, emotionlessly reiterating what was expected of him. The look in Fisher's eyes was terrifying—empty as death. With his usual sense of dread, Tim did what he had to, comforting himself with the fact that this nutcase was never getting out of here and could therefore do nothing with the information he was given but indulge his sick fantasies. At least that was what Tim prayed.

"Hey," he said quietly, standing close to the cell.

Fisher rolled over and rose from his cot, putting down his drawing materials and walking over to face Tim through the iron bars.

"What do you have for me?" he asked—a demand, not a question.

"The Stevens girl's file is being dug up from the Twenty-sixth Precinct's cold cases and sent to Forensic Instincts," Tim reported in a low tone. "It might take a little time, since the crime happened fifteen years ago. In the meantime, Casey Woods talked to Olson again last night. From what I'm hearing, she's definitely looking for some kind of connection between the past and the present."

"Good. That'll keep her busy. What about the cops?"

Tim shook his head. "There's no buzz at the Twenty-sixth Precinct about any connections to recent crimes. The same goes for the Ninth," he added, referring to the precinct that had jurisdiction over Tompkins Square—the district where Fisher had been set up and arrested.

"So Casey Woods is spinning her wheels." Fisher shrugged. "Just as well. It'll kill time. And make things interesting..."

He didn't elaborate. And Tim didn't ask.

Fisher continued to study him with that lethal stare. "I hear that things are going well for you. If that Lacy of yours keeps scoring goals like she did at last night's soccer game, you can spend my money on a nice vacation for you and the missus, because you won't need it for college. And Sarah? Between her GPA and that gorgeous red hair I keep hearing about, she's got an equally bright future. Incredible daughters you've got. Pretty, too. You should be very proud—and very careful. It's a scary world out there."

Tim's fingers curled so tightly around the cell bars that his knuckles turned white. He wished he could choke the life out of Fisher.

"Calm down," Fisher said, his lips curving a bit at Tim's reaction. "You already have high blood pressure. You don't want to make it worse. Besides, not to worry. You're doing your job. I've already arranged to have a payment wired to your bank account tomorrow." A long, drawn-out pause. "But we're just getting started. I want you to keep on this every waking minute."

Tim said nothing. He just turned and walked away.

He might be protecting his family.

But he had a sick feeling that he was digging himself an early grave.

# CHAPTER
## FOUR

Daniel Olson's house was a typical home in the Bensonhurst section of Brooklyn. A two-story Cape Cod on a quiet side street, it sat on a small parcel of land between two similar houses, and had a tiny front lawn and a stone pavement leading to the front door.

Olson opened the door himself when Casey, Claire and Hero arrived, along with a tote bag and their STU-100—or "canine vacuum," as Ryan called it—from which Casey would make scent pads for Hero. Casey introduced Claire and then Hero, both of whom Mr. Olson had expected.

Claire shook the older man's hand, almost wincing with pain upon contact. Casey had described his condition to the whole FI team. Still, Claire could feel death emanate from every pore of his body. She also felt a wave of bleakness when she looked at him. It didn't take a psychic to know that the man had very little time left. He was frail and wan, with deep, dark circles under his eyes. But the sadness in those eyes had nothing to do with

death, which Claire sensed he'd made peace with. It had everything to do with finding closure with regard to his daughter.

"Come in," he invited them, stepping aside so they could
cross the threshold into the foyer. "Can I offer you anything?
Maybe some water for your dog?"

"Nothing, thank you." Casey spoke up for the three of them.
The last thing they wanted was for this poor ill man to wait on
them. "As I told you last night, we just want to see Jan's room,
physically handle anything of hers that had special meaning and
make scent pads for Hero. We'll stay only as long as necessary."

Olson picked up on the compassion in Casey's voice and gave
a slight shake of his head. "I appreciate your consideration. But
please, take your time. Anything that can help you, any opportunity you see that can aid you in finding out what happened to
Jan—please take it. Quite frankly, you truly are my last hope."

"We'll do everything we can." Casey could already feel the
knot in her stomach tightening. She wanted to dash upstairs
and uncover their answers in one fell swoop. It wasn't going to
happen. She had to be patient. But she wasn't going to fail, either. She was going to give this man the closure he needed, and
maybe find that same closure for herself.

They all filed upstairs. Mr. Olson led them to the bedroom
on the left side of the corridor that belonged to Jan, gesturing
for them to go in. He himself hesitated in the doorway, glancing from Claire to Casey.

"I don't know how this works," he confessed. "Is it better if I
leave you to your own devices? Or is it better if I stay? Whatever
Ms. Hedgleigh's process is, I don't want to interfere."

Claire gave him that gentle smile of hers. "Please stay," she
said. "I might have questions for you. If I'm drawn to a particular object, I want you to tell me about it—everything you re-

member about its place in Jan's life. You're her father. You helped raise her. You'd be surprised how helpful your input can be."

The older man sighed. "I wish Jan's mother was still alive. She'd remember far more than I do. She was a traditional house-wife. She believed in staying home during Jan's younger years. She was so much more familiar with the details of her life than I am."

"Jan is an only child?" Claire asked, careful to use the pres-ent tense. There was no point in upsetting Mr. Olson, not until they had concrete proof that Jan was dead.

He nodded. "We wanted more children. But it wasn't meant to be."

Casey gazed at the room as Claire made her way slowly around. It was the bedroom of an average teenage girl—white furniture, peacock blue walls, a matching comforter and cur-tains and possessions that ranged from the eye shadow and lip gloss of a young adult to the figurines and stuffed animals of a young girl.

"When did Jan last redecorate?" Casey asked.

"In high school," her father replied. "The furniture hasn't changed, just the arrangement of the pieces. She painted the walls and picked out the matching bed and window coverings. But she kept her favorite things from childhood."

"Is this one of them?" Claire was holding a child's jewelry box, which, when opened, displayed a little spinning ballerina.

Olson nodded. "That was a gift from her grandparents. She got it when she was six. The jewelry that went inside it changed over the years, but the box itself stayed the same, right down to its position on her dresser."

Claire was only half listening. She wore a look of intense con-centration. "Happy memories," she murmured. "Lots of warm, positive energy." She fingered a few of the pieces inside—a slim bangle bracelet, a silver chain necklace, a pair of gold stud earrings—then placed the box back on the dresser and turned to squat beside a book bag. "When did she get this?" she asked, letting her fingertips brush the dark maroon canvas.

Mr. Olson's expression clouded. "Right before she left for college. Her mother and I used to tease her that it weighed more than she did because of the number of books she dragged around."

"How did it get to your house?" Casey asked at once. "Did Jan leave it here on her last trip home, or was it returned to you after she disappeared?"

"The latter." He swallowed. "Columbia returned it to us when they cleaned out her dorm room." He gestured at the book bag. "Feel free to look inside. Lord only knows that I have, dozens of times. Textbooks, notebooks and her calendar are all you'll find. I searched every nook and cranny."

"A calendar?" Casey jumped on that one. "You didn't mention that in our last conversation. And it wasn't in the material you brought me."

Olson sighed. "Like I said, I pored over it time after time. There's nothing in there but assignments that were due. No names, no specific dates, nothing. I saw no purpose in bringing it. If you feel otherwise, if you think I might have missed something, it's yours to review."

Casey nodded. She was watching Claire as she unzipped the book bag and searched the contents. She recognized the expression on Claire's face. And it didn't mean anything good.

"We'll take it with us," Casey responded. "Plus whatever else Claire zeroes in on."

Claire raised her head. "Do you have any other items that were returned to you by the university?" she asked.

"Jan's clothes. Her books. Anything she left at the school."

Mr. Olson spoke painfully. "I'm not a material person. When Jan didn't come home for a year, I donated most of her clothes to our church, thinking she could buy new ones when she returned. But if you're looking for whatever's left of her wardrobe, it would be hanging in her closet." He pointed to the double sliding pocket doors.

Claire opened them and studied a few articles of clothing, reaching for an occasional sleeve or collar. After a time, and in a deliberate manner, she squatted, picking up a pair of well-worn running shoes. "She wore these a lot. And not just to get around campus. She was an athletic girl."

"Yes," Mr. Olson said. "She played on several teams in high school. I'm not sure how many of them she continued on with at Columbia. Her workload was steep. But, yes, she wore those running shoes constantly. They were too beaten up to donate to charity."

"I see," Claire murmured. And she was clearly seeing a lot more than just the objects themselves. She didn't comment aloud, just turned the running shoes over in her hands and studied the soles. Then she glanced back at the book bag. Her fingertips skimmed Jan's belongings in a tentative, searching manner. Finally, she stopped. Still clutching the running shoes and book bag, she rose. "May I take these with me?"

"Of course," Mr. Olson said. "Why? Do you sense something from them?"

"I'm not sure yet." Claire was hedging. Mr. Olson didn't see it. But Casey did. Claire was picking up something specific— and negative—from those particular objects.

"I'd also like to take the jewelry box. It's energy is so positive, it's an ideal means of comparison." There was clearly more to that than Claire was saying. But, again, Casey remained silent. She waited for Mr. Olson's nod, and watched Claire add the jewelry box to her growing collection of Jan's possessions. "What about the rest of Jan's textbooks and notebooks? Whatever she wasn't carrying around?"

Mr. Olson pointed at a cardboard box that was nestled in the corner of the closet. "Anything like that would be in there. You're welcome to go through it."

"I'd like to take it with me," Claire said. "I want to sit quietly by myself and go through all the contents of the box as slowly and thoroughly as possible. Rushing the process would be a mistake. I need to get as strong an awareness of Jan as possible."

"Fine." Mr. Olson waved his arm. "Take it. As I said, take anything that might help you find my daughter—or what happened to her."

Casey sensed that Claire had finished her work here. She glanced down at Hero, who'd been sniffing the carpet this whole time.

"Besides the things we're taking with us, would you mind giving me a few more items right now? Things you remember Jan having in her possession as close to her disappearance as possible? Before we take off, I'd like to make scent pads for Hero."

"Of course." Daniel Olson walked immediately over to the bed. He picked up a stuffed bear and a throw pillow. "Jan had these from when she was a child. She never went anywhere without them. She kept them on her bed at home and then at school."

"Perfect." Casey unzipped her tote bag, which contained gauze pads, jars, tongs and latex gloves.

She had this routine down to a science. She'd pull on the latex gloves, set the gauze in place and put Jan's personal articles on them. Then she'd use the STU-100 to vacuum the articles for thirty seconds. The gauze would collect the necessary scents, after which she'd deposit them in the jar, storing Jan's scent for Hero's future use.

She wasn't worried about the items they were taking with them. She could make scent pads for those back at the office. They would be the objects most likely connected to Jan's disappearance, maybe even things she'd been wearing or carrying during an interaction with the offender. If that was the case, they could isolate the offender's scent for Hero and, if they were lucky enough to close in on any suspects, let the bloodhound do his work.

For the umpteenth time, Casey reminded herself that this wasn't supposed to be about apprehending the person responsible for Jan's disappearance, just about locating the young woman or her body. But Casey couldn't help herself. She was desperate to catch the scumbag who, if her instincts were right, was a serial killer. She wanted to give Daniel Olson the peace he required. At the same time, she wanted to nail Jan and Holly's killer.

She worked methodically with the vacuum, and then handed the stuffed animal and the pillow back to Jan's father. "Thank you. This is great for now. My whole team will be on this. I'll get back to you as soon as we have a lead."

"I appreciate it." The dying man looked so grateful, it was emotionally painful to witness. "Time is working against me. I'm aware of your reputation. So I feel my first sense of hope."

"Hang on to that," Casey urged, zipping up her tote bag and giving Hero's leash a light tug to let him know they were leaving. "We'll find the answers you're looking for." She knew she was making a promise she might not be able to deliver. But she couldn't help it. She had to give Jan's father something to hold on to.

It was up to her and the FI team to make that something a reality.

*Bottles, Wines and Spirits*
*Morningside Heights, NY*

The liquor store was a few blocks away from Columbia. Kendra and her friend Marie made a quick trip there after classes were over. They were eager to buy a large enough quantity of booze to impress the upperclassmen at the frat party they were going to that night. Kendra had her fake ID, so the age restriction wasn't an object. And they'd be paying in cash, so there'd be no credit card receipts to explain to their parents.

It didn't take long to make their selections. This place was great, because it was cheap. They picked up five bottles—three of vodka and two of rum—and carried them up to the register.

The guy behind the counter was in his early- to mid-thirties. With dark hair slicked back in a ponytail and wearing a T-shirt with a name plate that said "Barry" on it, he looked grungy, as if he didn't enjoy taking showers. He studied the two of them for a minute—during which Kendra was getting ready to produce her ID. Abruptly, he averted his gaze, ringing up their bottles one by one, and shoving them into two brown paper bags.

"Here ya go." He handed them the bags, eyeing them again in a way that was somehow creepy. He opened his mouth as if he was about to say something, when another customer interrupted, strolling up to the counter to make his purchase. So whatever he'd been about to say remained unsaid. He turned away, directing his attention to ringing up the next order.

The girls weren't sorry to get away from him.

They made their way back to campus, chatting as they walked.

"How sketchy was that Barry guy?" Marie asked with a slight shudder.

"Totally sketchy," Kendra agreed, grimacing. "I was happy to get out of there."

"Yeah, me, too."

"I think I've seen him before," Kendra mused. "It must have been at this store, although I didn't make the connection. Anyway, he's a creeper. I hope there's someone else at the counter when I go back."

Marie nodded. "What time do you want to meet tonight?" she asked. "And where?"

"Why don't we meet up outside the frat house. Say, nine o'clock."

"Works for me." Marie nodded. "I live closer to the frat house than you. I'll take the booze back to my dorm and bring it with me later."

"Perfect." Kendra handed Marie the bag she'd been carrying.

"I've got a take-home exam," Marie said, rolling her eyes. "I can't wait to finish it. Then I'll pick out something to wear."

Kendra grinned. "This should be a cool party." The two girls split up and went their separate ways.

And once again, a pair of eyes followed their motions.

# CHAPTER
## FIVE

Holly Stevens's police report arrived at the Forensic Instincts office late that afternoon. The contents were immediately scanned and stored on the server. Pages were printed out for each team member, all of whom stopped what they were doing to read and analyze it. Then they had a brief meeting to see how—and who—could best utilize the information gleaned from the two-page report.

Ryan was elected as the starting point. He'd already run a basic timeline search on Jan Olson's life. Now he'd cross-check it with Holly's.

Before heading down to his lair, Ryan swiveled his chair toward Marc.

"I found Brenda Miller," he informed him. "She's married, listed under the name Brenda Reins and living in Greenwich, Connecticut." He passed along a three-page printout. "I got a basic rundown on her, as well as digging up her address and phone number. She's a typical suburban mom, juggling a job at a nonprofit organization with raising three kids."

Marc glanced at his watch. "I can make Greenwich in a little over an hour—maybe longer, if I get caught in rush hour traffic." He took the printout. "I'll get on the road now."

"Since I know you like to go for the element of surprise, I called ahead to make sure you wouldn't be wasting your time," Ryan said. "A tween kid answered. I pretended to be a telemarketer. I heard a woman in the background. So I'm guessing she's home."

Marc shrugged. "Even if she wasn't, she probably would be once I showed up. There's nothing like dinnertime to bring the family together. And if she happens to be out, I'll wait."

"She drives a dark green SUV." Ryan gave Marc the year and the model, along with the license plate number. "So if you see the car in the driveway or the garage, you're in luck."

"Gotcha." Marc glanced across the conference room table at Casey, who'd been unusually quiet during this minimeeting. "Does that work for you or do you need me here?"

"It works. And I'm going with you." Casey set down Jan Olson's date book, which she'd been studying for the past hour. "We need to really probe the boyfriend angle with Brenda. Whether Jan was seeing one guy or ten, I want as much info on them as possible. And Brenda is more apt to be open with another woman than with a man. You can question her about everything else, Marc. But I'm taking the boyfriend route."

"Okay." Marc's eyes narrowed quizzically. He knew that expression on Casey's face. She was focused on something in particular—something she thought might be significant. "Want to share?"

Casey pointed at the date book. "Daniel Olson was right. Jan was a typical teenage girl, who made typical entries in her date book. One of the most common notations is something a father would never notice." She pointed at one page, then another, and finally a third.

"What are we looking for?" Ryan asked.

"Dots." Claire spotted them in an instant. "Each of those pages has a dot on it."

"And the dots show up every four weeks, almost to the day." Casey indicated a few more pages. "Jan was keeping track of her periods. Most women do. And hers came like clockwork, right up until two months before her disappearance. Then they stopped altogether."

"You think she was pregnant," Ryan concluded.

"I think the timing is too coincidental to be ignored. No period for two months, followed by an inexplicable disappearance?" Casey frowned. "That connection definitely requires investigation."

"Makes sense." Marc looked thoughtful. "Although it feels like a reach. A single young woman becoming pregnant, even fifteen years ago, wasn't an eyebrow-lifter. And it wouldn't be difficult to take care of quietly, especially on a college campus. Health services would be right there to give her a hand, no matter what she decided. And they'd keep it confidential, by law."

"True," Casey agreed. "But the Olsons are a very traditional church-going family. There were childhood photos of Jan receiving her First Communion in the living room. And Mr. Olson mentioned that he'd donated Jan's clothing to their church. If religion factored heavily into their lives, maybe Jan couldn't cope with a pregnancy emotionally, even if she could take care of it physically."

"Which brings us to the baby's father."

"Exactly." Casey nodded. "Who is he and how far would he

be willing to go to make this pregnancy—and the mother—go away?"

Marc still seemed pensive. "Did your friend Holly ever mention a boyfriend?"

Casey knew just where he was headed with this. "No. She definitely wasn't seeing anyone. We were pretty close. She would have said something to me if there was a guy in her life."

"Then if your theory turns out to be true, you've probably scratched the idea that we're dealing with a serial killer. The motives in Holly's and Jan's cases would no longer match. Jan's situation would be a personal, not a random, crime. For all we know, she took a fat check from the baby-daddy and disappeared. Or, at worst, he killed her. Either way, it dashes your hopes of linking this to Holly's death."

"I realize that." Casey met Marc's gaze. "And, no, it doesn't make me happy. But I told you from the beginning that my first priority was to find out what happened to Jan Olson. And that's what I intend to do—whether or not it links to Holly."

"Fair enough. Then let's interview Brenda together. Between the two of us, we'll get everything she knows about her best friend."

Brenda Reins was just popping a casserole into the oven when her doorbell rang.

She wiped her hands on her apron, glancing at the clock with more than a little annoyance. It was rare that her family was all together for dinner. Between Daisy Scouts, Little League, music lessons and sleepovers—not to mention Ronald's endless hours at his law office—it was a battle to get the five of them home and gathered around the table at the same time.

She'd planned tonight for a week, synchronizing all the schedules so they could enjoy a fun evening at home—right down to the popcorn and the movie. The kids were already upstairs, finishing their homework. And Ron was wrapping up a meeting and heading home.

If the person ringing that doorbell was one of her younger kids' friends, she was going to be one very irritated mom.

Determined to get rid of whoever was on her doorstep, Brenda marched into the foyer and flung open the front door.

Whoever she might have expected, it wasn't the couple standing there. "Can I help you?" she asked, brows drawn in question.

"I hope so," the woman replied. "I'm assuming you're Brenda Reins?"

"I am. And you are...?" She waited for an answer.

"My name is Casey Woods." Casey held up her New York private investigator's license. "This is my associate, Marc Devereaux. We're from the investigative firm Forensic Instincts. We've been hired to look into the disappearance of Jan Olson."

"Jan?" Brenda was taken aback. "She vanished over fifteen years ago. Why are you checking into this now? Have you learned something new about what happened to her?"

"We're not sure," Marc said frankly. "But the investigation has been reopened. We understand that you were her closest friend. We were hoping you could take a few minutes to talk to us, to tell us more about her."

Brenda hesitated. "You say the case has been reopened. By whom? Who hired you?" she asked.

"Technically, the NYPD hired us," Casey responded. "They don't have the resources to devote to such a long shot. We do. If you're asking who requested the investigation, the answer is Jan's father. He's gravely ill. He's desperate to find some closure to his daughter's disappearance before he dies."

Sadness clouded Brenda's face. "Mr. Olson was such a kind man. He used to take a bunch of us out to dinner whenever he visited—and he always included the kids who lived far away and couldn't get home to see their own families. I'm so sorry to hear he's ill. Please, come in."

"Thank you." Casey preceded Marc into the house. It was a richly appointed colonial, with a grand foyer and French provincial furniture to match.

Brenda led them into the living room and gestured for them to have a seat on the sofa. "Would you like something to drink? Coffee? Tea? Water?"

Casey waved away the offer. "We appreciate your taking the time to talk to us. We'll make this as brief as possible and then be on our way. Could you give us some insight into Jan Olson? Her personality, state of mind, friends, interests, classes—anything the two of you shared or that you were aware of?"

Brenda let out a long sigh. "It feels like a million years ago. Yet it still stuns me to think about it. Jan was a sweetheart with a heart of gold. I can't imagine anyone who'd want to hurt her. She was shy and studious, with just a small circle of friends."

"Did you know most of those friends?" Marc broke in to ask. "Would you able to compile a list?"

"Sure. Although, with the exception of our mutual friends, I have no idea where the others are now."

"Finding them will be my problem," Marc said, whipping out a notebook. "I just want you to detail every part of Jan's life that you recall."

"She wasn't all that social. She spent most of her time buried in her textbooks, trying to decide between premed and nursing. There was a lot of academic pressure, enough to make her quit the swim team. The only thing she kept doing to clear her mind was her morning run."

"What about guys?" Casey brought the subject right around to where she wanted it. "Did she have a boyfriend?"

A nostalgic smile touched Brenda's lips. "Chris Towers. The two of them met at freshman orientation. They really, really liked each other, and hung out from day one in the fall. They were definitely a couple—but not the kind who were all over each other or who isolated themselves in their own little world. Chris was in prelaw and on the debate team. He invested as much time in his schoolwork as Jan did."

"No other guys in Jan's life?"

"None." Brenda stated that definitively.

Casey cleared her throat. "Do you have any idea if Jan was pregnant?"

"Pregnant?" Brenda did a double take. "Absolutely not. Why would you ask that?"

"Because her father gave me her date book. And she kept meticulous track of her periods. Every month there was a dot marking the date. There were no dots the two months prior to her disappearance."

"That was stress, not pregnancy." Brenda shoved a loose strand of hair behind her ear. "Like I said, the academic pressure was crushing, especially in Jan's area of study. She was a wreck for weeks before she vanished. I remember her complaining that she'd missed her period. She went to health services. They confirmed that it was stress-related."

"You're sure?" Casey asked. "You said she was shy and quiet. She might have kept it to herself if she was pregnant."

"Very sure. Jan *was* reserved, but she and I confided in each other. Besides, she came from a very religious family. She and Chris weren't even sleeping together."

"Okay, then, tell us about her behavior during the last weeks before she disappeared." Marc took over from what he was obviously convinced had to be a dead end. "You said she was under pressure?"

"We all were. Jan more than others, because of her area of study. Plus, she was waitressing to make some extra cash. She was burning the candle at both ends and then some. That's why she quit the swim team, and why she intensified her running schedule. It was just too much. I really believe the overall tension is what made her snap."

"What do you mean by snap?" Marc asked.

Brenda's shoulders rose and fell in a defeated gesture. "She started staying out all night studying. I couldn't get her to take a break. She'd run a couple of miles at dawn, and then go from class to the library to her job and back. She barely stopped off at her dorm room, except to shower and change. And she withdrew—from me, from Chris, from everyone. Whenever I asked her to talk to me, she said she was too strung out. I was really worried about her. And then, abruptly, she disappeared."

"So you're saying you think she took off on her own?"

"We didn't know what to think. Chris called the police. And, of course, Jan's father. There was a brief investigation. But there was absolutely no evidence that Jan had been abducted—other than the fact that she didn't take anything except her purse."

"Nothing else was missing? No clothes or toiletries?"

"No." Brenda's brow furrowed. "Chris and I both practically ransacked her room. Neither of us could find anything out of place. That's why we filed a police report. It didn't make sense. But, given Jan's state of mind, I knew what the cops were thinking—that she'd either run away or worse. They searched for a body. None was ever found."

Marc didn't reply. But Casey knew his wheels were turning—and she also knew exactly the way his thought process was going. Suicide didn't fit. If Jan was going to kill herself, she wouldn't have vanished in order to do it. And running away? That didn't seem likely. Not without packing at least one bag of essentials.

True, there was nothing concrete for the police to go on. But the lead detective on the case certainly hadn't knocked himself out. All signs pointed to the fact that Jan Olson had been the victim of some kind of foul play.

Footsteps sounded from the second floor of Brenda's house, and a little girl of about eight burst in. She seemed surprised to see guests with her mother, and stopped in the doorway, twirling a strand of long brown hair around her finger.

"It's seven o'clock," she reported shyly. "I'm ready. So are Ben and Pammy. I reminded them. And I just called Daddy. He's ten minutes away."

Brenda smiled, reaching out her arm for her daughter. "Thanks for rallying the troops, sweetheart. Dinner should be ready in five." A quick glance at Casey and Marc. "This is my daughter, Annie. She's keeping track of the time for me. It's family dinner night." She gave them an apologetic smile. "Is there any way we can continue this another time?"

"Absolutely. We're heading out now." Casey rose to her feet. "I'm sorry for interrupting you. But I'm also grateful for your time and your input." She handed Brenda a business card. "My email address is there. If you could send me that list of Jan's friends and any addresses or phone numbers you do have, it would be appreciated."

"I'll take care of it right away," Brenda promised. "I'll even pull out our college yearbook to double-check that I've included everyone."

"Great." Marc put away his writing pad and stood up. "One more question. You said that Jan waitressed. Do you happen to know where?"

"The Lakeside Restaurant at the Central Park Boathouse. It was close to Columbia and the tips were really good. Plus, it was convenient if Jan wanted to get in an extra run. She worked there for about six months."

Marc nodded, adding that to his memory.

"Thank you again," Casey said. She flashed a smile at Brenda's daughter. "Enjoy your family time, Annie. We're sorry to have kept your mom for so long."

Outside the house, Casey turned to Marc. "Well, that shoots my pregnancy theory to hell. Brenda wasn't lying. Nor was she hesitating. She knew everything—including the fact that Jan went to health services about her missed periods. Of course, I'll want to interview Jan's boyfriend, Chris. But I doubt he'll give us a different story."

"Agreed." Marc nodded again. "But we have a lot of other ground to cover. Jan's friends, her sports, her job. This wasn't a suicide. Nor was it a random disappearance. There are too many indications pointing to an inciting incident, from Jan's anxiety to her change in behavior. I need that list of friends. As for right now, I'm sure Ryan's already found his way into the university's records. That'll give us insight into Jan's academic standing and her course schedule. There'll be professors to talk to and class-mates to look up. And we'll get Brenda's list soon. Patrick and I are going to be very busy."

"So am I," Casey said. "Knowing Ryan, I have no doubt that he's also run a cross-check on all the basic aspects of Holly's and Jan's lives. I want to look over those results and add any of the courses and activities I remember Holly being involved in."

"You're convinced the cases are related."

"Do you blame me?"

"No." Marc didn't hesitate for a second. "Actually, I'm start-ing to agree with you. The coincidence is just too real to be ac-cidental. If the pregnancy theory had held water, I would have felt differently. But it didn't. Which means the parallel victimolo-gies still stand, at least until a piece of evidence says otherwise."

"It's going to be another late night," Casey said grimly. "I'm not going to sleep until I sort out all the pieces."

Back in his cell, Glen Fisher pushed aside his empty dinner tray. The food sucked. But he wouldn't have to live with that for much longer.

He glanced at his watch. Eight forty-five. A slow smile curved his lips.

The fun was about to begin.

# CHAPTER
## SIX

Kendra reentered the liquor store a little before nine, barely noticing the drunk who staggered out ahead of her, metal flask in hand. The wall clock reminded her to hurry. She realized she didn't really need to be here, that it was probably overkill. But a handle of tequila would go a long way toward sweetening her and Marie's reception, especially when added to their earlier purchases.

That creeper Barry was still at the counter, eyeing her up and down as she paid for the booze. She kept her gaze averted and got out as quickly as she could.

She was late and she knew it. The party was already under way, and Marie would be pissed off that she had to wait.

Tucking the tequila under her arm, Kendra crossed West 113th Street, and headed directly toward the brownstone where the frat house was located. She was excited. She didn't go out often; she was too busy with her schoolwork. But she'd killed herself studying this week, all so she could have some fun to-night. All she could think about were the hot guys Marie had told her would be at the party.

She'd taken care with her appearance. Gone was the pathetic-looking geek who buried her nose in philosophy books. She'd straightened her curly auburn mane and tied it back neatly. She'd put on her favorite pair of skinny jeans, a V-neck sweater and some makeup. Not too much, not too little. Just enough to ensure that she wasn't lost in the crowd.

That was important to her. She didn't have much of a social life. She was an introvert and aware that people saw her as a bit weird. She studied not only to get A's, but because the philosophers fascinated her. Tonight would be different. Tonight she'd actually cut loose and have some fun.

She picked up her pace, eager to meet Marie and check out what promised to be a great party.

A flicker of light flashed from the alley, like a lighthouse warning an approaching ship of impending danger. Kendra was oblivious to it, as well as to the beam of light that bounced off the alley wall. She never saw the dark silhouette or smelled the acrid contents soaking through a handheld rag.

The fraternity house was just down the street. Kendra passed the narrow alley between two buildings.

Abruptly, a figure in black darted out of the shadows and grabbed her. A damp cloth was clapped over her nose and mouth. A powerful arm locked around her waist, pulling her into the dark alley.

Kendra began to struggle the instant she realized what was happening. But it was too late. The handkerchief was held in place. And the sharp point of a knife pressed against her abdomen. She felt its sting just as the sickeningly sweet smell pervaded her nostrils. Too terrified to move, too groggy to fight, she ceased her struggles.

The world went black.

It would never grow light again.


The fraternity party was already crazy when Marie showed up at the path leading to the front doors. She waited there as she and Kendra had agreed, which was just fine with her. As enticing as the thundering base was coming from inside, it always felt better to have at least one friend along when you made an entrance. Anyway, the liquor would be as welcome as the two of them, no matter how hot they looked.

Still, she found herself growing impatient as the minutes ticked by. She called Kendra's cell phone, but it went directly to voice mail. Marie hoped her friend hadn't gotten lost in the library stacks, immersed in one of her beloved Aristotle books.

Three phone calls and thirty minutes later, Marie gave up. She hadn't spent two hours tearing through her closet to find just the right outfit so she could stand outside and get odd looks from all the other partygoers. It was time for her to suck it up and go in on her own. She'd hand over the bottles and tell the frat guys that her friend was on her way. Then, she'd keep an eye out for Kendra. Hopefully, her friend would snap out of whatever trance had sidetracked her and show up.

On that thought, Marie marched up the path and went through the doors, ready to tackle the party on her own.


Claire had been sitting in a small dark office at Forensic Instincts all evening, handling Jan Olson's personal items. The energies she'd been picking up were dark and complex.

Icy coldness. That was the prevalent aura that emanated from Jan's clothing, her textbooks, even her notebooks. An icy coldness that was the absence of life. And the book bag, the running shoes—they held another energy. Fear. A powerful fear that Jan had internalized, shared with no one.

Whatever she'd been afraid of, it was key to their investigation.

*A killer's random learning curve.* The awareness slid into Claire's mind, then took root. Whatever had happened here, it was the initial part of a string of evil. Strategically planned. But a random choice of victims. At least it had been with Jan. Fine-tuning had brought with it a honed expertise. But Jan had been one of the first. A learning experience.

Claire could visualize Jan Olson running through a park. Water was glistening in the background. Her heart was slamming against her ribs. She'd peer over her shoulder, stumble on the uneven ground, then struggle on. Squeezing her eyes shut, Claire focused intently, trying to pick up something specific about Jan's surroundings—a landmark, a street sign, anything that could tell her about the locale. Butterflies...birds...

Abruptly, there was a loud buzzing in Claire's head, followed by an eclipse in time and a radical shift in scene. A jolt of ominous energy shot through her—one that was so powerful it caused her to physically double over.

Something horrifying was happening. Not in the past. Right this moment. Whatever energies Claire had been picking up from fifteen years ago had opened up a channel to a fatal crime that was occurring as she sat there. She fought her panic, trying desperately to zero in on the crime.

Pain. Agonizing pain. Terror. A woman. Struggling, clawing, fighting for her life. A monster who was overpowering her. The hard feel of a concrete floor. A warehouse? Yes, a warehouse. Dirty floor. Large wooden crates with shipping labels.

The smell of the river. The sound of bells. The flash of a clock tower. Not right there. But close by.

Clothing was being torn. The woman was screaming, begging. She was pinned to the ground. Naked. Helpless. Violated.

Large hands locked around her throat crushing her air supply as he raped her. Searing pain. Paralyzing panic. Heightening more and more and more…

Claire almost screamed aloud, the violent energies she was experiencing were so acute. Beyond excruciating.

She couldn't wait any longer. Drenched in sweat, she forced open her eyes and fumbled for her phone. Ordering her brain into rational action, she blocked out her vision and honed in on reality. Think. Think. The phone number. She'd called it a dozen times.

His direct line escaped her, so she settled for the general number and punched it in.

"Eighty-fourth Precinct," a voice answered.

"Is Detective Werner in?" Claire made her voice sound relatively normal.

"Just a minute." There was a short series of rings and then a familiar baritone.

"Werner."

"Tom? It's Claire Hedgleigh."

"Ah," Detective Thomas Werner replied with wry amusement. "The brilliant psychic addition to Forensic Instincts. I should be pissed that you're not consulting for us anymore. But I can't blame you for taking on a challenge like working for the FI team. How can I help you?"

"Something bad just happened. A rape. And an attempted murder. It could be a fait accompli already. I don't know. But it's in your district. A warehouse near the East River. Rows of wooden crates. And bells—I know those bells. They're from the clock tower at Dumbo." Claire pinpointed the enormously expensive Down Under the Manhattan Bridge Overpass penthouse in Brooklyn. "That's as specific as I can get. I wish I could tell you more. But I can't. All I know is that it's urgent. Search the area. And hurry."

"I'm on it." She could tell that Detective Werner was on his feet, ready to grab his partner and take off. He and his precinct had worked with Claire often enough to know she was the real deal.

"Please keep me posted."

"I will."

Claire disconnected the call, feeling ill as well as oddly attached to the vision. Like it was personal. But she'd never met the victim. She was sure of that. So why couldn't she shake this sense of personal dread? She'd consulted for the NYPD and local police departments for years before coming on board at Forensic Instincts. She knew the drill. And this was out of the realm of normal. There was something more going on here.

And that something involved her Forensic Instincts family.

She knew what she had to do next.


Casey had just arrived back at the office. She was on her way down to Ryan's lair to compare notes when her iPhone rang.

The number was blocked.

"Casey Woods," she answered.

"You're putting your energy in the wrong place, Red." The weird tinny words told Casey that, whoever the caller was, he was using a voice scrambler. "That girl's case is as cold as her body. But the one who just died? Her body is still warm."

"Who is this?"

"The last person you're going to see before you close your

eyes forever." A chilling laugh. "The blood chain is under way. It will end with you. Spin your wheels and try to stop it."

The line went dead.

"Casey?" Marc had been parking the van. He walked inside and was standing behind Casey in time to see her ashen expression. "What's the matter? You're white as a sheet."

Before Casey could answer, her phone rang again. She startled, then stared at the caller ID. It was Claire.

"Claire, I can't talk now," she said, trying to keep her voice steady.

"You have to." Claire was literally vibrating. "I just called the Eighty-fourth Precinct. Something's happening. Someone's being tortured and killed. It's happening in Brooklyn. And it's drawing me to you." Claire's voice broke. "Oh, my God—she's dead. He killed her. He raped her and he killed her. He's still with the body. He's doing something to it. But she's dead. And you have to know that. I don't know why. But you do."

Casey's own stomach was turning over. "Claire. Listen to me. I need you to focus. Tell me everything. *Everything.*"

"I did." It was clear that Claire sensed the rising hysteria in Casey's voice. "Why?"

"Because I think I just got a phone call from the killer."

# CHAPTER SEVEN

The body was located just after 1:00 a.m. at a warehouse on Jay Street.

Identification was no problem, since Kendra's purse hadn't been touched, so neither had her driver's license or student ID.

The medical examiner did his job and filed his report. The parents were notified. They lived locally, so they rushed over to identify the body. It was a heartbreaking scene.

Tom hated this part of his job.

Once he'd dotted his *i*'s and crossed his *t*'s, he dropped wearily back in his chair and rubbed his temples. His tired gaze fell on the phone and he stared at it for a long time. The case was now a wide-open homicide. No aspect of it should be discussed. But Claire had been instrumental in their discovering it. She had a right to know.

Tom picked up the phone and punched in her cell number.

Claire answered on the first ring. She was with the entire FI team, gathered around the second-floor conference table, down-ing cup after cup of coffee.

"This is an unofficial call, Claire," Tom stated flatly. "I shouldn't even be making it. But given our prior professional relationship and the fact that you initiated this entire search, I'll tell you what I can."

"Thanks, Tom." Claire put down her coffee cup. "You found the girl. I don't need to ask you if she was dead."

"No, you don't."

Claire nodded sadly. "I'm with my team," she informed him. "May I put you on speakerphone?"

"We're really pushing the envelope here. But fine."

Claire pressed the speaker button and set her phone in the center of the table. "Go ahead."

"It was pretty much as you described. The body was in a warehouse on Jay Street."

"Shit. That's my neck of the woods," Ryan muttered.

"She was nude," Tom continued. "Her clothing was torn to shreds. Her wrists were bound together. There was physical evi-dence of rape. The hyoid bone in her neck was fractured, indi-cating strangulation. The body was wrapped in a canvas tarp. Pieces of her hair had been snipped off. There was a red ribbon tied around her throat in a bow. And he'd applied lipstick to her lips. It was almost like he was leaving us a carefully wrapped gift, as sick as that is."

"Sounds like a signature mark of some kind." Marc spoke up. "Detective Werner, this is Marc Devereaux, one of Claire's colleagues. I realize this entire conversation is off the record. So can you give me a description of the girl?"

"Caucasian. Petite—about five foot three, a hundred and five pounds. Brown eyes, shoulder-length red hair."

There was a long moment of silence at the conference table before Casey spoke up.

"This is Casey Woods, Detective. What else can you tell us about the victim?"

"Her name was Kendra Mallery. She was a freshman at Columbia. Her family's been notified and they've ID'd the body, but they're in shock and not able to tell us much. I haven't spoken to any of her friends yet. So I don't know too many details about her habits or where she was headed when she was abducted." Tom paused. "I realize Claire is invested in this because she visualized the crime. But I get the feeling there's more at stake here. Why is your team asking so many questions?"

"Because it's possible the killer was in touch with me at the time of the murder." Casey tried to keep the emotion out of her voice.

*"What?"*

She went on to explain the call she'd gotten, reporting it as accurately as possible. She also told Tom about the cold case they were investigating and her caller's allusion to it.

"Shit," Tom muttered. "That's no coincidence. The killer is targeting you. And keeping tabs on you in the process. Do you have any idea who he is?"

"None." Casey fiddled with her pen as she spoke. "But the description you gave of the victim? It could as easily be a description of me. And not just the physical elements. I got my undergraduate degree at Columbia."

At this point, the tension in the conference room was suffocating.

"Look," Casey said at last. "We can speculate all we want. But the truth is, we have nothing but an untraceable, voice-scrambled phone call and a series of coincidences. That's not enough to take action."

"It's enough to assign you police protection," Ryan said.

"Minimal protection," Marc corrected. "Our team can provide a whole lot more." He cleared his throat. "Tom, based on Claire's tip, which led to your finding the body, along with the threats that were made against Casey—could you speak to your captain about Forensic Instincts working together with your precinct on solving this one? Our skills and resources can complement each other's."

"While working within the boundaries of the law?" Tom asked pointedly.

"That's always our intention," Marc responded. "We're not interested in being at odds with law enforcement. Just understand that we're protecting one of our own. Anything we do that falls into the gray area will be our responsibility and will in no way implicate the police."

"Fair enough," Tom agreed. "Let me finish the paperwork, including all the information you just gave me. We're in the process of checking for latent fingerprints on the tarp. We could get lucky. This bastard might be in the system. But first thing tomorrow morning, I'll take your request to my captain."

"Thanks, Tom," Claire said.

She disconnected the call. She didn't need to look around the table to see what was reflected on her teammates' faces.

With or without police assistance, they'd already taken on the case.

Claire remained in the conference room long after the rest of the team had taken off and even Casey had gone upstairs to make the attempt to catch some sleep.

No matter how hard she tried, Claire couldn't get the crime images out of her mind. They flashed through her head, one image after the other, like some old horror movie.

The visualizations had begun in sequence as Tom elaborated on what he'd found at the crime scene. Claire could see it all—Kendra's wrapped body, her hair, even the red satin ribbon tied around her throat. Worse, Claire could feel what Kendra had been feeling—everything from the panic to the blinding pain to the sense of futility, and then the moment when she'd given up.

The whole horrifying event had grabbed hold of Claire and wouldn't let go.

She dropped her face in her hands and rubbed her eyes, as if by doing that she could make it all go away.

It didn't work.

Shoving back her chair, Claire left the conference room, heading down the stairs, looking for escape. She had no desire to go home or to be alone in her apartment. She was totally freaked out and trembling, consumed by a sense of death.

She didn't remember passing the ground floor and continuing downstairs to the basement. But once she'd done so... She had no idea how she knew Ryan would be there. She just did.

The door to his lair was half-closed. Claire stepped inside, glancing at his usual spot behind the computer. He wasn't there. Instead, he was across the room, sitting on his bench and lifting weights. He was definitely a man with a mission, pumping iron with a vengeance, perspiration glistening on his bare chest.

He spotted Claire the minute she came in. Slowly, he lowered his weights to the floor and stood up.

"Are you okay?"

"No." She shook her head.

He crossed over to her, studying her drawn expression and wide, frightened eyes.

Neither of them said a word.

Claire reached behind her and shoved the door closed, turning the lock with a loud click. Then she took the few steps that separated her from Ryan and wrapped her arms around his neck.

"Make it go away," she whispered. "Just for a little while. Make the pictures stop."

He tilted back her head, kissed her once, hard, and then lifted her off the floor and flush against him. Claire wrapped her legs around his waist and they stumbled across the room, dropping onto the futon they'd used more than a few times for this.

Claire let her body take over, let the feel, taste and smell of Ryan permeate her senses. Making love with him was an all-encompassing experience, leaving no room for anything else. Which was exactly what she needed right now.

They drew it out as long as they could—blocking out the world, losing themselves in sensation. Claire's climax was explosive, and she cried out, feeling Ryan's body jolt with his own release.

Afterward, they were quiet, both of them loath to let go of the moment and allow reality to creep back in.

When Ryan spoke, it was in a rough, gravelly tone. "Don't cry."

Claire blinked. She hadn't realized she'd been crying. But her cheeks and lashes were wet, as was Ryan's shoulder where her face had been.

"I'm sorry." She ran her palm across his shoulder, then wiped her cheeks with the backs of her hands. "It's the emotional energy."

Ryan nodded, his chin pressed against the crown of her head.

Another moment passed, and Claire could feel the ugly ghosts threatening to crowd their way into her mind. Unconsciously, her nails dug into Ryan's back.

Ryan picked up on her panic.

"It's after three in the morning," he said. "We have to be upstairs in a couple of hours. For you to go home now would be ridiculous. Stay here."

Now *that* was unprecedented.

What Claire and Ryan had was very complicated. They were polar opposites in so many ways. They debated hard, they bickered constantly and they couldn't keep their hands off each other. Ryan was gorgeous and charismatic, with those smoldering Black Irish looks and the charm to match—all of which meant he attracted women like a magnet.

None of that impressed Claire. She was very much her own person, gentle and ethereal, yet strong and honest, unwilling to back down when she thought Ryan was wrong. They were, without a doubt, each other's weak spot, and despite their best intentions to the contrary *and* the fact that the two of them were like day and night, they continued to wind up in bed together.

They'd fast become a habit each of them was finding impossible to break.

After months of being involved, they'd relegated their sexual relationship to its own inexplicable but inescapable niche.

That niche didn't include spending the night together.

Still, what Ryan was saying now made complete pragmatic sense. It was hardly a romantic step forward. Just a time-saver and a few extra hours of comfort—hours Claire badly needed. She didn't want to think. She didn't have the energy to move. And she didn't have the mental strength to battle her demons.

Ryan didn't wait for Claire's reply. He rolled onto his side and reached for the fleece throw he kept at the foot of the futon. He settled Claire against him and covered them both.

"Go to sleep, Claire-voyant," he murmured. "Shut down that out-of-control mind of yours. You can pick up where you left off tomorrow."

Claire would never admit how relieved Ryan's words made

her feel, or how grateful she was not to be alone. She commanded her mind and her body to release the negative energy, and they complied. "I'm so drained," she heard herself whisper aloud.

"I know." Ryan lay down beside her, wrapping one arm around her waist, pausing only long enough to set the alarm on his watch.

By the time he put down his head, Claire was fast asleep.

Upstairs in her apartment, Casey was having no such luck.

She'd taken a hot shower to relax the tension from her body, plumped her pillows about twelve times and now lay on her back, one arm folded beneath her head.

She wished that damned voice on the phone hadn't been disguised. But the fact that it was—did that mean she knew the person at the other end? He wasn't threatening Forensic Instincts. Even if this was a personal vendetta against Casey's entire company, he was zeroing in on *her* as his target. That in itself was unnerving. But what unnerved her most was how detailed the offender's planning had been. He'd plugged into her current investigation and where she stood on it. That took time, patience and connections. He obviously had all three. And with regard to tonight's rape and murder? He'd carefully chosen a victim whose description matched Casey's.

All those things together added up to a systematic mind and strategic planning—a lethal combination.

Last, but far from least, he'd made sure to call Casey either right before or, even more macabre, sometime during his horrific crime.

That added a perverse twist….

What was his motive? Was it personal? Professional? And if

Casey was designated as the final target, what killing rampage did he have planned in the interim?

The questions bombarded Casey, growing more and more numerous as she lay there.

She had an impressive team in Forensic Instincts. They'd drop everything to work this crime and keep her safe. But there was only one person who had the expertise—and, yes, the personal investment—to get a handle on this case and solve it quickly.

She picked up her phone and punched in a number on speed dial.

Two rings, and then a sleepy voice answered. "Hutchinson."

"It's me. I need you."

# CHAPTER
## EIGHT

The FI team was exhausted, but vigilantly gathered around the conference table at 6:30 a.m. No single-cup Keurig today—they'd pulled out the big guns. There were two pots of coffee, neither of them decaf, already half-consumed within the first half hour of their meeting.

"I called Hutch last night," Casey informed the rest of the group. "Unfortunately, he can't get away from Quantico right away. But he'll consult with us by phone and arrange to get to New York as soon as possible."

"Good move," Marc said with a nod. "No one's better at profiling than Hutch. Although he'll probably be less objective than even we are."

"Probably." Casey didn't dispute that. "But it won't stop him from getting inside this psychopath's head." She dragged a hand through her hair. "Let's be blunt. We've been sitting here for almost an hour reviewing the details we know. We can continue ad nauseam, but we're not going to come up with a concrete lead. There's just not enough to go on."

"We were invited in by the cops," Marc said. "Or we will be once Tom speaks to his captain."

"That's not exactly the way it's going to work," Ryan corrected him. "We'll be kept on a short leash, and told what they want us to know. This is still technically their investigation, not ours. And you know as well as I do that we can't sit around waiting for them to toss us leads."

"Which is why we'll be making it *our* investigation." Marc spoke for them all. "We'll protect Casey. We'll find the killer."

"You can't protect me around the clock," Casey said.

"The hell we can't." Marc didn't bat an eye. "I brought my stuff over this morning. I'll be staying at the brownstone until we catch this son of a bitch. I'm the best qualified."

No one argued with that decision. Marc was formidable with or without a gun. He had physical skills that scared the crap out of most people. He also had the hearing and dexterity of a cat.

"I put my stuff in the third-floor meeting room," Marc informed Casey. "The couch in there is more comfortable than my bed. And I'll be one floor below you. Not to mention that Hero will be in your room. Between us and the alarm system, this place will be like Fort Knox."

"I'll program Yoda to respond to the slightest noise," Ryan said. "I'll start poking into Casey's cell phone records. And during the day, we'll take shifts watching her."

"That's not necessary," Patrick intervened. "Our efforts are needed in a proactive way. You know from our last case that I've got access to the best security guards in the business, all of whom are licensed to carry a gun. They'll go everywhere Casey goes, and watch the outside of the brownstone at night. She'll have 24/7 coverage. Ryan, that'll free you up to run the technology and strategic end of things, and Claire to focus on her psychic connections."

"I really appreciate all this." Casey set down her coffee mug. "And I'd be lying if I said I won't feel infinitely safer with all those plans set in motion." She stroked Hero's head. "But Patrick's right. Running interference isn't enough. Assuming the fingerprints turn up nothing, we have to put our efforts into figuring out who this guy is and why he has it in for me."

"You need to make two sets of lists," Marc told her. "One will be a list of everyone—both personal and professional—that you had even a slight disagreement with."

"I'll run all the FI case files," Ryan said. "Plus any cases from your consulting days. That'll give us the big-screen potential candidates."

Casey nodded. "And I'll dig into every nook and cranny of my life, every detail of my days, to add to that list."

"The other list will be of the killer's possible next target," Marc continued. "I want you to write down every single person you interact with who's a petite redhead." He thought for a moment. "If you know whether they're natural redheads, that would be better still. My guess is this killer wants the real thing if he can get it."

"Makes sense," Casey said. "I'll have plenty of time to do this tonight, since I doubt I'll be doing much sleeping."

"Tonight?" Claire shot her a quizzical look. "What about today?"

Casey blew out her breath. "We still have Jan Olson's case to pursue. I'm not being a martyr. I'm pretty fixated on what just happened. But there's a dying man waiting for us to find his daughter's body."

"Let me talk to Tom," Claire said. "I'll see how much police assistance we can count on. We have to work on both cases simultaneously. But, Casey, your life is our priority." She tapped the table thoughtfully. "I was connecting with Jan's energy when Kendra's murder took over. I sensed death. And fear. Fear that Jan wasn't sharing with anyone. She knew she was in trouble."

"What kind of trouble?" Patrick asked.

"Someone was watching her. Following her. She didn't know what to do."

"Exactly like Holly," Casey said at once.

"Yes." Claire nodded. "Exactly like Holly. And the stalker was new to this. Jan was practice." A deep breath as Claire let the recollections fill her mind. "I could see Jan running through a park. She was terrified. Stumbling. Looking over her shoulder. Her stalker wasn't just looking anymore. He was chasing her."

"Did he catch her?" Marc asked. "Rape her? Kill her? Could you make out his face?"

Claire shook her head in frustration. "I never got that far. Kendra's energy took over. I was gripped with it. It eclipsed everything I was sensing before that. There was simply no room for anything else."

At that moment, Claire's cell phone rang. "It's Tom," she announced, after checking out caller ID. "I'll put him on speaker."

"Hi, Tom, you've got us all," she greeted him.

"Good. Then I'll write down the office number, since I'll be dealing with the whole team from now on. After a lot of arm-twisting, my captain agreed to your request. He complained about getting some pressure from the captain of the Twenty-sixth." Tom was referring to the precinct where Columbia was situated. "Apparently, Casey Woods has pull there."

"I've consulted for them," Casey explained. "They have a great squad." No need to get into their ongoing partnership on the Jan Olson case.

"Well, we'll be joining forces on this case, since Kendra could very well have been kidnapped or killed on the Columbia campus and her body disposed of at the Brooklyn warehouse."

"What happened with the fingerprints?" Marc asked right away.

"Dead end. Whoever this scumbag is, he doesn't have a record." Tom sighed. "We were really hopeful on that score. Anyway, I also want you to know that, thanks to social media, word about Kendra's murder has gotten out. None of the details I shared with you, just the rape and the murder. There are counselors on campus talking to whoever needs help. And our detectives are there interviewing Kendra's friends."

"Anything yet?"

"Only that she was a studious, quiet girl who spent most of her time in the library. Her major was philosophy, so we'll be interviewing all her professors. As for her whereabouts last night, she was supposedly on her way to a fraternity party, but never showed up."

Claire had tears in her eyes. "The students must be planning something."

"Yeah, that's the other thing I wanted to tell you. There's a vigil being held on Morningside Campus at eight o'clock tonight. We'll have plainclothes detectives and video surveillance there."

"Since the killer will probably show up to get a firsthand look at the emotional devastation he caused." Marc spoke from his BAU training.

"Exactly."

"Our team will be there, too," Patrick told Tom. "We'll keep a low profile and let you do your thing."

"I figured as much." Tom's tone was grim. "Sometimes this job really sucks. But it sure as hell makes you want to solve a case." There was a pause. "Give me your office number. I'll keep you posted as information turns up."

Casey complied, giving him not only the office number, but each of their individual cell phone numbers, as well.

As soon as the call was disconnected, she glanced around the table, focusing specifically on Ryan. She knew what was coming.

And it did.

Ryan turned to Marc. "Our surveillance blows theirs out of the water."

"No question." Marc finished off his cup of coffee. "Looks like we'll be treading into that gray area sooner than expected."

It was 6:00 p.m. With two hours left before the vigil began, the area was deserted, except for Kendra's photo and a small circle of flowers surrounding it.

Ryan glanced out the window of the van as he, Marc and Patrick approached the campus. "Tom's right. This whole thing sucks."

Marc said nothing, although he didn't disagree. He'd seen some heinous things in his time. That didn't make a brutal crime like this any easier to comprehend.

Security was tight, as the FI team had expected it to be. Patrick got out of the van a block away and walked toward the campus grounds. He was wearing business casual clothes and had left his gun at home. He'd been given the necessary law enforcement okay. He'd have no trouble getting in. And he'd look like any professor or father paying his respects.

That left Ryan and Marc to do their own jobs.

The FI van pulled up to the security guard. Ryan reached into his pocket and produced his ID from New York Sound, one of the many corporate aliases Forensic Instincts had created to allow them to conduct surveillance operations without raising suspicion. As expected, New York Sound was on the approved vendor list. Once the guard verified that, he handed Ryan back his ID and nodded.

Ryan paused long enough to gaze around the area on campus where the vigil was about to be held.

"Where's the closest place for me to park?" he asked.

The guard pointed, uttering a series of lefts and rights, which Ryan memorized. Then he issued a mock salute and pulled slowly onto campus.

Situated where he wanted to be, Ryan turned and nodded at Marc. The two of them climbed out of the van, unloaded the tripod base speakers and positioned them strategically around the area where the vigil would soon commence. Next, Ryan connected the long cables to each speaker and attached the opposite ends to the special jacks protruding from the side of the van. He climbed inside and fired up the equipment.

Marc went from speaker to speaker, waiting to hear Ryan say, "Testing one, two, three," before he waved to acknowledge that Ryan's voice was coming through loud and clear. Next, Ryan gave Marc instructions at each speaker about how to position it. "Up five feet, turn left twenty degrees," he directed the first time, his voice emanating from the elevated speaker. The two of them continued the process until it was done.

To a passerby, it would appear as if Marc was adjusting a sound system. But inside the truck, Ryan was checking the angles of security cameras he'd concealed inside the speakers. Once the process was complete, he'd have a three hundred and sixty degree view of the entire vigil area. The output from each video camera would be recorded, allowing Forensic Instincts to analyze the footage, and use facial recognition software if needed. Casey had instructed Ryan to make the video available to her on the FI server as soon as they returned to the office.

Marc opened the back door of the van and climbed in. The place looked like a mini TV production room.

"Ready?" he asked, glancing around.

Ryan sat back on his heels. "Show time."

Kendra might have been a quiet and private girl. But the vigil was packed with students, some of them white with shock, some of them openly weeping. Whether or not Kendra was part of their individual social circles, her murder hit them all hard. She was one of their peers, one of their classmates. Any of them could just as easily have been the girl found in that warehouse. Knowing that, they hugged one another and stood in traumatized solidarity, overcome by the horror of the situation.

Patrick moved among the crowd, subtly but intently studying the vigil's attendees. No one paid particular attention to him, since there were other people his age, most of them parents who lived locally. They, too, felt a fearful kinship with the other parents—and not only out of grief for Kendra, although that was a huge part of their reason for being there. But they were also well aware that if this psychopath was targeting Columbia students, their own children could be in danger. Kendra's own parents were, understandably, absent. They were in no condition to be out in public when they were still utterly shattered and in shock.

Marie, Kendra's closest friend and the last known person to have seen her alive, made a brief but heartbreaking speech. She spoke about Kendra's kindness, her commitment to her family and friends, and her determination to graduate and make a difference in the world. When no more words would come, she wiped away her tears and bent down to place a bouquet of flowers at the foot of the pedestal holding the photo of Kendra.

After that, students all filed forward, placing everything on the grass from a single flower alongside Marie's bouquet to Columbia notebooks and T-shirts. The "pizza crowd," all of whom were among Kendra's small number of close friends, were huddled together. They each put a yellow rose—Kendra's favorite flower—on top of the pedestal, and then turned away, tears rolling down their cheeks. Even Robbie was there, squatting to place an empty pizza box near the flowers.

He walked over to Kendra's friends. "I don't know what to say," he told them. "She was a terrific girl. This is a nightmare. I hope the cops find the motherfucker who did this to her and lock him up for life." His voice got shaky. "The last time I saw her, she was trying to help me. Some car was blocking my delivery truck and I could barely get out. She would have gone up to the driver and blasted him if I let her."

"She told us about that," Amy said. "She went on and on about how miserably delivery people are treated."

"Yeah, well, I've gotten used to that." Robbie swallowed, obviously struggling to make mundane conversation. "I normally just let it roll off my back. But I would've been fired if the truck got dented. So I appreciated Kendra's concern. I'd be screwed without that job. As it is, I just took on a second one. But this new one lets me deliver pizzas by bike."

"That's good." Amy hadn't really heard him and he knew it. It didn't matter. Nothing mattered except the senseless and brutal crime that had taken away their friend.

The candle-lighting aspect of the vigil got under way. Everyone had been handed a candle when they arrived. Now they all lit them, standing silently and bowing their heads in prayer.

Not far away, a dark sedan was parked. Its driver was scrutinizing the campus through a zoom lens, watching each attendee, one at a time.

Watching and planning.

# CHAPTER
## NINE

Glen Fisher hadn't felt this aroused in a long time.

Pacing back and forth in his cell, his erection hardened along with his thoughts. His juices were flowing. Blood was pumping through his veins. Pooling at his groin. The next attack— he could actually feel it. His hands were around her throat. His penis was throbbing. He stared into her eyes as he drove into her body, coming harder and harder as he choked away her life. He ground her into the concrete floor as the last spasm surged through him. He was triumphant. She was violated and dead. It was a power like no other. And the best was yet to be.

In the meantime, he needed release, and he needed it now.

Dropping down on his cot, he threw a blanket over himself and reached for his drawing tablet.

One hand went to his crotch. The other grabbed the red crayon. He began to draw furiously.

Each slash of crimson corresponded to a pulsing surge of his climax as it shuddered through him.

The next two days were long and tedious as the FI team worked with the police and on their own to identify the sick bastard who'd killed Kendra Mallery and was now threatening to extend his killing spree to Casey.

Having done her part—compiling the two lists Marc had asked for—Casey was going crazy. She'd watched the video of the campus vigil three times, and other than feeling sick to her stomach, she'd seen nothing incriminating. All that it had succeeded in doing was to bring back a flood of painful memories from the past as she relived the vigil she'd attended for Holly. Different victims. Same nightmare. Same sense of helpless frustration.

Casey's existence was like being under house arrest. She was practically imprisoned in the brownstone, and when she went out, either Patrick or one of his hired bodyguards was glued to her side.

Her confinement only served to intensify the sense of responsibility she felt to solve the Jan Olson case. Jan's father had called each day, several times a day, to see if there was any news, even a tiny lead, to tell them where his daughter or her body could be found.

Casey couldn't ignore that. She'd made a commitment to this poor dying man. She intended to fulfill it.

She couldn't just rely on Claire's vision of seeing Jan racing terrified through a park, glancing fearfully over her shoulder. That was like looking for a needle in a haystack. There were countless parks in New York City, and that was assuming the attack had taken place here.

Holed up in one of the smaller conference rooms, Casey went

through everything they had. She followed up on Brenda's list, contacting as many people who'd known Jan as possible, particularly her boyfriend, Chris Towers, who now lived in Colorado with his wife and two kids. He was completely taken aback by the subject of Casey's phone call, but he answered every one of her questions, and his take on Jan was similar to Brenda's, only from a boyfriend's point of view. He confirmed that he and Jan were pretty much inseparable, but *not* sexually active, so pregnancy was out. And he agreed with Brenda that, in the week leading up to her disappearance, Jan had been acting unusually jumpy and nervous. She'd assured him it was just academic stress. But when she'd vanished without a trace, he couldn't help believing the two were related. He and Brenda had contacted the police, but no sign of Jan materialized. Eventually, they were forced to accept the fact that she'd taken off on her own. Any other theory was too horrific to live with.

"When was the last time you remember seeing Jan alive?" Casey concluded, asking it as a routine question. Frankly, she didn't count on his answer to shed any light on things. If he and Jan were as inseparable as it seemed, he'd doubtless seen her on the day she'd vanished.

Sure enough, Chris replied, "The afternoon she disappeared. I walked her to work. We made plans to meet up in her dorm room around eleven o'clock that night. She never came back."

Work.

Abruptly, something clicked in Casey's mind. Jan had been a waitress at the Lakeside Restaurant at the Boathouse in Central Park. If you coupled that with Claire's vision—a park with a backdrop of water—you got a strong potential scenario for the scene of the crime.

That was solid enough to act on.

Casey walked through the brownstone and found Claire in the main conference room finishing up a phone call with the police.

"Anything?" she asked.

Disconnecting the call, Claire shook her head. "Nothing yet."

"Then that frees you up to go with me."

"Go where?"

"To Central Park. To the restaurant Jan Olson worked in. We've been so wrapped up, we didn't get around to going there and questioning the staff."

Claire rose slowly from her chair, her mouth set in a firm line. "Number one, you're not going to Central Park—that's an open arena for people. Number two, Jan worked there fifteen years ago. Even if we find someone who's still around from back then, I doubt anyone would remember a college girl who waitressed there that long ago."

"I don't know. But we're going to find out." Casey wasn't letting this one go. "Take something of Jan's, something you feel connected to. I'll announce our outing to the team. I don't care if they barricade the door. We're going."

A half hour and a huge shouting match later, Casey and Claire, together with Dave Brinkman—one of Patrick's bodyguards—made their trip to Central Park. They walked all over the grounds, Claire tightly clasping Jan's calendar in the hope of picking up some of her energy and connecting it to their location.

Casey scanned the various areas of the park—the wide-open grassy spaces and the darker wooded sections.

"Could this have been the park you were visualizing when you saw Jan running away?" she prompted Claire, having purposely omitted any mention of the connection between Claire's vision and their trip to the Boathouse. She wanted anything that came from Claire to be spontaneous.

But now was the time to push it.

"Think," Casey urged. "Could Jan maybe have left her job and been tracked down and chased through Central Park?"

Claire started. Then awareness dawned in her eyes. She thought for a moment, turning up her palm in an uncertain gesture. "It's possible. I'm not sensing anything yet." She continued to walk, her forehead creased in concentration. Casey followed, noticing that, without realizing it, Claire was heading toward the lakeside approach to the Boathouse.

Abruptly, Claire stopped dead in her tracks, staring at the rowboats and gondolas moving across the lake. "The water," she murmured. "It was in the background when Jan was running. I'd forgotten. And there were butterflies. And birds. Those images are strong now—stronger than they originally were."

"The area around the Boathouse is known for its bird-watching," Dave commented. "There's even a bird registry to record observations." A corner of his mouth lifted when Casey turned to gaze at him, her brows arched in surprise. "I'm a trivia buff," he explained. "In fact, I can also verify the butterfly part. The last I recall, twenty-six species of butterflies have been spotted here."

"Wow." Casey sent him an admiring look. "And all Patrick mentioned was that you're a terrific bodyguard."

He shrugged. "I'm multitalented."

Claire was lost in her own world. "I'm starting to pick up on the sheer panic I sensed the other day. It's getting stronger. But it's still veiled—like there's a layer of gauze over it. I can't see through it."

"Maybe the attack happened farther away," Casey suggested. "Central Park is huge."

"True." Claire pressed her lips together. "I still need more."

"Then let's go inside and see if any of the staff remembers her."

"It's been fifteen years, Casey." Claire reiterated her earlier point. "Isn't that unrealistic?"

"Without a doubt," Casey concurred. "But that's why we're here. And we have to try, especially given the connection you're sensing."

Claire couldn't dispute that one. So she joined Casey and Dave as they went inside the restaurant.

But she was right. Interviewing people, seeking out information from fifteen years ago—it was like operating in a vacuum. Managers had changed, staff had come and gone and the clientele wasn't even the same as last year, much less fifteen years ago.

The best that Casey, Claire and Dave could do was leave with a printout of longstanding employees. It was a stretch to think that any of those people would remember Jan, much less who she'd been afraid of. But Casey was confident of one thing— that whatever had happened to Jan Olson, it had happened in Central Park.

A very weak lead, but a lead nonetheless—one that required Forensic Instincts' investigation.

The team wasn't going to be happy.

Despite their professionalism, their loyalty to Casey superseded all else. And right now, Ryan was scrutinizing the video footage from the vigil, Patrick was grilling everyone at Columbia that Ryan's research had spit out on the printer and Marc was poring over the two lists Casey had compiled.

The situation was lousy.

And Casey's nightmares were filled with fear.

Hutch threw the last of his clothes into an overnight bag, gulped down the rest of his coffee and glanced at his watch.

It was eight-fifteen, pretty late at night to begin a five-hour drive. He didn't give a damn. If he got on the road in the next few minutes, he'd be in Manhattan a little after one. He'd been working fourteen-hour days since the night Casey had called to say she needed him, just so he could get his piles of work done and get the hell out of Quantico. Yeah, it had been an exhausting stint, but he'd survived on next to no sleep before, and for less important reasons than this.

He was leaving—tonight.

It had taken him two meetings with the head of BAU-4 to agree to give him the days off. He'd accrued the personal time. But it wasn't that simple. The work wasn't going away. He'd had to plow through it in order to disappear for a while.

Casey hadn't pressed him to come. But just the fact that she'd called… That was something she didn't do. Hutch knew her well. They'd been involved for over a year now. The feelings were there. The words weren't spoken. It didn't matter. They both knew what they had. And it was more than enough to propel him to Manhattan.

He'd heard Casey's tone.

She was scared.

And, in his opinion, she had reason to be.

Hutch zipped up his bag and slung it over his shoulder. Then he scooped up his car keys and headed for the door.

Ten minutes later, he was on the road.


Maura Harris loved her job.

She'd worked in all aspects of veterinary care since she was a teenager and had volunteered at an animal clinic cleaning out kennel cages. Now she was applying to veterinary schools, hoping to one day fulfill her dream and run her own animal clinic.

In the meantime, she worked at the Canine Palace, a posh full-service inn for dogs, located in Tribeca. She handled everything from long-term boarding to doggy day care. Her time there had reinforced what she already believed: dogs were far easier and more delightful to deal with than their owners.

She commuted from Hoboken, a short ride on the PATH train that she could do in her sleep. With her credentials, she could easily have gotten a job closer to home, but she was too attached to her regular "clientele" to make a move.

Her hours were long. Sometimes she didn't get back to her apartment until after eight, especially when busy executives were picking up their pups after a very full day. But it wasn't a problem, since her boyfriend was an architect whose hours were as crazy as hers. Whoever got home first either cooked or bought dinner.

This particular night had been an exceptionally long one. A slew of professionals showed up to pick up their furry friends from doggy day care, and an equal number of folks had arrived to reunite with their pets after a week's or two-week vacation. Even that strange guy who'd been coming in every other day for a month to buy toys for a dog Maura had never seen showed up, examining the squeaky latex animals for an hour before he chose two of them to purchase.

By the time she got out the door, Maura's red hair was sweaty and stuck to her neck, and she was more exhausted than usual. All she wanted to do was take a hot shower, put something in her stomach and crawl off to bed.

She didn't pay a damned bit of attention to her fellow PATH train riders, nor did she glance around as she took the shortcut to her apartment. Her boyfriend hated when she went that way. It took her right by the sketchiest section of town. He'd rather she took a taxi. But she wasn't waiting around to hail one. Her sole focus was on getting home.

She was halfway by the projects when she got the eerie sense that she was being followed. She halted, turning to scrutinize the area behind her. No one. She was just being paranoid. Too many warnings from her boyfriend and too many TV shows.

Still, she picked up her pace. Commuting time was over, it was dark and she couldn't shake the creepy feeling in her gut.

Rough hands grabbed her from behind, and an arm hooked around her neck. A handkerchief was forced over her nose and mouth. The blade of a knife dug into her abdomen, just shy of piercing her body. Struggling wildly, she flung down her purse, hoping her assailant would take it and run off.

He didn't.

She fought harder, trying to shove away the knife blade as she thrashed her head, struggling for air. She'd watched enough cop shows on TV to recognize the sickeningly sweet odor of chloroform. She had to escape before the dizziness took over.

It was useless. Her assailant was too strong.

He began to drag her off.

In a last-ditch effort, she raised a leg and kicked him as hard as she could with the heel of her shoe.

He swore violently and stabbed the blade into her waist—not enough to kill her, but enough. Maura cried out in pain, but her cries were silenced by the handkerchief.

"You're not dying here," he muttered. "Not until I'm done with you."

He crammed the handkerchief into her mouth, pinching her nose closed and forcing the chloroform to do its job.

Blood soaking through her clothes, Maura collapsed against him, unconscious.


Claire was in her apartment, trying to relax. Sitting in the lotus position on her bed, she was taking deep cleansing breaths, letting the calming energy flow through her.

All of that ended in a surge of blinding panic, and a vision that was all too familiar. The same. Different. Terrifying.

Dear God, it was happening again.

*Patrick. She had to reach Patrick.*

# CHAPTER
## TEN

Casey had just stepped out of the shower and was towel-drying her hair when her cell phone rang.

She picked it up cautiously, glancing down at caller ID. Her gut clenched when she saw that the number was blocked. Still, she wouldn't allow herself to freak out. Lots of people preferred to have their cell phone numbers unidentifiable.

She punched on the cell. "Casey Woods."

"Hello, Red." The tinny scrambled voice sent chills up her spine. "Stop searching. That body is cold. There's a warm one with your name on it."

Casey sank down on the edge of her bed, trembling but determined to find out all she could before this psycho hung up on her.

"What cold body?" she demanded.

"The Olson girl. One of my first. Before I knew exactly the victim type I wanted. I like to think of her as practice."

*Oh, dear God.* Casey felt bile rise in her throat. "You killed…" She swallowed hard. "How do I know you're telling the truth?"

"I'll give her to you. It's ironic. You're doing such a thorough search, and she's right in your backyard. Worth Street, near Broadway. The newly renovated office building near the pharmacy. In a crawl space in the basement. She's still there. Pretty well preserved. I made sure of it."

Casey didn't—couldn't—speak.

"Worry about the present," the chilling voice continued. "I've just solved your old case. Put all your efforts where they belong. This new one—I've still got her blood on my hands. Find her while the body's warm. And know that it'll soon be your turn. Get ready for me, Red."

The line went dead.

It took Casey a few moments to get herself under control. Then she called Patrick's friend, Captain Sharp, at the Twenty-six Precinct, so that the NYPD could start digging for Jan Olson's body.

She had no doubt it would be where her caller had said.

Patrick was watching TV in the living room of his Hoboken brownstone when Claire's call came through. She was so overwrought he could barely understand her.

"Claire, calm down," he instructed, muting the sound. "Are you telling me there's been another murder?"

"Yes." Claire swallowed some water to compose herself. "It wasn't as clear as the last time. I couldn't see or hear anything to give me a clue as to where it was. But I had to call you. I had to…" She broke off, as if something were coming to her. "It happened nearby."

"Nearby where? The office?" Now Patrick was getting nervous. "Marc's with Casey. She should be safe."

"No. Not the office. Near you."

"In Hoboken?"

"Yes." Claire was getting agitated again. "Patrick, do you know anyone at your local precinct?"

"Of course."

"Call them. Now."

Casey nearly collided with Marc in the hall outside her bedroom. He was in special-ops mode, his entire body geared like a missile.

"Are you okay?" he demanded.

Still trembling, Casey stood there, white-faced, wrapped in her terry-cloth robe, her hair damp and tousled. "You know?" she asked Marc.

"I know there was allegedly another victim. Patrick called. He's worried about you. You didn't answer your phone. So he called me."

"I was talking to the police." Casey dragged a hand through her hair, trying to get her bearings. "I don't understand. How did Patrick know?"

"Claire. She says the crime happened in Hoboken." Marc's eyes bore into Casey. "You heard from the killer."

She nodded. "He told me about the new victim—and the old one."

Marc looked puzzled. "Old one? Which old one? Kendra?"

"No. Jan Olson. He told me where we could find her body. He said she was one of his first kills."

"Shit," Marc hissed. "He's claiming to be the same serial killer? Casey, there's a fifteen-year gap between the murders of Jan Olson and Kendra Mallery."

"I realize that. But I believe him. He didn't miss a beat. He gave me the location of Jan's body to get my focus off her and on to his current killing spree—with me as his finale."

Marc seized Casey's arm. "We're going downstairs to the living room. I'm getting you a drink. Then we'll talk."

Casey didn't protest. With Hero padding along behind her, she followed Marc down the staircase to the third floor, where the team's cozy living room was located. They didn't spend much time here; they were too busy doing other things that precluded relaxing. But the room was soothing, with decorative wood moldings and wainscoting, cushy sofas and a shag rug that Hero loved to roll around on.

He didn't play now. He climbed up on the sofa next to Casey and put his head on her lap. He was keenly aware of her tension. And he knew something was up.

"Thanks, boy," she said softly, stroking his head. "I could use the comfort."

Marc came in, carrying two glasses of bourbon. "Here." He shoved one in Casey's hand. "Drink."

"Yes, sir." She took a deep swallow, closing her eyes as the warming effects of the alcohol spread through her. "Just what the doctor ordered."

Marc lowered himself into the chair across from her. "Tell me exactly what he said."

After another swallow, Casey complied, relaying the conversation as close to verbatim as she could.

Marc whipped out his cell phone. "I'm sure the pervert used a burn phone. But we can try to trace it." He punched in Ryan's cell on speed dial.

Ryan answered on the first ring. "I'm already on it. Yoda pinged me. Tracing the call is a near impossibility. But I'm trying."

Ryan's tone told Marc there was more. "And?" he prompted.

"And I didn't mention it to Casey because she would've blown me away, but I installed an app on her cell phone. Every phone call she makes and receives is recorded and uploaded to our servers for analysis. I skip the calls with Hutch," he added, striving, in his customary way, for a flicker of levity. "Even I have a moral code when it comes to *that* kind of invasion of privacy."

"Admirable," Marc said dryly. He then filled Ryan in on the rest—Claire's intrusive vision and her call to Patrick.

"So the cops are searching for two bodies simultaneously." Ryan gave a grunt of disbelief. "This is crazy. If that sick wacko isn't lying—and I doubt that he is—we're talking about a career serial killer."

"Yup." Marc took a gulp of bourbon. "So, assuming the call can't be traced, what's your strategy?"

"I'm analyzing the killer's word pattern as we speak. The voice might be unrecognizable thanks to the scrambler, but the choice of words isn't." He paused. "How's Casey?"

"Holding up."

"Once I've got this running, I'm coming in. I'll do the rest from my lair."

"Good idea. I'll call Patrick and Claire and fill them in on the pieces they're missing. The whole team should be here."

And they were, gathered around the conference table when the first call came in just after midnight. It was from the NYPD's Twenty-sixth Precinct.

"We found her," Captain Sharp reported. "The body was precisely where your caller said it would be. It took a while to get through that narrow crawl space. But it's done. Now we wait for confirmation of her identity. We'll compare the victim's dental records to Jan Olson's. Oh, and she was wearing a brass locket.

We're going to examine it for partial prints. Who knows? We might get lucky. Especially if she was strangled."

"*If?*" Casey lost it. "Was she or wasn't she? And not only strangled, but raped, tortured, naked?" She tried, unsuccessfully, to stem her emotional outburst. "I know the M.E. has to do his job. But give me *something,* Captain."

The silence was oppressive. Obviously, Captain Sharp was taken aback by Casey's over-the-top response.

"Just tell us what you can, Horace," Patrick interceded. "We'll wait for the rest. It's been a rough night here."

"Understood." Captain Sharp accepted that, since he'd been made aware of the potential killer's claim about the current homicides. "I can tell you the body was nude, other than for the locket. As to any evidence of rape or strangulation—that's going to have to come from the M.E.'s office. We weren't able to identify any ligature or finger marks around the throat area, not with fifteen years of decomposition."

"The body's with the M.E. now?" Patrick asked.

"Uh-huh. I'll call you as soon as we get the report—after I notify Daniel Olson."

"The poor man," Claire murmured, disconnecting the call.

"On some level, he's been expecting this," Marc said. "It won't make the pain any easier to bear, but it will give him the closure he needs."

"And if the cops are lucky enough to get a fingerprint, we might get the killer—or at least his identity," Ryan added.

"Small consolation to a father who's just found out his daughter was brutally murdered," Claire said. "Fearing something and knowing it to be true are two different things. The latter eclipses any shred of hope."

Marc cleared his throat. "There's something else we have to discuss. Not about Jan's murder. About the one being investigated now. If Claire's right and the victim *was* killed in Hoboken, it obviously suggests a pattern."

"Damn right it does," Patrick agreed before Marc could even finish. "The offender is striking as close to home for Casey as possible—and taunting her in the process. First, a murder near Ryan's place. Now, a second one near me. That's no coincidence."

"It certainly isn't." A deep baritone came from the doorway.

The whole team turned around, just as Yoda announced, "Hutch has arrived. He operated the Hirsch pad correctly in order to gain access."

"Yeah, and I identified myself to the guard outside, too." Hutch tossed his jacket on a chair, dropping his overnight bag.

There was something about Hutch that dominated a room. He was a confident, take-charge man, powerfully built with hard features and piercing blue eyes, whose very presence screamed leadership. He'd been a D.C. cop, worked tough neighborhoods and had a scar on his left temple to show for it. He'd learned to keep his thoughts and feelings to himself, to remain silent until the person he was interviewing blurted out things that he or she wouldn't normally reveal. He'd also learned to capitalize on his strengths and to keep his weaknesses well hidden.

Casey was his main weakness.

She looked over at him now and blinked. "I didn't know you were coming this soon."

"Neither did I. Not until late this afternoon. Looks like I showed up at exactly the right time. What happened?"

"The cops recovered the body of a girl who was killed fifteen years ago—possibly by the same killer we're dealing with now—and who allegedly just killed again. At least according to what he said to me in our phone call." Casey blurted the whole thing out at once. "Aren't you glad you came to visit?"

Hutch narrowed in on Casey's face. He took in her ashen coloring, her huge, wide eyes and her tousled appearance. She'd thrown on a pair of jeans and a T-shirt and tied back her hair, but she wasn't the together-looking woman she always presented to the world.

"Yeah," he replied. "Actually, I am." His gaze flickered to Marc. "Can you fill me in?"

Nodding, Marc rose.

"The two of you macho guys aren't going off and closeting yourself in another room, and I'm *not* going to be coddled," Casey stated flatly.

"You're about to collapse," Hutch said, not backing down an inch.

"Then I'll do it here. We're waiting for a call from the Hoboken police. Plus, the M.E.'s examining the first victim's body. I'm not budging until I know what's going on."

Hutch shook his head. "The Hoboken police you might hear from soon. But an update from the M.E.'s office? Especially when the cops haven't spoken with the victim's next of kin? That call isn't going to come in for hours."

"Fine. Then I'll wait for the cop to call."

Hutch didn't change his expression. "Okay. Sit at the table and drink coffee. Let Marc fill me in." He was placating her, which he was more than willing to do if that was what it took. "We won't even leave the room. We'll stay in plain sight and talk over there." He jerked his thumb in the direction of the far corner. "Yoda can eavesdrop and give you a full playback later."

"That's correct," Yoda supplied.

Casey had that "it's my case" look on her face.

"Go ahead and run the show." Hutch read her expression easily. "But conserve your energy. I think Marc can handle a verbal briefing, don't you?"

"Fine. Yes. Go ahead." Casey waved her hand. "Marc's probably more coherent right now than I am, anyway."

As she spoke, Patrick's cell phone rang.

"Yeah," he answered. A brief silence. "What's her name and what did he tell you about her?" Another silence, this one a bit longer. Patrick's jaw tightened. "Thanks, Al. Call me as soon as you find something out." He punched off.

"What is it?" Casey demanded.

"A guy called into the Hoboken police to report that his girlfriend never came home tonight," Patrick answered. "She works in Tribeca and lives in Hoboken. She called her boyfriend around eight-thirty and said she was on her way. She never showed up."

"Tribeca," Casey repeated. "Where?"

"At the Canine Palace."

"Where we board Hero." Casey's voice was a monotone. "Is her name Maura?"

"Maura Harris, yes." Patrick studied Casey's reaction. "You obviously know her."

"She's great with Hero." Casey's reply was wooden. "I can also save you the description. She's a petite redhead, maybe late twenties. She's studying to be a vet." There was a pained pause. "Goddammit."

"She takes the PATH train."

"She took it," Claire said as fact. "She arrived at Hoboken. After that…" She swallowed, then fell silent. A flicker of awareness dawned in her eyes. "Affluence and poverty." The words seemed to come on their own. "Expensive condos. Low-income housing. One on one side. One on the other." A confused shake of her head. "And Andrew Jackson." She turned her palms up in non-comprehension. "A twenty-dollar bill? That doesn't feel right."

"Jackson Street," Patrick said. "Hoboken's west-east blocks

are named after U.S. presidents, sequentially from Washington Street. The projects and the condos you're describing are on Jackson Street—all the way over on the west side of town."

That resounded in Claire's mind and she gave a painful nod. "Have the police check there. They'll find the body."

# CHAPTER
## ELEVEN

The waiting game was under way. And the collective patience of the FI team was fraying.

They brewed multiple pots of coffee, read over their research until the words were swimming in front of them and paced the conference room with growing frustration.

It was Marc who finally broke the stalemate.

"We need some separation from this," he said, putting down his coffee mug. "Obviously, no calls are coming in anytime soon. In the meantime, we're banging our heads against the wall going over the same old information. Let's take a few hours and chill out. Hutch is here, so I'm going to the gym. I suggest you all follow suit. Do something to take it down a notch. Sleep if you can. Or whatever works. Keep your cell phones on. Stay close by."

"Good idea." Patrick rose from his chair. "I'll head home to Adele and maybe catch a few hours of rest."

"I'll stay here," Claire murmured, massaging her temples. "I'll be doing yoga in the third-floor office where I store my mats. With any luck, it'll calm me down."

"I'll join you at the gym," Ryan told Marc. "I really need to work off some of this stress. Waiting makes me crazy."

"Fine. Let's get going." Marc headed for the door.

Casey didn't budge from the conference table. Her stare was fixed on the telephone.

"And you get some rest." Hutch came up behind her and planted his hands on her shoulders. "You don't think you need it. But you do." He pivoted her chair around and pulled her to her feet. "You need to conserve your strength. It's going to be taxed to the nth degree until this case is solved."

"Okay." Casey nodded, forcing herself to see the wisdom of Hutch's words. She glanced around the room at each member of her team. "But whichever one of us gets news first, call the others ASAP."

"Agreed," Ryan said, speaking for the group. "And, Yoda?" he called out. "Remain on active standby."

"Active standby initiated," Yoda responded.

It was an hour later, and Casey's bedroom was dark and quiet—other than the thrum of Manhattan traffic from outside and the snorts Hero made in his sleep.

Hutch had been right. Casey was past the point of exhaustion. And she'd tried to rest, but without any success. Worn out or not, she'd been too wired.

Hutch had known just what to do about that.

Now, she blew out a breath—along with a wave of tension. "Have I mentioned that I'm glad you're here?" she murmured, draping her leg across his and resting her head on his chest.

"Not in so many words. But in actions? Yeah, I kind of picked up on the fact that you were happy to see me." Hutch ran his fingers through Casey's tangled mane of hair. "And, in case you didn't notice, I feel the same way."

"I noticed." Her lips curved a bit. "I still can't sleep. But staying awake did become infinitely more pleasurable. Your efforts are greatly appreciated, SSA Hutchinson."

"Glad to be of service. Diversionary tactics are one of my strong suits."

"You have many strong suits. Getting my mind off things I can't control doesn't even rank close to the top of that list." She raised herself up and kissed him. "Thank you for moving the mountains I'm sure you had to move in order to get here."

"This is where I need to be," he said simply. "I'll use whatever personal time I've accrued so I can stay until this threat to you is over. *If* that becomes necessary."

Casey's brows drew together. The only way it wouldn't be necessary for Hutch to use his vacation time would be if he was here in an official capacity. And she didn't see that in the cards.

"I doubt the NYPD is going to ask for the BAU's assistance on this one," she said. "Even if this does turn out to be one longtime offender—which I believe it will—the New York cops have the training and resources to conduct the investigation alone."

"You're right," Hutch said. "That's why I'm going at this from a different angle."

"Which is?"

"I spoke to Patrick. If things play out the way I think they will, he's going to put the bug in the Hoboken P.D.'s ear. We'll have a serial killer who's been active for fifteen years, and who chose a Hoboken resident as his latest victim. Not only that, but he disposed of her body in town. They'll have every reason to ask for help. Especially when there's an FBI agent who works at the BAU already in place—an agent who's ready, willing and able to assist with the investigation."

"You're not exactly objective on this one," Casey pointed out.

"No, I'm not. Which gives me extra incentive to solve it. You and I have done this dance before. I don't step over the line."

Casey glanced at him dubiously. "I doubt your supervisor's going to buy that, not this time. Every clash we've had in the past has been case-related. I've never been a potential victim before."

"Why don't you let me worry about handling my boss?" Hutch rolled Casey onto her back, that familiar smoky look in his eyes. "Are you planning on sleeping or not?"

"Not."

He shifted his weight, covering her body with his. "Then let's put this time to good use."

It was almost dawn when the Hoboken P.D. called Patrick on his cell phone to report that they'd found Maura Harris's body in a grassy area behind a string of buildings on Jackson Street between 5th and 6th. Her boyfriend had come in and made a positive ID, and the medical examiner had done a preliminary autopsy.

The description of the body they provided was practically identical to that of Kendra Mallery's. Maura Harris had been wrapped in a canvas tarp, beneath which her nude body was as limp as a rag doll. Her clothing had been shredded. There was physical evidence of rape—no semen, but severe vaginal bruising. Her wrists had been bound together. The cause of death was strangulation, and the hyoid bone in her neck was fractured. She must have put up a fight, because there was a shallow stab wound on the right side of her abdomen. Contrary to that destruction, lipstick had been applied to her lips as if to enhance her appearance. But locks of her hair had been snipped off, and there was a red ribbon tied around her throat in a bow.

The one addition to the scenario was that tucked beneath the red ribbon was another clump of hair. It didn't match the exact color and texture of Maura's.

"Tell your contact at the Hoboken P.D. to work with the Twenty-sixth Precinct and get the NYPD lab to run a DNA test," Hutch instructed Patrick as the team reconvened—yet again—around the conference room table. "I'd be willing to bet that the hair tucked into the red bow belongs to Kendra Mallery. The killer is putting his mark on the crimes, driving home the connection between the two and taunting us with his superiority at the same time."

"Yeah, I agree," Patrick said, making the phone call.

Casey leaned her head back and dragged a hand through her hair. "Kendra. Now Maura. It's my fault that they're dead."

"Cut it out, Casey." Ryan sliced the air with the side of his hand. "This guy is insane. His actions are his doing, not yours."

"Yes, but he's after me. He just has some sick need to prove something before he closes in on me. Why? Who the hell is he?"

As if on cue, the Forensic Instincts' landline rang.

Seeing the NYPD number on caller ID, Casey pressed the speaker phone button. "Forensic Instincts."

"Ms. Woods? This is Captain Sharp," the caller said.

"Hello, Captain. I have you on speaker. The whole team is here." She drew a deep breath. "What do you have for us?"

"A hell of a puzzle," he replied in a grim tone. "Word got through to me at the same time as it did to the First Precinct." That was the police precinct right there in Tribeca, where the body, presumably Jan's, had been found.

"And?"

"And, given the circumstances and the fact that all roads lead to my district, this case is now officially under my jurisdiction. However, between what I'm about to tell you and the call I got from the Hoboken P.D., my next phone call will be to the FBI. They need to be involved. This is way bigger and more complicated than anything I expected."

"Please explain." Casey was starting to get that ominous knot in her stomach. "Was the body Jan Olson?"

"Yes. Dental records confirmed that. The victim's father has been notified." There was a long, pensive pause. "But there's more. The police lab was able to apply heat to the brass locket. It's a complicated process—some chemical reaction I don't understand—but the result was that they were able to lift prints from it. They enhanced the prints by applying an electrostatic charge and dusted with a black fingerprint powder. The results were good enough to run through NCIC." He was referring to the National Crime Information Center, where all criminal offender data was electronically stored.

"Does that mean you found a match?" Marc asked, leaning forward with intense interest.

"Yes. The prints belong to a felon you've recently aided the NYPD in arresting. Glen Fisher."

"*Glen Fisher?*" Claire literally jumped up in her seat.

"Shit," Ryan muttered. "I don't believe this."

Casey said nothing. Her thoughts were racing too quickly to speak. She could still vividly remember that night last year when the FI team—who'd been approached at the final hour to assist the NYPD—had set up and apprehended Glen Fisher. His M.O. had been to rape and strangle redheaded college girls. Casey had posed as the ideal victim—a shy, vulnerable college kid hanging out alone at the bar near Tompkins Square Park where Fisher found his marks. She'd made sure she was the last patron to leave the bar, and walked right by the alley where Fisher was lying in wait.

The setup had paid off. Fisher had grabbed Casey at knife-point, dragged her into the alley and was yanking off her jeans when Marc exploded into the alley and slammed Fisher against the concrete wall, nearly breaking his neck until he exacted a confession.

The bastard had given up the locations of more than half a dozen bodies to the cops, and had been tried and sentenced to thirty-to-life. The FI team had pushed for life without parole, but Fisher's lawyer had played it well. He'd stressed the coercion Marc had used to get the confession, and the fact that the body locations Fisher had provided were pure hearsay and could have been information he'd blurted out under duress after having overheard them anywhere.

The jury didn't buy his innocence for a minute. The guilty verdict had come in fast and furious. But the judge didn't feel he had enough to render life without parole. So Fisher had gotten thirty to life and was sent to Auburn State—a maximum security prison.

Of course, he'd been a model prisoner there, the only noise he made being the appeals he continually filed on his own behalf.

Casey refused to entertain the possibility of his getting released—ever. She'd looked into those terrifying, empty eyes. She recognized a psychopath when she saw one. And she shuddered at the thought of him ever being allowed to walk freely in the outside world again.

"That means Fisher was committing his crimes long before last year's killing spree," Marc was saying. "We knew he was a sexual homicide offender. We knew he targeted college-age redheads. But we had no idea he was doing this over such a long interval."

"Exactly," Captain Sharp responded. "But he was. How many other victims he killed between then and when he was apprehended last year, I have no idea. That's what we have to determine."

*That* statement made Casey speak up. "I want to reexamine the Holly Stevens case," she stated. "Dig out whatever DNA evidence is stored in the evidence locker and have it tested. I'm willing to bet Glen Fisher killed her, too." A weighty pause. "And, Captain, with all due respect, please don't tell me there's no reason to believe Holly's was anything but an isolated crime. That reasoning doesn't fly—not anymore."

"I agree," he surprised her by saying. "I'll make sure the lab runs the necessary tests."

"Thank you." It was time to move on to the next, equally pressing issue. "One major aspect of this crime spree doesn't fit," Casey said. "The threatening calls I'm getting. The current crimes that are taking place, all of which my caller's taking credit for—how can those be committed by Fisher? He's in prison."

"That's the puzzle I was referring to. Obviously, they can't be. I called the prison myself and verified that Fisher is still there serving his sentence. Moreover, he has limited access to phone calls and every call he makes is on record."

"None of his calls was to me," Casey surmised.

"Right. So whoever's calling you and whoever killed the recent two victims isn't Glen Fisher—whether or not Fisher wants to take credit for them."

"The present-day killer probably knows Fisher," Marc said. "Maybe the two of them served time together. Or a dozen other maybes. But the current offender got his information from Fisher somehow."

"And he's likely carrying out a vendetta of Fisher's against Casey, whether by choice or via instructions from Fisher." For the first time, Hutch spoke. "He's also adding his own personal touch—the red ribbons wrapped around the victims' throats. Captain Sharp, this is Supervisory Special Agent Kyle Hutchinson. I'm with the FBI's Behavioral Analysis Unit. I've worked cases alongside Forensic Instincts in the past. Once you've called and made your formal request to the Bureau, I'm going to ask to be assigned to this case."

"That would be very much appreciated." Sharp sounded more than a little relieved. "Is it a coincidence that you're in New York? Or did you come up here to consult with Forensic Instincts on this case?"

"I actually drove up for a visit," Hutch replied easily. "But since I happened to walk right into this hornet's nest, I'm up-to-date on the details. My supervisor will send up another BAU agent to partner with me."

"Good. And I'll contact the Bureau's New York field office to get the Violent Crimes Squad involved." Sharp paused. "I don't have a good feeling about this new offender. His crimes are becoming more frequent and closer together."

"And, despite what Hollywood tells us, we all know there's no such thing as a copycat killer," Hutch said. "There are only new killers who capitalize on their predecessors' crimes, for various reasons. This guy is going for bigger and better than Glen Fisher's kills. And he's not choosing random victims. He's circling around Casey. She was the redhead who brought Fisher down. That means something—not only to Fisher, but to the new offender. He's not being subtle about her representing some sort of grand prize for him."

"I realize that." Casey had grown quiet again. She was thinking. "Captain Sharp, please, let's get Holly's personal items tested for a DNA match. You go ahead and make your FBI calls. Also, let's combine everything we have on Glen Fisher—his job, family, friends, anything. Maybe we can find someone in his life, however tangential, who's as warped as he is."

"One other thing," Claire inserted quietly. "I'd like to visit Daniel Olson, if you don't mind, Captain. He's been totally invested in finding his daughter's body. Now he's dealing with the finality of her death and the discovery of her killer. I know your precinct has reached out to him. But I feel that FI should do the same."

"By all means," Sharp agreed at once. "Forensic Instincts was instrumental in solving this case. I feel terribly sorry for Daniel. He's weak and frail, and he doesn't have much time left. He got what he wanted, but at what cost? I'm sure a condolence visit would be very much appreciated."

"We'll make that happen today." Claire's eyes were damp, her sensitive heart breaking for the dying man who was dealing with every parent's worst nightmare.

"I'll be in touch as soon as I have information and/or things in place," Sharp said.

Casey took charge the minute the phone call was disconnected.

"We've got two separate cases, linked by one killer, as far as I'm concerned," she told her team. "With regard to Fisher himself, we're going to learn every shred of information there is to learn about the bastard. That will help us figure out who's following in his footsteps. In the meantime, I want to contact the D.A.'s office. If it turns out that Fisher killed Holly—and you know he did—we'll have two old murders we can solidly link to him. I want him to be tried for them, for their families' sakes, and to ensure that Fisher gets back-to-back sentences that will keep him from ever seeing the light of day."

"Agreed." Marc turned to Ryan. "With regard to the current case, we still have video footage to review from Kendra's vigil.

Maybe we can spot someone suspicious on the scene. Hutch can use his trained eye to dissect it with us. By that time, we'll have word from the Hoboken P.D. on whether or not the clump of hair under Maura's ribbon belonged to Kendra."

His brows drew together thoughtfully. "We need to reexamine the list of potential victims. Kendra was found in Dumbo. That's near Ryan's place. Maura's body was in Hoboken. That's Patrick neck of the woods. If our theory is right, that leaves the East Village, where Claire lives, and Bensonhurst, where I live. We have to cross-match any of the women on Casey's list who has a residential or working tie to either of these two locations."

"What about Tribeca?" Ryan asked.

"That's iffy," Hutch interjected. "When he gets that close, he might want to perform his big finale and go after Casey. But it can't hurt to double-check the names on the list and see if any of them has ties to Tribeca."

"I'll pull the Glen Fisher file and start researching," Patrick said. He gave Casey a questioning look. "I hadn't come on board FI yet when you worked that case. I assume it was in conjunction with the Twelfth Precinct?" He referred to the area where Tompkins Square Park was located.

Casey nodded.

"Fine. I'll swing by there and see what they'll share with me."

Claire rose. "Casey, do you want to come with me to see Daniel Olson?"

"Yes." Casey got to her feet. "I also have some arrangements I need to make."

Hutch recognized the expression on her face. And he didn't like it. "What arrangements?"

"I plan to get permission to visit Auburn."

"You're visiting Glen Fisher?" Hutch looked more pissed than he did surprised.

"Damn straight." Casey raised her chin. "Fisher wants me up close and personal? Let's give him exactly what he wants."

# CHAPTER TWELVE

Later that day, Casey and Claire—with one of Patrick's body-guards glued to their side—visited Daniel Olson to pay their respects. There was little they could offer him except their con-dolences and offers to help with Jan's funeral arrangements. Mr. Olson quietly told them he had everything taken care of, and thanked them for getting to the truth, as well as for recover-ing his daughter's body. He begged them to make sure that the monster who'd done this to his child was locked up forever, so he could never hurt another man's daughter.

That plea doubled Casey's determination to ensure that Glen Fisher rotted in prison for the rest of his days. She drove away from the Olson house, watching Jan's father in her rearview mirror. He stood in the doorway, frail, broken, himself on the verge of death. Casey had to look away, the emotion was so great. But so was the resolve. That miserable son of a bitch was going to pay for the rest of his life. She would see to it herself.

She'd made the necessary phone calls to set things in motion. Now she just had to wait for the official word that she was on the visitors' list. As soon as that happened, she'd jump in the car and make the five-hour drive to upstate New York, where Auburn Correctional Facility was located.

There was plenty of time to ponder how she was going to handle Fisher as she left Brooklyn now and headed back to Tribeca. The van was silent, with Claire gazing out the window with tears in her eyes, and their bodyguard texting Patrick with an update on their whereabouts. There was nothing to say, anyway, no peace in this kind of closure.

But there was a world of planning to do. And Casey used that quiet time to do it.

Her cell phone rang just as she turned onto their street.

She glanced at the dashboard, recognizing the number in the display. "Hi, Ryan."

"Hey. You guys okay?"

"It was tough. But we expected that. Any news on your end?"

"Yeah. The cops got their search warrant for Glen Fisher's apartment. They'll meet us there at seven tonight. They're anticipating that his wife, Suzanne, will be home from work by then."

"*Us?*" Casey repeated. "Does that mean FI is actually invited to accompany the detectives on the search?"

"After a good word from Captain Sharp, yes. Remember, he owed us one because of the Olson case. Not to mention how central you are to the ongoing case." A wry note crept into Ryan's voice. "Why? Did you think the lack of an official invite would keep us away?"

"Not for a second. Still, it makes things a little easier when we get official permission."

"True. But not nearly as much fun. I kind of like when my creativity is tested."

"Oh, it will be," Casey assured him. "The NYPD's generosity toward us will only go so far. Especially now that the FBI has been notified and is on the scene. In no time at all, we'll be steering our own course."

"And you and Hutch will be fighting," Ryan pointed out in a teasing tone.

"No doubt." Casey sighed. "Anyway, I'm pulling up to the brownstone now. I see a parking spot right out front. So Claire and I will be inside in a sec. I want to sit down and review every shred of information you dug up on Glen Fisher."

"No problem. I've got plenty. But it's still a work in progress," Ryan reported. "I'm also running a full background check on Fisher's wife, Suzanne. From the interviews I read in the original police report, it sounds as if she's scared shitless of the guy—not that I blame her. That could work in our favor."

Casey pulled into the parking spot and turned off the ignition. "I'm sure Hutch will be on the scene during the police search. I want FI to meet with him beforehand. He'll give us a profile on a serial sexual homicide offender's spouse. Is he with the NYPD detectives now?"

"Nope. He's here. He figured you'd want to go over a few things before leaving for Suzanne Fisher's. He's upstairs somewhere, reviewing Fisher's case file and bringing himself up to speed."

"Good. We're on our way in."

Casey held up her access card to the card reader and punched her security code into the Hirsch keypad. Opening the front door, she stepped into the FI lobby.

She'd barely hung up her jacket when her iPhone rang. This time when she saw the blocked caller ID, she felt a wave of anger rather than fear.

"Yes?" she said cryptically, expecting the worst.

"You can sense when it's me. I'm flattered." The scrambled voice echoed in her ear.

"Is there another victim you want to tell me about?"

An eerie chuckle. "Even *I* need a little prep time. No, not yet. I called to commend you on your touching visit to the Olson father. Also to applaud you for your initiative on the Holly Stevens case. Your friend was an easy mark. Very submissive. She hardly fought me. Just cried and begged."

Casey's fist clenched until her nails bit into her palm. But she wouldn't give in and lose control. That was exactly what he wanted. She'd keep her cool, stay outwardly calm and collected.

"Was there any other reason for your call?" she inquired.

"You know what my reasons are."

"To scare me."

"To remind you," he corrected. "Your turn is sooner than you think. You'll be stripped of your bravado, of your supposed calm demeanor and of everything else. You won't be able to hide then, Red. Not your emotions. Not your body. Not your life. You'll be at my mercy. What exhilarating divine justice."

The call was disconnected.

"Son of a bitch!" Casey exclaimed as she punched off her phone.

"It was him again," Claire said quietly. "He wants to shove himself in your face, so you'll know he's watching your every move."

"He also wants you to know that, no matter which lead you pursue or how much progress you make, he's still in control." Hutch had come downstairs to the front hallway a few minutes ago, and was leaning against the wall, listening to Casey's end of the conversation.

Casey nodded, meeting Hutch's eyes. "Did I handle it right?"

"Yes. You didn't break, but you let him have the last word. If you challenge him too much, he'll lose it. That will escalate his rage and make him twice as dangerous. Plus, he might stop calling, and reserve his anger for acting out. That would up the number of victims. You've got to play this very carefully."

"Do I go along with the pretense that he's Glen Fisher?"

Hutch frowned thoughtfully. "It's interesting. He never refers to himself by name, never throws the whole Glen Fisher charade in your face. That goes along with our theory that he's a different offender, one who's alluding to—or pretending to be—Fisher, but is, in fact, eager to outdo him. I'd lay off any personal reference. Just keep treating him the way you are—as an anonymous enemy. The more he toys with you, the more he talks, the more likely he is to give something away."

"Okay." Casey sent Hutch a questioning look. "Are you officially on the case?"

"Yup. I got the call from my supervisor while you were out. Brian Gardiner is driving up as we speak. He's a good guy and a good agent. We've partnered up quite a few times recently. We'll be assisting the NYPD and the Hoboken police department in this investigation."

"Any other Feds coming that I should know about?"

A corner of Hutch's mouth lifted. "That you should know about or that you should avoid?" He shook his head. "Right now, it's just us. The NYPD is on top of things. If that changes, there'll be additional agents assigned."

Marc heard their voices, and came downstairs from the kitchen, half a sliced turkey sandwich in his hand. "I got a call from Captain Sharp." He took a bite of his sandwich, chewed and swallowed, holding Casey's gaze as he did. He was alerting her to the fact that he was about to deliver the news that she both wanted and dreaded.

"The lab ran the traces of semen found on Holly Stevens's clothing through NCIC," he said gently. "The DNA conclusively matched Glen Fisher's. You have your answer, Casey. Glen Fisher was responsible for both Holly Stevens's and Jan Olson's murders." He paused. "I'm sorry."

"I'm not." Casey's reply was firm, with absolutely zero element of surprise. "The horrifying part happened fifteen years ago. Putting a name to the offender is good news, not bad. Now Jan and Holly can get the justice they deserve. I'll make sure of it." She continued without missing a beat. "FYI, you're a minute too late with your announcement. I was just told about Holly from the horse's mouth."

"You got another phone call?"

"Indeed I did." Casey relayed the details of the phone conversation—as well as of Hutch's analysis—to Marc.

"This psychopath really wants to get all the accolades he feels he deserves," Marc responded.

Hutch's forehead was wrinkled in thought. "He wants to be Glen Fisher, but better than Glen Fisher. His technique is more polished than Fisher's. His signature red ribbon and the lock of hair is more intricate than anything Fisher did. All of that suggests he wants to outdo the master. On the flip side, he's obsessed with revenge against Casey, and with letting her know it every step of the way. That suggests he wants to convince us he *is* Fisher. Also, the original two bodies—Jan's and Holly's—had semen present. The current crimes have none."

Marc pursed his lips as he digested that. "There was no semen present on the bodies recovered last year, either."

"True," Hutch acknowledged. "Clearly, Fisher realized that DNA analysis had become far more sophisticated, and he didn't want to get caught. But that's not what this is about, at least not entirely. Sure, the new offender might be in the system and is protecting himself. But he's also taunting Casey. The lack of DNA evidence is meant to keep her off balance and wondering, on some level, if it just *might* be Glen Fisher committing these crimes—even though that's a virtual impossibility."

"Head games." Marc nodded. "Good point. So we can't assume the killer's in NCIC and is using condoms to avoid getting caught."

"Right. It could very well be that he *is* in the system. But it could just as easily be that he's not."

"So we're standing here with nothing." Casey sounded as if she wanted to slug someone—and that was exactly the way she felt.

"No," Hutch corrected her. "We're standing here with lots of information that we have to process in order to come up with answers." He glanced at his watch. "We're due at Fisher's residence in a few hours. Who from FI is coming?" He shot Casey a questioning look. "You and Marc?"

"I'm coming, too," Claire said at once. She and Casey had discussed this earlier in the day. "Casey and Marc will join you and the detectives for the search and questioning. I'll go where the energy takes me. Maybe I can pick up on something that will translate into a lead."

Hutch nodded, but said nothing. It was no secret that he was on the fence about the whole psychic phenomenon. The BAU operated on scientific and psychological principles that were all rooted in logic. But on a personal level, Hutch couldn't argue with Claire's success rate. He felt tremendous respect for her. So he might not be an active proponent, but he didn't condemn it, either.

"It looks like we'll have a full house," he noted.

"That's good. We'll cover all the bases." Casey inclined her head. "Hutch, can you give us a half hour of your time before you take off for the Fisher place? Anything you can share that would help us profile Suzanne Fisher would be great. Nothing from the classified section," she said. "Just something beyond the basics that might be useful."

Hutch seemed mildly amused. "I think I could make that happen—*if* I'm invited to the meeting you're about to have with Ryan."

"Fair enough." Casey was more than happy to meet him halfway.

"Good. Then we'll pool our resources." Hutch gestured toward the stairway. "The main conference room?"

"Yes." Casey quickly texted Ryan to meet them upstairs with everything he had on Glen and Suzanne Fisher. "Let's do this now."

# CHAPTER THIRTEEN

At a true New York pace, Casey, Claire and Marc strode from the Lexington Avenue subway stop to East 52nd Street and Glen Fisher's midtown apartment. Casey's gaze darted up and down the block. Tree-lined sidewalks. Low-rise brick buildings. A local deli. A few small restaurants. A produce store. A stream of people arriving home from work. Some were hurrying inside their apartment buildings, ready to call it a day. Some were walking their dogs. And some were carrying bags of groceries they'd stopped to pick up for dinner.

Everything seemed so normal, just as it probably had last year, when a homicidal monster was living here without a single person's knowing it.

A bone-chilling reality.

Ryan's comprehensive background check on Fisher had given the team—and Hutch—the big picture on what the killer was about. The original stats the cops had provided last year had listed his age as approximately thirty-two or thirty-three. As it turned out, he was older—thirty-nine to be exact—with a trim physique, close-cropped hair and a smooth-shaven face that made him look a lot younger than almost forty. Professionally, he was a CPA in a medium-size accounting firm, where everyone pretty much operated autonomously, the only interaction among them being in the coffee room.

Upon Fisher's arrest, all the employees had been interviewed, and it seemed that no one knew very much about him. They had, however, all thought of him as very sharp—a real go-getter with a long list of clients—and perfectly affable, and they'd been shocked by the details of the crimes he'd committed.

Personally, Fisher and his wife, Suzanne, had been married for ten years, and they had no children. Suzanne was thirty-six, and a piano teacher in midtown. Money wasn't an object, since Glen Fisher's parents were both deceased, and had left him a large sum of money. That, in addition to the sizable trust fund his grandparents had left him, alleviated any monetary concerns. He'd had one brother, ten years his senior, who, along with his wife, had been killed in a car accident a dozen years ago. Their nine-year-old son, Jack, had come to live with his uncle and had remained there until seven years ago, when he'd taken off on his own.

There was very little outside the norm about Glen Fisher—at least on paper. That made the whole situation more terrifying.

Casey knew that the NYPD detectives were already on the scene, as were Hutch and Brian Gardiner. She and her team had intentionally arrived a little late, when Suzanne would be preoccupied with the search taking place in her home, and might be more receptive to some human interaction.

The FI team climbed up the four flights of stairs to the Fishers' two-bedroom walk-up, and rang the bell.

Suzanne Fisher opened the door. She was just as Casey had remembered her from the media footage of the trial—a thin woman with straight, light brown hair that touched her shoulders, angular features and brown eyes that were currently wide with apprehension. She looked like a frightened deer, one who wanted to run but had no idea in which direction to take off.

"Mrs. Fisher?" Casey asked politely. It was a rhetorical question, not only because Casey recognized her but because diagonally behind her were two detectives, rummaging through a rolltop desk in the living room.

"Yes." Suzanne studied Casey quizzically, as if trying to place her. "Are you with the police?"

"No." Casey steeled herself for the inevitable reaction. "I'm Casey Woods. This is Marc Devereaux and Claire Hedgleigh. We're with Forensic Instincts."

Sure enough, Suzanne's entire demeanor altered like the flick of a light switch.

"I remember you. What do you want?" she asked in a clipped tone.

"Just to talk to you." This was a time when candor was Casey's best ally. "I realize you have no great love for us. But we're hoping that, by speaking with you, we can help make sure that justice is done."

"You're the reason Glen was arrested in the first place."

"We were assisting at the request of law enforcement," Casey responded in a calm, straightforward tone. "Unfortunately, your husband attacked me at knifepoint in an alleyway. He was trying to rape me when Marc stepped in."

Marc didn't say a word. Casey understood that he was letting her take the lead, which was exactly what she wanted. A woman would have much more success with Suzanne. Not to mention that, between his powerful build and hard features, Marc was the epitome of intimidating. He could scare off a timid woman like Suzanne with one wrong response.

Suzanne's lips had tightened at Casey's statement, but the fear in her eyes didn't fade. "That's hearsay," she replied. She'd been well-coached, but Casey could see that she didn't believe a word of her own denial.

"No, that's fact," Casey told her. "Not hearsay and not supposition. But that's not the issue. As of now he's been linked to additional homicides. I wasn't present for those. So I want to do some information-gathering, to make sure we get the most comprehensive picture possible, without being influenced by last year's events. That includes not just the facts, but the nuances. We want to paint an accurate picture of your husband and his state of mind. Will you give us that chance?"

Suzanne balked. Obviously, Casey's psychological approach had found its mark.

"The police are already here asking questions and rifling my apartment." Suzanne was waffling in her decision. "What could you add that would have any positive impact?"

"Nonprocedural elements. We can probe areas that the police don't feel are important. We can concentrate on *your* perceptions, on your assessment of your husband and his activities. Claire, for example, is an intuitive. It's possible she can sit in a room or handle specific objects and pick up on your husband's energy—what he was thinking or feeling. That might help us humanize him. And humanizing him could turn out to be the only way to soften the hard-core evidence the police have uncovered."

Suzanne turned to Claire, gazing at her with the typical expression of curiosity that Claire had come to expect. "You're a psychic?"

"In a matter of speaking, yes," Claire replied, opting to bypass the accurate definition of an intuitive.

"Bottom line," Casey continued, "the evidence is stacked against your husband. You can't hurt him by speaking to us. You might even be able to help him," she repeated. "If there are mitigating circumstances, details that have been overlooked or a personal perspective that didn't come out in court the first time, now is your opportunity to rectify that."

A long pause ensued.

Finally, Suzanne gave a reluctant nod. "Okay. Come in." She stepped aside so they could enter.

The three of them walked in. Casey glanced around, making a quick assessment of the apartment. Hardwood oak floors. Modern furnishings. Lots of space. More or less what she'd expected.

The detectives were going through the desk, drawer by drawer. Hutch was perched on the edge of a swivel chair, reading over bank statements, his eyes narrowed in concentration. His head came up at the sound of Casey's voice, and he briefly met her gaze, his lips twitching at the realization that she'd talked her way in. Unsurprised, he went back to his work.

"Can we sit down somewhere and talk?" Casey asked Suzanne.

"Why don't we take a few kitchen chairs and go into Glen's study?" Suzanne replied. "The police have finished going through it. The place is a mess, but it's comfortable. And we won't be interrupted."

That choice piqued Claire's interest. "Did your husband spend a lot of time in his study?"

"Yes. That was his sanctuary. He spent long hours there, doing work or just thinking."

"Good. Then I'll have the best chance of connecting with him in that room."

The study was a richly paneled room with a wall of bookshelves, a traditional desk and swivel chair, and a window ledge of potted plants. Although there were quite a few disconnected wires, the components of a state-of-the-art computer system remained on the desk and printer stand.

Casey got the immediate sense that Fisher kept things in strict order. The books were alphabetically arranged on the shelves, the plants were lined up equidistant from one another and the desk was in the exact center of the room.

"A total control freak," Marc muttered behind Casey.

She gave a curt nod, then sat down on one of the chairs they'd moved in from the kitchen.

"Is there anything you'd rather Claire not touch?" she asked Suzanne.

That particular psychology worked well on people. It put the ball in their court, gave them control of the process. This way, they relaxed, and Claire wouldn't have to worry about setting them off if she picked up some off-limits treasure.

Sure enough, the guard-dog look vanished from Suzanne's face.

"I'm fine with you touching whatever you choose to. We have no valuables in this room." She seated herself behind the desk in an unconscious attempt to erect a wall between herself and the FI team.

"Thank you." Casey gestured for Claire to get started. Meanwhile, her own mind was already on the process at hand.

Marc lowered himself into the chair beside Casey's, draping one arm across the back in a relaxed position. The less formidable he appeared, the better. As it was, Suzanne kept edging nervous glances his way.

"What can I tell you?" she asked, tucking a lock of hair behind her ear.

"Let's start with how and where you and your husband met," Casey suggested.

An innocent enough question—one that was usually greeted with some sign of tenderness or nostalgia.

There was none in Suzanne's reply. It was almost as if she were reciting a well-memorized speech. "We met eleven years ago in a pharmacy right here in midtown. We both had the flu and were hunting down medications to make us less miserable. We ended up comparing notes on home remedies. Glen was charming, even with a fever. I gave him my telephone number. He called a week later to see how I was feeling and to ask me out to dinner. We dated for about five months. Then he proposed. We were married a month after that."

"Wow." Casey's brows rose. "You planned your wedding in record time."

"We didn't have a traditional wedding," Suzanne explained. "Neither Glen nor I have any family. Nor are we religious. So we went to a justice of the peace and said our vows."

"I hope you at least had a honeymoon."

"We took a cruise." Once again, Suzanne tucked a lock of hair behind her ear. "It was lovely."

Clearly not. The woman was so strung out when she spoke about her husband and their relationship that it screamed dysfunctional. Suzanne's body language was a manifestation of fear. No surprise, given the monster she was married to.

"I heard that you teach piano," Casey continued, still sticking to safe ground. "Are your students adults or children?"

"Both. Mostly children." A hint of a smile. "They're challenging. It's hard to make Mozart cool. But I love watching their reactions when they get it right."

Mission accomplished. Suzanne had relaxed.

"You're obviously good with kids," Casey noted. "What about your husband—does he like children, as well?"

The mask snapped back into place. "He has no problem with them. But he's not the paternal type, if that's what you're asking."

Time to abandon that subject.

"What about music? You're clearly into classical. What about Glen?"

"He's not a huge music fan." Suzanne shifted in her seat. "He spends most of his time on his clients. Since accounting is not my strong suit, I don't ask too many questions."

"Different interests can be good for a marriage," Casey said. "What things did you do together?"

This time Suzanne flinched, ever so imperceptibly. "We watched movies. Glen did crossword puzzles. I read. We were homebodies. Nothing too exciting."

Homebodies? Casey suspected that Suzanne was more of a prisoner.

Casey went in a little deeper.

"Was Glen an easy man to live with? Was he good to you?"

Suzanne was on her guard again. Her gaze flicked away from Casey's. "I realize Glen hurt you. I'm not stupid. But, in his defense, he's a complicated man. He doesn't talk much about his past, but I know he lost his mother when he was six and his father when he was eight. His brother, Clark, was ten years older, so he kept Glen out of the foster care system and basically raised him. Clark got married when Glen was in college. Not too many years later, Clark and his wife were killed in an automobile accident. That left Glen on his own. I know what that feeling is like. It's frightening. It changes you. It changed Glen. I'm sure of it."

Casey was sure it had made him angry, introverted. But it hadn't turned him into a psychopath. That sickness had been with him all his life.

She glanced down at her notes. "You mentioned that Glen

had no family. What about his nephew, Jack? As I understand it, he lived with Glen after his parents died in the accident."

"He did." Suzanne swallowed. "Glen thought of it as a chance to give back. Clark took Glen in when he was young and alone. Glen did the same thing for Jack. He became his legal guardian."

"Yet you didn't mention him before. Had he moved out by the time you and Glen married?"

Suzanne's shoulders lifted in a shrug. "On paper, he lived with us for a few years after we got married. But he didn't spend much time with us. Jack was a typical teenager. Wild and reckless. He was always with his friends. He took off when he was sixteen. He didn't stay in touch."

"So he and your husband weren't close?"

"They were fine. They got along. As I said, Jack wasn't around much. So, even though Glen was Jack's guardian, Jack didn't factor heavily in our lives."

"I understand." Casey's eyes shifted, ever so briefly, to Claire, who was standing at the edge of the desk, her fingertips resting on top of a Newton's cradle. Her fingers slid down the wires of each ball, lingered on the metal sphere at the bottom, then slid back up to the base.

Her expression was intense, and she was visibly recoiling from something she was sensing.

Casey turned her attention quickly back to Suzanne. She had to keep her engaged, so that her focus was *not* on Claire. When Claire was locked into whatever energy she was picking up on, her emotions were written all over her face.

"I can see that you believe in your husband," Casey concluded. "Is that because you love him or because you think he's innocent?"

"I don't know how to answer that." Suzanne was staring at the carpet. "I know what the evidence says. I know Glen made a confession. I believe that confession was coerced—not only by you, but by the police. I think Glen was intimidated. I don't think he realized what he was saying. That's all I think."

Another memorized speech.

Interesting that Suzanne hadn't responded to the question about loving her husband, only about her doubts concerning his guilt. And even those responses had been halfhearted.

"Mrs. Fisher, was there ever a time when your husband hurt you?" Casey asked the question as gently as possible. But she needed to get a total read on this woman.

"Never." The pulse beating at Suzanne's neck said otherwise. "Glen has a temper. Sometimes he yells. But nothing more than that."

"Does his yelling frighten you?"

"No." Her pulse beat faster, and her reply was blurted out much too quickly. "I know he'd never act on his anger. Most of the time, he'd work out his feelings by going out for a long walk. That always calmed him down. He'd come home in much better spirits."

*I'll bet he did,* Casey thought. *After raping and killing another woman.*

"He's a good man, Ms. Woods," Suzanne said, defending her husband to the last. "Yelling is hardly a crime. Every marriage has its challenges."

"I agree." Casey watched Suzanne shove an invisible strand of hair behind her ear—clearly a habitual gesture and a glaring tell. "Do you visit him in prison?"

"Almost every Sunday. I don't teach on Sundays. So I drive up to Auburn on Saturday night and visit Glen the next morning."

"That's wonderful. I'm sure your visits are the highlight of his week."

"I hope so."

The woman looked completely unstrung. Casey's verdict was that she was afraid of her husband, but that, at the same time, she needed and admired him. It was classic battered-wife syndrome—pretty much the assessment Casey had expected to come away with.

Marc slanted a sideways glance at Claire, who had picked up a handsome silver ballpoint pen and was rolling it between her fingers, studying it. Abruptly, she dropped it onto the desk, pulled away her hand as if she'd been burned and took a step back from the desk. "I'm very sorry for what you've had to go through, Mrs. Fisher," Marc said, speaking up for the first time and trying to stall so Claire could compose herself. "First the trial and conviction, and now a bunch of detectives rummaging through your home. I'm sure it's upsetting to have to go through all this again."

"It is." Suzanne was visibly puzzled. She clearly felt she should be hating the FI team, but was finding it exceedingly difficult to do so.

Which meant they were doing their job. The more ambivalent Suzanne Fisher was about Forensic Instincts, the more likely they were to get her cooperation later, should they need it.

"I appreciate your consideration," she said. "It's...unexpected."

Marc shot another swift glance at Claire, who had pulled herself together. She met his gaze and nodded, telling him that she was okay and that she was finished.

He took her cue and stood up. "On that note, I think we've kept you long enough."

"I agree." Casey—having picked up on all the same signs Marc had—rose to her feet, as well.

Abruptly, Suzanne turned to Claire. "Did you sense anything?"

Claire was in the hot seat and she knew it. She also knew it was time to put on her game face and to give Suzanne something the woman could live with. Otherwise, the tentative connection she'd so painstakingly established would be severed, and FI would be written off as the enemy.

Claire wasn't about to undo all the progress that Casey and Marc had just made.

*Stick to the truth. There's less to remember.*

"You're right that your husband is a very complex man," she replied. "He's also a very pensive man. He did a great deal of planning in this room. I can feel the intense level of concentration." Claire gave one of those gentle smiles that lowered the defenses of even the shrewdest subjects. "You understand your husband well. He knows that. He counts on that. And he appreciates that."

Her declaration had the desired effect, although, unsurprisingly, Suzanne looked more relieved than she did happy. "Thank you. That's good to hear."

She was a lot more relaxed saying goodbye than she'd been saying hello.

"She's scared shitless of him," Marc said as soon as they were outside the building, heading for the subway.

Casey nodded as she strode, New York City–style, down the street. "I can't make up my mind how deep the abuse goes. Does he strike her or just manipulate her emotionally?"

"My guess?" Marc responded, keeping pace with Casey. "He manipulates her emotionally. He's highly intelligent and shrewd. He can get what he wants through mind games. That would challenge and please him a lot more than physical abuse. She's malleable. She loves him and fears him in equal proportions. He has a powerful hold on her, even while he's in prison."

"She's malleable, but she's not stupid," Casey said. "She's found a way to justify her husband's actions—at least the actions she knows about. It's the only way she could find to live with herself, or with him. Which leads to the next question—how much of who he is and what he does is she aware of, and how much is she totally oblivious to?"

"You know how we get that answer, don't you?"

"Absolutely," Casey replied. "We follow her. Patrick is the best one of us for the job. He's great at tailing people and staying inconspicuous. Plus, Suzanne Fisher has never met him. So even if she does spot him in the crowd, she'll have no idea who he is or what he's doing."

"We can't forget the nephew, Jack."

"We aren't. I have Ryan digging into his background and trying to find his whereabouts. It stands to reason that he was fine for money, assuming that Clark's inheritance and trust fund filtered down to him after his father's death."

"Yeah, but after seven or eight years, money has a way of running out," Marc said dryly. "Who knows how Jack's living now."

"Or why he was so eager to get away from his uncle."

"Glen Fisher is an evil, evil man," Claire declared out of nowhere. She stopped walking, reaching into her pocket and pulling out the silver ballpoint pen that had been on Glen's desk. "I took this. I shouldn't have, but I did. His wife won't miss it. If she does, I'll claim to have taken it by accident, and return it immediately."

"It's significant?" Casey asked.

"It's emanating powerful energy." Claire eyed the pen, still glassy-eyed and unhinged from the enormity of what she'd picked up on in Glen Fisher's study. "He used this for sketching out his crimes, and for taking notes on future crimes. He's done unspeakable things. His wife has good reason to be terrified of him—even if he is in prison. He has a way of reaching the outside world even from his cell."

That brought Casey's head up. She'd planned on waiting until they were back in the office to grill Claire. But what she'd just said shot those intentions to hell.

"What does that mean—he reaches the outside world from his cell? Did you pick up something about whoever he passed the baton to? Who the new offender is? What their arrangement is?"

"No. Maybe. I'm not sure." Claire shoved the pen back in her pocket. Ignoring the stream of pedestrians who were muttering as they veered around her, she remained at a standstill, massaging her temples.

"My brain is about to explode, there's so much pounding at it right now," she said. "I need to go home. I need to be alone and think. There are too many stimuli shouting at me. The traffic and city noise doesn't help. Outside stimuli. Inside stimuli. I need to be in my own private space so I can sort things out and make sense out of chaos. Give me some time." Her complexion was ashen. "I'll call you the moment I make sense of things."


The evening hours rolled by.

Suzanne spent them pacing around her bedroom. She was worried. She was scared. And she was ready to jump out of her skin.

Finally, her cell phone rang. She snatched it up, quickly accepted the charges and waited to hear Glen's voice at the other end.

"Glen." She breathed his name. "I've been waiting to talk to you for hours—ever since the detectives and the FBI agents left." Her voice trembled. "They practically ransacked the apartment."

"I'm sure they did," her husband said in an offhand tone.

"Just as I'm sure they found nothing." A pointed pause. "Because there's nothing *to* find, right?"

"Of course, right." Suzanne shoved her hair behind her ear. "I did what you asked. I answered their questions and gave them free access to the entire apartment. I cooperated fully."

"Good girl. What did they take with them?"

"Just bank statements and our address book. There was nothing else that jumped out at them."

"Speaking of bank statements, did you handle this month's withdrawal and payment the way I asked?"

"Yes. I withdrew the cash two days ago, right on schedule. But I spoke to our landlord, and held off on making yesterday's rent payment. I'll make it first thing tomorrow—along with the other necessary installment."

"Good. That'll keep our bank record seamless for the cops' eyes. But it'll also defer our financial exchange until their emphasis is totally on me and off you." There was a smug note in Glen's tone. "You're a sweet, gentle soul. After today, you'll be scratched off law enforcement's list. You did a fine job. I'm proud of you."

Suzanne soaked in the praise, but she didn't relax. She wasn't sure how Glen was going to receive the next segment of information she was about to impart.

"They weren't the only ones who were here for the search."

"Oh?"

"Three members of the Forensic Instincts team showed up. I let them in. I hope that wasn't a mistake." She held her breath, praying Glen wouldn't go ballistic.

He did anything but.

"Forensic Instincts? What a nice added bonus. Which three members?"

"Claire Hedgleigh, Marc Devereaux and Casey Woods."

"This just gets better and better." There was a smile in Glen's voice. "Tell me about the meeting."

Suzanne replayed the entire conversation, as close to verbatim as she could.

"They're doing reconnaissance," Glen noted. "Just a fishing expedition, since you didn't give them a thing to work with. But I'm very pleased that they're involved. Feel free to answer their phone calls and visits. Be gracious, but be tight-lipped."

"You think they'll come back?" Suzanne tensed. "You just said I'd be scratched off the list."

"*Law enforcement's* list," Glen clarified. "Forensic Instincts is an entirely different animal. They're the most challenging of adversaries. So, do I think they'll come back? I know they will. In fact, I'm counting on it."

# CHAPTER FOURTEEN

"There's next to nothing here. Not even a damned credit card statement."

Hutch tossed down the monthly bills he'd reviewed for most of the night. He was perched at the edge of FI's conference room table, gulping coffee and poring over all the paperwork that law enforcement had collected at the Fishers' place.

It wasn't much.

"Glen Fisher was all about cash," he said. "Every month on the exact same day of the month, he withdrew precisely eight thousand dollars from the bank and used it to pay all his bills, including his rent. That's weird, but not illegal. He had that generous trust fund from his grandparents, and a wad of cash inherited from his parents. The other half went to his brother, Clark, whose assets were inherited by his son, Jack. I have no idea if the kid blew it all or gave it to his uncle for managing."

"I can fill in some of those blanks." Ryan entered the conference room. "Yoda," he instructed. "Display background check on Jack Fisher."

"Retrieving requested information," Yoda responded.

A moment later, up popped a webpage displaying a three-column table. In the first column were the dates of various documents in descending order. In the second column was the source of the information—everything from high school transcript to Experian. In the third column was the result of the background check. Where the query had returned some information, the result column displayed a link to a PDF document that contained the details of the search and the results.

The first PDF document stopped everyone in their tracks.

It was Jack Fisher's death certificate.

"Shit," Ryan muttered. "I was hoping this would be a productive avenue."

"Well, it's not," Hutch said. "Put it on the back burner for now, and let's focus on more viable leads. Is Patrick tailing Suzanne?"

"As of dawn today, yes," Casey replied. "He hasn't called in yet. But she probably hasn't even left her apartment for work. It's early."

"I wish we'd started following her a few days earlier," Hutch said, studying the bank statement again. "Yesterday she made her eight-thousand dollar monthly withdrawal. I'd love to know how she allocated it."

"And I'd love to hear back from Claire." Casey frowned. "I'm not going to bug her. She'd call if she had anything solid to tell us. But we really need her input—especially if it implicates Glen or hints at who his successor is. As for me, I'm waiting for official word that I'm on Fisher's visitor list. Once that happens, I'll be driving up to Auburn. My getting in his face might provide us with something."

"Or it might provoke him to go after you sooner," Hutch said, his expression as hard as his tone. He still wasn't happy with Casey's plan to see Glen Fisher.

"I'll risk it. You'll coach me as to how I can best approach him. If I piss him off enough, maybe he'll lose it and inadvertently give us a lead."

Glen Fisher was in a fine mood.

He hadn't been sure that the cops would let Forensic Instincts take part in yesterday's search. But clearly Casey Woods had the kind of connections that opened doors—including the door to his apartment.

He wondered just how frustrated she'd been to learn nothing, to actually be in his living space and yet not be able to capitalize on it. There was something deeply exciting about the thought of having her in his home, going through his things and still being a fly in his web. She was at his mercy. He was the master of her fate, whether she knew it or not.

She'd know it soon enough.

And she'd be begging to die.

Claire nearly jumped out of her chair when her doorbell rang.

She'd been sitting at her kitchen table, nursing a cup of green tea, and eyeing the ballpoint pen that was in front of her. She'd handled it a dozen times, and each time a barrage of dark energy had assailed her, nearly suffocating her with its intensity.

She was steeling herself to go through the onslaught again.

The doorbell was a startling, but in some ways relieving, interruption.

She rose, checking the wall clock as she did—8:30 a.m. She barely remembered when night had turned into day.

Blinking, she forced herself to reorient so she could deal with her first outside interaction since yesterday. She glanced down at herself, just to make sure she was decent enough to be seen. Oh, right. She was wearing her oversize college T-shirt and black yoga pants. She'd showered and put them on sometime after dawn.

Wow, was she out of it.

Still somewhat off-balance, Claire picked up a hair band and tied back her still-damp hair. With that, she headed for the door.

Habit made her peer through the peephole. Brows raised, she opened the door.

"Hey," she greeted Ryan in surprise. Their time together rarely included early morning drop-bys—or any other conventional dates.

"Hey, yourself." He walked in, carrying a white bag containing something that smelled wonderful. "Croissants," he explained. "Fresh from the bakery down the street. I'm assuming you haven't eaten?"

Claire looked from the bag to Ryan and back. "No, I haven't."

"Good. Then let's eat." He placed the bag on the kitchen table. "I see you're drinking some of that foul-tasting tea. I'll have coffee."

"Of course you will." Claire walked over to brew a single K-cup of coffee. No matter how hard she tried, she couldn't convert Ryan to a green tea drinker.

"Are you okay?" he asked, studying her as he did. "Casey said she hadn't heard from you since yesterday. It's not like you to fall off the grid."

"You're right." Claire handed Ryan his coffee. "I lost all sense of time. This pen and all the horrifying visions it's conjuring up are consuming me."

Ryan took the cup of coffee with a nod of thanks. He didn't have much faith in psychic connections. But he'd be a fool to disregard all of Claire's successes. And whatever she'd been experiencing now had taken a huge toll on her. She was pale, her eyes haunted, and she wasn't a hundred percent steady on her feet. Altogether, she looked as if she was on the verge of collapse.

"Let's sit down." Ryan took her arm and guided her over to the sofa. He put both their cups on the table in front of them and sat, pulling her down beside him. "Did you get any sleep last night?"

"Not really. Then again, I didn't really expect to. The connections I'm making with Glen Fisher are really freaking me out. I've dealt with evil before, but this is in a class by itself. The man is a psychopath. The things he did to those women, the strategic planning that went into each attack—every time I pick up that pen, I get flashes of a different scene, a different victim. Nobody—not FI and not the authorities—have so much as scratched the surface. These brutal murders have gone on for years."

She pointed at where she'd been sitting at her table. "I have a notebook and my own pen next to Fisher's. I've been writing down each energy event I experience. It's the only way to keep track of all Fisher's crimes—that's how many of them there were. And I have no sense of a timeline. That's part of what I was hoping for. I wanted to not only collect but to organize my thoughts before I came back to the team."

"Sounds like a plan, but a complicated one." Ryan's knuckles caressed her cheek. "You need more than I realized. The croissants can wait. You need a break, and something to relax your body and clear your mind." He slid off her hair band, massaging the back of her neck as he did. "I can provide both."

Claire smiled. Now *this* was the Ryan McKay she knew.

"I'm sure you can," she murmured. "But it's a tall order. My mind is pretty locked up right now."

"I'll unlock it." He fanned her hair out over her shoulders. "You know how I feel about a good challenge. I always rise to the occasion."

"True." Claire was unbuttoning his shirt. "Your methods are impressive. Your results are even better."

"Uh-huh." Ryan's hands were under her T-shirt, gliding up and down her back, leaving goose bumps in his path. "But you're really wound up this time. It might take a while to get the desired results."

"I can wait."

"I can't." Ryan yanked the T-shirt over her head, drew her to him and covered her mouth with his.

After that, it was an eruption of the senses, just as it always was.

Claire never let herself go quite the way she did when she and Ryan were together. And he knew it. He drew out every touch, every sensation, until the pleasure was almost painful. Then he slowed down, backed off and started all over again. He brought her to the edge and kept her there, savoring the urgency in her body—sometimes satisfying it, sometimes making her wait.

The experience was anything but one-sided. Ryan was an accomplished lover who was used to being in control. Claire blew that talent to bits. She drove him crazy and she was acutely aware of it. Every touch, every taste, every shivery twist of her body, elicited a harsh groan and an equally hard shudder from him.

They were explosive together.

Afterward, they lay quietly on the couch, an afghan thrown over them, their heart rates gradually slowing to normal.

"Feel better?" Ryan asked as he let shimmering strands of blond hair run through his fingers.

"Much." Claire shut her eyes, savoring the boneless satisfaction that seeped into every pore of her body. "Challenge met and overcome."

"Glad to hear it." There was a sexy smile in his voice. "Call for reinforcements anytime."

"I will." Claire smiled, too. "And don't sound so smug. I rocked your world, too."

"Yeah, you kind of did." He sounded as if the admission was dragged out of him.

"It's okay, techno-hottie. Your secret is safe with me."

"Good. I have a reputation to protect." Ryan stretched. "Well, now I'm starving. Carb time?"

"Your coffee is cold." Claire reached down for her T-shirt, and pulled it over her head. It hung down to her upper thighs, so she didn't bother with anything else. "I'll microwave it." She walked into the kitchen, glancing down at Glen Fisher's ball-point pen as she did.

She came to an abrupt halt.

"He's planning something," she whispered. "It's dark and it's evil. And it's bringing him one step closer to Casey."

Patrick followed Suzanne into the subway at Lexington and East 51st Street, keeping a discreet distance while making sure she was directly in his line of vision. Unaware of his scrutiny, she proceeded to the Uptown platform and waited. The number 6 train arrived. The doors opened. She stepped inside.

Quickly, Patrick followed her.

Suzanne took the nearest seat, clutching her purse tightly to her side. To the average straphanger, she looked every bit the typical New Yorker, protecting her belongings from a "hit and run" purse snatcher. But Patrick wasn't any average straphanger. His trained eye detected Suzanne's heightened awareness of her surroundings and her even greater concern for the contents of her purse.

He stayed where he was, standing just a short distance away, close to Suzanne, equally close to the exit doors. Suzanne was visibly impatient and uneasy, staring at the doors as the train stopped at 59th, 68th St.–Hunter College, 77th, 86th, 96th, 103rd, 110th.

Finally reaching 116th Street, the train stopped, and Suzanne rose from her seat. Winding her way over, she stood right up against the doors and rushed out of the train as soon as they opened. With calm purpose, Patrick exited behind her and continued his tail.

There was no doubt that Suzanne was a woman with a mission. She blew out of the subway station, crossed 116th Street and headed west. She strode under the elevated tracks at Park Avenue and continued past the small shops on the south side of the street. Then she crossed Fifth Avenue, and veered sharply into a storefront with a large sign in the window that read Halal Meat.

Patrick remained outside, leaning against the wall and reading the newspaper—holding it up so his face was hidden. He was curious as hell as to why Suzanne would take this long trek just to pick up dinner.

Ten minutes later, he was even more puzzled. Suzanne left the store without making a single purchase. She headed back toward the subway, retracing her route.

Patrick didn't break stride. He continued behind her, whipping out his iPhone and calling Ryan on speed dial.

Ryan sounded distracted when he answered.

"Hey, Patrick." His mouth was clearly full.

"Sorry to interrupt your breakfast, but I need some help."

"Shoot."

"I need you to investigate a butcher shop for me." Patrick went on to explain the events that had just taken place.

"Yeah, that's weird." Ryan was back on his game now. "Why would anyone go so far out of their way for a specialty butcher shop and then not buy anything?"

"Exactly. And she was gripping her purse like she was carrying the Hope Diamond inside it."

"This sounds like it could be something. I'm on it."

Claire put down her cup of tea and eyed Ryan quizzically. "Patrick has a lead?"

"Yup." Ryan was pulling on his clothes. "I've got to get back to my lair and get on it." He hesitated for a second, studying Claire in an oddly protective way. "Are you going to be okay?"

"I'm fine." She waved him toward the door, gathering up the rest of her clothes. "I'm going to jump in the shower and come into the office, too. I've got more than enough to start reviewing things with Casey."

"And you'd better do it fast, because the minute she gets the green light, she'll be driving up to Auburn." Ryan walked over, raised Claire's chin and kissed her. "That's for later, when we're killing each other."

# CHAPTER
## FIFTEEN

Casey had gone out for a long walk with Hero—and, of course, one of her bodyguards. She was so tense that even playing tracking games in the dog park with Hero didn't release her excess energy. She felt as if she were circling Glen Fisher and his plans, making narrower and narrower rings, but not quite getting close enough to grab him.

The clock was ticking. And another woman was going to die.

It didn't take a psychic to figure that one out. The killer had made it crystal clear. He hadn't said when or where, but Casey sure as hell knew why. And, irrational or not, she felt guilty and responsible. The rapes and murders might fulfill some sick fantasy, but she was the psycho's ultimate target. His other victims were selected to taunt her, to drive home his absolute control and dominance.

There was no such thing as a copycat killer. Hutch had taught her that a long time ago. There were only killers who wanted to establish themselves as bigger, better, craftier—even if they did view the original offender as a hero. So who was this psychopath who'd chosen—or been chosen—to take over for Glen Fisher?

She returned to the brownstone just as tense and edgy as when she'd left. She unleashed Hero, who took off for the living room.

Puzzled, Casey followed him to see what the attraction was. She found Claire waiting for her, perched on the edge of the sofa, with Hero now sitting at her feet, a captive audience. Claire reached into her pocket and pulled out a dog treat.

"Here you go, boy." She offered it to Hero, who gobbled it up without hesitation. Well aware of who the softie of the team was and who was therefore his meal ticket, Hero settled himself against Claire's leg. Claire looked up. "Hi," she greeted Casey. Her voice was high and thin, and her expression was haunted.

"Why didn't you call me?" Casey demanded at once. "I would have come back sooner."

"I've only been here for a few minutes." Claire scratched Hero's ears as she spoke. "I was pacing around my apartment, hoping to put the horrifying images in my mind in some kind of understandable order. I couldn't. And then I got this wave of darkness—we're almost out of time, Casey. The next murder's already been planned."

"Dammit." Casey dragged a hand through her hair. "You have no idea who? Or when?"

"No."

"What did you see?"

"A redhead. College-age. I didn't see a face. Only a shadow hanging over her, closing in until it hid her from view. No matter how hard I tried, I couldn't bring the shadow into focus. I couldn't see *him*."

Claire's eyes welled up with tears, and she kept talking, faster and faster, as if by blurting everything out, she could empty her-self of the evil, make the images go away.

"I've spent the past eighteen hours focused on the black, black energy that's Glen Fisher. I've felt him torturing women. Pin-ning them to the cold, hard ground until rocks or branches tore at their flesh. I could feel him raping them and then choking the last breath out of their throats. I could see their faces at the end, the terrified panic in their eyes as they realized they were dying. It made me sick."

She dashed away the tears with the backs of her hands. "I wish to God I could get the gory details out of my head. They're for-ever etched in my brain. I threw up twice on my way over here."

"I'm sorry," Casey said gently. "What about this next murder?"

"It's outside Glen Fisher's realm. He's on the periphery, but not at the heart of what's going to happen. I don't know who is."

"Whoever's taken over the killings." Marc had come into the room, and he was studying Claire through intense, know-ing eyes. "If you're really living inside all these brutal killings, you're going to have to talk to someone."

"I know," Claire said. "But not now. Not until we've caught this monster." She leaned forward and picked up the pad she'd placed on the coffee table. "I wrote down everything I saw and felt—about Fisher and about the next victim. I only pray there's something here to help us."

As she spoke, Hutch walked into the room, his concentration on rereading a text message he'd just received. He raised his head and focused on Casey. "It's a done deal," he announced. "We're on Glen Fisher's visitor list. Throw some clothes in a bag and let's hit the road. If we leave now, we can be in Auburn after din-ner, catch some sleep and meet with Fisher tomorrow morning."

"*We?*" Casey did a double take. "I don't remember asking for an escort."

"You didn't. But law enforcement isn't happy with your going alone. Neither am I. Not under these circumstances. You're a targeted victim, and Fisher has potential ties to the killer. They don't want you facing him by yourself."

"So they're sending a Fed in with me? Do they honestly think he'll spill his guts with you sitting there?"

"They don't think he'll spill his guts at all." Hutch gave it to her straight. "But I'll make the ultimate call. If I think it would be beneficial for me to take a stroll to the vending machine, I'll do that, and you can have a crack at Fisher alone."

"How gracious of you." Casey was pissed. "I'm not a child who needs a nanny, Hutch. As it is, I have a security team surrounding me 24/7. Now I'll have a guard dog accompanying me to the prison."

"And you also have a psychopathic killer who wants you dead." Hutch was equally blunt. "Look, Casey, you and I each have different training and different methods for reading people. Let's not fight each other. Let's just say that two heads are better than one and leave it at that."

"Because I'm not getting in to see Fisher unless I do."

"You got it."

"Fine." Casey didn't give in gracefully. "But no censoring what I say or how I say it."

"Translated, you're going to do what you want, how you want—the way you always do."

"Play nice, kids," Marc inserted dryly. "Otherwise, that long drive you're about to make is going to seem even longer."

Casey nodded. "I'll go pack."


Prison guard Tim Grant approached Glen Fisher's cell. It was late, and just about all the inmates in the cell block had gone to sleep. Tim himself was looking forward to going home and getting a good night's rest.

But first he had some business to take care of.

Big payoff or not, he hated these meetings with Fisher. The guy scared the shit out of him. Tonight, however, would be relatively pleasant. He'd done his chore, and he'd also gotten the information Fisher was hoping for.

This meeting should be quick and easy.

Grant heard Fisher climb off his cot. An instant later, he was facing Grant down, watching him through the cell bars with that chilling stare.

"Did you get me the new burn phone?" he demanded in a low tone.

"Yes." Tim passed the cell phone through the bars. "I loaded it up with sixty minutes. You should be set for a month."

"Nice job." Fisher studied the phone. He was in a good enough mood to offer a compliment.

"I also got some details on that visit you're waiting for. It's happening tomorrow morning at ten. You wanted to know who from Forensic Instincts would be coming. It's just Casey Woods."

Fisher's teeth gleamed in the dark. "Excellent. So she and I will have our privacy."

This was the one snag Tim hadn't been looking forward to relaying. "Not exactly. They're sending a Fed along with her. An agent from the BAU."

"*Shit.*" Fisher's oath was muffled, but he slammed his fist against the iron bars. "That's not acceptable." The scary intense look crossed his face. "I'll politely ask him to excuse us. If that doesn't work, I'll find a diversion to get rid of him. Be around. I might need your help."

"Okay." Tim felt that gripping fear starting to tighten his gut. "I'll do what I can."

"I know you will."

Ryan had been researching that damned butcher shop all day. And he had turned up absolutely nothing. The store held its required licenses, and passed the usual health inspections. Everything seemed in order—at least on the surface.

But that wasn't good enough. Ryan's sixth sense wouldn't leave him alone. Suzanne's trip to West 116th Street was just too bizarre to be meaningless. Ryan wouldn't be satisfied until he checked it out himself.

He glanced at his watch—1:30 a.m. He wasn't discouraged. He knew Marc would still be awake and working.

Sure enough, when he went upstairs, he found Marc cross-checking the employee background searches Ryan had done on the Auburn Correctional Facility staff.

"Anything?" Ryan asked.

"Nope. Not yet." Marc stretched. "I need a break."

"Good. Because I need a date."

Marc's eyebrows rose in amusement. "Do I get a corsage?"

"You get to play a video surveillance game with me, from setup to stakeout. Interested?"

"Sure." Marc rose, looking down at his T-shirt and jeans. "At least I don't have to change my clothes. I hate playing dress-up."

"Just bring refreshments," Ryan advised. "We're going to get bored, cramped and hungry. But I'm hoping it'll pay off."

"Lead the way."

It was 3:00 a.m. Most of New York was fast asleep, other than the occasional car and private sanitation truck removing garbage from West 116th Street before the restaurants opened.

Marc and Ryan blended right in. They looked like construction workers getting an early start to the work day. Across the street from the meat market was the building Ryan had selected. It was under construction—the perfect place to mount one of his video cameras.

He and Marc got immediately to work.

Marc picked the padlock on the construction fence. That done, he and Ryan went inside and climbed the makeshift stairway to the roof. Squatting down, Ryan mounted his camera to the building wall. The camera had a large battery pack attached, and a solar cell on top. That would ensure it had adequate power to stream video wirelessly to the FI van, which Ryan had parked on West 115th Street.

And, just for kicks *and* to make sure no one disturbed his setup, Ryan affixed a Department of Homeland Security decal on the camera, with a warning that tampering with the equipment was a federal offense.

Marc chuckled at the forged decal. "Nice touch."

"Hey," Ryan said with an amused shrug. "People will believe anything if it sounds official and is spelled correctly."

With that, he went back to work. He used his iPhone to remotely access the video server in the van, which was recording the camera feed. He made sure he could clearly see the meat market and would have no trouble checking out who entered and exited.

Everything was a go.

Marc and Ryan left the building, locked the construction entrance and returned to their van on West 115th Street.

It was going to be a long, long night.


Casey and Hutch drove through the institutional gates of Auburn State Correctional Facility at 9:45 a.m. The prison was almost two hundred years old—the second oldest state prison in New York—with twin guard towers on either side of the building and an American Revolutionary War soldier atop the apex. Stringent security measures were in place, and Casey and Hutch presented their proper ID before they were frisked and allowed to proceed to the cold, barren visitors' room.

They took a seat at a table, waiting. Ten minutes later, the door opened and a guard escorted Glen Fisher in.

The instant Casey saw him, a jolt of fear shivered up her spine. She fought the urge to flinch, instead commanding herself to hide her trepidation behind a composed veneer. It had been months since the trial, when she'd last seen Fisher. She'd submerged the memories—the soulless evil in his eyes, the cruel angle of his jaw, the arrogance of his stance. It all flooded back now, along with the memories of his hands on her as he tore at her clothes, the knife at her throat as he threatened to slit it—the entirety of what had happened in those moments before Marc burst into the alley, tore Fisher off her and slammed him against the wall, practically choking the life out of him.

Part of Casey wished Marc had succeeded.

The damned case hadn't even been FI's. The police had come to them at the last minute and requested their help in a setup. They'd already identified Glen Fisher as the perp. But they needed proof. And what better way to get it than to catch him in action? Fisher's victims were redheads. Casey was a redhead. She was also the president of a maverick investigative team, with a great track record, that was known to push boundaries and to take risks.

So Forensic Instincts had come on board at the eleventh hour. They'd arranged to have Casey pose as a lonely college girl at a bar—one where Fisher chose his victims. She'd timed her departure from the bar perfectly, and then walked "home," taking a route that took her right past the alley where she knew Fisher was lying in wait. The rest had played out just as planned.

And they'd brought down Glen Fisher.

*Casey* had brought down Glen Fisher. She'd become his first and only failure, and the last pair of terrified eyes he'd looked into before being roughed up by Marc and cuffed by the cops.

From that moment on, she'd become the embodiment of all his internal rage. She'd seen it in his stare when he looked at her during his trial.

He blamed her for everything, even the things that went deep into his past and made him the monster he was today.

Yet, in spite of all that, Casey was about to face him.

Swallowing hard, she battled her inner turmoil, dead set on keeping the upper hand in this interview. Hutch had prepped her. She knew what to expect and what to do. And, dammit, she was going to do it, no matter what the cost.

She knew Hutch sensed her reaction. But he didn't glance her way. He kept a laser gaze on Fisher, hardly blinking as the killer ignored him, his stare locked on Casey. But, in an almost imperceptible motion, Hutch slid his hand over and squeezed Casey's fingers beneath the table.

Casey felt some of the tension ease from her body. Maybe it wasn't such a bad idea to have Hutch along for this meeting, after all.

Fisher reached the table and his lips curved into a cocky smile as he took a seat. "Hello, Red. This is quite an honor."

*Red.* That was what the scrambled voice on the phone had called her. Fisher was using it purposely.

"An honor? It's not meant to be one." Casey spoke in an even tone. "It's meant to be a face-to-face meeting. You're obviously determined to see me. So here I am."

"I was delighted to get word about your visitation request."

Without averting his eyes, Fisher jerked his thumb in Hutch's direction. "Is this your ventriloquist?"

"Supervisory Special Agent Kyle Hutchinson," Hutch supplied. "FBI Behavioral Analysis Unit."

"Of course." Fisher gave a tight nod. "You disappoint me, Red. I thought you'd be feisty enough to talk to me alone. What's Agent Hutchinson's role here—to protect you or to offer his professional take on me?"

"Neither. Protocol." Casey interlaced her fingers on the table in front of her, her fear receding beneath a wall of resolve. "Frankly? I didn't want or need an escort. I wanted a one-on-one meeting. My request was denied."

That explanation seemed to please him. "So the decision wasn't yours. I'm glad to hear that. It means I was right about you, after all. You are a little hellcat." He paused. "For now."

"Let's skip the veiled threats," Casey said. "And the cat and mouse game."

"Fair enough. I'm listening."

"We've linked you to several old, cold murders."

"Have you? I hope you didn't drive all this way for confirmation. You know I'm appealing my conviction. I won't be admitting to anything. I wouldn't have done so in the first place if you hadn't used that barbaric navy SEAL to torture me and extract false confessions under duress."

"Funny, that's not how I remember it."

"Then your memory is poor."

Casey shrugged, calling on her training and Hutch's prep work. "Either way, it never occurred to me that you'd be making a full confession right now. You're too smart to offer yourself up. If I've learned anything about you, it's that we underestimated you. We won't do that again."

"A wise decision."

"But you should know we found DNA evidence in both the Jan Olson and Holly Stevens cases."

"Did you? Fascinating."

"You were a novice in those days," Casey continued. "Plus DNA evidence hadn't come nearly as far as it has now. Which would explain why you left semen on both victims."

Fisher didn't respond.

"We aren't the only ones who knew about the cold cases. My new BFF used his voice scrambler to call me and share the info. He's been very busy, and very communicative. He's on a brand-new crime spree, which I'm sure isn't news to you. He calls me after every one of his brutal murders. And he obviously admires you a great deal. Because his implication's that he *is* you."

A fine tension emanated from Fisher. "Why? What did he say?"

"He just gave snippets of information about where we can find the victims and made direct threats to me. It's as if you trained him—and you did a hell of a good job."

Again, no answer.

"He's embellished on your work, you know," Casey added. "He doesn't simply leave the bodies as is. He's very artistic and refined in presenting his work. Clearly a cut above the crude way you worked."

Anger flashed in Fisher's eyes. "Artistry is in the eyes of the beholder."

"True." Casey nodded thoughtfully. "So, theoretically, if you were the one committing those crimes now, you'd opt not to go for the dramatic?"

"I'd opt for saying that the end results are dramatic enough. Embellishments like red ribbons and lipstick? In my mind, that's overkill."

"I see your point." Casey gave herself an internal high five.

Getting Fisher to supply those details was a win. But she wasn't done. "Still, he's very clever," she said, pushing the envelope. "He hasn't left one shred of evidence. He's pretty remarkable."

Fisher was tapping his foot on the floor. Clearly, Casey was getting to him.

"Do you disagree?" she asked. "Am I missing something?"

"You're wrong as usual," he retorted. "I thought you'd want to live. I thought you'd come here to beg for help."

Casey jumped all over that. "Would you offer it to me? Would you tell me what kind of danger I'm in? Do you even know?"

A cruel smile—one that said Fisher felt back in control. "I know more than anyone. What I do with that knowledge is another matter entirely."

"You're toying with me again." Casey inserted a touch of nervousness in her voice. "You're the one who wants me dead."

"You're scared, Red. That excites me."

"You're sick."

"And you're vulnerable."

Casey rose, giving the appearance that she'd snapped. "I'm getting out of here," she said, her eyes huge and frightened. "You're not telling me anything. All you want is to intimidate me." She took a few steps toward the door.

"Leaving so soon?" Fisher called after her. "I'm disappointed. I thought you had a greater purpose in coming here today."

Casey whirled around. "Listen, you sick bastard. You're so full of yourself. Don't be. You're not even a man anymore. The medical examiner concluded that the real reason there was no semen on any of last year's victims is because you're impotent. You brutalized those women any way you could. But not in the way that mattered. You failed miserably in that regard. So if I feel like I'm in danger, it's because your successor can at least perform."

*"Bitch."* Fisher was on his feet in a second, a vein bulging at his temple. "Leaving physical evidence is a *choice*. Whoever's after you now is smart enough to make the right one. But never doubt that he'll do to you exactly what you deserve—violate and torture you before he ends your pathetic life. I'll make sure you bleed for what you did to me. You'll suffer unbearably. Sleep on that."

"This interview is over." Hutch shoved back his chair and stood up. "Come on, Casey. We're leaving." He signaled at the guard.

"I'm ready." Casey was all composure, triumph glistening in her eyes. "Thank you for the information, Glen. You've just linked yourself to the killer. Say goodbye to ever leaving this cesspool."

Anger blazed in Fisher's eyes. "And you've just made your death a hell of a lot more painful, Red."

# CHAPTER
## SIXTEEN

Casey wasn't sorry when Hutch drove out of the penitentiary gates. She'd been pushed to her limit during this visit. She felt drained from the interview and as if she needed a bath from being so close to Glen Fisher.

She sank into the passenger seat, staring out the window at the side-view mirror and watching the drab, gray complex disappear into the distance.

"You holding up?" Hutch asked as they pulled onto the highway.

"I'll live." Casey's answer was frank. "But this was tougher than I expected."

"You did a great job. And you got us just what we needed—an inadvertent admission from Fisher that he's somehow tied to these new killings. Not because of his bullshit threats, but because of the details about the victims. The ribbons, the lipstick—none of that was released to the public."

"I know." Casey massaged her temples. "And the rage he feels toward me came through loud and clear. He's communicating with the new killer in some way, maybe even running the show."

A corner of Hutch's mouth lifted. "Nice touch about the impotence. The scumbag almost had a coronary. He'll stew over that one. And he may even act on it." Hutch's smile faded. "The only thing that worries me is figuring out when he's going to aim that psychopathic rage directly at you. You definitely poked the lion with a sharp stick."

Casey's cell phone rang. She glanced down at the caller ID. "Marc," she announced.

She punched on the phone, hitting the speaker button so Hutch could be part of the conversation. "Hey. We're on our way back. I'll fill you in then, okay?"

"Good," Marc replied. "Ryan and I are doing our surveillance. But I wanted to let you know that I just heard from the Manhattan D.A.'s office. They've agreed to file new charges against Glen Fisher for the rapes and murders of Holly Stevens and Jan Olson. Given the circumstances, they're expediting things. The necessary papers are being filed and arrangements are being made to transfer Fisher from Auburn to the Rock." The Rock was Rikers Island, New York City's maximum security prison.

"So this should happen quickly," Casey clarified.

"Yup."

"I can't wait for Fisher to hear the news."

"It'll probably be tomorrow or the next day. Otherwise, I'd suggest you stick around and see the expression on his face firsthand."

"I couldn't stick around, anyway," Casey reminded him, steeling herself for the reaction she knew she was about to get from Hutch. "I've got a full calendar tonight. A six o'clock haircut. Then my class at eight." She was referring to the biweekly human behavior seminar that she taught to a class of psychology students at NYU. "I'm going to both," she stressed, trying to avoid a blowout fight with Hutch.

It didn't work.

"Like hell you are!" Hutch nearly shouted. "Considering what's going on, you'll cancel the haircut and the class."

"No way." Casey shook her head. "I'll take one of Patrick's bodyguards with me. But I'll repeat what I said when I first started getting these phone calls—I am not changing my life. And I'm not hiding. I'll be sensible. But I won't be a prisoner."

"You two can kill each other on the ride home," Marc interjected. "I just wanted you to know about Fisher's impending transfer."

"He won't be surprised by that turn of events," Hutch said, tabling his showdown with Casey for a few minutes. "Casey pretty much shoved the news in his face—and got him agitated enough to slip up. We've got what we need to go after Fisher for the past *and* present crimes."

"Nice work," Marc commended.

"What about at your end?"

"Like I said, still doing surveillance outside the meat market. It's tedious. And we've got nothing yet except a massive headache. But we're keeping on it. We'll check in as soon as we have something."

The truth was that it had been eighteen hours since Ryan had set up his surveillance.

He and Marc were bleary-eyed and no closer to the truth. All morning long, they'd watched as customers—mostly female— had entered the meat market, then exited with their purchases. A handful of times, customers had left without making a purchase. Interestingly, all of those customers had been men.

But that was the one, unimpressive, concrete observation the day had brought.

"Goddammit," Ryan said, sitting back in disgust. "Technology did shit for us this time. Outside video surveillance isn't enough. We've got to find a way to see what's going on between the customers and the owner."

"You want me to break in to the store?" Marc asked, still squatting in front of the computer screen. "You could install Gecko inside the ventilation system."

Gecko was Ryan's small robotic invention—a little R2D2 that traveled through tight spaces and provided both audio and video feed.

Ryan didn't seem too enthusiastic. "Gecko could do the job— if we knew exactly what we were looking for and if one of us spoke Arabic. And even if we could manage both, I'd have to eyeball the ventilation system first and figure out the best location for Gecko."

"All of which takes time," Marc agreed. "Not to mention the fact that we'd have to plan the break-in."

"I don't like it." Ryan fell silent, rubbing a hand over his jaw. "There has to be another way," he muttered.

Abruptly, he raised his head. "I just came up with a great idea. If it works, we could have our answers immediately."

"I'm listening."

"Listen while I tell Casey." Ryan reached for his iPhone. "I need her approval on this one."

The call from Ryan interrupted Casey and Hutch's verbal battle.

"Hey, Ryan." She was grateful for the interruption. "Marc told me you'd be calling. What's up?"

"I have an idea. I need to run it by you and get your okay."

"Shoot."

★ ★ ★

Leilah Milani was a struggling actress Ryan had met at a bar several years ago. She was a dark-haired Persian beauty—a free spirit, with a thirst for life, and a body that was so hot, it sizzled. She and Ryan had had an on-again, off-again thing that was ten percent conversation and ninety percent sex. Leilah's acting career had started to take off about eight months ago, and Ryan's career at Forensic Instincts was thriving. So they hadn't touched base in a while.

That didn't stop Ryan from picking up the phone now.

He gave Leilah a call right after he hung up with Casey, and met her at the Forensic Instincts brownstone a few hours later. She was the same exquisitely beautiful woman he remembered, and she was dying to hear the acting job Ryan's company wanted to hire her for.

Ryan led her into a first-floor interview room. "You look great," he said.

Leilah's smile was radiant. She walked up to Ryan, wrapped her arms around his neck and planted a long, lingering kiss on his mouth. "So do you," she murmured.

"Oh…excuse me, I didn't know this room was occupied."

Claire's tone was as startled as it was cold.

Ryan glanced past Leilah to see Claire leaning against the door jamb, arms folded across her chest as she observed the overfriendly exchange between Ryan and the exotically stunning woman with him.

"Hey, Claire-voyant, come on in." Reflexively, Ryan released Leilah, dropping his arms to his sides. This was a new and unwelcome situation for him. He'd never before given a damn if two women he was involved with at the same time ran into each other. No strings meant no strings. But with Claire… this was weird.

"This is Leilah Milani," he introduced, waving Claire in. "She's an old friend who's going to be helping us out with this case. Leilah, this is Claire Hedgleigh. She's the Forensic Instincts—" he paused, cautioning himself not to use the dreaded word *psychic* "—intuitive. She's a core team member."

"Nice to meet you, Claire." Leilah walked over and extended her hand, shook Claire's. "An intuitive? Is that like a medium?"

"We have different sensitivities. We operate through different communication channels," Claire replied. Having gotten past that first awkward moment, she reverted to her usual gentle, even-tempered self. "What about you? What's your profession? How are you helping us with this case?"

"I'm an actress," Leilah informed her. "And I don't know the details of my assignment yet, but apparently Ryan is giving me an exciting opportunity to assist you."

"I'm sure he is. Ryan is all about excitement." Claire couldn't resist that one barb. "In any case, I won't keep you." She turned her gaze on Ryan, her demeanor one hundred percent professional. "I just wanted to tell you that I spoke with Casey, that her outing yielded some success, and she'll be back by dinnertime."

"I know. I spoke with her." Ryan had the absurd desire to grab Claire, shake her and explain. At the same time, he was inexplicably angry at himself for even thinking he owed her an explanation.

Reading the warring emotions on his face, Claire opted to extricate herself. "Talk to you later," she said. "And good luck with your assignment, Leilah. I'll get back to what I was doing and give you two some privacy."

She shut the door behind her.

"She's lovely," Leilah commented, eyeing the closed door for a minute. Then she turned to face Ryan. "And you're sleeping with her," she added. "Is it serious? I'd hate to think you're off the market."

Ryan kept his expression nondescript. "We're not here to discuss my sex life, Leilah. We're here to set up a sting. Are you game?"

Another one of those radiant smiles. "As I said, I'm game for just about anything with you."

"Good." Ryan ignored the double entendre. "This isn't going to require an Oscar-worthy performance. But it *is* going to be an integral part of solving this case."

"I'm honored," she said teasingly. "I've never been asked to capture a criminal."

"Well, there's a first time for everything. Let me start by saying that this has to be conducted with the utmost discretion. It's not a role you can publicize or put on your résumé."

"Got it." Leilah nodded.

"It also has to be done ASAP—as in tomorrow. Can you swing it?"

Another nod. "I'm in between roles. Give me the details. Then, I'm all yours." She winked. "In any way you want me."

Violent porn.

It was just the charge he needed. He'd been operating in hyperdrive all week, his adrenaline pumping as he raped and tortured the bitches one by one, then choked the life out of them. His mind was still revving, but his body was depleted from expending all that energy. He needed to jack himself up, get ready for the next step. And this was the night to do it—the only free night he'd have for a while.

He turned the key in his apartment door and let himself in, making sure to lock the door behind him. He went through his customary room-by-room check, just to ensure that nothing had been disturbed. You could never be too careful.

Everything was exactly as he'd left it.

He tossed his duffel bag in the bedroom, walked into the kitchen and popped a microwave meal in to heat. When the timer beeped, he took out the dish and carried it into the living room where his big-screen TV was.

He set his dinner on the coffee table. Then he went back to the bedroom, opened his closet and squatted down over the brown cardboard box that was brimming with DVDs. He took each of them out, scrutinizing them as he made his selection.

He chose one of his favorites, *Scream If You Can,* in which women were choked almost to the point of asphyxiation during violent intercourse. Their pain, their gasps for air—it all really juiced him up.

He replaced the other DVDs and put away the box.

Returning to the living room, he turned on the electronic equipment and slid the DVD into the player.

His dinner was still warm. He picked it up and settled himself on the secondhand couch.

It didn't take long to accomplish his goal. Soon, his heart was thumping in his chest, his breath was coming faster and his erection was throbbing.

Dinner was forgotten.

He could visualize his next victim, pleading as she lay beneath him, trying to escape the brutal pounding of his body as it tore hers to shreds. He could feel his hands around her throat, hear her choked cries of pain, revel in the power that was his as he— The ringing of his cell phone was a shrill, intolerable interruption.

At first he ignored it. He was too far gone, lost in the surges of his own release. His head fell back against the sofa cushion, and he gasped in air as the warm aftermath of triumph flowed through him.

The damned phone wouldn't shut up.

It began ringing again, an insistent discord violating his peace.

He turned his head and looked down at the phone, recognizing the familiar number—a number he never dared to ignore.

"Yeah," he said, having punched on the phone and brought it to his ear. He listened for a few minutes, his annoyance transforming to puzzlement. "A clump of her hair? How the hell do you expect me to pull that off?" He listened again. "Okay, yeah, I guess I can do that. I'll start figuring it out tomorrow...*Now?*" His eyes snapped open. "You mean as in right now? I can't possibly—" Another bout of listening, this one longer and more intense. "Fine, I get it—you know where she is every fucking minute, and now is when she's there," he snapped, kissing his plans goodbye for the rest of the evening. "I'll take care of it....Yeah, half and half. I'll let you know when it's done."

# CHAPTER
## SEVENTEEN

There were very few things that made Casey relax.

Her monthly hair salon appointment was one of them.

As soon as they lowered her in the chair and cradled her head in the indented curve of the sink, her type A+ personality ebbed into an uncustomary type A−. She shut her eyes and let the warm water work its magic. The scent of the shampoo, the gentle massage of her scalp, it all eased the tension from her body. And then afterward, sitting in Louis's chair—half watching him performing his artistry and half zoning out—it was a monthly experience that was like a minivacation for her.

Having a security guard reading a magazine in the waiting area and frequently eyeballing her for safety put a definite damper on things. But she refused to let that ruin her experience.

The next few days were going to be manic. This time was hers.

"I'm leaning toward creating a wispier look," Louis announced. "I'll take about a half inch off the bottom, and do more pronounced edging up the sides."

"Sounds good." The agreement was perfunctory. Louis did what he chose and his decisions were *not* open to debate. But that was fine with Casey. Louis was a genius with a pair of scissors. She was never disappointed when she left his chair. He went to work, alternately combing, snipping and scrutinizing his handiwork. Casey watched with half-shut eyes, thinking about grabbing a sandwich at the deli next door before she hailed a cab to NYU.

The salon was bustling. Upscale as it was, it attracted a high-end crowd, many of whom made their appointments for right after work. That gave them a chance to wind down before dinner.

None of the patrons paid much attention when the handyman entered the salon. He was wearing a gray uniform jacket and carrying a tool chest.

"Hi," he greeted the receptionist. "I'm with Superior Plumbing. The deli next door is having water pressure problems. The landlord asked me to stop in here and measure your water pressure to make sure you're not being affected."

Charisse, the receptionist, looked worried. "Does he think we're having an issue? We're a hair salon. Any problems with our water would be a disaster."

"Yeah, I know." The guy nodded. "That's why he wants to be sure. He doesn't want you to have any disruption to your business."

"I appreciate that." Charisse cast a nervous glance around the salon. "Please, go ahead and check," she urged, pointing toward the rear of the salon. "And, while you do, I ask that you do your best not to upset the clientele. They won't react well to a snag in their salon experience."

"Got it." He snapped off a salute. "I'll make it quick and painless."

With that, he headed toward the back, well aware that the bodyguard sitting up front was scrutinizing him. Purposely, he walked past the workstation where Casey Woods was sitting, having her hair cut, without breaking stride.

The bodyguard went back to reading his newspaper.

The instant there were no eyes on him, the repairman let a pen drop from his pocket. It fell onto the marble tile floor with a clatter and came to rest near Louis's station. The repairman squatted down and scooped up the pen—along with a few wisps of Casey's hair. Rising, he continued to the back, going straight over to the deserted area where the water meter was situated. Making sure he had no audience, he slid Casey Woods's hair in a small Ziploc bag and sealed it. He opened his toolbox and placed the small bag inside.

Mission accomplished.

He waited a respectable period of time, then returned to the front of the salon.

"All good," he told Charisse. "Your water pressure's fine."

"Oh, thank you." She heaved a sigh of relief. "And please thank the landlord for us."

"Will do. Have a good night."

He got out of there as fast as he could. Getting the hair was only step one in what he needed to do. He had to split the clump of hair in half, keeping a section of it for future use and arranging to have the other half delivered to Auburn Correctional Facility.

He glanced at his watch.

He had half an hour to meet his contact.

Glen Fisher was awake most of the night.

His moods cycled rapidly as he replayed his meeting with

Casey Woods. Sometimes his rage would eclipse all else, forcing him to clench his fists at his sides to control the urge to choke her. Sometimes his lust took over, and he had to seek his own relief to calm the obsession to possess her. And sometimes, a smug sense of peace took over, reminding him that he'd have a chance to do it all, feel it all, inflict it all.

It was a relief when Tim the prison guard showed up at his cell.

"I have a few things for you," he muttered through the bars.

Glen rose. "A *few* things?" He only knew about one, and he'd been itching to receive that since last night.

"Yeah." Tim passed the Ziploc bag containing Casey's hair through the bars. "You wanted this." He hesitated, looking down at the papers in his hands. "I'm sure you *didn't* want this. But I thought you deserved a heads-up. These legal documents arrived late today. The Manhattan D.A. is filing charges against you for the murders of Jan Olson and Holly Stevens."

Glen snatched the documents and pored over them, his eyes narrowed in concentration. Then he raised his head.

Tim resembled a cringing child, as if he expected to be lambasted—maybe even threatened—for giving Glen the papers.

He was pleasantly surprised.

"I was expecting these," Fisher said. "Casey Woods all but handed them to me herself." He glanced briefly at the packet of hair, then back at the legal documents, that eerie look coming into his eyes. "This round is hers. The next one won't be."

Tim cleared his throat. "They're transferring you to Rikers in a few days."

"Excellent." Glen turned that crucifying stare on Tim. "I want you to get me an iPhone. Immediately. I don't care how much it costs. Just get one. Bring it to me tomorrow morning—same time as today."

★ ★ ★

Leilah was prepped and ready.

She and Ryan left Tribeca around 11:00 a.m., making their way up West End Avenue in Ryan's equipment-laden truck. Crawling up Tenth, they turned onto West 116th Street, headed east and parked a block away from the meat market. Climbing out of the van, Ryan paused long enough to place a forged "Clergy" card in the windshield—a personal statement on his part because he hated paying for parking in Manhattan.

Garbed in a traditional burka, Leilah walked ahead of Ryan, keeping a half block distance between them. By the time Ryan entered the store, Leilah was waiting in line, pacing up and down the length of the meat case. Ryan took his cue, and went over to examine some of the prepared foods—or at least pretended to. In reality, he was scanning the locations of the HVAC supplies and returns. It was a start. He'd need to get his hands on detailed drawings in order to put Gecko into play.

Leilah was still pacing. The owner of the store began darting irritated looks at her. By the time the patron ahead of her had completed her transaction, the shop owner was visibly agitated.

"May I help you?" he asked her in heavily accented English.

Leilah responded in Arabic. The owner reverted to his native Arabic, as well.

A heated conversation ensued.

Ryan had no clue what they were saying, but Leilah's raised voice and her accusing finger pointing at the lamb kabobs in the case launched the owner on a tirade. He ended with a few tightly controlled, furious words, and then stormed into the back.

Leilah met Ryan's eyes and nodded, letting him know that this was his opportunity. Ryan nodded back. He'd already used the time when Leilah was doing battle to select the ideal location to plant a bug—just beneath a wooden railing. To the untrained eye, it looked like a piece of used chewing gum. It felt like one, too. So, anyone coming across it by accident would leave well enough alone, too grossed out to touch or to closely inspect someone else's disgusting leftover.

A man entered the meat market and glanced around, looking for the owner. On his heels, a woman with a shopping bag came into the small store, also gazing quizzically around. She asked Leilah where the owner was.

Before Leilah could respond, the owner returned, emphatically shoving what was clearly a newly cut batch of lamb kabobs at her. He turned to the two new customers, forced a smile and said he'd be with them in just a minute. Then he turned back to Leilah, who was peering at the bright red contents on the brown paper. After a thorough inspection, she gave a nod of approval.

The owner quickly weighed the meat, wrapped it up and told Leilah how much she owed him. She handed him a hundred-dollar bill. He rang up her purchase, pulled out change from the register and handed over the meat and her money.

It was blatantly obvious that he couldn't wait for her to leave.

Ryan checked his watch, frowning as he ostensibly realized how late it was. He put down the container of prepared couscous that he'd planned on buying, and headed for the door.

A few minutes later, he and Leilah were back inside the van.

"What the hell happened in there?" Ryan demanded. "I thought the guy was going to bust a gut."

Laughing, Leilah peeled off her burka, tossed back her head and shook out her full mane of hair.

"I told him the lamb in the case looked like a dead carcass cut up into pieces. I asked him if his meat was halal or did that just apply to the sign in the window. He was livid. He told me to go elsewhere to buy my meat. Then I told him I needed five pounds of kabobs—five *fresh* pounds—which I demanded he cut for me on the spot." A lighthearted shrug. "I guess he wanted my money, so he forgot about my insult."

Ryan began to laugh. "A brilliant strategy and an equally brilliant performance. I'm totally impressed."

"I aim to please." Leilah preened like a beautiful peacock.

"I knew you spoke Arabic. But where did you learn how to pull off a scene like that?"

"From my mother," Leilah replied. "She was quite the force to be reckoned with. As a little girl, I would go with her to the meat market. The shopkeepers would cringe when we walked in. But they tolerated her badgering because she was a good customer." She gave him a sunny smile. "And while we're on the subject of badgering, you owe me five hundred bucks for my performance, another hundred for the meat, and I'm hungry. When are you going to cook these kabobs I so painstakingly acquired?"

"Later," Ryan promised. "After we get what we came for. I promise I'll fire up Big Bertha and char this lamb to perfection." Big Bertha was Ryan's homemade grill that looked more like a midnight requisition from an oil refinery than a typical gas grill. "In the meantime, I brought you a snack as a substitute."

He opened a cooler, placed the meat inside for safekeeping and removed a Ziploc bag, offering it to Leilah.

She glanced down at the contents. "You remembered!" She leaned forward and gave him a long, sensual kiss—one that might have gone somewhere if Ryan had let it.

He eased back on his haunches, preparing to get the audio information off his bug.

"I hope you brought something else for yourself." Leilah spoke between mouthfuls of the buffalo jerky that was her favorite.

"I'm fine. I just want our venture to pay off." He fast-forwarded the digitally recorded audio stream from the bug he'd planted. Oddly, the woman who'd entered the store after the man was being helped by the owner first. The transaction seemed normal enough. She made her purchase, paid and left.

Ryan could hear the door slam shut. Immediately thereafter, the two men began speaking in Arabic.

Nudging Leilah, Ryan hissed, "Translate."

Leilah nodded, dabbing at her mouth with a napkin. She then translated, speaking in fits and starts. "The customer is talking." A pause. "He said, 'I want to send one thousand dollars to my uncle in Quetta, Pakistan, and another thousand to my brother in Dubai,'" she reported. "He asked the owner, 'What are your fees?'"

Another intent pause. "The owner said 'three hundred dollars.' The customer told him that was a lot of money." Leilah frowned, her forehead creased in concentration. "The owner is explaining. He's saying that this is a very risky business, that the authorities are trying to pull the plug on all of them and throw them in jail. He wants to be paid for his trouble."

Leilah reached for another piece of jerky. "This will take a while. The two guys are haggling over the fees." She resumed her munching as the heated conversation continued. Eventually, she raised her hand, swallowing quickly. "The owner agreed to take only two hundred and fifty dollars, since he was dealing with a repeat customer. The man asked him when the money would be ready. The owner said three days for the brother in Dubai and five days for the uncle in Quetta. The men agreed."

Leilah listened again. "The customer is counting the money out loud. Two thousand. Two hundred. Fifty. The owner is accepting payment and advising the man that his uncle and brother can pick up the money in the same places as before. He's reciting the addresses." One final pause. "Now they're saying goodbye."

Ryan took in everything Leilah had just said. He steepled his fingers as he thought about what was going on and how it related to Suzanne's visit earlier in the week.

His gut told him that she'd be visiting the store again soon. His bug would then pick up the interaction between her and the meat market owner.

At that point, it would be time to put Gecko to work.

Glen Fisher despised waiting.

Nevertheless, in this case patience was essential. Things had to proceed in a precise order so that he could reap the rewards.

Outdoor exercise was over. Time to file in from the yard and go to the cafeteria for lunch. Dutifully, he got in line. While he waited, he groped inside the fold of his prison jumpsuit. His fingers slipped inside the Ziploc bag he'd crammed in there, rubbing her lock of hair between his fingers. A sense of power surged through him. He was so close he could taste it. Taste her.

Taste victory.

# CHAPTER
## EIGHTEEN

Deirdre Grimes put down her psychology textbook, rose from behind her desk and stretched.

She meandered over to her dorm room window and glanced down at Third Avenue. It was jammed, as usual. For her, that was one of the beauties of attending NYU. Growing up in a tiny rural Midwestern town where everything shut down at five, the constant activity of Greenwich Village was a whole new and exciting world.

Most of all, nothing beat New York City pizza.

She grinned, thinking that she ordered so many pizza deliveries, the guys at her favorite place knew her phone number by heart. It was always the same order—a meat lover's pie with a delicious combination of sausage, pepperoni and meatball. She'd eat a few slices, after which she'd store the rest in her minifridge to enjoy over the course of the week.

She'd finished up her last slice yesterday. So she'd be placing her order in a little while—her reward to herself after completing her calculus problem set and beginning to tackle the assignment Ms. Woods had given them in Human Behavior.

Normally, Deirdre didn't add to her already-heavy course load by taking evening classes. But she was a psych major and Ms. Woods's course was totally fascinating. It delved into what made people tick, how to read body language and how to zero in on different "tells."

Last night's lecture had focused on passive-aggressive personalities. The class assignment was to write a short paper describing a specific interaction with that type of individual, and what the indicators were that defined the person in question as passive-aggressive.

The paper wasn't due for two weeks. But Deirdre was actually looking forward to writing it. She knew just who she'd be writing about.

A knock on the door made her turn away from the window. She brushed a strand of red-gold hair off her face and crossed the dorm room, turning the knob to see who her visitor was.

Opening the door was the biggest mistake of her life.

The Forensic Instincts team desperately needed a break. They'd been working for days without rest. The wear and tear was beginning to take a major toll on them.

Ryan provided that break—for the team, for Hutch, for the security guys and for Leilah. He took over the patio out back, setting up an impromptu dinner courtesy of his and Leilah's shopping spree at the meat market. He spent an hour or so tinkering with Big Bertha to get things rolling.

"Big Bertha" had earned her name. Ryan had built the huge contraption from two steel drums, strategically cut and welded into a fire trough. But the real magic of the grill was its custom burners that Ryan had fabricated along with an "oxygen" boost that almost doubled the flame temperature, searing the meat like no other cooking apparatus.

While Ryan was adjusting the flame thrower he called a grill, Leilah was busy in the FI kitchen checking on the lamb that had been immersed for hours in her family's traditional marinade, a recipe passed down from generation to generation. The aromatic blend of lemon, garlic, mint and other spices permeated the town house, making everyone hungry for dinner and keeping Hero glued to Leilah's side.

The meal was delicious, but there was an unmistakable tension.

Claire was visibly aloof to Ryan. He'd tried several times to approach her and neutralize the strain between them. But it was clear that while Claire completely understood why Ryan had summoned Leilah for her help, she did *not* understand the overtly affectionate nature of their interaction. Nor did she want to.

"You're screwing things up," Marc commented as he walked out to the patio and perched beside Ryan, who was doling out seconds.

Ryan's jaw tightened. "Why? Is your meat too rare?"

"You know what I'm talking about. And it's not the food."

For whatever reason, that infuriated Ryan more than he already was. His head snapped up and he glared at Marc. "Are you about to give me relationship advice? You, who haven't been involved with a woman in as long as I can remember?"

Marc was unperturbed. "Yup. Because, whether or not you admit it, your relationship with Claire is more than casual— which means you have parameters to adhere to." He paused. "And for the record, just because I like to keep my private life private, it doesn't mean I spend my nights alone."

"Fine." Ryan took it down a notch. "Point taken. Actually,

both points taken. How the hell am I supposed to convince Claire-voyant that I'm not hitting the sheets with Leilah?"

"You could start by not being so responsive to her flirting. It doesn't take a body-language specialist to figure out that she's trying to rekindle whatever you once had. And you're not exactly discouraging it."

"Yeah," Hutch agreed, having strolled over to join the men. "Cut the charm. I know you eat, drink and sleep it, but it's not doing you any good tonight."

"So what am I supposed to do—blow her off?"

"Just cool it, take it down a notch," Hutch advised. "I don't know what kind of arrangement you and Claire have, and it's none of my business. But even if you're keeping it light and easy, doesn't mean she wants another woman shoved in her face. Do what you want, but do it on your own time—not when Claire's around."

A corner of Ryan's mouth lifted. "Our boss has really taught you well. Nice analysis of the female brain. Okay, I'll try my best."

Back in the dining area, Claire sat by herself, playing with her couscous, and trying to deal with her own new and raw emotions. She was being unreasonable, and she knew it. Ryan had every right to renew whatever personal involvement he had with Leilah. There were no promises between them, no labeled relationship and no exclusivity clause. Still, all Claire could see was a beautiful, dark-haired woman all over Ryan. It was clear that they'd been hot and heavy at some point, and equally clear that Leilah was interested in picking up where they'd left off. As for Ryan, he was being too damned accommodating, despite needing Leilah's help.

She had no idea how to approach this one.

"Hey." Casey came over and sat down beside her. "You okay?"

"I guess not. But you already know that." Claire shot her a helpless look. "Why am I letting myself feel this way and how do I stop it?"

"I'm not sure you can." Casey's smile was wan. "Relationships are hard. They're complicated and confusing. And they make you feel and act like you usually don't."

"Leilah's gorgeous," Claire blurted out, listening to the tinkling laughter of the curvaceous, dark-haired beauty as it emanated from the kitchen. "Even Hero's transfixed."

"Hero's transfixed by her family recipe. But, yeah, she is gorgeous." Casey wasn't going to lie to her friend. "And she's being pretty obvious about what she wants. But it takes two to make that happen. And I think Ryan has too much respect for you to respond to Leilah's one-liners."

"We're like day and night," Claire said, referring to herself and Leilah. "And I'm not about to compete, no matter how crappy this makes me feel."

"You don't have to compete." Casey paused, carefully weighing her next words. "Ryan cares about you a lot more than even he realizes. He hates clingy women. Before you, he'd never think of giving any woman he was involved with an explanation of his actions. It wouldn't even be on his radar that she might be hurting. And if it was, he wouldn't feel any responsibility to alleviate that hurt. I see a whole new Ryan these past months."

Claire fell silent. "You're right," she said at last. "Relationships *are* hard. I liked it better when I was—" She broke off, dropping her plate to the carpet and letting out a gasp. "Oh, no."

"What is it?" Casey recognized the frightened, faraway look in Claire's eyes.

"It's happening again," Claire whispered, still staring off into space, her breath fast and ragged. "Another woman. Feeling terror. And pain. She's clawing to get away. But she can't. She can't." Claire covered her face with her hands, as if by doing so she could block out the images.

Casey's own heart was racing, the fear that had dominated her life all week consuming her yet again. "Can you see the surroundings? Think, Claire. Try to concentrate. Is it indoors? Outdoors?"

"Indoors," Claire said in a shaky whisper. "Institutional setting. Cinder-block walls. Woven multicolored area rug. He's dragging her down onto it. There's nothing she can do."

Casey's mind was processing. Institutional setting with cinder-block walls. Not an apartment. A college dorm? Maybe. But which college? Which dorm?

They could call the police. But they had nothing to give them, nothing concrete.

They were helpless.

Casey's cell phone rang. She didn't need to look at the caller ID for the all-too-familiar "unavailable." She knew who it was.

Woodenly, she punched the phone on. "Don't bother," she said in a tortured voice she couldn't conceal. "I already know."

"Really?" the scrambled voice answered. "I'm impressed. That psychic of yours is worth her weight in gold."

"Who's the victim?" Casey was past the point of playing games. "Just tell me."

"And ruin the fun? Not a chance, Red. You'll find out soon enough. She respected you, you know. You'd be proud. She fought hard. Just as you will. This one's ironic. We've come full circle."

The sound of the connection ending sent chills up and down Casey's spine.

Full circle? What the hell did that mean?

★ ★ ★

It was 10:00 p.m.

Robbie chained his bike to a pole on Third Avenue, and lifted the soft, thermal box out of the basket. He headed for the familiar dorm, where he made a meat lover's pizza delivery at least once a week. Deirdre Grimes was predictable. She always ordered the same thing, and she always gave him a generous tip.

He climbed the two flights of stairs to her second-floor dorm room. He then headed down the corridor, stopped outside her room and rapped at the door.

No response.

"Hey, Deirdre," he called, knocking again. "It's Robbie. I've got your pizza. Eat it while it's hot."

Again, no reply.

Robbie glanced up and down the hallway. He spotted Anita Lerner, another of his college customers, on her way to the showers.

"Hey, Anita," he yelled out to her. "Have you seen Deirdre?"

Anita stopped and shook her head. "I've been locked in my room studying. Deirdre was about to do the same the last time I saw her." She sent him a grin. "Probably fell asleep. Knock louder. She wouldn't want to miss her meat lover's."

"Yeah, okay." Robbie turned back to the door as Anita continued on to the showers. He knocked loudly and repeatedly, calling out Deirdre's name a few more times.

Nothing.

He tried the doorknob. It turned, and the door swung open.

"Deirdre?" Robbie was greeted by a semidarkened room. He wasn't about to just march in, but he could reach the light switch from the doorway. He flicked it on.

The overhead lit up the place, revealing an empty room. There was blatant evidence of a scuffle. An overturned desk chair, a throw pillow on the floor and a potted plant knocked down and spilled across the woven rug.

And that wasn't all. There was a large red stain on the rug.

Blood.

Robbie stood dead still for a moment. Then, he took out his cell phone and called 9-1-1.

There was none of the merriment of a few short hours ago at the Forensic Instincts brownstone. All of that had come to a grinding halt after Casey had gotten her chilling phone call. She'd immediately called Captain Sharp with as much information as she had—which wasn't much. Now all they could do was wait.

The phone rang at ten-thirty.

Casey punched the phone on speaker. "Yes," she responded. "Do you have something for us?"

"There's been an incident at NYU," Captain Sharp informed them. "The pizza delivery boy called it in about a half hour ago." He described the condition of the door room that Robbie had walked into. "The crime scene unit is doing its job. I have nothing solid to give you. But Claire's description of the scene was accurate. The only difference is that, this time, the body was removed. We've got cops combing the area to find it."

Casey sucked in her breath and asked the question she dreaded the answer to. "What's the name of the girl who's missing?"

"Deirdre Grimes."

"Oh, no." Casey sank down on a chair, her face as white as a sheet.

"Obviously you know her."

"She's one of the students in my evening class." Casey provided the information on autopilot, bile rising in her throat. "She's bright, enthusiastic…and a redhead." She squeezed her eyes shut. "Damn this scumbag. Why doesn't he just go after me and leave these poor girls alone? Deirdre is nineteen. She had her whole life ahead of her."

"We haven't found a body yet," Sharp reminded her gently. "Maybe there's hope."

"No. There's not," Claire replied. She turned away, her lashes damp with tears. "He killed her. And then he moved the body and prepared it for us." A shudder went through her. "Somehow the body is close to me."

"In Tribeca?" Casey demanded.

Claire shook her head. "No. Not close to the office. Close to me."

"He dumped the body near Claire's apartment," Hutch concluded. "Think about it. The killer already left bodies in both Ryan's and Patrick's neck of the woods, and one body in Tribeca, as well. All that's left of the FI team's neighborhoods are Claire's and Marc's. NYU isn't far from Claire's apartment. Following the killer's pattern, I think we should concentrate our search in the East Village."

Abruptly, he broke off, a flicker of realization dawning in his eyes.

"You already know where the body is," Casey deduced.

Hutch met Casey's gaze. "He told you that you'd come full circle. We thought he meant it emotionally. But he meant it in a real sense—full circle from where Glen Fisher first attacked you."

"Which was in the East Village," Casey breathed. "He put Deirdre's body in that alley near Tompkins Square Park."

# CHAPTER
## NINETEEN

Tim Grant peered up and down the prison corridor. It was nighttime. No one in sight. And all the prisoners were confined until morning.

He approached Glen Fisher's cell and glanced inside. Fisher was visibly impatient, pacing back and forth, pausing only long enough to finger the lock of hair Tim had brought him the day before.

That damned lock of hair had made Fisher terrifyingly happy. It was as if he was a predator, and the hair was a trophy from one of his quarries. Tim didn't know the details. And he didn't want to. He just shut them out and did his job.

Tonight he had another delivery that would brighten Fisher's night, thanks to some help from Bob Farrell, his NYPD contact.

"Fisher," he muttered, his lips close to the bars.

Glen's head whipped around. "You have something for me?"

"The iPhone you asked for." As always, Tim felt a wave of

relief when he satisfied Fisher's demands. The alternative wasn't something he wanted to contemplate.

"Excellent," Fisher said, a victorious smile curving his lips. He reached through the bars and took the slim cell phone. "This is precisely what I needed. You can go now."

Tim didn't need to be told twice.

He turned around and retraced his steps, getting as far from Fisher as he could.

Glen waited until the sound of the prison guard's steps faded away and disappeared. Then he went to the far side of his cot and squatted down, where he couldn't be seen. He huddled over the iPhone and turned on the power. Waiting only until it was ready to go, he punched out a text message. It read: Is "Find iPhone location" visible?

He waited, knowing that an answer would be forthcoming.

He wasn't disappointed. A few minutes later, a return text arrived. Auburn State NW, it said.

Those were just the words Glen Fisher wanted to see.

He leaned back against the bed frame, taking out the lock of Casey Woods's hair and rubbing each silky red strand between his fingers.

The contact felt good.

The real thing would feel better.

Casey lay quietly in Hutch's arms, listening to the sounds of the city outside her window, yet hearing only the cries of pain that her mind conjured up—cries that Deirdre Grimes must have made before they were choked into silence.

For reasons she couldn't explain, Casey had insisted on visiting the crime scene. Hutch had gone with her. The crime scene unit was still at the dorm room, as was Robbie the pizza guy, who looked green at the gills. He'd answered the detectives' questions, but had agreed to hang around for a while, just in case something else turned up that he might be able to help with. The poor guy was a wreck. He couldn't pull it together, nor could he stop staring at the bloodstain.

Casey didn't blame him. The image was horrible. What it implied was worse.

Sure enough, Deirdre's body was found in the exact alley near Tompkins Square Park where Glen Fisher had attacked Casey last year. She'd been posed just the same as the others, right down to the red ribbon, lipstick and the lock of hair. The hair would be checked for DNA. They all knew that the DNA would belong to the killer's previous victim. The only difference between Deirdre's murder and the previous murders was the evidence of blood at the crime scene. The police were certain the bloodstain they'd found on Deirdre's dorm room rug would match the bloodstain on the tarp she'd been wrapped in and the clumps of blood that were matted in her hair. She'd put up one hell of a fight, and it was clear that the killer had had to slam her head against the floor repeatedly to gain control of the situation.

In the end, her brave struggles hadn't mattered. The killer had won. Deirdre was dead.

Casey closed her eyes, bombarded by feelings of rage, anguish and guilt.

"It's not your fault," Hutch murmured. "You're on his victim list, too."

"How did you know what I was thinking?"

Hutch reached for her hand, which was on his chest, her fingernails digging into his skin. "Because you're stabbing me. You only do that when you're angry at yourself."

She smiled faintly. "Sorry." Casey relaxed her hand. "But how can I *not* blame myself? Deirdre—as well as the others—they were all killed because of me."

"You did everything in your power to stop it. Deirdre was on the list of redheads you know that you made up for Marc," Hutch reminded her. "In fact, almost all the victims were on that list. And we ran checks on every one of those young women—to see if they were being followed, harassed, even in a bad relationship. They all came up clean."

"Yet they all wound up dead," Casey said. "How many more of them are there going to be?"

"My guess? One. Someone to dump near Marc's place and complete the circle. After that..."

"After that, it's my turn." Casey finished his thought.

"It's not going to happen." Hutch had that hard edge to his voice.

"We don't know, Hutch." Casey spoke softly. "He's good. And between his skill and Fisher's direction—we might not be able to stop it."

Hutch rolled Casey onto her back, gazing down at her with fire in his eyes. "We'll stop it. *I'll* stop it. However good he is, I'm better. And I'm not going to lose you. So don't even think of going down that path."

Casey smiled and gave a sarcastic salute. "Yes, sir, Supervisory Special Agent Hutchinson. I don't know what I was thinking."

Hutch didn't smile back. "You threw Fisher off his game when you got in his face. He'll make a mistake."

"He's not the one doing the killing—at least not currently."

"But he's the lynch pin. If he screws up, his partner will screw up."

"We still don't know the connection between them—or even who this supposed partner is."

"We will. In the meantime, you're never alone. No one can get at you."

Casey gave a small nod.

"It's okay to be scared." Hutch's tone grew gentle. "I know you keep your emotions locked up tight, but when you're with me, you can let down your guard."

"Look who's talking. You, who are always in total control."

"Not always."

"True," Casey conceded. "Not when we're in bed."

The intense look was back on Hutch's face. "No," he agreed. "Not when we're in bed. Maybe that should tell us something."

He lowered his head and covered her mouth with his, passion laced with tenderness.

That poignant tenderness dominated their lovemaking—each kiss, each caress, each movement, of their joined bodies speaking volumes and overshadowing all else.

When it was over, they lay quietly together, their fingers intertwined. There was a very new, very raw emotion that permeated the room, speaking volumes about what just happened between them, what was still happening in the aftermath.

Hutch found his voice first.

"Don't you think it's time we acknowledged what we have?" He spoke roughly into Casey's hair. "We dance around it. We exert boundless energy and maximum effort to avoid giving it a name—even though we both know it's there."

"I'm not afraid of saying it." Casey put her hands on Hutch's shoulders and pushed him slightly away so she could gaze straight into his eyes. "I'm afraid of what happens once it's been said. What do we do with it? Where do we go from there? Our lives are so complicated. Our worlds are so different and so far apart. How do we reconcile that?"

"The same way we reconcile it when we avoid saying the words—day by day, need by need."

Casey swallowed. "Okay. Here it is. I'm insanely in love with you. I can't imagine my life without you in it."

Hutch's knuckles caressed her cheek, an incredibly intimate expression crossing his face. "I've been in love with you since I first laid eyes on you. You're as impossible as our situation. But I wouldn't change you or the way I feel about you. This will be hard work. But we're both die-hard perfectionists. We'll make it right."

"I'm too stubborn to accept anything less. And so are you." Casey's lashes were damp. "This killer doesn't stand a chance, does he?"

"Nope. Not with us closing in on him. He's as good as done."

Hutch visited both crime scenes the next day—the dorm room where Deirdre was killed and the alleyway where her body was left. Patrick—who was a trained pro at this after three decades of FBI investigative work—joined him.

The dorm room yielded nothing. From there, the two men searched every inch of the alley, hoping one of them would find the tiniest something that might have escaped the crime scene unit.

No such luck.

"This murder was more violent than the others," Patrick commented, hunkering down beside the trail of blood that ran across the cracked concrete. "Based on what I got from the police, he really brutalized her."

"Sexually, as well," Hutch said. "The details were pretty gruesome. I kept them from Casey. She's got enough to deal with. The killer is getting angrier and more violent. Something is provoking him. The question is what?"

"Casey's visit with Fisher?" Patrick suggested. "Couldn't that have set him off?"

"It definitely set *Fisher* off," Hutch responded. "But there's a disconnect here. If it was Fisher who'd committed this crime, your theory would make a world of sense. But it wasn't. It was our unsub." Hitch resorted to FBI-speak, using the common term for Unknown Subject. "And even if that unsub is taking orders directly from Fisher, this is the kind of rage that's personal. It's not a third party delivering a message."

Patrick's expression was grim. "So this lunatic is either furious at Casey or furious at law enforcement."

"That would be my guess."

"Hey." A male voice from the sidewalk summoned them. "Are you the police?"

Both Hutch and Patrick turned to see a well-dressed guy in his mid-to-late twenties hovering just outside the alley. His hand was wrapped around a leash with a Boston terrier at the end of it. The dog sat patiently while his owner talked.

"Why?" Hutch asked, taking the lead on this one. "Do you need the police?"

The guy shrugged. "I don't know. I just read that a dead body was found in this alley. I figured if you were the cops, I'd talk to you. I might have some information."

Hutch pulled out his ID. "Supervisory Special Agent Hutchinson, FBI," he said. "What can you tell us?"

The guy blinked. "The Feds. Wow. This must be a big deal."

"What's your name?" Patrick asked.

"Jason. Jason Franklin. I live in that apartment over there." He leaned over and pointed past the canopied overhang on Avenue B to one of the apartment buildings down the street.

"And what information do you think you have for us, Jason?"

"Maybe nothing. But I was out walking Rocco last night—"

Jason indicated his dog "—and there was a big silver pickup truck blocking the sidewalk right where I'm standing now. There's construction being done in the area, so I figured that's why the truck was there—either to load or unload. Or maybe it had broken down, because there was no one in it. Either way, I didn't give it much thought. Then I read about the body they found in this alley and I decided I should tell someone what I saw. I planned on calling the cops right after I walked Rocco. But now I'm telling you in person." He looked at them. "Do you think the truck was here to dump the body?"

"I don't know," Hutch replied, pulling out his iPhone, ready to type in the information. "But you did the right thing, telling us what you saw. Do you remember anything about the truck, other than the fact that it was silver? A make? Model? License plate number?"

The guy shook his head. "I take the subway. I don't know anything about cars or trucks. So I'm the wrong person to ask about specifics. The only reason I noticed the truck at all was because Rocco and I had to squeeze by it to take our walk."

"Understood." Hutch's finger was poised over his phone's touch screen. "Give me your address and phone number, Jason. That way a detective can contact you and ask any further questions."

"Sure." Jason provided the details they needed. "It's creepy to have something like this happen in my own neighborhood. I hope you find the psycho soon."

"We intend to."

At seven o'clock that evening, Ryan's basement lair became a flurry of activity.

Having set up his audio equipment, Ryan planted himself at his desk, swiveled his chair around and played back the voice recordings of each and every customer who'd been at the meat market that day. Leilah perched on the edge of the desk beside him, listening carefully to every verbal exchange. With each new customer, she indicated with a thumbs-up or a thumbs-down whether or not the customer was engaged in illegal money transfers using hawala—an international operation often used for money laundering. Ryan made copies of the thumbs-up recordings, along with the date/time stamp, and skipped over the others.

His work was meticulous, and not only for FI's purposes. When this case was over, his intention was for the FBI's New York field office to receive an anonymous email containing the audio files and a suggestion that they investigate the meat market on West 116th Street. That would take care of the illegal activities going on there.

Once in a while, as the tapes played, Leilah would throw back her head and laugh aloud in reaction to what she was hearing. Ryan would cock his own head in puzzlement, and wait for her to explain. She responded by translating. Twice, the exchanges involved cranky men, complaining about their wives—annoyed that they were asked to pick up meat for dinner when they already had enough on their agenda. One of those men confided in the butcher that the contents of the meat case were more lively than his wife in bed.

On the flip side were the wives who'd argue about who had the worst husband. One woman asked the other if she had a recipe that would insure that her husband choked on the meat she was buying.

That one even made Ryan chuckle.

Overall, the work was long and tedious. It was 10:00 p.m. before they reached the last few recordings of the day. Partway through, Claire walked in, giving Ryan an update on the police reports.

She hesitated in the doorway when she saw what was going on. "I'm sorry. I seem to be making a habit of interrupting you." This time her voice was sincere. She'd come to grips with her infantile emotions. Ryan and Leilah were working. If they were doing more than that on their own time, that was none of her business, and she was just going to have to deal with it in a gracious way. "I just wanted to give Ryan a police update. But there are no major details. So it can wait." She turned to go.

Before Ryan could respond, the day's last verbal interaction at the meat market began playing on the tape—a woman's soft voice, speaking English.

Claire stopped in her tracks, veering around to face them.

"What's that you're listening to?" she asked, pointing at the equipment.

"Voice recordings of everyone our bug picked up in the meat store today." Ryan was taken aback by the intensity of Claire's tone. "Why?"

"Because that voice—it belongs to Suzanne Fisher."

Ryan shot straight up in his chair. "Are you sure?"

"Without a doubt," Claire replied. "I was with Casey and Marc when we questioned her. We talked at length. I remember her voice. I'm positive that's her. What's she doing in the meat market?"

"Let's find out." Ryan rewound the tape and played it from the start of the conversation.

Suzanne Fisher was counting out five thousand dollars in cash, plus an additional five hundred for the transaction fee, and tendering it to the owner. "Would you please send that to my husband's nephew in Brooklyn?" she requested.

"Of course," the heavily accented owner replied. "It will be ready for him tomorrow morning."

*"Shit!"* Ryan exclaimed. "She's sending money to Glen Fisher's *dead nephew?*"

"Clearly, he isn't dead," Claire said. "He's alive and well and living in Brooklyn."

"How could that be?" Ryan was livid—mostly at himself. "We all saw the death certificate. Which means the death was staged. But why would Jack stage his own death? Glen must have been involved the whole time. I'm such an asshole. I should've dug deeper and made sure the death certificate was legit. In the meantime, why is Glen transferring cash to Jack? Is he supporting him? Or is it more?"

"More as in working with him?" Claire asked. She swallowed hard. "Or even killing for him?"

"Anything's possible." Ryan had already grabbed his iPhone and was punching in Marc's number on speed dial. "I'll take a better look at Jack's background later tonight. But for now, we've got to get to him—fast. We have no time to lose. When he collects his cash, we'll collect him."

# CHAPTER
## TWENTY

Marc groped for his iPhone and saw Ryan's caller ID pop up on the screen.

"What now?"

Ryan's brows rose. It wasn't like Marc to sound so irked, and maybe even a little distracted.

It was a moot point, because Marc's mood changed the instant Ryan told him about Suzanne's impending money transfer to Jack.

"Tell me what you need," Marc said.

"I need your help breaking into the meat market and planting Gecko. Tonight."

"I'll be at the office in an hour."

Right before Marc disconnected the call, Ryan heard the distinct sound of a woman's disappointed voice in the background. So Marc really did have a sex life. And Ryan had just screwed it up—at least for tonight. That explained his foul mood when he'd answered the phone.

Good thing Marc always showed such iron control. Otherwise, he'd probably kick Ryan's ass.

There was a ton to do before Marc arrived—all of which had to be done without noise or interruption. Ryan was already inside his own head, oblivious to everything and everyone around him.

Claire and Leilah took the hint, climbing the stairs to the first floor.

There was an awkward silence as they stood in the hallway together, neither of them quite sure what to say.

Finally, Leilah made a disgusted sound and rolled her eyes. "This is ridiculous," she declared. "I admire you, Claire. You're intelligent, you're strong and you speak your mind. We're not that different, except that you keep your thoughts private and I wear mine on my sleeve. I can't speak for you, but I think we could be friends, if we could get past this absurd rivalry. One thing I've learned for sure—no man is worth it."

Claire's lips curved in a smile. "I like you, too, Leilah. And I apologize if I acted like a high-schooler. You're right. We have a lot in common. As for Ryan, he is who he is."

"Exactly." Leilah glanced at her watch. "It's still early. Why don't you and I go out for a drink and you can explain to me the difference between a psychic and a claircognizant."

"You're on."

Ryan's first course of business was to double-check Gecko and make sure that his mechanical and electronic marvel was fully charged and ready for action. He needed his little critter's mission-critical capabilities to pull this off.

There would be no second chances.

He connected Gecko's USB port to his computer, fired up the diagnostic program that would run Gecko through a thorough analysis of all his subsystems, as well as calibrate his internal gyro, GPS sensors and servo motors.

While Gecko was undergoing his "physical," Ryan turned to the next order of business—getting as much information about the meat market and the building it was located in as possible.

Ryan's first digital stop was the Department of Finance's Digital Tax Map online service. Once the site was up, he entered the address of the meat market and quickly found the block and lot number of the building. Exploring the public records available, he saw several building permits from a few years ago related to the heating and electrical system upgrades that had been performed. Since the building was owned by a Columbia University trust, a tier-one contractor, Gotham Mechanical, had completed the work.

Next, Ryan opened up another independent X window session on his computer, retrieved the hacking script he had written for just such occasions and began the process of circumventing the firewalls sitting between him and the Gotham Mechanical projects server. A few minutes later, Ryan was looking at the "as built" drawings of the upgraded HVAC system Gotham had modified just three years ago.

With a few quick mouse clicks, Ryan initiated the download of the AutoCAD files to Lumen, one of FI's servers. There were three that made up the team's expansive server farm: Lumen, Equitas and Intueri, named after the Latin words for light, justice and intuition—a perfect description of Forensic Instincts.

Ryan then immediately began to generate a 3-D file from the AutoCAD drawings so he could visualize the best place to introduce Gecko into the HVAC system, as well as how to navigate through the maze of ducts inside the building. It was important to minimize the number of changes in height and direction for Gecko to perform. The best solution was to cut an access panel in the supply ductwork located in the basement utility room.

Ryan had just started assembling the tools he would need when Hero's bark and Yoda's voice simultaneously announced Marc's arrival.

Claire and Leilah strolled into Weather Up, a trendy bar on Duane Street in Tribeca, and settled themselves on stools. Bypassing the more elaborate drinks, they ordered glasses of wine.

There were a fair number of good-looking guys in the bar— all of whom noticed them, many of whom appeared to be on their way over for introductions.

Leilah eliminated the problem immediately. She turned her back to the rest of the room. Sipping her cabernet, she tossed her hair away from her face, and angled her head to gaze at Claire. Her body language was clear. She was having an intense conversation with her friend. Now was *not* pickup time.

The disappointed guys went back to their drinks.

"Why don't we get the Ryan part of the conversation over with first, so we can actually talk?" Leilah surprised Claire by suggesting.

Claire found herself smiling. She brought her wineglass to her lips and drank a bit of her merlot. "You're incredibly up front," she said. "It's not exactly a shock—I've watched you in action the past few days. But I assumed I'd find the trait annoying. Actually, it's very refreshing."

Leilah shrugged. "I hate playing games," she responded. "And I refuse to circle around with you like a couple of cats. Let's make it simple. I'll tell you about Ryan and me, and you tell me about Ryan and you. Then we can dismiss the subject and go on, get to know each other."

"Sounds fair." Claire had never met anyone quite like Leilah. She couldn't blame Ryan for being attracted to her—she was the whole package.

"Ryan and I met at a bar," Leilah began. "We were both on the verge of career breakouts. But neither of us was totally settled in yet. So we decided to enjoy our free time while we still had some." Leilah smiled, that glowing smile that lit up her whole face. "We spent most of our time in bed," she stated honestly. "Ryan excels there, as I'm sure you know. But he's also brilliant and funny and spontaneous. We did everything from long-distance marathons to holding shot contests together. Those were crazy, exciting days." She paused. "Would I want to revisit them? Of course. Do I think that's going to happen? Not anytime soon." Leilah regarded Claire without a trace of jealousy or anger. "He's crazy about you."

Claire's eyes widened. "He said that?"

"Of course not. He probably doesn't even know it. And he wouldn't admit it if he did. But, trust me, it's true. I've never seen Ryan like this. He cares if you're upset. He worries if you're in danger. And he's put up an emotional wall between him and me, because he doesn't want to give false signals." Another smile. "You must be quite a challenge for him. You two are like day and night."

"You're right about that part." Claire sighed. "Most of the time, we annoy the hell out of each other. He has very little respect for what I do, and I don't understand a word of what he does. We argue like teenagers. It's ridiculous."

"Except when it's not?" Leilah asked.

Claire nodded. "Except then." She took another sip of merlot, feeling as exposed as if she were under a microscope. "I'm sorry. I'm just not used to discussing my sex life."

"You don't have to. I can feel the pull between you and Ryan whenever you're in the same room. Is it just the sex? Because I don't think so."

"No," Claire admitted. "It's not. There are genuine feelings involved. I'm just not sure what they are or what they mean."

"Then why dissect them? Let them be what they are and unfold as they're meant to."

"That's what Ryan and I have been doing. I don't want to complicate things with labels and analysis. We are what we are. Which is already more than I can handle."

Leilah chuckled. "I hear you. And I think that's a good plan. Guys like Ryan are best taken a day at a time." Pushing aside her wine, Leilah moved on, clearly done with the subject of Ryan. "Tell me about you. All I know is that you're blonde, you're gracious and you have a princess-in-a-tower kind of beauty. And I know that Ryan calls you 'Claire-voyant' and you call yourself claircognizant. What's the difference?"

"You mean besides the fact that Ryan believes it's all a bunch of crap?"

"Yes. Besides that. I'm intrigued. Fill me in."

Claire hesitated. "Do you really want to get into this?"

"Would you prefer not to?"

Claire took another sip of her wine. "It's just not something I normally discuss."

"Because it's private, or because people don't understand?"

"Both." Claire was frank. "But mostly the latter. It's not fun to be treated like some sort of witch."

Leilah made another sound of disgust. "That's sheer ignorance. I think spirituality is more grounding than reality."

Claire looked surprised. "I didn't realize you felt that way."

"Well, I do. I believe there's a world of power in things you can't actually see or touch. So, please, share whatever you're comfortable sharing. I'd love to learn more about your gift."

There was something about Leilah that encouraged Claire to do just that—an open, nonjudgmental quality that was very rare.

Claire began with the basics. "Well, to start with, there are four metaphysical senses. Claircognizance, or clear knowing, is just one of them. Clairvoyance, or clear seeing, is another. Then there's clairaudience, which is clear hearing, and finally, clairsentience, which is clear feeling. With claircognizance, your conscious mind is not in control of your thoughts. Those thoughts come to you at random. I don't know how or why."

Leilah seemed fascinated. "When did you discover you had this gift?"

"I was young," Claire said. "In kindergarten. It's hard to explain but I became attuned to things—things I'd have no way of knowing. It was a kind of inner awareness that told me what was happening or was about to happen. It scared me and it fascinated me, but I didn't really understand it—not then. When I got older, I did some research and found a group of kindred spirits in upstate New York. We corresponded. They taught me how to channel my thoughts through meditation. Not only did my abilities become clearer, but the meditation made it easier for my thoughts to come through without all the noise surrounding them."

"Wow. That's amazing." Leilah had propped her elbow on the bar and was leaning against her hand, hanging on to Claire's words. "What about your family? How did they react?"

"Not well." Claire felt that all-too-familiar twinge. Somehow the pain of rejection never really went away. "I'm an only child. I come from a well-respected, very visible family. They're well-known in the community, and as traditional as they come.

Their image is important to them. I didn't fit that image. I tried. They tried. It didn't work."

Leilah was studying Claire's face. "Old money," she deduced aloud. "Your ancestors probably came over on the *Mayflower*."

"Something like that, yes."

"That must have been terrible for you." Leilah's tone was rife with sympathy. "I come from a big, huggy-kissy family. They supported my dreams even during the endless months when I couldn't get a single acting role. I don't know what I would have done without them."

"You would have become totally self-reliant," Claire told her. "That's what I did. But you didn't have to. You're fortunate."

"I know." Leilah traced the stem of her wineglass with one finger. "I admire you. You're strong and independent. It's no wonder everyone at Forensic Instincts thinks so highly of you."

Claire was about to respond, when a dark, eerie wave swept over her, nearly knocking the breath from her chest. Her wineglass slipped from her fingers, crashing to the floor and spilling merlot everywhere.

She never noticed. She was inside herself, trying to focus on the cause of her awareness. It wasn't another murder. But it was creepy and it was ugly. A prelude to something sinister.

"Claire?" Leilah's voice seemed to come from far away. "Are you all right?"

"I...I don't know." Claire had one foot in each reality. "Something's going on. Our killer is preparing, like an animal circling its prey. He's chosen his next victim. He's looking at her, making plans. Dammit!" Claire dragged a frustrated hand through her hair. "Why can't I see his face? Why can't I get inside his head and wrap my mind around the identity of his next victim? I never connect until the murder is actually under way. And by then, it's too late."

"Should we tell someone?" Leilah asked, visibly shaken.

"Yes." Claire nodded. "Let's go back to the brownstone. The team needs to know."

Jack shut his apartment door, and opened the envelope he'd just picked up from the Duane Reade photo center. He removed the prints he'd made, sifting through them one at a time.

Wow. This girl was beautiful. He would have really enjoyed this job.

Too bad it wasn't meant to be. She wasn't his for the taking. His uncle Glen had dibs on that.

# CHAPTER
# TWENTY-ONE

The building on West 116th Street was becoming way too familiar for Ryan. At this point, the thought of smelling meat and fat scraps made him want to puke.

He and Marc approached the building. Through the front window, Ryan pointed the blue-green light of his argon laser at the alarm keypad inside. He could see a concentration of oils from the owner's fingers on the number keys "3," "4," "7" and "9." The last four digits of the meat market's phone number was 4-7-3-9. Not even a challenge, Ryan thought in disgust. Human beings were too damned predictable.

Marc fiddled with the lock, releasing the last pin, and manipulated the bolt back inside the door. Depressing the plunger on the handle, he opened the door and they entered the dimly lit market.

Immediately, the keypad tone began beeping, indicating

the start of the alarm system countdown. Ryan calmly entered 4-7-3-9 and silenced the tone.

Quickly, the two men made their way down into the basement. Ryan would have preferred placing Gecko behind an air vent in the owner's office, but that wasn't about to happen. A steel-clad door and Medeco cylinder lock required them to shift to plan B. Fortunately, the utility room was unlocked, so in they went, straight to the air vent. Just to be on the safe side, Ryan cut a square access hole on top of the supply duct, so no one would notice that the duct had been compromised and repaired.

Then he turned Gecko on.

He watched as the little fellow whirred to life, and then set him inside the duct. Slowly and methodically, Gecko executed the 3-D navigation plan that Ryan had generated. Both Ryan and Marc listened as the "tink, tink" sound of Gecko moving from duct to duct echoed in the basement.

Ryan pulled out his iPhone and started the monitoring app he'd created. Marc, always impressed by Ryan's abilities, peered over his shoulder as Gecko turned on his camera and LED light, illuminating the air vent in the market's locked office. Ryan could see the desk. On top were a telephone, fax machine and a large black ledger. On the walls were maps of the world with time zones clearly delineated. It looked more like a bookie's office than a butcher's.

With Gecko in place, Ryan turned off the little critter's LED light, and put him in "vigilant" mode, where Gecko would conserve power waiting for noise, light or motion to trigger a status change to "active." When that happened, all sensors would go on and data streamed in real time to FI's offices.

Ryan sealed up the duct, closed the utility room door and he and Marc headed upstairs. Marc stood outside while Ryan pressed 4-7-3-9 to reactivate the alarm and then exited. Marc expertly relocked the door and the two men walked toward their truck.

The whole FI team knew that Ryan treasured his sleep, and how miserable he was when he didn't get his eight hours. But tonight, he had no thought of hitting the sack—not until he'd done some heavy-duty digging into Jack Fisher.

He pulled up the information Yoda had compiled. Jack's parents' death certificates. Trust fund documents. Glen Fisher being appointed Jack's guardian after his parents were killed in a car accident. Jack disappearing when he was sixteen.

He'd been a minor back then. Therefore, Ryan's normal background search procedures wouldn't work. Usually he would access credit reporting, criminal and other databases. But a disappearing teenager presented a unique challenge.

Ryan started by using school districting maps to determine what elementary school Jack had attended. He then followed the boy's progress from elementary school P.S. 59, to Simon Baruch Middle School and finally the Honors Academy at Fort Hamilton High School in Brooklyn.

Assembling the assorted pieces, Ryan determined that Jack had disappeared sometime between his sophomore and junior years in high school. That was consistent with his death certificate, which listed him as seventeen when he died.

"Bullshit," Ryan cursed at the monitor. "The fucker's still alive."

Time for some real investigative work. Using the dates he now had, Ryan dug up yearbook and other intermittent pictures. He fed the time-sequenced images into the system, and used photo-aging algorithms to project a current picture of Jack at age twenty-four.

He printed copies of Jack's photo on FI's high-resolution color laser printer, and then continued his research.

A decade ago, blogs and social media were in their infancy. Ryan searched the local newspapers around the time of Jack's disappearance for any clues.

One story popped up and Ryan's antennae rose.

It was an article about a sixteen-year-old girl being molested outside a nightclub on 88th Street in Bay Ridge—The Suite, which was today known as the Capri. The girl, Angela Minutti, was the daughter of local mobster Paul Minutti. Two male teenagers were found the next day, beaten to death and dumped in front of the nightclub. Another boy was missing and presumed dead.

Angela Minutti was in shock and uncertain who'd attacked her and who'd rescued her. There were ski masks, brutality and finally the police. One thing she did recall—and that was that Jack Fisher was on the scene. But she couldn't remember if he'd helped her or hurt her.

Ryan found an interesting video taken the day after the attack. Angela had just been helped into an ambulance, where she was huddled, wrapped in a blanket and shaking. There were visible bruises around her neck.

Ryan paused the video, extracting and enhancing the frame he was interested in. Then he made a snap decision. He needed Hutch to weigh in on this.

Quickly, he composed an email to Hutch detailing the key points of his research, including a link to the video. He attached the still video frame he'd extracted and enhanced. Then he pressed Send.

It didn't take three minutes before his cell phone rang.

"I got the email," Hutch said. "I'm reading your points right now." A pause. "Looking at both the video and the picture."

"And?"

"And those are definitely choke marks on her neck."

Ryan cleared his throat. He was getting into dicey territory. He couldn't reveal the fact that Jack Fisher was alive—not without telling Hutch how he'd found out. Illegally.

"Hutch, let's say this incident happened before Jack Fisher died. Let's say he was responsible. What can you read between the lines here?"

Hutch's silence told Ryan that he was in think-mode. But he must have sensed that Ryan was hiding something. Whatever it was, he obviously didn't want to know. So he just addressed Ryan's question.

"Glen became Jack's guardian when the boy was nine," he said. "In my experience, those are formative years. Who knows what Glen exposed his nephew to during that time? Violent porn? Maybe more. There's also growing evidence that psychopathy is inherited. But even if the Fisher DNA has a predisposition toward violent psychopathy, my guess is that Glen probably triggered those impulses in Jack, the way someone or something did the same for him."

Hutch paused, skimming the material again. "Anything else?"

"Nope," Ryan replied. "After this, the story ceased to exist. Media silence."

"I'm sure Angela's father took care of that."

"Agreed." Ryan was already eager to get back to work. "Thanks, Hutch. You've been a big help." He ended the call.

*Yeah,* he thought, still staring at the screen. *The story had ceased to exist.*

*And so had Jack Fisher.*

Glen had convinced a court that his nephew had been killed, the victim of a no-body homicide—the third boy in the videotape. Once Jack had been declared dead, Glen must have absorbed whatever remained of Jack's inheritance and kept the whole damned legal proceedings—including Jack's supposed death—from Suzanne.

Ryan sat back in his chair, lips pursed in thought. It was no wonder Jack had wanted to disappear. If he resurfaced, word would go out and Paul Minutti would make sure he was dead within a week.

But Glen Fisher had had other plans for his nephew's future.

So Jack Fisher was alive—somewhere. In Brooklyn. Hiding.

It was up to Ryan to figure out where.

He took his printed pages over to the futon and settled down to scan them for clues.

The next thing he knew, Marc was standing over him, shaking his shoulder to wake him up.

Jolting awake, Ryan found himself crumpled on the futon, where he must have collapsed out of sheer exhaustion.

He whipped his arm around so he could see his wrist and check out his watch—5:00 a.m. He'd slept for an hour. The owner of the meat market should be arriving any minute.

Sure enough, it wasn't fifteen minutes later that Gecko "woke up." The audio channel came alive with the sound of a key being inserted into a lock, followed by a loud "thunk" as the bolt slid back into its place in the door. The heavy door creaked open. Then a brief hum of a fluorescent ballast and the office was bathed in a bluish light.

Sensing the video opportunity, Gecko's camera activated and Marc and Ryan watched. The face of the owner appeared on the large monitor as he walked toward his desk.

He sat down, obscuring the phone keypad with his body. All Marc and Ryan could see was the back of his head and shoulders. His arm reached forward, dislodged the receiver from the cradle and punched in eleven digits.

When the receiving party answered, the owner identified himself in Arabic.

"Shit," Ryan muttered, hitting pause. "Where's Leilah?"

"My guess?" Marc replied wryly. "Asleep in her bed. It's five-something in the morning."

"Yeah, right." The ramifications of that were lost on Ryan. He picked up his iPhone and punched in her number.

Leilah's groggy voice answered. "Ryan? What do you want?"

"I need you to translate for me."

"Fine. I'll be there in a couple of hours."

"Now." Ryan's was gripping his cell phone, his mind singularly focused.

Leilah was getting pissed. "I'm in my nightshirt, in my bed. I worked more hours for you yesterday than I ever have studying lines. I'll come in later."

"Wait." Ryan stopped her from hanging up. "I'll let you hear the one-sided conversation through the phone. It's the meat market owner. Please, Leilah. This is urgent."

"Okay." She sighed. "Play the conversation for me."

Ryan put the phone on speakerphone and pressed the pause button again.

The shop owner's voice resumed, speaking in a transactional way. His conversation was brief.

The instant he hung up, Ryan hit Pause again, and addressed Leilah. "Did you get that?"

"Uh-huh." Leilah began translating. "The owner told whoever's at the other end to give a man named Jack five thousand dollars. He told him that, as they'd previously agreed, he would receive a handling fee of two hundred and fifty dollars. The owner ended by saying that Jack would be there this morning to collect his money, so to keep an eye out for him." She broke off. "Is that what you were looking for?"

"Exactly. I owe you a steak dinner." Ryan was watching the screen again. "Just wait two minutes until I'm sure he's finished talking. Then you can go back to sleep."

"If I'm lucky," Leilah muttered in a grouchy voice.

Ryan and Marc watched as the owner opened the large ledger book, scribbled something inside and closed the book with a loud thud. Then he rose from his chair, walked toward the door, flipped off the light and closed the door behind him.

The last sound they heard was the locking of the door.

"We've got to get moving," Ryan told Marc. "We have no idea how early this morning Jack will be showing up to get his money."

"Good night, Ryan," Leilah called out.

"Sleep tight. Dream of steaks." Ryan punched off the call.

"What now?" Marc asked.

"Now we find out where Jack is headed so we can beat him there."

Ryan got on his computer and fired up his audio analysis toolkit. First, he extracted the initial portion of Gecko's audio recording—the exact timespan during which the owner was dialing the phone. Using a spectrum analyzer and applying different Fourier transforms, he isolated and then amplified the touch tones generated during the dialing process.

The first set of dual tones corresponded to a frequencies of 697 Hz and 1209 Hz. Ryan checked his table, which translated DTMF key presses into pairs of tones. Frequencies 697 and 1209 together was the number 1. Next was 852 and 1209 Hz. Number 7. Frequencies 697 and 1209 Hz again. Number 1. Soon Ryan had decoded the phone number from the touch tones: 7-1-8-8-3-6-6-6-1-3.

A quick Google search revealed that the phone number belonged to a Kwik Pik Convenience Store at 8595 Fourth Avenue, Brooklyn. Ryan switched to Google Maps, locating the store in the Bay Ridge section, not far from the Verrazano-Narrows Bridge.

That was going to present a problem. Rush hour was already under way.

"I'll take my bike," Marc said, referring to his motorcycle. "I drove it here this morning. It's the fastest option."

Ryan agreed. "And you know the turf." Marc lived in Brooklyn, so he'd know just where he needed to go.

"I'm outta here," Marc announced.

Leaving the brownstone, he jumped on his motorcycle, revved it up and turned on West Street. From there, he drove toward the Brooklyn–Battery Tunnel.

Once through the tunnel, he took the first exit and zigzagged his way through Red Hook, avoiding the Gowanus like the plague. Finally, he turned onto Fourth Avenue and headed south to 86th Street.

Jack Fisher exited the Kwik Pik, his elbow guarding his zippered jacket pocket—and its contents—carefully. He hurried down the stairs into the 86th Street subway station.

As he did, he could hear the whine of an approaching motorcycle at full throttle heading in his direction.

Marc parked right outside the Kwik Pik, facing the convenience store. Time to activate his helmet cam. Ryan had wirelessly connected it to Marc's iPhone. As he saw a person appear on his iPhone screen, one tap and the image from his helmet cam along with a time stamp was saved on the smartphone and simultaneously uploaded to Intueri, where it was processed through facial recognition by Yoda. In a matter of seconds, Yoda's voice would report the results to the Bluetooth-connected speaker in Marc's motorcycle helmet.

Great idea in theory.

A bust in reality.

A few hours later, Marc was tired of hearing "unknown," "traffic offender," "felon on parole" and "pervert." His balls were killing him from the pothole-ridden Brooklyn streets taken at breakneck speed. Not to mention that he was starving and had to pee something wicked.

None of that would have broken his resolve and made him leave.

What made him do that was the fact that his gut told him he'd missed Jack. Son of a bitch, but he'd missed him.

Disgusted, Marc called Ryan and filled him in.

Then he went home. He wanted to grab a shower and a few hours' rest while he could.


Suzanne Fisher arrived home, hung up her coat and put her purse neatly on the end table—just where Glen wanted it. He insisted that everything had its place.

Then she took out her cell phone and punched in a number.

She had no way of knowing it, but the NYPD had legally secured a wiretap on her phone, and a stakeout team was perched in their car across the street. From that vantage point, they watched through a pair of binoculars, hoping that Suzanne would make a phone call.

This was their chance.

Detective Oliver Michaels elbowed his sleeping partner. "Wake up, Lou. She's got a phone in her hand. Have Verizon patch you in."

Lou was instantly awake. He called a special number, then identified himself and the wiretap request number.

The Verizon operator paused. "Neither the cell phone nor the landline is being used," she reported.

Lou turned to his partner. "She's not on either phone," he barked out.

"Yeah? Well, look." Oliver pointed. Both men could see Suzanne holding a phone and waving her free hand emphatically.

"Shit," Oliver said as the reality hit him. "She's using a burn phone. By the time we got the phone companies to look through the tower information, and to reverse-engineer the phone number that's outgoing from Suzanne's apartment, both her burn phone and her husband's would be tossed."

"And new ones gotten and in place," Lou added.

"Shit," Oliver said again.

Suzanne smiled and hung up the phone. Glen would be pleased. Jack had received the money she'd sent at his request.

She had learned long ago never to question anything Glen asked her to do. The absence of pain was a strong motivator. Glen ordered. She obeyed. Questions begged for answers—answers she was afraid to hear. She knew. But she didn't want to know. She blocked it out and just did her tasks. It was better that way.

She went into the bedroom and made sure all the blinds were drawn. Carefully, she removed the dried flowers from a large ceramic vase in the corner. Slowly, she reached inside it, applied downward pressure with her fingers and turned the false bottom inside the vase. Removing the threaded rubber plug, she extracted a large Ziploc bag. Inside was a woman's wig. A red-haired wig. When he was especially agitated, Glen would make her put on the wig. Then came the rough, powerful sex. He'd wrap his hands around her neck. At times she couldn't breathe. But his praise and his affection were worth the bruises and difficulty with swallowing that lasted for days.

When she'd last spoken to Glen, he'd instructed her to wash the wig and make sure it looked nice. That could mean only one thing. Soon he'd be with her. Soon his strong hands would be crushing her windpipe.

She curled up on her bed in the fetal position and began to tremble.

# CHAPTER
## TWENTY-TWO

The prison transfer was set to take place tomorrow.

Glen was more than ready to go—and not to Rikers.

He waited in the dinner line, positioning himself near Dave Norman, the inmate he'd made the deal with. He edged forward, spying the two scraps of paper in Norman's right hand.

With the slightest movement, Glen pressed the wad of bills into Norman's left hand. Norman's fist closed around the cash. He shifted his other arm back and slipped Glen the pieces of paper with the necessary information scribbled on them.

The whole transaction took thirty seconds.

But it would pay off big-time.


Morning finally arrived.

The NYS Department of Corrections van pulled out of Auburn Correctional Facility promptly at 8:00 a.m., heading to New York City and Rikers Island.

Neither of the two armed corrections officers was looking forward to the endless drive ahead of them—more than six hours on the New York State Thruway, assuming no traffic. And there was *always* traffic.

Opting for the thruway meant the drive would be an hour longer. But the shortest route would take them from New York into Pennsylvania, then into New Jersey and back into New York. Bad idea. Neighboring states hated having prisoners transported on their roads, especially out-of-state prisoners. And this prisoner was a convicted rapist and murderer, definitely an undesirable.

So the short route was out.

Then again, there was an additional plus to taking the thruway. It was a restricted toll road—and that meant minimizing the stops that were necessary. The fewer stops, the fewer possibilities of something happening en route.

So the corrections officers were just going to have to suck up being on the road for the extra time.

Jack plugged his iPad car charger into the twelve-volt accessory outlet of the silver-colored Dodge Ram pickup. He grinned as the Find My iPhone app located the device in question—at Route 34 and the New York State Thruway. He secured the iPad to the dashboard so he could check out each and every location update.

That done, he reached for his iPhone and sent a brief text message: I see you.

Glen Fisher felt the phone vibrate at his crotch, where he'd taped it before leaving Auburn. The guards hadn't even bothered to check that area of his body. Then again, he couldn't blame them for not wanting to pat down the fresh urine patch he'd made on the front of his bright orange jumpsuit.

A brilliant idea on his part.

He completed the strategic move by faking embarrassment as the two moronic guards howled, pointing at Glen's crotch and elbowing each other as they taunted him about how "the tough guy" had freaked out and peed his pants.

Let them laugh. They wouldn't be laughing four hours from now.

The pickup truck headed for upstate New York.

In the back of the truck, two all-terrain vehicles were loaded. A U-Haul car trailer was hitched to the rear of the truck, holding a silver Ford Fusion, which rested securely, hidden beneath a car cover.

There was a lot of setup that still had to be done.

Three hours later, everything was in place. The Ford Fusion was innocently parked in the Hudson Valley Mall, along with dozens of other vehicles whose owners were shopping. The car trailer was dumped in a nearby field, obscured from view by tall grass.

From there, Jack navigated the truck through local roads and onto a farm-to-market road alongside the thruway. He got out and rolled the ATVs down wooden planks, hiding them from view behind some evergreens that had been planted by the state to diffuse the noise emanating from the thruway.

Done.

He hopped back into the pickup and turned onto Route 28, taking the thruway entrance. He pulled a toll ticket from the machine, then drove north toward Albany. A couple of miles ahead, he located the emergency vehicle turnaround between the north- and southbound lanes. Slowing down, he turned left, stopping perpendicular to the southbound lanes.

He stared at the iPad. Just a few more minutes. The thruway was quiet. Jack could see the Department of Corrections van in the distance, cruising along in the left lane. He waited, and then veered sharply left, accelerating into the fast lane as he headed south. The corrections officer at the wheel cursed, swerving into the right lane in an attempt to avoid the pickup that had just cut him off.

Jack wasn't finished. He veered right, sideswiping the van and causing it to swerve out of control. It crashed into the divider and rolled down the small embankment into a drainage ditch along the highway.

Slowing, Jack eased onto the shoulder, then shifted the truck into Reverse and backed it up to the crash site. He got out, pulled a ski mask over his face and then shrugged the backpack he'd brought with him over his shoulders. Cautiously, he walked down the embankment, creeping toward the driver's side.

The driver's side window was shattered, shards of glass everywhere. The corrections officer himself was unconscious. The second CO—the one on the passenger's side—was pinned in his seat, groaning in pain. He wasn't going anywhere in a hurry.

Jack moved quickly. He removed a pry bar from his knapsack and worked at the driver's door until it sprang open. He dragged the officer from the vehicle onto the grass and began searching his pockets until he found the keys he was looking for.

Rushing around back, he unlocked the back of the van and flung open the doors.

"Hey," Glen greeted him from the inside. "Nice job. You did me proud." He was bruised from being banged around when the van rolled, and he was bleeding from being struck in the face by pieces of flying glass. He barely noticed.

"You okay?" Jack asked.

"I will be when you get me out of here." Glen indicated his hands and feet, which were locked to the security bars welded to the van's interior.

"Give me a minute." Jack tried one key after the next, until he found the magic one. He released Glen's hands and feet, and helped steady him as he rose.

"Let's go," Glen urged, hearing the banging as the second CO attempted to get free. "We don't have much time."

Jack looped an arm around Glen's shoulders and guided him back up to the southbound lanes of the thruway. Together they crossed the paved highway, walked across the grassy strip between south- and northbound traffic and waited for a break in the light stream of vehicles before traversing the lanes of northbound traffic.

Jack yanked off his ski mask, and motioned toward the hole in the fence he'd cut. The two men made their way through the chain-link fence, and ran to the row of evergreens where Jack had hidden the ATVs. They fired up the vehicles and Jack led his uncle across farms, local roads and parking lots until they reached the mall. There, they left the ATVs running and jumped inside the Ford Fusion that Jack had parked earlier. Quickly, Jack drove south on 9W to Route 55 and the Mid-Hudson Bridge. From there, he headed east on Route 55 until he reached the Taconic State Parkway.

Driving south, he obeyed the speed limit on the winding road as he made his way to New York City and the plan they'd be putting into place.

After all, there was no point in breaking the law.

Casey and Ryan were in the conference room. Casey was leaning over Ryan's shoulder, watching as he ran the silver pickup truck—reported by the witness with the dog—through every car dealership and every car rental company's computer base.

He came up empty.

"It was a long shot," he said, swiveling his desk chair around to face Casey. "Either a buy or a rental would leave some sort of paper trail. So I'm not surprised. Pissed, but not surprised. The killer doesn't want us to trace the car to him. My guess is that it was stolen. I'll call Captain Sharp and have him check out all the police reports that have come in on car thefts in the past week. Hopefully, we'll find a match."

The FI office phone rang.

Casey walked over and picked up the receiver. "Forensic Instincts."

"Hello, Casey." It was Captain Sharp. And he sounded oddly strained. "I'm glad I reached you."

Warning bells began screaming in Casey's head. She perched on the edge of the conference room table, her fingers tightening around the receiver. "What is it? Has something happened?"

She heard a heavy sigh. "There's no easy way to tell you this, so I'll just say it. Glen Fisher escaped a few hours ago during his transport from Auburn State prison to Rikers. It was obviously well planned. He had major assistance, both inside and outside the prison."

Casey had gone deadly quiet. "And the status now?" she asked finally.

"We have no idea where he is. Every branch of law enforcement is combing the area for him—the state police, the NYPD and the FBI's New York field office. We'll find him."

"How could this happen?" Casey was still trying to process what she was hearing.

"As I said, it was meticulously planned." Captain Sharp relayed whatever information he had on the highway collision. "We found a U-Haul dumped in a field of tall grass near the Hudson Valley Mall, and two all-terrain vehicles abandoned adjacent to the mall. Clearly, that's where Fisher's accomplice parked the vehicle they ultimately escaped in. The silver pickup—obviously the one we've been trying to locate—was abandoned at the crash site."

"So we have no clue where he is, what he's driving or who's helping him," Casey summed up. "That's a whole lot of nothing to go on."

"I realize that." Captain Sharp didn't try to pretend. "But he can't have gone far, not in a couple of hours. We have police stationed at all the airport, bus and train terminals, in the event he tries to take off. We've also got full-time surveillance at Fisher's apartment, and cops following his wife everywhere she goes. In the meantime, I want you to stay inside and stay safe."

She started to speak, but Sharp's tone hardened. "I know how proactive you and your team are. But no heroics. No taking matters into your own hands. We both know that getting to you is one of Fisher's primary goals. Don't help him achieve that."

"I understand." Casey was rubbing her forehead, as angry as she was fearful. The son of a bitch had bested her. He'd accomplished exactly what he wanted. "Please keep me posted the instant you know anything."

She hung up the phone.

"Your pulse is elevated, Casey," Yoda announced. "And your breathing is labored. You are distressed."

"Yes, Yoda, I am." Casey was trying to keep her emotions in check.

"What the hell just happened?" Ryan demanded, coming to his feet and walking over to Casey. "You look sick. What did Sharp tell you?"

Casey met his questioning gaze with her sober one. "Get the team together. Call an emergency meeting. Glen Fisher escaped today."

# CHAPTER
## TWENTY-THREE

Suzanne took the most indirect route possible, leaving her Manhattan apartment the instant she heard from Glen. He'd called her as soon as he and Jack got on the road and were driving south. His instructions were to wear a turtleneck shirt, grab the red wig and be on the move.

By the time the police received word of Glen's escape, Suzanne would be too far away to tail. Of course, this would be the one and only time she'd get to see him—until they vanished for good. It would be too risky to make this trip once her apartment was under surveillance. As it was, she'd return today to a waiting team of law enforcement officials, who'd be firing questions at her.

Glen had prepared her for all of them.

Suzanne glanced at her watch. Even with time on her side, she'd taken mass transit and taxis in a roundabout route that finally landed her at the motel where Glen was staying. Jack would probably still be there, talking over the outstanding details of whatever they needed to take care of before they were done.

She didn't want to know what those details were.

She just wanted the normal life she'd always dreamed of having.

She paid the taxi driver and walked through the motel parking lot, stopping at Room 8.

Two quick knocks. "It's me," she said in a subdued tone.

An instant later, the inside lock turned and the door opened just enough to allow her to squeeze through.

She barely noticed Jack, who greeted her with a grunt. Her eyes were fixed on the man sitting at the wooden desk with photos and notes spread out in front of him.

"Glen." She rushed over and put her arms around him. "Are you all right?"

"Just fine." He rose, pulled her against him and gave her a hard, demanding kiss. "You brought the wig?"

"It's here in my tote bag." Suzanne patted the bag that was draped over her shoulder, and let it slide to the floor.

"Good." Glen shot a brief glance at Jack. "Make yourself scarce for an hour. Pick up some food. We haven't eaten all day."

"No problem." Jack didn't look surprised. He looked bored. "I'll see you then." He scooped up his jacket and left.

Glen gripped Suzanne's shoulders, his thumbs biting into the hollows of her chest.

She winced, but said nothing.

"Put on the wig," he commanded. "Then get undressed and get into bed. We have a lot of time to make up for."

Jack took an extra fifteen minutes away from the motel just to be on the safe side. Glen had been on edge all day. It was like walking on eggshells—something Jack was *not* in the mood for. With any luck, a good lay would have put him in better spirits.

He knocked once, and waited for Suzanne's response. She called out for him to come in. She sounded hoarse. He wasn't surprised.

He turned his key in the door and walked in.

Glen was back at the desk where he'd been earlier, poring over the photos Jack had taken. Suzanne was curled up tightly on the bed, her fingers wrapped around the turtleneck collar of her shirt. She was trembling.

Business as usual.

"McDonald's delivery," Jack announced, putting a few bags of food and a tray of drinks on the nightstand. "Get it while it's hot."

Glen put down his pages and strode over. McDonald's was something he'd missed. Good old junk food. There was nothing like it.

He gave Suzanne a backward look. "Time to eat."

"I'm not very hungry," she managed.

"Yeah, you are. You have to be after our...recreational break."

It wasn't a request. It was an order.

Suzanne eased gingerly to her feet. Her entire body ached and her throat hurt so much she wondered if she could swallow. She walked unsteadily across the room, and then sat down on the other double bed, the one closer to the nightstand.

"Cheeseburger or fish?" Glen asked.

"Fish, please," Suzanne rasped. Her hope was that fish would go down easier than meat.

"Here." He handed her the wrapped sandwich and a tall cup of soda with a straw. "This'll make you feel better." He frowned as he saw some bruise marks peeking over the top of her turtleneck. "Pull your collar up higher before you leave," he instructed. "We don't want to give the cops any ideas."

"Of course, Glen." Suzanne took a sip of soda, and winced at the pain. "I'll do exactly what we discussed."

Hardly glancing at Suzanne, Jack swallowed a cheeseburger and gulped down a root beer. Then he walked over to the desk, collecting the photos he'd taken of their next victim and bringing them over to Glen.

"She's hot. I'm jealous."

Glen arched a brow at his nephew. "Don't be. This isn't about fun. It's about inflicting as much pain on Casey Woods as possible. This will be the final emotional blow. After that, she'll experience it all firsthand."

"I want to do this one with you," Jack stated.

"Do you?" Glen pursed his lips. "That might be interesting. Definitely more crushing for the victim—and for Casey Woods."

"Yup." Jack's eyes lit up. "And I can come up with all kinds of embellishments."

"That you *won't* do." Glen slammed his cup onto the table and bolted to his feet. "You shouldn't have been doing it in the first place. I already told you that."

"It's creative. And amusing." Jack wavered a bit, but held his ground.

"Listen." Glen took two steps and loomed over him, grabbing his shirt with both fists. "I don't know who you think you are, but you're nobody. *Nobody.* You're a punk kid who's followed orders while I've been locked up in that shithole. But I'm here now. And I'm running things."

Jack shrugged out of his uncle's grasp. "I'm not the same kid you left behind when you were sent to Auburn," he said with a defiant look. "Just read the papers. I'm the killer everyone's afraid of now."

Glen tensed up like a bowstring and slammed a fist into Jack's jaw, knocking the younger guy onto the floor. "Who the hell do you think you're talking to? Watch your mouth. You couldn't do shit without me. I'm the one who took you in and taught you everything. You want to play big shot for everyone else? Go ahead. But don't try it with me. Not if you want to keep all your teeth in your head."

A vein was throbbing at Jack's temple, but he said nothing. He just rubbed his jaw, scrambled to his feet and walked over to the desk. He gathered up the diagrams they'd been reviewing.

"This is the campus layout," he told Glen, giving him the sheets of paper. "I circled the areas that are more deserted at night. Those are our best bets for grabbing her and getting away."

Glen reviewed the diagrams. "Over here," he said decisively, pointing at one of Jack's designated areas—a narrow passageway between buildings. "It's behind the library. The chapel is the only building nearby. None of the kids are going to be hanging around waiting to pray. They'll either be inside the library or partying elsewhere."

Jack nodded. "She's a studier. She usually heads to the library around seven and leaves when it closes at eleven forty-five. We can take her then. I've still got the Fusion right here in the parking lot."

"Wrong." Glen shook his head. "Talk about being compromised. Every cop in the state is going to be looking for that car. It's a liability to us now. Get rid of it."

Jack looked annoyed. "I could just change the plates."

"I said get rid of it." There was no give in Glen's tone. "Tonight. Then get yourself back here. We'll find our way into Manhattan when the time is right. I'll take care of getting us a new car."

"Find our way how?" Jack was bristling again. "Suzanne's

car isn't here, and we couldn't risk hiding out in the back of it, anyway. I still think I could lift some plates and we could get home in the Ford. We'll dump it afterward."

The look in Glen's eyes was chilling. "Shut up. This isn't a democracy. I give the orders. You follow them. The next time you challenge me, I'm going to break your scrawny neck. Now get out of here. Dump the car in East New York. Rent a motel room. Get yourself back here in the morning."

"Then what?" Jack was visibly controlling himself. His hands had balled into fists at his sides.

"Suzanne will go out now and buy me hair dye and a change of clothes. Tomorrow she'll go back to Manhattan the same way she came. You and I will take the bus." A cutting pause. "Anything else?"

"Yeah. Where did you plan on us staying in the city—at my apartment? The cops will eventually track down where I live and start swarming the place."

The anger building inside Glen was a palpable entity—one that made Suzanne tremble all the more. "We'll get a room in Brooklyn. I have the name of a place. It's a couple of miles from where you're dumping the car. It's off the beaten path, and it'll keep us off the grid. We'll take care of that when you get back. Now shut your punk mouth and do what you're told."

Jack didn't answer. He walked over and stuffed two more cheeseburgers in his pockets. "I'm on my way—*boss*."

He made no move to temper the sarcasm in his voice.

Without looking back, he left the motel room, slamming the door behind him.

Suzanne watched the pulse throbbing at Glen's throat, and the terrifying gleam that came into his eyes. Then she stared at the closed door.

Dear God, now there were two of them.

★ ★ ★

It took less than an hour after Captain Sharp's call to round up the entire FI team and assemble them around the main conference table so they could create an immediate action plan.

Before one word was said, Hutch strode into the room, a grim expression on his face. He went right over to Casey, who was seated at the head of the table.

"I just got out of a task force meeting. Are you all right?" he asked, squeezing her shoulder.

"I'm hanging in there," she replied. "I've had better days, but I'll survive."

"Yeah, you will." Hutch's jaw was working. He was clearly furious about Fisher's escape. "I'll make sure of it."

Casey glanced up at him in surprise. "I assumed the Bureau had you on the move—that they'd asked you to drive up to Auburn to dig around."

"They tried. I told them Brian could handle it alone. I'm staying here with you."

"Not happening." Casey gave a shake of her head. "You're the best there is. I want you grilling the Auburn prison staff and inmates with Brian. Not staying in Tribeca babysitting me."

"Casey will be fine, Hutch," Marc interceded. "I'll be staying at the brownstone around-the-clock. Fisher would have to get through me to get to Casey. And he already knows what I'm capable of." Marc's gaze shifted to Casey. "You're my assignment, by the way."

"So I gathered." Casey's tone was dry. "Okay, fine. If it'll get Hutch to do his job, I'm game."

Hutch and Marc exchanged a glance. Knowing Marc as well as he did, Hutch conceded. "I'll leave tonight. It's obvious that someone—probably a prison guard—helped Fisher escape. I'll find out who, and what, he supplied Fisher with. I'll interview every damned prisoner Fisher interacted with if I have to. I'll get the information we need. I'll also check out any motels near the crash site, just in case. Fisher is staying somewhere. And I doubt it's with Jack. That's way too risky."

"Yes, and he sure as hell isn't going to his apartment," Marc added. "Although he might get in touch with Suzanne through a burn phone."

"Let Suzanne Fisher be my project." Claire spoke up with quiet assurance. "She felt a connection to me when we visited last time. I'm not law enforcement. I'm not aggressive. I'm a safe person for her to turn to. If I play my cards right, I might be able to get something out of her. If nothing else, I might pick up on some new energy—something Suzanne is feeling now that her husband is a free man."

"That's definitely a good match." Casey gave an emphatic okay to Claire's suggestion. "Drop in to make sure she's okay. I saw the way she acted around you. She'll let you in. You'll make her feel as if you're an ally."

"Exactly."

"Let me do some legwork," Patrick suggested. "I'll backtrack through all of Fisher's previous crimes. That might give us some insight into his future behavior. He wants Casey, yes. But he has to have a plan to get her. He knows we'll be keeping her under lock and key. So let's see what methods he's used to draw people out in the past."

"That's a good idea," Casey said, nodding. "Anything we can do to get inside Glen Fisher's head is significant." She glanced at Ryan. "Are you still digging up data on Jack Fisher? Because he's the obvious suspect as Glen's co-conspirator. We need to draw him out."

"Yeah." Ryan was thinking. "Now that it's been found, I'm abandoning my investigation into the silver pickup. I've got to

find out what kind of car Jack got his hands on and how he or-
chestrated it—the wheres and whens. The minute I get downstairs, I'm going to start digging to see what auto thefts have been
reported within a two-hour driving radius of the crash site."

"Also, someone has to talk to the corrections officers who
were driving the van." Casey turned to Hutch. "I could do it.
Marc would come with me."

"Nope." Hutch made quick work of that offer. "Brian and I
will stop at Kingston Hospital on the way home. If the corrections officers are conscious, we'll interview them. I'm hoping
that at least one of them can give us a description of the driver.
Also, Ryan, they might be able to describe the make or model
of the car that sideswiped them."

"And here I'll sit, playing indoor catch with Hero," Casey
muttered.

Hero's head came up at the sound of his name and he gave
an enthusiastic "woof."

"Fine, boy." Casey scratched his ears. "I'll divide my day between romping with you and playing gin rummy with Marc."

"I've never been beaten," Marc said. "So don't plan on an
easy time of it. Not from Hero and not from me."

Casey grinned. "Thanks for trying to take me down a notch.
I'm pretty freaked out."

"Don't be." Hutch checked his watch. "Fisher's going down
and so is his partner. This spree of his is about to end." He
bent down and kissed the top of Casey's head. "I'm going to
find Brian and take off for Auburn. You stay put. I'll keep you
posted."

Jack drove the Ford Fusion to Cypress Hills Houses in East
New York. He was still ripping pissed off about the way Glen
had spoken to him. Things had changed since his uncle went to

prison last year. Jack wasn't an apprentice anymore. He was now the sexual homicide offender who was feared by all the redheads in the tristate area. He didn't intend to alter that.

Pumped up, Jack rolled down the car windows, left the engine running, got out and slammed the door. By the time he was settled on the B13 bus, a couple of teenagers had hopped into the Fusion and taken off.

Jack wasn't in the mood to rent a room in a moldy motel yet. He could do that later. For now, he needed some recreation. With that in mind, he stopped at Peyton's. Nothing like a strip club to release some of his pent-up aggression.

His cell phone rang three or four times during his stopover. He knew who it was. He ignored his uncle's attempts to contact him. Somehow he derived great enjoyment from the realization that his mentor was enraged.

It would put the old guy in his place.

# CHAPTER
## TWENTY-FOUR

Hutch and Brian arrived in Auburn that night, caught some sleep and were up and ready to go as soon as the prison opened for visitors. Hutch had spent a good chunk of the car ride in heated conversation with the NYS Department of Corrections. Time was of the essence, so protocol and procedures were *not* going to slow him down. He wasn't waiting for some bureaucrat to bless his interviews with the prison staff.

Finally, the right buttons were pushed, the process was expedited and Hutch and Brian's early morning visit was granted.

Their first meeting was with the warden, who had himself started an internal investigation. He had nothing to report, which didn't surprise Hutch. An investigation like this was going to take some major digging, and involve some ugly revelations. Neither of those things was going to be welcomed by the warden, who had a vested interest in conducting a superficial investigation—one that exonerated his chain of command and blamed the entire escape on a fortuitous traffic accident.

Hutch wasn't buying his bullshit theory. The escape required perfect timing. Luck had nothing to do with it. Any thought of a coincidental driver causing the collision was absurd.

With that in mind, Hutch and Brian asked for and received permission to interview everyone who had come in contact with Fisher—guards, chaplains, work supervisors, fellow inmates. The warden had no choice but to cooperate. Any resistance on his part would give the appearance of having something to hide. He had to provide the FBI with full access. Hutch knew that and capitalized on the warden's weak bargaining position.

His feeling of forward motion was short-lived.

After six hours of intensive interviews, Hutch was seething. His every instinct was screaming that guards had smuggled contraband items to Fisher—although no one would name names—and that the two prison guards who had searched Glen just prior to his being transported to Rikers were either lazy or morons. He didn't care which. But he needed to find out what they'd overlooked.

He took out his cell phone and called Ryan.

"Hey," he said. "I need your help figuring something out."

"Okay." Ryan was pounding at his keyboard. "Shoot."

"Long story short, I think Fisher hid something in his crotch when he left Auburn. The guards who were supposed to search him said he peed his pants, so they were too grossed out to run their hands up his legs to check."

"Isn't that what latex gloves are for?"

"Yeah, unless the guards don't bother using them. My question is what's the most likely thing that Fisher would be hiding? A knife? A handcuff key? A cell phone? You're the gadget guy. Help me out here. Oh, and one other thing—I get the feeling that some of the other guards are supplying inmates with contraband. So, don't restrict your thinking to what could be made or purchased in prison. Fisher could have arranged for anything. Get back to me ASAP."

"You got it."

Trish Brenner finished dinner at the dining hall and went back to her dorm to prepare for her evening ritual—four or five hours at Firestone Library. She knew she studied too hard and that her social life was an epic fail because of it. But she'd worked like a demon to get into Princeton University, and she wasn't going to blow it by partying and letting her assignments slide.

She had a huge paper to write this week, one on all of Shakespeare's tragedies, and it was going to take a lot of effort to write it, much less ace it. So she was getting an early start, reviewing several plays each night and taking copious notes on each of them.

She packed up her wieldy textbook of Shakespearian plays, and shoved it in her book bag, along with her laptop, a notebook and assorted writing and highlighting implements.

She pulled on a light windbreaker and ran a brush through her long, red hair.

Time to hit the stacks.

It had been a frustrating day for Hutch and Brian.

Brian pulled off the thruway at Exit 19, paid the toll and took Route 28 East. Five minutes later they were sitting in front of Kingston Hospital.

They left the car out front and strode inside the main lobby. Immediately, they were accosted by a security guard, who'd spotted them through the glass door, ignoring the no parking signs.

Hutch displayed his FBI credentials and informed the now-cooperative guard that they were there on official business. The guard escorted them to the information desk.

Hutch addressed the receptionist behind the desk. "Which room is John Nessman in?" he asked, referring to the corrections officer who was driving the prison van. "Also, Frank Rumson," he added, referring to the second officer.

The woman checked her list. "Room 323 and Room 347." She pointed down the hall, then called after them to take the Blue Elevator.

Hutch and Brian reached Room 323, flashed their credentials again—this time at the local cop who was stationed in the doorway—and went in. Nessman was bandaged and in obvious pain from the concussion, broken wrist and severe lacerations he'd sustained from flying glass. His wife was sitting at his side, comforting him. When Hutch and Brian appeared, and identified themselves to her, she agreed to get a cup of coffee and return in a few minutes so they could talk. She requested that they please go easy on him, given his pain and the ordeal he'd gone through. They agreed, and she slipped out of the room.

Despite his condition, Nessman responded to each and every one of Hutch and Brian's questions, explaining how the pickup truck had suddenly pulled into the fast lane, cutting him off. After that, he'd swerved into the slow lane to avoid hitting the truck, but the driver had intentionally sideswiped the van. There was no question that there was malicious intent involved.

"I did my best to defend against the attack, but the debris in the road caused me to lose some control. The truck hit me again, and that sent the van off the road." He sighed, grimacing in pain. "The rest is a blur, and then everything went black. I woke up in this hospital bed."

"Is there anything else you can tell us?" Hutch asked. "Anything that might help?"

Nessman gave a tentative nod. "I know this sounds farfetched, but I had the gut feeling that the truck was waiting to ambush me. It's as if the driver knew exactly where I was and when. I don't know how he'd manage that, but he did."

Hutch was about to ask more about the correction officer's assessment when his wife returned. She was visibly concerned about the effect the FBI's visit was having on her husband.

Instinctively, Hutch and Brian rose to leave. Hutch paused only to tell Mrs. Nessman that her husband was very brave and had done everything he could to prevent what had happened.

"He's going to be fine," Brian assured her. "A little TLC and he'll be as good as new."

She nodded, her eyes filled with tears.

Hutch and Brian went on to Room 347 to repeat the process with Frank Rumson. Unfortunately, the poor guy was so out of it from the morphine they were giving him that he was barely conscious. So they weren't getting any more information here today.

Back in the car, Brian got behind the wheel, and Hutch slid into the passenger seat.

"Now that was interesting," Brian said as he steered out of the parking lot. "Nessman felt as if his attacker was lying in wait."

"And that he knew just when and where to show up." Hutch's forehead wrinkled in thought. "This looks more and more like a plan that was finely tuned and perfectly executed. I have no doubt Fisher's capable of both. What I want to know is *how*."

Hutch punched in Ryan's number again.

"Still on it," Ryan answered.

"Well, add this to your list of specifications." Hutch relayed the correction officer's insights about being tracked.

"That gives me an idea," Ryan said. "Let me call you back. I'm going to try an experiment."

Ryan hung up.

He pulled out his iPhone, went to Settings, clicked on iCloud and turned the Find My iPhone service on. Next he grabbed his iPad, downloaded the Find My iPhone app from the app store and installed it.

Having launched the app, he could see his iPhone listed with a green dot. When he clicked and highlighted that line on his iPad, a map appeared with the location of his iPhone. He ran upstairs with both devices, went outside and started to walk down the street. He touched the refresh circle/arrow and watched as the location moved. He walked faster down the street, pausing to refresh again. New location displayed. He sprinted to the corner and turned right, running halfway up the next block. Stop. Refresh. New location.

He had his answer.

Ryan's breath was coming fast when he flung himself into his chair at his basement desk. He speed dialed Hutch.

"What took so long?" Hutch asked dryly.

Ryan didn't laugh. He told him about his experiment—and his conclusions.

"Fisher taped an iPhone to his crotch—plastic-wrapped, no doubt," he said. "The iPhone reported its location to another iOS device—an iPhone or an iPad. Whoever his accomplice in the truck was—let's say Jack Fisher—watched his progress in real time as the prison transit van traveled down from the Auburn prison. The kid had no problem preplanning several interception points. When and where the ambush took place depended on which route the van took."

Ryan paused. "I've got to give Fisher kudos for this one. Even I'm impressed by his ingenious application of off-the-shelf technology."

"Yeah, well, I'm more impressed with his ability to manipulate people—through fear, intimidation and, obviously, raw intelligence. Thanks, Ryan. You clued me in on just how formidable an opponent Glen Fisher is."

Hutch disconnected the call.

For the first time since this case had begun, he was deeply concerned about Casey's safety.

# CHAPTER
## TWENTY-FIVE

Suzanne stopped at her local Starbucks, as Glen had instructed. She was grateful that he'd selected this as her alibi—the location she'd give the police to explain where she'd been for the past hours. It was perfect, for various reasons.

The coffee store was in Midtown. It was jammed, and Suzanne was a newbie there. So no one would remember when she'd arrived. Equally important, she could buy a hot cup of chamomile tea, sit down at a far corner table and just sip the beverage, letting it ease the stinging pain in her throat.

Reflexively, her fingers went to her neck. Glen had been particularly brutal this time. She understood that he'd been without for months on end. So she'd tried to hold back her cries of pain. But he'd felt the dampness of her tears, and it had really pissed him off. Her job was to absorb his needs, and to take them in stride. Usually, she could. Today, she couldn't.

She took another grateful sip of tea, glancing at her watch as she did.

It was late. Time to head back to her apartment—and the interrogation that would be awaiting her.

She took her cup with her, as planned, and left the store, wincing as she walked home. She'd have to hide the stiffness of her gait. She'd soak in a hot tub later, after the flood of law enforcement had gone.

As she walked, she rehearsed the answers she'd soon be supplying. Pretending wouldn't be hard. After years of marriage to Glen, playacting was second nature.

She reached the building, and was about to climb the stairs when two men marched over to her.

"Mrs. Fisher?" the taller one said. It really wasn't a question, just an affirmation. He flashed a badge at her. "I'm Detective Malcolm. This is Detective Rayburn. We'd like to talk with you about your husband."

Suzanne's brows lifted slightly. "I don't understand. I told you everything I could possibly think of the day you searched my apartment."

Malcolm had a dubious expression on his face. "Are you saying you don't know?"

"Know what?"

"That your husband escaped yesterday during his transfer to Rikers Island?"

Suzanne's eyes widened and she started. "What? When did this happen?"

"Yesterday afternoon, in upstate New York. Where did you spend the night?" Rayburn wasn't mincing words. "Not to mention the past two days. We checked. You canceled all your piano lessons."

"Yes, I did." Suzanne knew this would be one of the biggest hurdles. "I called all my students. I wasn't up for work, not with Glen being charged with a whole new set of crimes and being brought to Rikers Island. The thought of him serving an even longer sentence, especially when he was working so hard on an appeal—I couldn't bear it. I took a train out to Montauk. I sat at the lake all day and watched the boats, the way Glen and I used to. I slept on the train back. I wasn't myself, so I spent most of the day at Starbucks, thinking." Suzanne made sure her Starbucks cup was visible.

Rayburn drilled her. "You slept on a train and didn't stop at home to shower or change clothes before you spent an entire day at Starbucks?"

"I was upset. An empty apartment was the last place I wanted to be." Suzanne held up her palm, holding his questions at bay. "Please tell me about Glen. Is he all right?"

The detective studied her from narrowed eyes. "I wouldn't know. He's vanished."

"How? How could this happen?"

"We were hoping you could tell us." Malcolm gestured toward the stairs. "Let's go upstairs to your apartment. We can join the other crime scene investigators, detectives and FBI agents who are, once again, going through your home. Maybe you can answer our questions and we can answer yours. Sort of tit for tat." His voice oozed sarcasm.

Suzanne steeled herself. She'd expected this to be hard. Her instincts now told her that it would be even harder than she'd imagined.

*Stick to the script.* She could hear Glen's voice echoing in her head. *Answer as briefly as you can. They have nothing on you. Don't give them something.*

She nodded politely at the two detectives and—being careful to keep her physical discomfort totally in check—led the way upstairs.

Hutch glanced up when the two detectives escorted Suzanne Fisher into the apartment. He and Brian were there, along with the rest of the law enforcement crew. Brian was talking to one of the crime scene guys, getting information on any new personal belongings that might be present now but weren't there during their initial search.

Suzanne reminded him of a trapped bird—terrified, overwhelmed and desperately in need of escape. There was a pinched expression on her face. She was trying to hide it, but she was in physical, as well as emotional, pain.

Now *that* bore looking into.

Hutch walked over. "Hello, Mrs. Fisher. I don't know if you remember me."

"I do." Suzanne nodded. "You're the FBI agent I talked to. I'm sorry, but I don't remember your name." She eyed him, waiting to see what he'd ask, readying herself to supply the answer. Like a kid at a spelling bee—one who'd been drilled to deliver the correct response.

Suzanne Fisher had been prepped.

And there was only one person who could have prepped her.

"Agent Hutchinson," Hutch filled in. "And, yes, we talked a little the last time I was here. I'd like to talk to you again, if you don't mind." His glance darted quickly from Malcolm to Rayburn, tacitly telling them to give him some time alone with the subject.

"I don't mind," Suzanne replied, visibly relieved when the two detectives walked away. "What is it you want to know?"

"Let's sit down." Hutch guided her over to the living room

sofa, watching her carefully as she lowered herself to the cushion. No, he hadn't imagined it. She was hurting—badly. Her
entire body went rigid as she sat, and she gritted her teeth to
bite back any sound of pain.

"Do you have any tea left?" Hutch asked, pointing at her cup.

"What? Oh. No. I finished it." Suzanne stared at the empty
cup.

"I'll toss it for you. And I'll bring you a glass of water."

"Thank you." Suzanne handed it over. She was clearly struggling for self-control. She'd been told to stay strong. And she
was trying to obey that order.

Hutch went into the kitchen and came out with two glasses
of spring water, one of which he pressed into her hand.

"I hope you don't mind that I grabbed some water for myself."

"Of course not."

Hutch sat down on the tub chair that was positioned across
from Suzanne. "I presume you've heard about your husband's
escape?"

"The detectives told me. I still don't understand. He just vanished?"

Hutch explained the details of the escape, studying her intently as he did.

"So, no one has any idea where he is," he concluded. "We
were hoping you could help us."

Suzanne's spine went rigid again. "How can I help?"

"Just by knowing him so well." Hutch eliminated her defensive reaction by taking a nonthreatening approach. "He's your
husband. You know little things about him that no one else
does. Does he have a favorite place to hang out? Somewhere
he goes to be alone with his thoughts? Friends in upstate New
York he'd go to for a place to stay?"

Hutch's plan had the desired effect. Suzanne's whole body

eased. "We have no friends in that area," she said. "And, as far as relaxing, I told all of you last time that Glen likes to take long walks to clear his head. He must be terrified right now. He could walk for hours."

"Do you think he'd contact you?"

Suzanne's shoulders lifted in a shrug. "He'd want to. But Glen is a very intelligent man. If he really did escape, he'd know full well that all of you—" she made a sweeping gesture with her arm "—would be swarming the apartment and tapping my phone. So I doubt he'd take the chance."

Okay, Ryan was right. The two of them were communicating by burn phone. No surprise there.

But they'd had much more than a verbal communication these past two days.

Suzanne was rolling the water glass between her palms.

"Go ahead and drink," Hutch urged. "This whole event has come as a huge shock to you. Would you like something stronger?"

"No. Water is fine." Almost against her will, Suzanne raised the glass to her lips and drank. The wince she gave was glaringly evident.

Hutch's attention shifted to her turtleneck shirt. An interesting choice of attire, given the fact that it was a warm spring day.

"Do you think your husband would reach out to his nephew?" Hutch asked the throwaway question. He knew how she'd respond. But he was buying some time, calming her as he led up to what he wanted to accomplish.

"Jack?" she asked in well-coached surprise. "No. They haven't been in touch in years. So there'd be no point in trying to contact him."

"That makes sense." Hutch leaned over to wipe a scuff mark

off his shoe. In the process, he tipped his glass and spilled some water on the pristine area rug.

As he'd guessed, Suzanne sprang into action. With everything in the apartment lined up and maintained just so, it wasn't a leap to assume that a water spot on her rug would freak Suzanne out.

"I'm so sorry," Hutch said.

"That's all right." Suzanne was already on her feet, grimacing in pain as she hurried toward the kitchen.

Moments later, she was on her knees, placing a dry dish towel over the wet spot, absorbing the liquid. "It shouldn't stain," she said aloud to herself. "It's only water."

Hutch wasn't listening. He was leaning over, peering at the back of her neck, which was exposed now that her motions were jerking down the top of her turtleneck.

He could see the marks even on her nape. Red, angry welts. He could just imagine what the hollow at the base of her throat looked like.

If Hutch had had any doubt that Suzanne had been with her husband, those doubts were eradicated.

"Can I help?" he asked, averting his gaze from her neck.

"No. It's okay. The towel dried it." She sounded so relieved, it was pitiful. There were tears in her eyes—tears of pain, of fear, of desperation.

"We can protect you," Hutch tried. "If there's something you want to tell us, we can help."

Suzanne blinked back her tears, regained control and rose from the floor. "I've told you all there is to say," she responded. "I'm just worried about Glen. If you hear any news about him— where he is, if he's safe—please let me know right away. You might think of him as a murderer. I think of him as my husband."

"I realize that." Hutch assisted her to her feet. "But that doesn't mean you should risk your own safety for him."

All traces of tears were gone. "I know what I have to do, Agent Hutchinson."

Glen Fisher unfolded the first slip of paper he'd brought with him from the prison and punched in the telephone number on his burn phone.

"Yeah?" a voice at the other end answered.

"Eddie Weber told me to call you," Glen said. "I need a car with a full tank of gas. Tomorrow night."

"Where are you headed?"

"Jersey."

"Then do you want swapped plates?"

"Swapped plates?" Glen's brows knit. "Eddie didn't say anything about that."

"These days, there are cameras all over the place that read license plates, looking for people like you. If you're going to use the car for more than a quick hit, I'd swap plates with another car—same year, make, model and color. That way, the license-plate reader won't spot you. And it usually takes the owner a day or two to notice the different plates and report them to the cops."

"Good idea. Do that."

"You've got the money?"

"Twenty. In cash."

"Make it twenty-two. I charge extra for the plate-swapping. Finding two matching cars is a lot more work."

"I get it. Fine. Twenty-two. I'll have it."

A grunt of approval. "Be at Ninth Avenue at West 39th Street, southwest corner. Ten o'clock."

"That works. It'll give me a direct shot to the Lincoln Tunnel," Glen said, thinking aloud. "Who am I looking for?"

"A guy who leaves an old black Honda Civic double-parked at the corner with the engine running and asks you for Eddie's duffel bag."

"I'll be there."

"So will he."

# CHAPTER
## TWENTY-SIX

The next afternoon, Hutch broke away from the task force to go over to Forensic Instincts. They all gathered around the conference room table, where he filled the team in on his interview with Suzanne Fisher, and the ongoing search for her husband.

"She was with him," Hutch announced without hesitation. "And the bastard did a real number on her. She could barely walk without wincing and there were red welts on her neck."

"He obviously uses the poor woman as a punching bag to act out his sick fantasies," Patrick muttered.

"She's afraid of him." Casey was pacing, unable to sit still. "Battered wife syndrome at its worst. The question is how much is she helping him with his plan? Is she just his eyes and ears, or is she an active participant in all this?"

"At the very least, she's subsidizing Jack—and she's doing it under the radar." Ryan finally had the chance to report his findings to the team—findings that had gotten buried beneath the events of the past few days. He explained the money transfer Suzanne had made at the meat store, and how he and Marc had tried, and failed, to catch Jack at the pickup site.

"Do I want to know the details of how you got this information?" Hutch asked.

"No." Ryan didn't miss a beat. "What you want to know is that it's all being compiled and an anonymous document will be delivered to the FBI's New York field office. Everything that's needed will be in there."

"That's gratifying."

"So the butcher shop is a front for a hawala broker," Patrick mused aloud, his forehead creased in concentration. "That explains why Suzanne uses cash to pay for everything. She withdraws eight thousand dollars a month, uses six thousand for expenses and sends the remaining two thousand to Jack. No credit card receipts, no bank entries, nothing."

"This is Fisher's idea, and Suzanne's executing it." Hutch had moved on from legality to fact. He folded his hands behind his head and leaned back in his chair. "Very clever. It keeps Jack's whereabouts and his communication with his uncle untraceable and off the radar."

"So Jack's been in their lives all this time." Casey stopped pacing to think. "He could very well be his uncle's protégé. But why disappear to begin with?"

"I can answer that one, too." Ryan told them about the mob daughter's attack and Jack's presence at the crime scene. "I'm sure he vanished to stay alive."

"And he *is* alive," Casey said. "The question is doing what? Hiding out and living on his uncle's money, or following his uncle's lead by becoming an even more twisted sexual homicide offender?"

"One more reason to tail Suzanne." Marc was nursing his cup of coffee. "Not only could she be going out to see her husband, she could be meeting up with Jack. And, if she's got a hands-on role in their crime spree, she could be scouting victims. We just don't know how deep she's in. Or exactly where Glen's job ends and Jack's begins." Marc looked around the table. "We do know that Glen Fisher is a smart SOB. He'll be expecting us to have eyes on Suzanne. So we'll have to figure out how to get around that."

"Yup," Hutch agreed. "That's why Suzanne took off for their little tête-à-tête first thing yesterday, before news spread that Fisher had escaped. That way, Suzanne could leave her apartment and go to him, and no one would be watching her yet." He frowned. "We all know that Fisher doesn't plan on hanging around upstate. He's heading for Manhattan. But when? And what's his agenda? Is he operating alone or teaming up with Jack? Is he going straight for Casey or does he have other interim victims in mind?"

"At least one more interim victim," Claire supplied in a haunted, faraway tone. "One who's vivid enough for me to pick up on. I'm not getting much, just a vulnerable, exposed energy. But I do know that Fisher has selected a target and a timetable. Soon. I just can't sense who or where."

"Well, it doesn't take a sixth sense to know where we're going to find this body." Marc looked and sounded grim. "I'm the missing link."

"Bensonhurst," Hutch muttered. "Somewhere near your place. We'll share that probability with the task force. Still, it doesn't give us a hell of a lot to go on."

"No, it doesn't. Not to mention that we'd be finding our victim dead, not alive." Claire swallowed. "What good is that? It's not the disposal site we want to get a jump on, it's the assault site. *Dammit*." She slammed her fist on the table. "I hate this. I get snatches of energy, but never enough to prevent a crime. Innocent women are dying, and there's nothing I can do about it."

"Don't be so hard on yourself, Claire-voyant," Ryan said, covering her hand with his and giving it a squeeze. "We're all still one step behind Fisher. But one thing's for sure. He's not getting his hands on Casey. Not on our watch."

Ryan's words echoed with confidence.

He just wished the reality was as certain as the intent.


Glen and Jack Fisher walked down Ninth Avenue right on time.

Their contact was equally prompt.

The streets were dark. Nobody driving by would pay the slightest attention to the three men talking and the one old black Honda Civic parked next to a fire hydrant, engine running.

In mere minutes, the transaction was complete. The duffel bag was handed over, and the money was counted. The car keys were given to Glen. Eddie's guy strolled off into the night.

Glen and Jack hopped into the car and took off, heading for the Lincoln Tunnel.

On the other side of the tunnel was their next victim.


"You didn't have to cook dinner for me." Claire was sitting on Ryan's sofa, her head leaning back against the cushion. Eyes shut, she sipped the glass of wine he'd poured her. Reflexively, she pulled up her legs and folded them under her in lotus position.

Under the circumstances, this was about as relaxed as she was going to get.

"You needed the break—and the meal," he said. "I haven't seen you eat a bite of food all day." Ryan checked the vegetable lasagna to see if it was cooked enough. Perfect.

"Are you sure you're not just showing off your culinary talents?"

"Very sure. I wouldn't get too excited if I were you," he added, cutting and transferring portions of food onto plates. "I'm not exactly a gourmet. It's a pretty basic meal. On the other hand, if you thought I ate out of a can every night, you'll find this very impressive."

"I'm sure I will."

Ryan carried the two plates over to the coffee table and put them down. Then he refilled their wineglasses and sat across from Claire. *"Voilà."*

"This is lovely." Having lifted her head, Claire glanced at her plate and smiled. "And not a speck of trail mix to be found. Here I thought I'd finally discovered all your hidden talents. Looks like I was wrong."

"You were. My talents are limitless." Ryan gave her a wink, settled in and prepared to eat. "I'm starving. You must be about to faint. Dig in."

Claire tasted the lasagna and made an appreciative sound. "Mmm… Delicious. And you're right. I'm a lot hungrier than I realized." She paused, staring at her plate. "I'm really torn up over this case. I not only feel horrible about the murders, I feel guilty that I can't pick up precise enough energy to stop them before they happen. And worst of all, I'm coming up empty on anything that would protect Casey. It's like…it's all just out of my grasp."

Ryan set down his wineglass. "You're not the only one who feels like you're coming up short. I've got some of the best forensic tools around and I'm still a step behind Glen Fisher. If science can't do it, I doubt metaphysical energy can," he said with a rueful look. "Sorry. I didn't mean to diss you. Your insights have been dead-on."

"No problem." Claire wasn't insulted. As much as Ryan tried to accept the value of her gift, Claire knew the whole thing was hard for him to swallow. "It doesn't really matter whose technique comes through in the end. As long as one of them does."

"Agreed. Now let's change the subject," Ryan suggested. "That was the whole point of this dinner. Shutting out the frustration and the intensity of this investigation. Just for a few hours. We're entitled to that."

"You're right. We are."

From that moment on, they intentionally kept the conversation light, steering clear of anything relating to Glen Fisher. There was nothing more they could do that night, and recouping their emotional and mental acuity was important.

"Thank you," Claire said as she finished her cup of herbal tea. "Dinner was wonderful. I didn't realize how badly I needed it. But I did."

"Me, too." Ryan rose and closed the gap between the two sofas, taking Claire's hand and pulling her to her feet. "There's one thing I *did* know I needed. And that's this."

He kissed her, long and hard, tangling his hand in her hair and deepening the joining of their mouths.

Claire responded, wrapping her arms around his neck and returning the kiss with the same level of passion.

Ryan backed her across the apartment to his bedroom, never breaking contact as he did. They broke apart only to tug off each other's clothes, and then fell onto the bed.

It was the way it always was—mind-blowing, all-encompassing sex. Sex that wasn't just sex at all, but a kind of raw joining that dominated their senses and took them by surprise every time it happened.

Afterward, they lay quietly together, their legs entwined, Claire's head pillowed on Ryan's chest.

"Wow," he said in a harsh rasp.

Claire nodded, too winded to speak.

"I don't know what the hell this is," Ryan said bluntly. "But it's like nothing I've experienced before."

"Me, neither." Claire was quiet for a moment. "I swore I wouldn't tell you this, but I was insanely jealous of Leilah," she blurted out. "It was irrational and totally out of character for me. But I couldn't shake it."

"Well, shake it. Whatever Leilah and I had is over."

"That's good. But it's not enough. I don't want you with other women." Claire stunned herself with the unyielding quality of her tone. "I realize that's contrary to everything you're used to. But I'm not willing to share—not this time." She tilted back her head, gazed up at Ryan. "Is that a deal-breaker?"

Her choice of words made him grin. "No." He shook his head, feeling as bewildered as she obviously was as he spoke the truth. "Ever since you and I have been together, I haven't wanted anyone else. And if you hooked up with any guy but me, I'd probably beat the shit out of him. I never saw this coming. But it's here."

"Yes. It is. Whatever *it* is."

"Does it matter?"

"No."

Ryan pulled Claire over him. "I say we celebrate *it*."

"I second the motion."

During the hours that followed, all of Claire's senses were alive and focused on Ryan.

There was no room for anything else—not even the powerful dark energy that she would normally have felt like a knife twisting in her gut.

★ ★ ★

Trish Brenner stayed at the library longer than usual.

When she glanced up, the stacks were almost empty, and a few last-minute students were packing up and getting ready to leave.

She sighed, rubbing her eyes, and making peace with the fact that she needed some sleep in order to continue at her current pace.

Wearily, she pushed back her chair and rose from the table, shoving a strand of red hair behind her ear as she gathered up her work and slid it into her book bag. After analyzing a half dozen of Shakespeare's tragedies, she was still grappling with the psychology of his antagonists, the mastery of which was a crucial part of her grade.

She paused, playing with the same thought she'd been entertaining all week long. She had an older cousin who was a specialist in human behavior and had even formed an investigative firm around it—a really renowned one. Casey Woods's office was in Manhattan, just a train ride away. Problem was, their families had been estranged for so long that Trish and Casey didn't know each other, and never spoke. So reaching out to her would take balls.

What if Casey got pissed off about being bothered by a college kid she barely remembered?

Trish weighed the options. She needed this grade. She knew someone with expertise. What was the worst that could happen? Casey would blow her off. And as the saying went, if you don't ask, the answer is always no.

Trish would call Casey tomorrow.

With that, she scooped up her cell phone, slung her book bag over her shoulder and headed back to her dorm for some sleep.

She never made it there.

★ ★ ★

The last vestiges of night were lingering outside Ryan's bedroom window. His bed was in shambles, as very few of the long, dark hours had been spent in slumber.

"Stay," Ryan murmured into the tangled cloud of Claire's hair.

"I think I already did." Claire opened one eye, sensing that night would soon be turning into day. "What time is it?"

Ryan glanced at the illuminated dial of his clock radio. "Four-fifteen."

"And you're not grumpy? You, who needs his solid eight hours to function?"

"Some things are worth losing sleep over."

A small smile curved Claire's lips. "I'm honored." She gave a huge yawn. "Also half-dead."

"That's because you ravaged my body."

"Me? I think you've got that backward. My body aches in places it never knew it had."

Chuckling, Ryan pulled the blanket up around them and settled Claire by his side. "We'll call it a draw, okay?"

"Okay." She was already drifting off.

"Good night, Claire-voyant."

"Good night, techno-whiz."

Casey's cell phone rang.

She felt Hutch tense up next to her even as she jolted awake.

Her gaze fell on the alarm clock on her nightstand—4:35. That could mean nothing good.

She grabbed the phone, looking at the illuminated screen. Another blocked call.

Her insides went cold.

"Who is this?" she demanded.

"It's me, Red." The scrambled voice rasped against her ear. "But you already knew that."

"What do you want?"

"Didn't your psychic come through for you this time? I guess not. Too bad she slacked off. This one was worth watching."

"Who was it? Who's the girl?"

"Let's just say that your next family get-together is going to be short a member."

Casey felt as if she was going to vomit. "Tell me who your victim was," she managed.

"It was obvious she had your blood running through her veins. Feisty little thing. She put up quite a fight. That made the whole experience better. It was the best one yet."

*"You bastard."* Casey had jumped to her feet, gripping the cell phone so tightly her knuckles had turned white.

"Don't spend too much time grieving, Red. You're next. Start saying your goodbyes."

The line went dead.

# CHAPTER TWENTY-SEVEN

Casey stared at the phone for a long moment before turning to Hutch. "It was one of my relatives."

Hutch rolled off the bed and went directly to her. He gripped her shoulders tightly, calming and steadying her all at once. "Let's figure out who. We know the victimology. Who in your family is a redheaded female, younger than you—probably late teens to early twenties—most likely living within a reasonable driving distance of here?"

"I have a small family." Casey was still reeling with shock. "And we never see one another. There was some kind of falling out between my mother, my aunt and my uncle years ago. I don't even know what it was about. But I never got to know my cousins. And my father has no family at all."

"Small means less work for us. We'll go through every family member, estranged or not. Start with the nucleus."

"There's me, my brother, my sister and my parents."

"Kids?"

"My brother and sister-in-law have one—a son. My sister and brother-in-law opted not to have kids."

"Move on to your aunt and uncle," Hutch said. "I know you don't have relationships with them. But let's review their kids."

Casey frowned. "My aunt and her husband live in Boston. They have a son and a daughter who live near there, too."

"Daughter's age? Description?"

Casey frowned again. "I haven't seen her since I was in my teens. Her name's Allison. She's either a year older or younger than I am. And she's got short black hair."

"So if she has kids, they wouldn't be teenagers."

"No." Casey shook her head. "And her brother's younger than she is. No spouses. No kids."

"Move on to your uncle."

"My uncle is the major outcast of the family. He and his wife moved out to Seattle. I think their two daughters live there, too."

"Daughters?"

"Yes." A niggling thought popped into Casey's mind. "My uncle's the baby of the family, so his kids are a lot younger than I am."

"How young?"

The color drained from Casey's face. "College age."

"What can you tell me about them?"

"I don't remember." Casey drew a hand through her hair. "But I'll call my mother and find out. Falling out or not, she keeps tabs on everyone."

She reached for her phone and punched in her mother's number.

Five minutes later, she disconnected the call. Her hands were shaking. "My cousins are in college, like I thought. They're both girls, and both redheads. Maggie is twenty and goes to Williams. Trish is twenty-one and goes to Princeton."

"Let's run with that." Hutch snatched up his own cell phone. "You track down one. I'll track down the other."

It didn't take long to discover that Maggie had spent the night out with a bunch of her friends—and that Trish was nowhere to be found. Not a single one of her friends had seen her since she left for the library early that evening.

Hutch called the Princeton police department so they could begin a localized investigation and search.

But both he and Casey knew that wasn't where the body would be.

Even before making the painful call to her uncle and aunt, Casey called Marc.

"Yeah, Casey," he answered, instantly alert.

"I got a call from the killer." She went straight to the point. "He said there'd been a new victim and that she was a member of my family. Hutch and I made some calls. My twenty-one-year-old cousin Trish is missing. She's a student at Princeton. No one's seen her in hours."

"I'll get a hold of the guys I know in the Sixty-second." Marc referred to the police precinct that serviced the Bensonhurst section of Brooklyn. "They'll contact the other precincts already involved in this case. Hutch will call in the Bureau's New York field office. The more law enforcement we have out there searching, the better." The muffled sounds in the background told Casey that Marc was getting dressed. "We don't need to guess. The body's somewhere in Bensonhurst."

Trish's lifeless body was found stuffed behind a trash can between two apartment buildings on 79th Street.

Casey and Hutch were already in Bensonhurst, working with

the FBI, when the call came in. Casey took off by foot, racing to the crime scene before anyone could stop her. She pushed her way through the crowd until she reached the spot where the medical examiner was squatting down, examining the body.

"Oh, no," Casey whispered, staring at her cousin. Even if she hadn't pulled Trish's Facebook photo, she'd know her. The family resemblance was undeniable.

Trish was crammed inside a canvas tarp, her head drooping awkwardly to one side, a chunk of her hair cut away. Stripped naked, her body was battered from what had obviously been a brutal rape. Her throat had heavy bruises on it—the signs of a vicious strangulation. Some of those bruises were hidden beneath the red ribbon that was neatly tied around her neck. In the center of the bow, two locks of hair had been tucked, side by side, at the base of her throat. And lipstick had been carefully applied to her mouth.

This time, Casey couldn't control herself. She turned and leaned over the garbage pail, heaving until there was nothing left inside her. Shoulders still bent, she dragged air into her lungs, tears pouring down her cheeks.

Hutch came up behind her, gently rubbing her back in an effort to soothe her. There was no point in telling her it was all right when it clearly wasn't. Casey's cousin—a vibrant young woman with her whole life ahead of her—had been horribly violated and murdered. There were no words to make that reality go away.

"There was more than one assailant," the M.E. announced, studying the strangulation welts. "They used gloves, but there are two sets of different size finger and hand marks on the body."

"Glen Fisher." Casey heaved again. "He did this to Trish, together with the other offender. They both... Oh, God." She wrapped her arms around herself, shivering uncontrollably.

"Also, these two hair samples didn't come from the same body," the M.E. continued. "That's visible even to the human eye. But we'll have them analyzed for DNA evidence."

"If the killer is following his usual pattern, one lock of hair belongs to our previous victim, Deirdre Grimes," Hutch said. "I don't know about the other."

"Well, it isn't the victim's," the M.E. told them. "The shade of red is different."

*The shade.* Something about that was bothering Casey. She forced herself to turn around and stare directly at her cousin.

"Her lip gloss," Casey said, her voice hoarse and unsteady. "It looks exactly like the shade I wear. Can you have it checked?"

"Of course." The M.E. rose to her feet. "Do you have a sample of yours with you?"

"Yes." Casey dug through her purse, and came up with a tube of pale peach lip gloss. "Here. Check it against Trish's. Then compare it to the lipstick on all the bodies. If it's a consistent match, this whole lipstick thing is more than just an arbitrary fetish."

"It's yet another link to you," Hutch said. He studied Casey's expression, and recognized that she was a nanosecond away from melting down. "Let's go home." He pulled her jacket more closely around her. "There's nothing more we can do here."

"I have to call my uncle," Casey murmured, talking more to herself than to anyone else. "I have to let him and his wife know. What in God's name am I going to say? That a psychopath who's after me raped and killed their twenty-one-year-old daughter for practice?" Tears welled up in her eyes. "This is my fault. I never thought of Trish or Maggie when I wrote up that list. They weren't even on my radar. I don't care if we were estranged, I should have thought of my own family members. We should've had Patrick's security friends assigned to them. If we had, Trish might still be alive."

"Stop it, Casey." Hutch hooked his finger under her chin and raised it, forcing her to meet his gaze. "There's nothing to be gained by blaming yourself. Even if you'd thought of her as a possible target, Trish was a college kid. She couldn't have been shadowed 24/7. Glen Fisher, Jack Fisher, whoever the hell is the offender, would have found a way. Now let's go home. You'll call your aunt and uncle in the car. And then you'll call your team. It's time to close ranks. The killer made it clear that he's coming after you now."

The entire Forensic Instincts team was already at the brownstone when Casey and Hutch arrived, thanks to the phone chain Marc had initiated. Hero went straight to Casey as she walked in, greeting her with that loving instinct animals possess when they know something is wrong.

"Hey, boy." Casey crouched down to scratch Hero's ears and stroke his silky head.

"Are you okay?" Claire was the first one out in the hall, anxiously searching Casey's face for signs of strain.

It wasn't hard to find them. Casey was a basket case.

"I'll never forget the sound of my uncle's voice when I told him," Casey replied, rising to her feet. "He was shattered. So was his wife. Part of their lives was taken away. And what could I say? There were no words to ease the pain."

Claire walked over to Casey and gave her a tight hug. "I'm so sorry. I didn't pick up on any of this. I should have."

There was something odd in Claire's tone—a deep sense of personal guilt. Casey was about to ask her about it, when Ryan stepped into the hall behind her. The expression on his face, the protective way he hovered near Claire—both of those answered

Casey's question. They'd been together last night. Claire's intuitive instincts had been directed elsewhere. And now she was beating herself up over it.

"Don't do this," Casey told her quietly. "I have enough guilt for all of us. But Hutch is right. Guilt won't flush out Glen Fisher or the other offender. That's going to require skill."

"Yeah," Ryan said. "Especially since they're clearly on their way to you."

Patrick joined them in the foyer. "This place is like a fortress. I doubled the number of security guards stationed outside the building. And if you *have* to go out—and I repeat, *have* to—it will be with two men, not one."

"Thank you," Casey said gratefully. "But we can't keep taking a defensive stance. It's time to be proactive."

"You're not baiting the guy." Hutch's words were a flat-out command.

"I wasn't going to. I'm not suicidal. There's got to be another way. Fisher is going to make me sweat. Let's use that time to come up with something."

Jack pedaled his bicycle past the Forensic Instincts building for the third time that morning. He'd pulled his Yankees cap down low and his jacket collar up high. So his face was pretty much concealed.

Glen had told him to do surveillance, to see what the deal was at Casey Woods's office. The fucking building was like a prison, with two guards standing outside the door and who the hell knew how many more inside. Plus there was her tough, cop-looking boyfriend and that navy SEAL who'd pounded the shit out of his uncle. Neither one of them was going anywhere.

Getting to her was going to be like getting inside Fort Knox.

Jack rounded the corner and took a break. He swung off his

bicycle and bought a pretzel and a soda from a local hot dog vendor. Pedaling around was a pain in the ass, but he was in too good a mood after last night to let it bother him.

Taking care of that girl with his uncle had really gotten his juices going. He'd forgotten how awesome Glen was at this. Not just the sex or even the strangling, but the head games, the taunting threats. Casey Woods's cousin had been scared out of her mind even before they'd laid a hand on her. And then, taking turns, prolonging the end—it had been great. Dumping the body near that navy SEAL's place had completed the ritual.

Now it was time for the real deal.

He took a bite of his pretzel, thinking that, while he hated to admit it, he was glad his uncle was with him on this one. Glen was creatively brilliant. He'd work out how to get past the barricade surrounding Casey Woods. He was probably planning it right now.

And then they'd be on their way.

Glen stared at himself in the bathroom mirror at Jack's apartment. He'd automatically gone in there to shave, before remembering that he now sported a mustache and the beginnings of a beard—both dyed the same deep red as his hair. He could have picked any color other than his own dark brown. But red seemed like the most ironically pleasing choice. So he was now a bearded redhead with brass-rimmed glasses and a limp—thanks to the two-inch lift he'd placed in his right shoe.

The new and unrecognizable Glen Fisher.

Exiting the bathroom, he reached into his pants pocket and pulled out the second carefully folded scrap of paper he'd brought from Auburn. Like the previous scrap, it had a name and phone number on it. This one read Henry Rand. Rand was a pawnshop owner with a useful side gig: identity forging. He was supposedly the best, at least according to the Auburn inmate who owed Glen.

Glen was about to find out just how good he was.

The timing of all this had to be perfect, like a well-choreographed ballet. Glen was setting up an exit strategy. And Rand was a key player in keeping that strategy on track.

Glen punched in the number on his burn phone and waited. One ring. Then two.

"Yeah?" the gruff voice at the other end said.

"It's Fisher. You're expecting me."

"I got word. What do you need?"

"Three new identities, including one for me. Full sets of papers for each."

A low whistle. "That doesn't come cheap."

"I know. I've got twice your normal fee, since I need them twice as fast."

"How fast?" Rand sounded much more amenable once he'd heard that.

"As quick as you can turn them over."

"Then let's get started. Be at my shop tonight at eight. Use the back door. Bring all the necessary information. I'll take your picture. The other two will have to come in separately to get theirs."

"Not a problem. I'll arrange it."

Glen disconnected the call, very pleased.

He wasn't so pleased when Jack called him much later that night, as he was getting back from his meeting.

"We have a problem," Jack said, leaning against his bicycle, which he'd tucked in a narrow alcove about two blocks from the Forensic Instincts office.

"I don't want to hear that." Glen shut the door to the apartment.

"I'm sure you don't. But it's true. I've spent the whole day checking out the Forensic Instincts building and the activities of Casey Woods—which, by the way, are nonexistent. She's holed up in there with her army of guards and her FBI boyfriend. Even the rest of her team doesn't come out too often—just for quick errands or to walk the dog. There's no way we're getting our hands on that bitch. I can't even get close to the building, that's how many video surveillance cameras there are. This sucks."

Ingesting that information, Glen went into the kitchen and poured himself a drink. "Chill," he instructed Jack. "Just keep watching and keep track of all the comings and goings. The rest you'll leave to me. Trust me. I'll get our firecrotch where we want her."

"If you say so." Jack sounded dubious.

"I do."

# CHAPTER
## TWENTY-EIGHT

The FI team disbanded late that night, and everyone went home to get some much-needed rest.

Ryan had been eyeing Claire all night—her pallor, her tight expression—and he knew exactly what she was thinking. He wasn't planning on letting her think it.

When she left the brownstone, he fell into step beside her. He hopped on the subway that went to her stop, exited along with her and walked her home.

They didn't speak a word the entire way.

Once they were inside her apartment, Ryan marched her over to her wicker sofa, put his palms on her shoulders and pressed her down into a sitting position. Then he poured her a glass of wine and pushed the glass into her hands.

"Drink."

Claire looked up at him, her eyes dazed. "You don't have to babysit me."

"I'm not. I'm trying to get you to stop beating yourself up. Clearly, what Casey said didn't get through. So it's my turn."

She didn't respond. She just stared into her glass as Ryan went to the kitchen and got himself a beer.

"We both know why I didn't pick up on Casey's cousin's energy." Claire finally stated her feelings when Ryan returned to the living room. "If you and I hadn't been so caught up in each other…"

"Then you would probably have lived through the pain and suffering of Trish's murder," Ryan finished for her. "Just the way you did with the others. And, just like with the others, you would have prevented nothing. The only good you could've accomplished is speeding up the search for the body. Which means squat. Trish would still be dead."

"Maybe. But maybe I would've seen something, heard something, that would have helped the next time—Casey's time. What if that's true? What if I could have saved her from what's to come, but I blew it?"

"Then you'll do it now."

"I plan to. Before all this happened, I was going to pay Suzanne Fisher a visit. I'll wait till she's home from work tomorrow night. Then I'll drop by. If there's any telling energy I can get off her, I'll get it."

"Good idea," Ryan said. "I'm sure she'll be receptive to you. You have a very soothing nature. It'll lower her defenses."

"Let's hope so. I've got to make some inroads, and fast. We're running out of time."

"There's another way, too."

"Which is?"

Ryan took a deep swallow from his bottle. "Look, we both know that I don't understand your visions, or your energy-tapping, or any of that stuff. But I do know that you seem to do it really well when you're holding something of the victim's in your hands. We'll get something of Trish's—something that makes you sense whatever you sense off it—and then you'll sit down in a dark, quiet room and do your thing."

A flicker of hope flashed in Claire's eyes. "I hadn't thought of that. But you're right. The cops can't release anything from the crime scene, but that doesn't mean I won't find some object in Trish's dorm room that she was deeply connected to. Maybe I can pick up some energy that'll give me a glimpse into her mind. Maybe I can even sense a thought or an emotion from last night."

"And if you do, it's going to eat you alive," Ryan warned.

"I'm sure it will. But if it brings us closer to the killer, it'll be worth it."

"Okay, then." Ryan nodded, pulling out his iPhone. "I'll call Casey. She'll get us permission from Captain Sharp. We'll drive down to Princeton in the morning."

Claire picked up on Ryan's use of the plural. "*We?* You don't have to come with me, Ryan. This isn't even your thing."

"True. But you'll need some moral support. I can do that."

Claire found herself nodding in surprise. The softer side of Ryan McKay. She'd never thought she'd see the day.

"You're right," she told him. "You can."

Casey didn't shut an eye that night.

She'd gotten the necessary permission for Ryan and Claire to enter Trish's dorm room so Claire could try to connect with Trish's energy. Hopefully, that would yield some results.

It still didn't help Casey sleep.

Finally, after staring at the ceiling for five hours, she rose and went into the kitchen to brew herself a cup of coffee.

Hero padded in after her, acutely aware of the tension that

continued to permeate Casey's apartment, as well as the office itself. He sat down on the kitchen floor, his huge eyes fixed on her.

"Whoever said men weren't sensitive?" Casey murmured, walking over to scratch Hero's ears. She poured some of his food into his bowl and placed it on the floor. "You've been up all night with me," she acknowledged. "The least I can do is offer you a 5:00 a.m. meal."

"Does that apply to me, too?" Hutch was leaning in the kitchen doorway, hair tousled, eyes almost as red as Casey's.

She gave him a rueful smile. "I'm sorry. I know I was thrashing around all night. You should have grabbed your pillow and gone to sleep in the den."

"It wasn't a sleep night for me, either." Hutch poured himself a cup of coffee and sat down at the counter beside Casey. "I was too busy putting pieces together."

"That whole lipstick thing is really bothering me," Casey said, gripping her coffee mug. "I hope we get the chemical analysis back soon. Because I know in my gut that it was my shade. And if it is…"

"Then it makes you question Suzanne Fisher's role in all this."

Casey angled her head toward Hutch. "Does that mean you were thinking along the same lines?"

"I was thinking about Suzanne Fisher as a whole. She's an enabler, which makes her a perfect victim for Glen Fisher's abuse. She's a conduit to what he needs to get done. We knew that. But now we're taking it a step further. Now we're wondering if she actually has some input into the murders."

"Creative input, in this case," Casey clarified. "Men don't come up with the idea of matching lipstick shades. That's a female thing."

Hutch nodded. "A man would think about the overall concept

of dressing up a victim to make her look like a gift to satisfy his ego. He might even zero in on making her look like you. But a specific color or brand of lipstick? Doubtful."

"So if that added touch belonged to Suzanne Fisher, what other contributions is she making?"

Hutch's expression was grim. "Right now, I'm more concerned with how she knew what makeup you wear. Did she follow you when you bought it? Or did she somehow get her hands on your things?" His eyes narrowed. "Do you remember where and when you last bought your lipstick?"

Casey racked her brain. "About a month ago, I guess. I bought it in Macy's."

"That's a huge store. It would be easy enough to eavesdrop on your purchase." Hutch processed that piece of information. "Do you remember any time your lipstick was missing? When you dropped it or thought you'd misplaced it?"

"No. And I'd notice that. It's always in my purse. I use it all the time."

"Then I opt for the spying at Macy's. Which, like we said, tweaks the profile on Suzanne Fisher. She might be much cleverer and less passive than we've been assuming. Obeying instructions, yes, but also coming up with her own ways to help."

"Do you think she's sick enough to have an actual hand in murdering these women?"

"Not directly, no." Hutch shook his head. "She's not dominant or vicious enough. More likely, she sees her husband as some kind of wronged hero. That would make it possible for her to justify his abusive behavior toward her. And, if she does view him in that light, she can also convince herself that he's doing the world a service, ridding it of women he's labeled as evil, including—no, especially—you."

"That's sick."

"So is Glen Fisher." The more Hutch considered that theory, the more sense it made. "It's clear that Suzanne adores her husband, no matter how terrified of him she might be. He manipulates. She rushes to his aid. And if she's smart and creative, she could be doing anything from scouting victims to researching your ties to people..."

"...to finding out what lip gloss I wear so she can add a special touch to the posing of the victims." Casey shuddered. "How twisted."

"Did any hatred come through when you interviewed her?" Hutch asked.

Casey considered that, and then wiggled her hand from side to side. "That's a hard question to answer. There was definite anger and wariness. I had no doubt that she blamed me for her husband's conviction. I played with her head a little, so she vacillated from livid to uncertain to vulnerable. Most of her attention was focused on Claire. She was fascinated with the whole psychic angle. That might have watered down any rage directed at me. The woman is a psychological and emotional wreck." Casey paused. "Speaking of which, Claire is going back to visit Suzanne tonight. She's not calling ahead. She wants to go for the element of surprise. That, combined with Suzanne's open reaction to her last time, could pay off."

"Smart move." Hutch's cell phone rang. "Hutchinson," he answered. A lengthy silence. "Okay, thanks." He disconnected the call. His expression was *not* happy.

"What is it?" Casey demanded. "It must have been pretty important for whoever it was to call you at 5:30 a.m."

"It was." Hutch took a belt of coffee. "The chemical and the DNA analyses are back. You were right. The lipstick *is* your shade. But that's not all that's yours. So is the hair."

"The hair?" Casey stared. "You mean the second clump of hair tucked under the ribbon on Trish's neck?"

"That's the one. Now how the hell did the killer get it?"

Casey didn't have to ponder that question. "I got a haircut the other day. There were pieces of my hair all over the floor. He could have taken it from the floor or the garbage or... Wait a minute." She clutched Hutch's arm. "There was a repairman in the salon that day. I didn't give it a second thought until now. My view was obscured. But he walked by me. He could easily have picked up a piece of my hair."

"That means the killer stood right beside you." A muscle worked in Hutch's jaw. "Shit. Even with our tight security, he got that close."

Casey swallowed hard. "I'll talk to the salon receptionist, and see what I can find out about the repairman. I doubt she'll know much, though. He probably just walked in, did whatever he was there to do and left."

"I'll go with you." That was Hutch's no-choice tone.

Casey didn't argue with it.

"Maybe the receptionist will remember something about the way he looked," Hutch suggested. "Glen Fisher was still in prison at that time, so this was killer number two. Anything we can learn about him would be a plus."

"The salon opens at nine."

"We'll be waiting at the door."


Claire gazed around the Princeton dorm room that had been Trish's home for the school year. The energy here was strong. Trish's aura was everywhere. This room was her nest. That made it easier to connect with her.

Claire stood there for a long minute, immersing herself in the energy. Then she walked straight to the desk. Her fingers brushed over the textbooks lying there. She picked up one general psychology book and one small, well-worn copy of *Othello*.

"What a sad, ironic choice," Claire murmured, her tone hollow. "Of all Shakespeare's works, this was Trish's favorite—the play in which Othello suffocates Desdemona." A shiver ran through her. "There's a lot of Trish in this room. She spent hours studying, sitting right here at this desk. She was a good student. She pushed herself hard."

A pained pause, during which Claire pressed her lips together. "More irony. She was working on something that involved psychology. She planned on calling Casey. She was thinking about that last night when she left the library. But it never happened."

Ryan wasn't sure whether or not he was supposed to comment. He had no idea what Claire was seeing, if it was fact or fiction, but that didn't mean he didn't have a hundred questions. He was clueless about how psychic connections worked. And he didn't want to break the chain of whatever Claire was feeling. So he kept quiet.

"The library..." A series of images flashed through Claire's mind, and that faraway look came into her eyes. "Trish dropped her backpack when they grabbed her. It was still at the crime scene, which was between the library and the chapel. She tried to scream. They chloroformed her. She put up quite a fight. It took both of them to subdue her and get her off campus. The rest of it—the torture, the rape, the strangulation—that all happened in the alley where they found her body. What they did to her was barbaric." Claire's lashes were damp with tears.

Ryan couldn't remain silent anymore. He touched Claire's shoulder. "You don't have to do this."

"Yes, I do." Claire's breath was coming faster, and she switched to the present tense. "I can make out their forms. I want to see their faces, but I can't. I can tell that one man is older, in good physical shape, solid. He's the cruel one when it comes to mind games. The other guy is younger, leaner. He moves faster. And he hurts harder. God, the physical pain—it's excruciating. Twice. First one man, then the other. Oh, God, Ryan, they're tearing her apart."

Claire was gasping now, but she refused to stop. "She can't fight them anymore, not when she's fighting for her life. She can't breathe. She's struggling for air." Reflexively, Claire's hand went to her throat. "Their hands keep squeezing. Squeezing. The blackness is coming. She's going limp. Fading away." She paused, suddenly very still. "It's done," she managed. "She's dead. They're not even waiting. The older guy is getting the tarp ready. The younger one is doing the artistry—the ribbon, the hair, the lipstick. I can feel both their energies. Why can't I see them? *Why can't I see them?*"

"Claire, no more." Ryan couldn't watch her go through this. He turned her around and gave her a shake. "It's enough. Stop torturing yourself."

Dazed, Claire looked up at him, still caught in her vision. "I can make out their bodies, their builds, their actions—all but their faces." She blinked, and the vague look faded from her eyes as realization struck. "This is the first time I was able to envision everything. I experienced it from inside the victim's head and from a third-person angle, as well. I've never seen the killers before, not in any way. I'm getting closer. But how do I close the distance, go the rest of the way?"

She noted the helpless expression on Ryan's face, and smiled. "Who am I asking? The man who thinks Yoda is human but psychic energy is bullshit?"

"You're right, I'm probably the wrong person to ask. Still, logic tells me that your plan to meet with Suzanne Fisher tonight is the next step. Maybe the two experiences back-to-back will give you what you need."

Claire gave a thoughtful nod. "While I'm linked in with the killers' aura, I might be open to receiving more. I also have Glen Fisher's pen that I took from his apartment. Now that he's out of prison and taking part in these rapes and murders, I might get something off that." Her chin came up and she met Ryan's gaze with a look of sheer determination. "Let's go home. I have work to do."

Ryan dropped Claire off at home, and then headed back to the office to see if anything was up. The team was milling around in the conference room, reviewing theories. Ryan described Claire's experience at Princeton and her plans for that evening.

"That's good," Casey said. "It seems as if we're all focusing on Suzanne. Especially since we got the chemical breakdown from the lipstick applied to Trish's mouth." She went on to tell Ryan about the lip gloss and the lock of hair. "Hutch and I spoke to the salon receptionist this morning. She didn't remember much. Just a guy in his midtwenties wearing a uniform. She was pretty sure he was on the thin side, but his cap covered up his hair and shielded his face. So there wasn't much for her to tell us."

"We also called the plumbing company he allegedly worked for," Hutch added. "No service call was requested, so no technician was dispatched. We even checked with the landlord, and with the store that supposedly had a water problem. All fictitious."

"You think Suzanne did recon at the salon?" Ryan asked. "It would be seamless. She'd go for a haircut, and figure out the layout of the place while she did. She'd make the appointment under an assumed name. She could even have checked the appointment book to see when Casey was coming in. And she'd have done all of this while Fisher was in prison, so the police wouldn't be following her yet."

"I definitely think that's the case," Patrick agreed. "Because the cops are having absolutely no luck with their tail. Suzanne goes to work, does her chores on the way home and then holes up in her apartment. She hasn't so much as seen a friend, much less her husband. And the wiretapping has yielded nothing, either. According to that, there's been zero contact between husband and wife. It's looking more and more like she and Fisher have burn phones. And how do we deal with that? It's frustrating as hell."

Ryan was quiet for a long moment. His thoughts were coming faster than he could keep up with.

"Suzanne is at work," he announced abruptly. "So are her neighbors. That gives us all afternoon." He turned to Marc. "I'll need your help."

"You've got it. What do you need me to do?"

"Give me two hours. Then meet me in my lair."

# CHAPTER
## TWENTY-NINE

Ryan was hunched over his workbench. Periodically, a plume of white smoke would rise, along with the acrid smell of solder and flux as he connected several miniature circuit boards inside a waterproof, black metal box.

He'd chosen the box specifically for this purpose.

He leaned back and inspected his work. "Yes," he said aloud, congratulating himself on his success. The results were damned good.

"I take it from your smug smile that you're ready," Marc said, standing in the doorway to the lair.

"Yup. Just need to run a test." He twisted a co-ax cable onto a spare connector on the wall marked "Time Warner Cable raw" and from there to the co-ax connector inside the box. Next, he connected the power cable to the battery and waited as his contraption came alive.

Blinking red lights turned solid as the device completed the boot cycle. "Yoda," Ryan called out. "Initiate sniffing."

"Sniffing on," Yoda responded seconds later.

With that, Ryan took out his iPhone and placed it on the workbench, then dialed Claire's cell and pressed speakerphone.

"Hi." Claire seemed surprised. Ryan knew full well how involved she was this afternoon. "Everything okay?"

"Just sniffing you."

"Excuse me?" Claire sounded as if she was about to drop the phone.

"A technical term." Ryan grinned.

"Very cute. In that case, I'll give you my scarf to carry with you. Then you can sniff me whenever you want."

Marc nearly choked with laughter.

"Okay, okay. Sorry I interrupted." Ryan quickly said bye and hung up.

"Call intercepted," Yoda announced. "But I did note Claire's surprise, and it does make logical sense. Why did you choose her to call after initiating sniffing?"

"Just a test, Yoda." Ryan rolled his eyes. "No explanation required. Sniffing off, okay?"

"Very well, Ryan. Sniffing off," Yoda replied.

"Nice pickup line," Marc commented dryly as he helped Ryan pack up the tools they would need. "Remind me to use it sometime."

"Don't bother." Ryan ignored the loud inhaling noises Marc was making. "You couldn't pull it off."

"Obviously, neither can you. Claire's reaction trumped your line."

Ryan shot Marc a look. "Let's put on our workmen's clothes and get going."

★ ★ ★

A half hour later, Marc and Ryan left their van and made their way toward Suzanne's building.

As Ryan had predicted, the street was busy but the building was quiet. The entrance door, however, was locked, able to be accessed only by residents.

Ryan blocked Marc from view, so no passersby could see him pick the lock. A minute or two later, the task was done. Marc carried the extension ladder through the hallway and toward the back door, which led to a common backyard for all the residents of the building. Ryan followed behind with a large toolbox and a black metal box.

Once in the backyard, Marc raised the ladder and placed it strategically against the brick wall and alongside a metal conduit that ran from top to bottom. Ryan opened the toolbox, removed a leather tool belt and strapped it to his waist. He scaled the ladder, carrying the black metal box. Halfway up the wall, Ryan attached the metal box to the conduit, using large cable ties. Not a permanent solution, but strong enough to suit his purposes. Next, he removed the access cover on the conduit junction and saw the CATV lines. Selecting one, he quickly cut the line, crimped a co-ax connector on each end and inserted a splitter between the two. Ryan reached around to a pouch, removed a portable tester then clipped it to a metal ring on his tool belt. Finally he connected the attached cable to the empty connector on the splitter and glanced at the test gauge.

Internet tested perfect.

After disconnecting the test cable, he went down the ladder, drilled a hole in the access cover and inserted a rubber grommet in the hole. Then he made up a short cable to connect his box to the cable company's line. He inserted it through the grommet. Heading back up the ladder, he connected the cable between his metal box and the splitter. He unlocked his metal box, plugged the loose connector to the + terminal on the battery inside and watched as the series of circuit boards powered up and all status lights turned solid.

Satisfied, he locked the metal box, reattached the access cover and climbed down the ladder.


Ryan pulled out his iPhone, went to his contacts and selected Yoda. "It's me again, Yoda. Begin sniffing."

Yoda replied, "Sniffing on."

"Okay, I have to ask." Marc glanced from the contraption to Ryan. "What the hell is sniffing and how does this thing of yours work?"

A corner of Ryan's mouth lifted in a grin. "I figured your curiosity would eventually win out. Sniffing looks at network traffic by intercepting the flow of information and trying to decipher it. In this case, I've married two femtocells—one CDMA, the other GSM—to a Raspberry Pi computer and a cable modem for backhaul to our office."

"Well, now that that's clear..." Marc shook his head in disbelief.

"Okay, translation," Ryan said. "I've created a short-range cell phone network that will intercept any calls Suzanne makes. The calls will be routed over the internet connection I just tapped into, while a mirror copy of the back-and-forth phone conversation will be sent to our office, where Yoda has just turned on my tracking and analysis system. Let's see if it works. Try each of the burn phones I gave you."

Marc dialed Patrick.

Yoda's voice came on. "Call intercepted from 718-123-4567 to 347-123-4567."

The latter was Patrick's cell number. The call went through.

Marc could hear a muddied version of his own voice echoing through Ryan's iPhone, as well as Patrick's response. He hung up and tried the same thing again, using the other burn phone and placing the call to Casey.

Yoda responded the same way, this time noting Casey's as the transfer number. And this time it was Casey's voice that came from Ryan's cell phone.

Marc gave another stunned shake of his head. "You're good," he told Ryan. "You amaze even me. Although, thanks to the past half hour, I've decided never to use my cell phone again, except to order takeout."

Ryan chuckled. "Yeah, this kind of stuff does tend to make you feel paranoid."

Marc retracted the ladder while Ryan removed his tool belt and packed everything back into the toolbox. Silently, the two men exited the building and returned with their equipment to the truck.

The waiting game would now begin.

Since she and Ryan had left Princeton, Claire had been plagued by the strong feeling that she was coming close to some kind of crucial energy that was just out of her reach. She determined that, by going home and shutting herself off to everything but that energy, she'd be able to grasp it. The more zoned in she was, the more productive her talk with Suzanne Fisher would be later.

The key differences between this coming visit and the earlier one were that, first, the sphere of killings was now tightly wrapped around Casey, with all the pieces locked into place. That pushed Casey's vulnerability—and the energy she exuded— to its peak. And, second, was the fact that, for the very first time, Claire had come in contact with Glen Fisher's energy. She'd felt it powerfully when she'd touched Trish's books, and when she'd envisioned the attack. Having that to work with opened a whole new door.

Claire turned down the lights in her apartment, drew the blinds and lit a candle or two. She then went to her kitchen drawer and took out the pen from Fisher's office. It was carefully wrapped in a Ziploc bag, so nothing could come in direct contact with it and compromise its integrity.

The instant Claire removed the pen and touched it, she felt a jolt of negative energy shoot through her fingertips. The feeling was so strong she almost cried out. Evil. It was pure evil.

Flashes of imagery ran through her head. Like an old-fashioned movie reel, they played out in fast motion, some of them so grotesque that they couldn't disappear fast enough for Claire.

Woman after woman. Rape after rape. Murder after murder. It was a barbaric collage of Fisher's crimes that zigzagged in order of magnitude, with the more recent ones in chronological order, culminating with the two-man attack on Trish.

Abruptly, an icy sense of total vulnerability and exposure came over Claire. She felt stripped naked, struggling, helpless, terrified.

With a soft cry, she dropped the pen. It clattered to the floor, the sound echoing inside her head. Her breath was coming in frightened pants. But she didn't care. Because now that she wasn't holding the pen, the vision was fading. She was back in her apartment, safe, with no invasion of her person or her space.

Hands trembling, she made herself a cup of nettle tea, although she had no false illusions about its ability to calm her. She just wanted the comfort of a familiar friend, the herbal tea that always warmed and grounded her.

After she'd finished a cup and a half, she went into the living room and sat on the sofa, trying to make sense out of the horrifying images.

The clarity and detail of what she was seeing made her suspect that the nightmare was about to come to a head. And the chilling image of herself in the role of a victim made her wonder if she was walking into danger tonight.

Was it possible that Glen Fisher would be at his apartment when she stopped by?

That didn't feel right. Fisher was anything but a stupid man. He hadn't so much as called his wife these past few days. And, with the apartment crawling with cops, he'd never take the risk of walking into their trap.

Could Suzanne herself be a threat?

That was a more viable possibility. True, Claire had picked up more sadness and fear than hostility the first time she'd been in the woman's presence. But things had changed since then. Suzanne's husband was out and free. What details of his plans had he shared with her? How much, if anything, had she contributed to those plans?

All of that was untapped information.

Still, Claire had something working in her favor. Suzanne believed in her abilities. That much, Claire had sensed from the onset. So, if Suzanne was curious enough, if she let her guard down enough—there was no telling what Claire might gain from this visit.

She rose and walked over to her yoga mat. A solid one-hour session, A hot shower. And then a subway ride to midtown.

She wasn't leaving that apartment without getting answers to her questions.

# CHAPTER
## THIRTY

Glen was horny as hell.

He made his way to a secluded area along Shore Road Park in Brooklyn near the Verrazano-Narrows Bridge. The view was spectacular, as was the memory of the redheaded jogger he'd raped and killed there just over a year ago.

It was the perfect place to call Suzanne.

He'd told her to expect his call—right about now.

He pulled out his burn phone and punched in the number.

Suzanne answered on the first ring. "Hello?" Glen had taught her never to say his name, just in case there was a crosswire.

"It's me." Glen didn't waste any time. "Are you wearing the wig?"

"Yes." Suzanne tucked a strand of it into place. Glen liked it just so. She made sure to keep it that way.

"Good. Very good." He settled himself on the bench.

★ ★ ★

Ryan was in his lair, poised and ready when the phone call went through.

It didn't take ten seconds to recognize what the call was about. Ryan wanted to puke. Lucky him. He'd be spending the next ten minutes listening to Glen Fisher having phone sex with his wife. Well, puking wasn't an option. Not when time was of the essence. He'd just block out the content and get the information he needed.

Taut with frustration, Ryan kept banging the table with his fist, trying with each thud to encourage his hacking script to pierce the wireless carriers' billing systems and triangulate the location of Glen and his cell phone, based on cell tower geometry. Shit. Shit. Shit.

Finally the coordinates appeared in a small window on the screen.

"Yes," Ryan hissed. He cut and pasted the coordinates into a widget he'd written—one that translated the longitude and latitude into a large red X superimposed on Google Maps. Ryan zoomed in. Son of a bitch. Fisher was practically underneath the Verrazano-Narrows Bridge, in Shore Road Park.

Majorly pissed off, Ryan headed upstairs to the conference room to tell Casey and the rest of the team the bad news.

"My system worked perfectly," he announced. "Unfortunately, Glen Fisher was having phone sex with his wife and jerking off on a park bench in Brooklyn. By the time I could've gotten there, the perv would have been long gone."

"So we've got nothing," Marc said in disgust.

"Not a fucking thing."

Suzanne Fisher put down the burn phone, removed her red wig and curled up on her bed as soon as the call was over.

Wearing it during her more explicit talks with Glen wasn't her favorite thing. But it put him in such a good mood, and made the phone sex so much more intense, that it was worth it.

She'd have to buy a backup wig before they left the country.

She'd just stood up to put the wig away when a knock sounded on her apartment door.

She froze, uncertain what to do. The police had backed off on their interrogations, the press had been pretty successfully blocked and she'd followed Glen's instructions and told all her friends and coworkers that she needed her privacy when she was at home. So who could be at her door?

Timidly, she walked into the living room, hovering near the sofa, trying to decide what to do.

"Mrs. Fisher?" Claire called out. "It's Claire Hedgleigh. I came to see how you are. May I come in?"

It was that lovely young woman who was a psychic.

Suzanne felt an unexpected surge of relief. There was something about Claire Hedgleigh that she found very comforting. She was a kind person, with a generous soul and an amazing gift. She'd obviously sensed that Suzanne needed female companionship—someone to share a cup of tea with—and she'd responded to that awareness.

And if Suzanne was wrong, if Claire had come as a member of Forensic Instincts and had concocted some kind of offensive agenda, she'd be swiftly shown out.

But somehow, Suzanne didn't think that was the case.

"Just a minute," she called back.

She was halfway to the door, when she realized she was still holding the wig. Hurrying over to the sofa, she stuffed it under the closest cushion and returned to the hallway.

She unlocked and opened the door, giving Claire a guarded smile—one that curved her lips but didn't quite reach her eyes.

"This is a pleasant surprise," she greeted her.

Claire drew her brows together in a quizzical look. "I hope I'm not intruding. I know this is a difficult time for you. I just got the feeling I should drop by."

So she was right, Suzanne thought. This wasn't a fishing expedition. It was simply a caring gesture—one that was based on the gut feel of a psychic.

"That's very nice of you," Suzanne said. "I *was* feeling out of sorts tonight. I was just about to make myself a cup of tea. Would you like one?"

"That would be wonderful."

"Please, come in. Sit down." Suzanne swept her arm in a welcoming gesture.

"Thank you." Claire entered the apartment, crossed over and settled herself on the sofa.

"I have every kind of tea imaginable," Suzanne told her. "I was about to brew chamomile to help me relax."

"That's my favorite for relaxing, too."

"Then I'll make two cups." Suzanne disappeared into the kitchen.

While she waited, Claire folded her hands in her lap and gave herself a stern talking-to. For whatever reason, she was having a hard time staying put and keeping her expression serene. She hadn't expected this kind of reaction. She hadn't had it the last time she'd been here. But this time, there were new and complicated energies filling the rooms—energies that screamed of Glen Fisher.

He hadn't physically been here. Claire felt certain of that. But his presence was as powerful as if he had. Recently. Which meant he'd definitely been in touch with his wife and that he was calling the shots about whatever was going on. His personality was so strong that Claire could hardly breathe. And his aura was so evil that it caused her physical pain.

There was the panicky feeling again. Claire swallowed hard, determined to go with the feeling and not to follow her instincts and bolt. She had to figure out the source of that suffocating panic.

She was exposed, in danger. It was a very personal danger, not one that was routed to her from another source. No one was touching or assaulting her. Yet she was at the mercy of the evil that enveloped her. She couldn't escape it. She was desperate to run—now, right now—to get away from this apartment and the threat that existed here.

But she didn't.

She remained where she was, seated on the sofa, battling to understand. Suzanne Fisher wasn't going to harm her. No one else was in the apartment. So what was causing the panic that kept coursing through her?

Eyes shut, Claire forced her body to relax on the sofa.

That made things worse.

Prickles of fear shot up her spine. Besides the panic, she started picking up an odd and creepy heated sensation on the underside of her thighs. Rather than dissipating, the sensation intensified, and then spread upward to her bottom. It closed in on her from the waist down and it took all her mental strength not to leap to her feet.

Instead, she focused on the sensation. It wasn't actually painful, but it came damn close. And it was more frightening than painful. Again, there was no sense of being touched or violated by human hands, just that insistent heat.

Claire ignored the fine sheen of perspiration that broke out all over her body. She shifted on the sofa cushion, wondering if her position would alter the feeling. Resettling herself on a diagonal, she crossed her legs and waited.

A burst of heat.

Her eyes flew open, and she bit her lip to restrain the startled cry that rose in her throat.

In her peripheral vision, she spied a flash of red under the original spot where she'd been seated. Her head turned in that direction.

A cap of hair shoved beneath the sofa cushion. Red hair.

Claire didn't think. She just glanced behind her to confirm that Suzanne was still in the kitchen. Seeing that she was, Claire grabbed the hair and tugged it out.

A red wig. Shoulder-length. Expensively made. And screaming with myriad energy. Claire realized that some of the energy was the heat that had been building up beneath her and was now rapidly fading.

For a brief instant, she stared at the wig. Then she shoved it into her tote bag, pushing it way to the bottom and covering it up with the rest of the bag's contents.

She now had to conduct a civil, believable conversation, and then get out of there as fast as she could.

She wasn't sure she could pull this off. She wasn't much of a con.

Time to become one.

"Here we are." Suzanne returned to the living room with a tray containing two cups of tea, milk and sugar, two linen napkins and a dish of cinnamon cookies. "I thought you might like to try these. I baked them myself. They're very light." She set down the tray, serving Claire like a proper hostess.

"How thoughtful." Despite her best intentions, Claire was operating on only a few cylinders. Her mind was in emotional chaos. But the few prevailing instincts she still had cautioned her that she couldn't give herself away—not when she'd just stolen something crucial from Suzanne Fisher's house.

"I can't think of a more relaxing snack," she added, reaching for a cookie and a napkin. First eat. Then drink. Both would keep her mouth occupied and her emotional turmoil from registering on her face. She took a bite of the cookie. "Mmm. These are delicious."

Suzanne looked pleased. She settled herself on the opposite side of the sofa, taking her own napkin and cookie. "I'm delighted you dropped by."

"I took a chance that you'd be home," Claire said. "As I mentioned, I had the feeling you needed some company."

"Was it a psychic premonition?" Suzanne asked eagerly.

This was familiar turf. Trying to explain to people the nature of her gift. Normally, this conversation was a frustrating one for Claire. Right now, it was a welcome reprieve.

"No, it wasn't a premonition, just a gut feeling. Some of it was based on fact—you've been bombarded with difficult stimuli these past few days—and the rest of it was instinct. I felt a connection with you the first time we met. Maybe that's why I sensed what you were feeling. I don't know."

Suzanne's eyes were wide with interest as she sipped her tea. "It must be wonderful and frightening at the same time to know things without actually knowing them."

"I wouldn't say that I *know* things. I just sense them. Sometimes I'm right. Sometimes I'm wrong. Either way, it's a huge responsibility. And, yes, it can be frightening." Claire answered that one with total candor. "As for wonderful, it's only wonderful when it produces positive results. When it agitates me and leads nowhere, it's more upsetting than it is good."

"I see your point."

"I'm glad. It's a hard one to explain." Claire sipped her tea.

"Speaking of frightening, has the press backed off and left you alone?"

A shrug. "The police have kept them in check. I wish they'd just go away. I want to live a normal life, to go to work, or to the market, without being followed and harassed."

"It'll die down. Right now, it's overwhelming because your husband just escaped. Once that's resolved, he'll be in custody and you'll be able to go back to your normal life."

Suzanne's back stiffened, and a flicker of suspicion darted across her face. "I don't want to talk about Glen's escape or the posse that's after him. If that's what you came here to discuss, I'll have to ask you to leave."

"On the contrary." Claire kept her composure calm, shaking her head from side to side. "To be frank, I'm just as happy not to discuss your husband at all. I assumed you were feeling isolated and wanted to express your feelings for him. If you don't, all the better. Because the truth is, you love and believe in him. I don't. So why should we be uncomfortable or argue? I'm sure we have other things in common besides the issue of your husband's guilt or innocence."

Relief flickered in Suzanne's eyes, and the tension in her body abated. "I appreciate your sensitivity. It would be refreshing to talk about something else for a change."

"Great. Why don't you tell me about your interest in the piano? When did you learn to play? And what made you decide to teach?"

Claire's digression worked. Suzanne spent the next half hour talking about how she'd played the piano since kindergarten, how her love for it had been passed down by her mother and how much she enjoyed educating others in the beauty of classical music. Especially children, who were more open and eager to explore—even if they did hate practicing during the week.

From the piano they went on to discuss the symphony, and how much Suzanne loved both that and the theater.

Every time Claire lifted her cup of tea, she glanced at her watch.

When a little over an hour had passed, she knew she could leave without arousing any suspicion.

"This has been lovely," she said, setting down her empty teacup. "Can I help you with these dishes before I go?"

Suzanne rose, waving away Claire's offer. "Don't be silly. It'll take me five minutes. I really enjoyed this visit. I hope we can do it again soon."

"Next time I'll call and arrange something in advance," Claire lied with a smile. "I don't want to infringe on your privacy."

"You didn't. But, yes, we'll make arrangements next time."

Suzanne showed Claire to the door.

Claire couldn't get out of there fast enough.

Suzanne was humming as she washed the teacups. She hadn't realized how lonely she'd been for female companionship until Claire arrived. It had been so nice to pass an hour talking about shared interests. They would definitely have to do it again.

Just before preparing herself a light dinner, Suzanne went into the living room to shut off the lights. That was when she remembered the wig. She'd better put it away before she forgot. Glen might call at a moment's notice and ask for a repeat performance.

She reached under the sofa cushion. Nothing. Frowning, she removed the cushion, and then the second and the third.

The wig was gone.

And there was only one person who could have taken it.

Her heart began to pound furiously. Fear superseded all the other emotions she was feeling. She had to call Glen, to tell him what had happened. She'd have to explain how stupidly trusting she'd been. He despised weakness. When he heard that she'd let her guard down, succumbed to her need for company, he'd be livid.

God help her.

She marched back into the bedroom as if she were a prisoner on her way to the death chamber. There was no point in putting it off. She might as well face the inevitable right now. She wasn't supposed to call Glen. He prearranged their calls, and he was the one who made them. But this was an emergency. He had to know what had happened.

Picking up the burn phone Jack had gotten her, she punched in the number Glen had recited to her over the phone just hours earlier.

Glen had been looking forward to this next hour. The phone sex had eased his pent-up tension—just what he needed to enjoy the perfect meal…a couple of Nathan's Famous hot dogs, a large order of French fries and a cold beer.

As it was, he'd been preoccupied all day, racking his brain to come up with some way to get Casey Woods alone. Based on Jack's reports, that would be next to impossible. Well, that wasn't going to fly. Somehow he had to figure out how to finish what he'd begun.

He was deep in thought and halfway through his long-awaited meal when his burn phone rang.

He glanced at the caller ID, and anger rose inside him like a tidal wave. "Why are you calling me?"

"I'm sorry." Suzanne swallowed. She curled up on the bed and covered herself with a blanket, unconsciously shielding herself from what was to come. "I need to tell you something. It's important."

"What do you want? I'm busy."

"Claire Hedgleigh came to visit me tonight. I didn't invite her," Suzanne added hastily. "She just sensed that I...needed some company. I remembered that you told me not to make the Forensic Instincts team suspicious. So I asked Claire in for tea."

"Interesting." Glen's mind was processing a mile a minute. There was no way Claire Hedgleigh had come over for a cup of tea. She had an agenda. The Forensic Instincts team had probably chosen her for a recon expedition because she was the least threatening, and because she was just the kind of woman Suzanne would gravitate to for female companionship. Smart move on their part.

Time to find out what damage had been done.

"What happened?" he asked his wife.

"I screwed up."

Glen's jaw clenched. "What did you tell her?"

"Nothing. In fact, she didn't even want to talk about you. We discussed the piano."

"How quaint. So how did you screw up?"

In a quavering voice, Suzanne told him about the incident with the wig. "I don't know how she found it. Either by accident or maybe she got some vibes that it was there. But she has it. And I don't know what to do."

Glen began to laugh, first a little and then a lot. The idea of Claire Hedgleigh communing with Suzanne's wig struck him as very funny.

"Why are you laughing?" Suzanne demanded. "I've put you in danger."

"Cut it out, Suzanne. Yeah, it was stupid of you to leave the wig lying around. But other than that, the whole thing is ridiculous. Ms. Psychic probably thinks she's going to find me through some cosmic connection."

Suzanne wasn't laughing. "It's possible. That wig is very personal to us. She could get damning energy off it."

"What kind of 'damning energy'? That we like to keep things spicy in the bedroom?"

"What if she puts it on? What if that helps her figure out where you are?" Yes, Suzanne was weak with relief that Glen wasn't furious with her. But she was still worried to death over the ramifications of Claire's having the wig.

"And how would she figure that out?" Glen threw back at her. "Even if she's the psychic of the year, she has nothing to use. Since I left Auburn, you wore that wig only once in my presence—in that motel room. The rest of our encounters have been over the phone. There's nothing either substantive or metaphysical for her to use to figure out my whereabouts. Let her parade around midtown Manhattan with the wig on for all I care. We'll get you a new one."

Suzanne was calming down now. "I was thinking we should get two so we always have a spare."

"Good idea. Only let me take care of it. I don't want you drawing any more attention to yourself. No sense raising any red flags." He chuckled at his own play on words.

"Do you think I'm more at risk now than I was before?"

"The only thing that's at risk is your modesty, if your friend Claire Hedgleigh visualizes anything graphic pertaining to you and that wig. Other than that, just keep going about your regular routine."

He ended the call, still chuckling at the idea of Casey's psychic friend trying to gain info from a cascade of hair. He knew the Forensic Instincts team was tight. He had to give Claire Hedgleigh points for balls and for creativity. Balls for dropping in on Suzanne with no backup. And creativity for deciding to play dress-up to gain insight into his plans for Casey so she could protect her friend. Suzanne was worried about what would happen if she put the wig on. Hell, maybe she'd learn a thing or two.

Abruptly, Glen's head came up, and his laughter faded. Of course. What an asshole he'd been. He was so busy trying to conjure up a way to infiltrate Casey Woods's impenetrable world and grab her that he hadn't thought of the obvious.

He'd forget going after her.

Instead, he'd force *her* to come to *him*. And he knew just how to do it.

Adrenaline pumping, Glen rose from the table and chugged the rest of his beer. He walked over to the condiment area, dropped his cell phone in the garbage and walked up to the counter, where he asked one of the servers for a paper bag. He opened the bag, dumped the remainder of his French fries inside and then placed an uneaten hot dog on top of the fries. Folding the top of the bag, he polished off the last bite of hot dog on his tray, picked up the bag and left.

No sense letting good food go to waste.

Especially since the next Nathan's he'd be eating would be in Dubai.

# CHAPTER
## THIRTY-ONE

After leaving the Fishers' apartment, Claire went straight to the brownstone rather than home.

She knew the FI team. They'd all still be there, hard at work. And she was eager to report what had happened during her visit with Suzanne Fisher. After that, she'd seclude herself in her preferred small office, and see what kind of energy she could pick up off the wig she'd taken.

She was racing against the clock and she knew it.

Suzanne had probably gone to pieces when she realized the wig was missing. And that would trigger some reaction from her husband. Claire just wasn't sure what that reaction would be.

She only prayed it wasn't one that would accelerate Fisher's plans for Casey.

Claire had to do some yoga, calm down and free her mind of all the chaos it was experiencing. Then she could concentrate and, hopefully, put her efforts where they belonged.

Calming down was *not* in the cards.

Claire practically collided with Patrick in the front hallway, where he was talking with a few of his security guards, reassigning different people to different posts and letting others go home for a rest. He paused when Claire blew in, and angled his head in her direction.

"Lose your cell phone?" he inquired.

"Excuse me?" Claire gave him a baffled look.

"Your cell phone. The thing we reach you on. It's been going straight to voice mail."

"Oh." Claire groped in her tote bag and pulled out the phone. She glanced down at it, feeling like an idiot. "I turned it off while I was meeting with Suzanne Fisher. I must have forgotten to turn it back on." She quickly remedied that as she spoke.

"Well, don't bother checking your twelve voice mails. Just brace yourself."

"For what?"

"For me." Ryan was leaning against the second-floor bannister, glaring down at her.

Totally puzzled, Claire climbed the stairs to the second level. "What's wrong? You knew where I was."

"Yeah, I knew." Ryan was clearly furious. "Are you out of your friggin' mind? You were going over there for a visit, to commune with the energy in her apartment. Instead, you ripped off her sex toy? What did you *think* was going to happen?"

Claire blinked. "How did you know I took the wig?"

"Because I'm tapped into every cell phone call the Fishers make. Because I've had the outstanding fortune of listening to their before and after conversations—first, their make-me-barf phone sex, and then Suzanne's hysterical call to her husband, telling him you'd stolen her Barbie doll hair."

"I assume, from your reaction, that Glen Fisher was mad?"

"Shouldn't that question have occurred to you *before* you took the wig?" Ryan wasn't letting this go.

"Probably," Claire admitted. "But the truth is, I didn't stop to consider the fallout. I just saw an opportunity and I took it. That wig was screaming with energy. I could barely breathe. All I wanted was to sort out the aura." A pause. "You didn't answer my question—how did Glen Fisher react?"

"You're lucky. Apparently, he's not a big believer in psychic readings. He laughed off the whole thing and told Suzanne he'd buy her a new wig. Plus a second one for the road."

Claire searched Ryan's face. "They're planning on killing Casey and then taking off."

"Sure sounds like it."

"Did you trace the phone calls?"

"Dead ends. One from a park bench in Brooklyn and one from a Nathan's at Coney Island. No chance of tracing them. And now it looks like Fisher's dumped the burn phone. He's probably got another one."

"But you don't think he's coming after the wig?"

"No. It was still a stupid thing to do."

"I guess." Claire was eager to start her process. "But what's done is done. I've got to get busy to see if my hunch pays off."

Ryan waved his arm toward the third floor. "Have at it. But let me know before you take off on any more excursions."

"I will." Claire was already halfway out the door.

Glen was lying on the sofa, arms folded behind his head, smiling, when Jack let himself into their rented Brooklyn hideout that night.

"Hey." Jack sent his uncle a curious glance. "You look like your day went well."

"It did." Glen swung his legs over the side of the sofa and rose. "Did you keep your eye on Claire Hedgleigh the way I asked?"

"Followed her with my binoculars nonstop until a half hour ago." Jack went into the kitchen and got himself a beer. "The security on her is nil," he reported, uncapping the bottle. "She comes and goes as she pleases. I've seen that dude Ryan go home with her sometimes, but he usually doesn't stay. I guess he gets laid and goes home. Not a bad deal. She's pretty hot."

"Good. Do your job right and you can enjoy her."

Jack perked up. "We're taking her? She's a blonde."

"Yes, I know. I have eyes," Glen snapped.

"Then what? You're going to use the wig?"

"I'm going to use *her*. She's going to help us draw out Casey Woods."

Realization dawned in Jack's eyes. "I get it. The Forensic Instincts team is tight, and Casey is their leader. There's no way she'll do nothing if she thinks Claire Hedgleigh is in danger."

"You got it." Glen gave him a mock salute. "We'll be threatening what she cares about most."

"And maybe have some fun in the process?"

"Like I said, she's all yours. But we need to keep our eye on the prize. A life for a life. They can have Claire Hedgleigh. We'll be long gone when they find her."

"The new identities will be ready for pickup tomorrow, right?" Jack asked. "Suzanne and I sure went to enough trouble to get those photos taken without being tailed."

"Yup. I'll take care of getting them while you're waiting to grab your hot psychic on her way home. We'll bring her to the new warehouse I scouted out on South 2nd Street, and use your iPhone to take clear, explicit photos."

Jack gave a smug nod. "Casey will be out the door the instant she can shake the guards."

"Which she'll do as soon as she gets a look at what we're doing to her blonde friend." A cruel smile twisted Glen's mouth. "What the hell. Maybe I'll put the red wig on her and go at it. I'm in such a good mood that I'll even take sloppy seconds."

Claire squirmed as she sat on her mat in the third-floor office, then took two or three deep, cleansing breaths.

It was no use.

She'd been perched there for what seemed like forever, and she still couldn't clear her mind. All her impulses were pulling her toward the tote bag across the room—the one with Suzanne Fisher's wig.

She finally gave up and gave in. Crossing over, she rummaged through her bag and pulled out the wig.

The instant her fingers closed around it, a cascade of different images and energies accosted her at once. It was like opening Pandora's box and trying to escape its contents.

This time, Claire fought the onslaught of emotions and forced herself to ride them out. She was sucked into graphic sexual moments between Suzanne and Glen Fisher—most of those moments filled with fear and pain on Suzanne's part. Suzanne couldn't breathe. She was tossing her head back and forth to suck in air. Her body was being torn apart, battered to the point where she prayed for it to end. And yet she wrapped her arms around her husband, absorbed his anger along with the pain he was inflicting.

It wasn't excitement, not for Suzanne. There was a serenity about her that overrode the physical torment—the sense that she was alleviating her husband's demons on whatever level she could.

She loved him. She shut her mind to who and what he was.

And when the thoughts crept in, uninvited, she justified his behavior by focusing on his past.

*His past.*

Claire squeezed her eyes shut and went deeper into Suzanne's energy.

Glen Fisher had been sexually abused. Claire couldn't visualize it happening, but it was vividly part of his wife's consciousness. Suzanne hadn't been part of his life when it happened. That was many years ago, when Glen was in middle school.

A math teacher. Redheaded. Petite. Beautiful. Perverse. She'd taken an already twisted adolescent and screwed with his body and his mind. She played into all his sick fantasies and dragged him into all of her own.

The control had been hers, the scars his.

He never actually discussed it. Instead, he revealed snatches of it when he was in a rage, venting. Suzanne had put together the pieces. And they made her sick. How could she fault him for the residual effects? His tightly leashed rage, his hatred toward women who reminded him of her?

She couldn't. She feared who he could sometimes be. She hated what she knew in her gut he did. But she understood it.

She'd helped him in ways she could justify to herself—starting with supporting Jack when he needed her. He couldn't do it alone; he didn't have his uncle's strategic brilliance. But he did have a flair for the creative. So Suzanne had put her touches on that.

The lip gloss. Claire envisioned Suzanne standing several yards away from Casey in the department store that day, listening. Casey had asked for the lip gloss by name, and then purchased it. Suzanne had waited until she was gone, after which she'd bought five tubes of the same product and had them delivered to a post office box for Jack.

Claire tried to visualize the address on the package, or the post office it was mailed to. Nothing. She then tried to see Jack with the package in his hands. Mentally, she groped for an image of his face, his build—*anything.* But she kept coming up empty. The only psychic connection she seemed able to make was with Suzanne.

*What else did you do, Suzanne?* she asked herself, tightening her grip on the wig.

Surveillance, of a sort. Claire could see Suzanne driving her dark sedan to the Columbia campus to watch a particular girl—Kendra Mallery—as she joined a bunch of kids eating pizza. That wasn't Suzanne's only visit. She'd returned to the campus on the night of Kendra's vigil to take pictures of the attendees, and then to text the pictures to Glen—along with a dozen other pictures of different girls he'd asked her to watch.

Suzanne didn't want to think about the reasons he requested the photos. But she knew. God help her, she knew. He was hunting down potential victims.

Potential victims.

Claire's breath caught in her throat, and she was plunged into that same terrifying place she'd been in before, during the time she'd been holding Glen Fisher's pen. Vulnerable. Panicked. Gasping in air. Crying out. Screaming.

This time she could feel herself being stared at by two pairs of eyes—eyes that were filled with evil. Cruelty.

She was lying on a concrete floor in an industrial building. She was cold. So cold. She couldn't get warm. Couldn't escape.

Abruptly, the image changed, and it was Casey who was living the nightmare. Only it was worse, more violent. There was a physicality taking place that hadn't existed for Claire. They were hurting Casey, forcing her to the concrete floor, striking her when she fought back. And Claire had to watch the whole thing.

The scene was dizzying. Claire alternated between being an active participant and an observer. First, she was right beside Casey, flat on her back, her head turned toward her friend. Casey was bound, nude, thrashing her head from side to side as she was held down. Then Claire was floating above the scene, watching it as a viewer.

The two men were hovering over Casey now, binding her wrists and tying a rope around each ankle, keeping her legs apart. They were fumbling at their own clothes, readying themselves for a long-awaited vengeance.

And Claire was once again removed, fighting with all her might to get to Casey, to free her, to somehow help her escape.

But escape was impossible.

In the midst of Claire's vision, a beam of light sliced through the room she was seeing, illuminating the face of one of the attackers.

It was Glen Fisher.

Claire willed the light to expand, to include Fisher's accomplice. But it wouldn't. His face remained in darkness. Why?

The images were fading. Despite her own sense of dread, Claire battled to hold on to them. She needed to see more, to find something to focus on that would provide her with a clue. Something she could give to the team to stop this heinous occurrence.

Her efforts were futile. She was back in the office, huddled on the carpet. Tears were coursing down her cheeks, and terror was pervading her body. She sank onto the floor, shaking violently, dragging huge gasps of air into her lungs.

She had to think. To make sense of what she'd experienced. Now. While the images were still vivid and fresh in her mind.

With the backs of her hands, Claire dashed the tears off her face, focusing hard on what she'd just gone through as well as what she'd just witnessed. As an active victim, it was like being a bug under a microscope. She'd felt the probing scrutiny. But she hadn't felt any hands on her. No contact whatsoever. Why? If she was being attacked, why were her attackers just staring at her?

That hadn't been the case with Casey. They'd struck her, brutalizing her body. There wasn't the slightest doubt in Claire's mind that they were preparing to rape and kill her. The image had been as powerful as any reality.

Why had she and Casey been lying side by side during that brief period of time? Had this been an actual premonition or was it a symbolic apparition meant for Claire to interpret?

One thing was for sure. Whatever was going to happen was imminent.

And it was evil.

# CHAPTER
## THIRTY-TWO

Patrick was the only one in the conference room when Claire walked in. He was poring over the financial data Ryan had extracted on the Auburn State prison guards. Since it was clear that someone on the inside was helping Fisher, Patrick was trying to figure out just who that someone was by searching bank records that showed hefty deposits. He hadn't asked Ryan how he'd gotten these records. He was certain he didn't want to know.

Patrick's attention shifted the moment Claire entered the room. Her strained expression and the dazed look in her eyes told him she needed to talk.

He put down his paperwork and frowned. "You okay?"

"I don't know." Claire sank down at the conference room table in an adjacent chair.

"Ryan didn't upset you, did he? I know he was angry, but that's because he was worried about you."

"What?" Claire seemed puzzled, almost as if Ryan's name was unfamiliar to her.

"Okay, it isn't Ryan," Patrick said. "Then what? You look lousy now, and you looked pretty high-strung when you came in. What's going on?"

Claire hesitated for a second. Then, she blurted it all out—her meeting with Suzanne Fisher, the wig she'd taken, the weird visions she'd been having.

Patrick listened quietly and objectively. He might be in his early sixties, but he was an open-minded man. He'd never heard of claircognizance before he'd met Claire, but that didn't mean he was a flat-out nonbeliever. It just meant he had a hard time accepting the premise of energy-sensing to solve crimes, especially when there were no hard-core facts to support it.

But he'd seen the results of what Claire could do. And they were inarguable. So he listened carefully, and digested what Claire had to say.

When she was finished, she caught her breath and studied Patrick's expression. "You're thinking it's a bunch of crap."

"No, I'm trying to figure out what the symbolism is."

"Claire saw herself in the role of a restrained victim because she feels responsible for me." Casey's voice reached them from the doorway, where she was leaning, arms folded across her chest. "She's upset because she can't pick up anything that could help prevent what Glen Fisher has in mind."

Claire started, swerving in her chair to see Casey. "I didn't know you were in the room."

"I'm glad I was." Casey crossed over and sat down with Claire and Patrick. "I don't want you keeping things from me. I don't need shielding. I need to know everything. And, by the way, there's nothing you said that I haven't already thought of."

"I'm so frustrated." Claire raked a hand through her hair.

"And, yes, I'm freaked out, too. These images are starting to really mess with my mind and make me physically ill."

"But they're intensifying," Casey pointed out. "That's got to mean we're getting closer to Fisher's end game." She raised her chin. "Except that we're going to alter the results of that end game."

"Without a doubt." Patrick rose to his feet. "Marc's here tonight. Obviously, so is Hutch. You're in good hands."

"I know that," Casey said. "Just as I know that we're going to get to Glen Fisher before he gets to us. So let's all try to rest."

"I agree. We should all call it a night. It's late. We'll pick this up in the morning." Patrick glanced down at Claire. "How'd you like an old-fashioned guy to drive you home tonight? I took the car rather than the train today, since I had no idea what time I'd be heading home."

Claire felt—and showed—a surge of relief. "That would be great. I'm still feeling off balance. Once I've taken a hot bath and curled up in bed, I'll feel better."

"Then let's go." Patrick rose and gestured toward the door. "My car's right across the street."

Claire said good-night to Casey and preceded Patrick down the stairs. They left the building and walked over to Patrick's car.

As Claire opened the passenger door, an icy chill shot through her—just for a second, then it was gone. She caught her breath, her head immediately coming up as she searched the city street.

There were no creepy figures lurking about. And no suspicious-looking vehicles, either.

Still, she was very glad that Patrick was driving her home.

Unlike his nephew, Glen Fisher didn't sleep much that night. There was too much to do.

He waited until almost four in the morning before visiting the

Brooklyn warehouse he'd so carefully chosen. The padlock on the outside door was tightly locked. He unlocked it with a key and went inside. Everything was in order. He'd set up a couple of chairs, a video camera and his tools of the trade. How many of those he used was up to Casey Woods.

He'd made sure the chairs were padded. He and Jack were going to be here for quite a while, and they might as well be comfortable.

The whole setup was ready.

Glen sat down and linked his hands behind his head. It felt damned good to be in control again. He was running things, issuing the orders. He'd told Jack and Suzanne to pack lightly. Anything they needed, they could replace once they reached Dubai. Their new identities were in place. Their flight out of the U.S. was scheduled to leave JFK at 6:00 p.m. the night after next. That would give him and Jack more than enough time to flush out Casey Woods, do what they needed to do and take off.

Considering how deep her loyalties ran, she'd get here the instant she knew how high the stakes were. The quicker she showed up, the less torture Claire Hedgleigh would endure.

It was a no-brainer.

Rising, Glen gave the place one last look. Then he left. He'd be back soon enough.


Ryan was bored with the waiting game.

It had been a good fifteen hours since the last phone call between Fisher and his wife. Since then, nothing.

He had some time to kill, so Ryan decided to dig around in Glen Fisher's past, curious about what made the psycho tick.

It sucked that there were no computer files dating back thirty years. Ryan would have enjoyed hacking into Fisher's school records, to find out what sort of kid he'd been—visibly off or charismatically controlling. Psychopaths came in many forms, as Hutch had taught him. They didn't automatically become serial killers. They were born with certain personality traits, and those traits were influenced by the way they were raised, their early childhood experiences and their particular psychological profiles.

What Ryan did know was that Fisher was highly intelligent, arrogant, consumed with his own self-importance. That couldn't have played well once he hit secondary school.

For the hell of it, Ryan starting digging around in newspaper archives, looking for criminal incidents involving kids in Fisher's middle school and high school during the years he'd attended. It didn't take long for him to hit the mother lode.

The first article on the scandal was hidden on page three of the local paper. The second and third articles weren't so discreet. They were splashed across the front pages of metro New York newspapers, as well as being highlighted in two or three gossip rags.

It was at Fisher's middle school, the year he was in seventh grade. Evidently, a twenty-eight-year-old female math teacher had initiated sexual relationships with several of her students, all of whom were minors. Ryan studied the reports, trying to find the names of the students. But, as he suspected, they were being withheld to protect the poor kids, who were probably already so messed up they were living on psychiatrists' couches. What Ryan did find was the name of the math teacher. Colleen McCoy.

He fed her information into Google.

Some of the same articles he'd already read came up, but there were others, as well, that went into more detail as they discussed Ms. McCoy's dismissal from her job and the pending criminal charges being brought against her.

It seemed the teacher had seduced at least three of her students behind the gymnasium during after-school hours. One of them eventually had the balls to tape the encounter, and then go to the guidance office with the facts. That had set everything in motion and resulted, ultimately, in the full discovery of Ms. McCoy's sexual deviance when it came to her victims.

Could Glen Fisher have been one of those victims?

Ryan leaned forward, his eyes narrowed as he read. The woman was clearly a sicko. But the details of her perversions were no longer what Ryan was looking for.

He skipped over the newspaper pieces. That wasn't where he'd find what he wanted. He went straight to the tabloids.

Bingo. A color photo of Colleen McCoy, being led away in handcuffs. Ryan zoomed in and enlarged the photo so he could scrutinize the teacher.

Pretty. Petite. Redheaded.

Just like Fisher's victims.

Ryan leaned back in his chair, continuing to stare at the photo as he processed this new piece of information.

It might end up being an extraneous factoid.

On the other hand, it might not.

It was a long day in the manhunt for Glen Fisher. The killer had done a remarkable job of keeping himself and his nephew, Jack, concealed from the public. None of the toll-free calls from people claiming to have spotted Fisher held any merit. The sands of the hourglass were running out, and there wasn't a single new lead to go on.

Hutch returned to Forensic Instincts at dinnertime, weary and tense. The team had spent the day much as he had, hunting down leads and waiting for Fisher to fall into their telephone trap.

Nothing.

When Hutch walked into the conference room, the team was sitting around the table, discussing Ryan's findings. Claire had already confirmed Ryan's suspicions that Glen was one of Ms. McCoy's victims, by sharing what she'd picked up on earlier.

"What's your take?" Ryan asked Hutch.

Hutch read over each of Ryan's printouts. "Based on what I'm seeing here, it's not a leap to say that Claire is right, and that Fisher was one of Colleen McCoy's victims. Nor is it a leap to say that she was the catalyst who triggered his future behavior. The guy was fifteen. Sexually, that's a vulnerable age for a kid. So she messed with his mind and his body. Combine that with a psychopathic profile, and you've got all the components of a ticking bomb, ready to go off."

Casey nodded, scrutinizing the math teacher's photo. "The resemblance to the victims is creepy," she murmured.

"Not just to the victims." Marc leveled a stare at her. "To *you*."

"I know." Casey let her head rest against the chair cushion. "You don't need to drive home that point. It freaks me out enough as it is."

"We still haven't figured out what to do about it," Claire said.

"Verifying our theory is a waste of time," Patrick argued. "At least until we're building a case against Fisher. Right now, it's a poor use of our resources. It would take a bunch of man-hours to get the appropriate police report and to get permission to unseal the names of the kids involved. And for what? Just to know we're right? We need to stop Glen Fisher, not psycho-analyze him."

"Yes and no." Hutch looked thoughtful. "It's definitely not worth our time yet to confirm that Fisher was one of the victims, especially since this happened too long ago for Ryan's hacking skills to come in handy. We'll do it the legal way—later. But for now? It's a great bit of ammunition to hold on to in case Fisher calls and starts playing head games with Casey. She can retaliate, rev him up and maybe get him to say something he'll wish he hadn't. I saw her do it when we met with him in prison. She pushed his buttons. He really lost it."

"You're thinking he'll call Casey again?" Claire didn't seem happy about that.

"It's a definite possibility. He's locked and loaded. Whether or not he wants to up the fear factor as part of his game plan for Casey—that's an unknown." Hutch's expression grew grim. "What worries me more is why he seems so confident that he can pull off the grand finale. He knows the level of security we have on Casey, and that she rarely leaves the building. So why is he so damn cocky?"

"That's my concern, as well," Marc said. "He's way too sure of himself. That means he's devised a specific plan and is ready to carry it out. We've got to be extra diligent."

"With regard to brownstone access, I increased the sensitivity of the alarm system and put Yoda on continuous high alert," Ryan informed them. "That means no one outside of the team can switch him into sleep mode. He'll react to every coming and going—from room to room, as well as from entry point to entry point."

"What about the fourth floor?" Hutch asked, referring to Casey's apartment. Normally, Yoda didn't intrude into that personal space.

"The added security extends to the fourth floor, too. Sorry about the lack of privacy. But desperate times and all that." A corner of Ryan's mouth lifted. "The good news is that I didn't plant any video or audio surveillance up there. So you can hook up to your heart's content."

Hutch didn't smile, nor did he look as if sex was on his list of priorities at the moment. "I think we should call it a night.

The sooner we lock up and activate all our security, the better. Tomorrow, the task force is going to tap into all its resources to see if Glen Fisher is setting things in motion to leave the U.S. If Casey is his last hurrah, it would make sense for him to get out and get settled in a country with no extradition policy."

"You don't have to wait until tomorrow." Ryan rose. "I'll do a little digging before I head home, and see if I can come up with some names to add to your list of identity forgers."

"And I'll take the combined lists and pay every dirt bag on them a visit tomorrow," Patrick said. "Fisher could be leaving alone, or he could be taking Jack and Suzanne with him. I'll find that out, too."

"Nice." Marc nodded. "I'll keep you company—in case a little extra persuasion is in order. Shut your eyes if you have to."

"Not necessary. Not when it's Casey we're protecting. Screw the straight and narrow."

Marc whistled. "You really are one of us now, Patrick. Impressive."

"I shouldn't be hearing this," Hutch said.

"Hearing what?" Marc shot him an innocent look. "I didn't say anything. Neither did Ryan. He's just surfing the web and I'm just visiting some colleagues. Right, Ryan?"

"Right."

Casey gave them a faint smile. "Thank you all," she said, coming to her feet. "I'm going to grab something from the kitchen and then go up to bed. I'm exhausted." As soon as Casey moved, Hero scrambled up, too, staying close to his mistress's side. She reached down to stroke his head. Hero wasn't the only one who bolted to his feet. Hutch was right behind them. "I'll be joining you."

"Sentry duty?" Casey asked.

"If that's what you want to call it."

"I'd say I'm a lucky girl. Two loyal men sleeping in my bed to make sure I'm safe."

"You can't have enough guard dogs." Ryan glanced around the table. "Everyone else going home now?"

Patrick and Claire nodded.

"Good. Then I'll wait and see that the security systems are fully engaged before I leave." He waited until Claire was easing her way around the table before catching her arm and speaking in a quiet voice that only she could hear. "Want company?"

"Not tonight." She shook her head, her troubled gaze asking him to understand. "It's not that I don't want you there. I just need to be alone. I need to concentrate all my energy on one single focus—Casey."

"Understood." His knuckles brushed her cheek. "Just call if you need me."

"I will."


Claire took the subway home.

She was so damned wired. It seemed to take forever for the train to reach her stop. Her mind was on overdrive, but not in a controlled way. More like a wild stallion at a rodeo. The images in her mind were flashing wildly and randomly, and the tension pounding at her temples was heightening.

Talk about energy. Its intensity was nearly paralyzing.

She needed to find a way to calm down and channel it.

Stopping only long enough to pick up some Chinese takeout, she walked the block and a half to her apartment, trying to decide whether a hot bath or a hot shower would do her more good.

She relaxed more in a bath.

But she thought more in a shower.

It was a toss-up.

Still trying to decide which would yield the best result, she rounded the corner of her block.

Abruptly, a chill shot up her spine.

She sensed the man behind her a split second before the barrel of a gun was shoved into her back.

"Hello, Claire." His voice was unfamiliar. But it was close— so close that it ruffled her hair. "Keep walking. Don't make a sound. My car is right over here. Let's hop into it like a couple bringing home Chinese takeout."

"Who are you?" she managed.

"I think you know the answer to that. Now get in."

He opened the backseat of the sedan, and pushed her in. Then he slid in beside her and locked the doors. There were no streetlights nearby, and the car's windows were tinted, so it was virtually impossible to see inside. Using that to his advantage, he worked quickly, stuffing a handkerchief into her mouth and binding her wrists and ankles.

Claire struggled as hard as she could. It only made him tighten the ropes until they cut deep into her skin. He was wearing a ski mask, so she couldn't make out any of his facial features. But his hands were that of a young man—probably in his twenties. And his build was lankier than Glen Fisher's. So it definitely wasn't him. It had to be Jack.

She would have tested her theory by using his name, but the gag crammed in her mouth made that impossible. She tried to focus on his energy, but her own fear overrode any metaphysical connection she might have established. So, instead, she concentrated on her breathing, keeping it slow and shallow, so she could conserve her energy and her oxygen. She had to remain as physically strong and mentally alert as possible.

She refused to allow herself to think ahead to what he had in store for her. The present. Just stay in the present.

Her assailant snatched the bag of Chinese food she'd been carrying. "I'll take this," he said, leaning forward to place it on the passenger seat. "I skipped dinner. I'll eat while I drive."

He pushed Claire down on her side, reaching over to grab a black sack he'd stashed on the floor. Something lying beside her on the leather seat tickled her nose, and Claire pulled her head back, trying to see past the empty junk-food bags scattered around her.

Suzanne's red wig.

She looked at it and started.

He must have seen her reaction, because he glanced at the wig and chuckled. "I paid a visit to your apartment before I came to pick you up. Nice place. Didn't have time to take the full tour. I just took what I needed and left. I'm looking forward to the blonde *and* the redhead."

He yanked the sack over her head until she could see nothing but blackness.

"Stay down," he warned, climbing over the console and into the driver's seat. "It's a short ride. Then the fun begins."

# CHAPTER
## THIRTY-THREE

Suzanne wasn't the one who was conducting surveillance—not this time.

The FBI and NYPD were crawling around her apartment building nonstop, and there was always one unmarked car parked at the fire hydrant across the street, where the pair of detectives could have a clear view of her apartment.

They weren't even trying to hide the fact that they were keeping close tabs on her.

So, even though she usually handled things herself, this time was different. She and Glen had discussed the strategy he'd come up with. He'd had her contact Bob Farrell, the retired NYPD detective from the Twenty-sixth Precinct who'd provided Auburn State prisonguard Tim Grant with all the useful information Glen had required. Bob was well acquainted with Suzanne. She was the one who'd handed him his payments.

Given Glen's escape and the high-profile attention it was receiving, Bob wasn't thrilled to hear Suzanne's voice—until he heard how much money she'd be paying him for a relatively simple assignment. Then, his tune had changed, and he'd happily accepted.

He used sophisticated binoculars to keep an eye on the Forensic Instincts brownstone. There were more security people there than he could count, and he wasn't stupid enough to place himself in their line of vision. He kept his distance, just scrutinizing the fourth-floor window Suzanne had instructed him to. The blinds were all drawn, so he couldn't make out people. But he could get brief glimpses of activity through the sliver of space between the blinds and the window moldings. Clearly, the room was a bathroom. And the hint of space was enough.

Bob watched, and waited patiently.

He got what he needed at around nine-fifteen.

A light went on. And the silhouette of a male figure filled the narrow sliver of space. The man was walking into the bathroom.

Bob remained as he was, staring intently. Sure enough, condensation began to build up on the windowpane.

He pulled out his burn phone and punched in a text to the phone number he'd been given.

He's in the shower.

Glen Fisher smiled when he read the message. Agent Hutchinson was a creature of habit. Time to use that to his advantage.

He switched screens to his own text and attachment, which he'd readied for delivery an hour ago.

He gave it a quick glance. Then he hit Send.

Casey was thrashing around in her bed to the background noises of Hutch's shower spray when her iPhone went "bing." That meant she had a text message. Sitting up in bed, she scooted over to her nightstand and picked up the phone to check it out.

Unknown sender. No message header.

With a sick feeling in the pit of her stomach, she opened the text.

Your life for hers, it read. Find a way out of there now. Come alone to 55 Ludlow Street, south of Grand. Use the gray steel door. It's unlocked. If you bring any company, your friend dies.

Casey's entire body went rigid. Fingers trembling, she clicked on the attachment.

It was worse than she'd imagined.

Claire was lying on a concrete floor, nude. Her arms were tied over her head, and her legs were separated, each ankle bound to a different post. There was visible bruising around her neck, and a look of stark terror on her face. The red wig was carefully arranged on her head.

God only knew what they'd done to her.

Casey was already in motion, on her feet and dressed in less than two minutes. Hutch wouldn't be a problem; he'd be in the shower another ten or so minutes. The problem was getting out of the building without cluing in a security guard, tripping the alarm system or—most difficult of all—alerting Yoda.

Clandestine wouldn't cut it. She'd have to go for a direct strike.

Glancing over at Hero, who was watching her intently, Casey formulated a quick-and-doable plan.

"Time for a walk, boy," she told him.

His head came up, his soulful eyes brightening with enthusiasm.

"Right answer," she said. "You're going to be my decoy."

With a sideways look at the closed bathroom door, Casey slid her hand behind her nightstand and into the narrow space between the base and the floor. She pulled out her pistol, made sure it was loaded and tucked it in her purse. Then she grabbed Hero's leash and called him over.

He scrambled to her side.

"Good boy," Casey murmured, leashing him up. She paused only long enough to use her iPhone to forward the text message to Hutch. After that, she dropped her phone in her purse, wrapped Hero's leash around her hand and left the bedroom.

By the time Hutch found the text, it would be too late for him to catch up with her. But if the unthinkable were to happen— if she failed in her plan to swap places with Claire, and Fisher decided to kill them both—then Hutch would know what was going on so he could do what needed to be done.

She couldn't let herself think that way. There'd been enough bloodshed because of her. Claire was *not* going to be another notch on Glen Fisher's belt.

Taking a deep breath, Casey forced away thoughts of the painful acts Fisher might already have inflicted on Claire. She walked down the three flights of stairs to the main level, Hero padding beside her. The two security guards looked up as she reached the door.

"Hero needs to go out," she explained. "And I need some air. I thought one of you could keep us company."

Both guards shook their heads. "No air for you, Ms. Woods," one of them said. "You stay inside. I'll walk your dog."

"He's kind of fussy," Casey tried. "I'm not sure he'll do his business with an unfamiliar hand holding his leash."

The guard wasn't budging. "I'm good with dogs. I'm sure I can get him to cooperate. You wait here."

He transferred Hero's leash from Casey's hand to his. Casey wasn't surprised by the refusal. Nor did she argue. She just tensed up, ready and waiting.

She moved the instant the door was open.

Shoving past the startled guards, she dashed down the front steps and took off at warp speed. She could hear Hero's agitated barking and the yelling of the guards behind her. But she didn't turn around and she didn't slow down.

She had to get to Claire.

It was a good two miles away. It was also nine-thirty at night. The streets were quiet. A taxi could make it there faster than her feet.

She stopped a short distance from the office, waited until she spotted a familiar yellow car and then stepped off the curb, holding up her arm. "Taxi!"

The cab pulled over. Casey leaped inside, blurted out the address and begged the driver to hurry.

He took off, heading for Chinatown.

Casey perched at the edge of her seat, her heart racing a mile a minute.

And throughout the ride, she prayed.

Hutch knew something was wrong the moment he stepped out of the bathroom.

There was no sign of Casey. There was no sign of Hero. But he could hear the frenetic barking of the bloodhound coming from downstairs. Simultaneously, he could hear a few of the guards shouting back and forth.

Something had happened.

Hutch yanked on his jeans and a sweater, snatched up his Glock and his cell phone and took off down the stairs.

He nearly collided with a guard in the entranceway. The guy was gripping Hero's leash and staring after his partner, who was racing down the street.

"What the hell is going on?" Hutch demanded.

"She took off," the guard reported. "The minute we opened the door, she bolted."

"Casey *left?* Of her own accord? No one forced her?"

The guard shook his head. "She said her dog needed a walk. She wanted to take him herself. We refused. I was all set to go, when she pushed me aside and ran that way." He pointed.

Hutch shook his head. "That makes no sense. Why would she…" He didn't know what made him do it, but he stuck his hand in his pocket and pulled out his cell phone.

The red message light was flashing.

Thirty seconds later, he knew exactly where Casey had gone and why.

"Shit." He was out the door, waving his arm at the unmarked car that had already pulled over.

"Get in." It was Hutch's partner, Brian, at the wheel, with one of the NYPD task force detectives riding shotgun. Brian glanced from Hutch to the scene that was unfolding in front of him. "We just picked up a couple of burgers. This is what we came back to."

Hutch jumped into the backseat and slammed the door shut. "Start driving. I'll explain on the way. Fifty-five Ludow Street, south of Grand. Hurry. As it is, I'm sure we'll miss her. God-dammit, Casey." He punched his leg in frustration.

Brian didn't ask questions. He just screeched off in the direction Hutch had indicated.

Hutch glanced at his cell phone. He had to let the rest of the FI team know. Especially Ryan. This wasn't going to be pretty.

He texted all the team members, alerting them to a crisis situation and telling them he was about to forward them a text with an attachment.

I'm on my way, he told them. Go to the office. I'll contact you as soon as I have something.

* * *

Casey instructed the cabdriver to stop a half block from her destination.

He pulled over, frowning as he did. "Are you sure you want me to leave you here, lady? This isn't exactly a great place to be late at night."

"I'm sure." Casey stuffed a wad of bills in his hand. "Thanks."

She got out and sprinted to the sidewalk, then strode off at a rapid pace. She anchored her purse against her side, her fingers gripping the barrel of her pistol. She slowed down as she neared the gray steel door, her gaze darting around.

The street was deserted.

She was just reaching for the handle when a dark hooded figure lunged up the cellar stairs adjacent to where Casey stood. He grabbed her, holding her in a vise-grip, while wrenching the pistol from her hand and yanking away her purse.

"Forget it, Red," he muttered. "You lost."

He clapped a chloroform-soaked cloth over her nose and mouth, locking her in place as she fought.

It was a fight not destined to be won.

Casey collapsed, unconscious, and Jack let her sink to the ground. He shoved her pistol in his jacket pocket. Then he rifled her purse to make sure her iPhone was inside. Yup. There it was.

Leaving the phone in her purse, he tossed the whole thing in a nearby Dumpster and returned to Casey's crumpled body.

He scooped her up, carried her to his car and threw her inside.

Turning on the engine, he texted Glen.

Package on its way.

# CHAPTER
## THIRTY-FOUR

Hutch was out of the car before Brian had come to a complete stop.

*"Casey!"* Hutch hit the pavement running, yelling Casey's name as he grabbed the steel door handle and yanked on it. *"Casey!"* He pounded on the door, then pressed his ear against it, listening intently to see if there was any sound.

Nothing.

He turned around, his head whipping to one side and then the other as he studied the deserted area. No sign of anyone.

"Hutch?" Brian was squatting down, holding a damp handkerchief. He brought it close to his nose and took a sniff. "Chloroform."

"Shit." Hutch's heart sank, even though he wasn't surprised. He knew Fisher wasn't going to keep Casey in a warehouse whose address she'd probably passed along. This had just been the capture point.

Nearby, a cell phone rang.

Hutch raised his head. "That's Casey's ring tone." He followed the sound. "It's coming from the Dumpster." He hurried over and rummaged around in the garbage until he found Casey's purse.

He pulled out the cell phone. Ryan's caller ID.

Hutch punched on the phone. "Neither of them is here," he informed Ryan. "They dumped Casey's purse and cell phone in a Dumpster. We found a chloroformed handkerchief on the sidewalk."

"Fisher has her." There was a note of panic in Ryan's voice. "Fisher has them both."

"Yeah." Hutch rubbed his forehead. "And we don't have much time to find them."

"Are you coming back?"

"We'll check out the area. Then I'll head back to the office."

"Bring the phone with you," Ryan said. "Maybe I can find something else on it—anything that could tell us where she is."

"I'll bring the whole purse. But we both know it's not going to do us any good."

"What will?" There was a note of desperation in Ryan's voice.

"I have an idea."

Patrick got the phone call as he was driving in from New Jersey. He tensed when he saw from caller ID that it was Hutch.

"You found something?" he asked.

"Not a thing." The road noise said that Hutch was back in the car. "But we've got a couple of hours, tops." He didn't need to specify what he was referring to. They both knew he meant until Claire and Casey were raped and killed. "I came up with a plan. But I need your help."

"Name it."

"It's time to call in the favor your friend Captain Sharp owes you. I need him to assemble a SWAT team—now. Can you make it happen?"

"I'll find a way. What's it for?"

"I'll explain in the office. How long until you get there?"

"Twenty minutes."


Hutch burst into FI's second-floor conference room.

Ryan, Patrick and Marc were all there, poised and ready.

"What's the plan?" Ryan demanded.

"I've got Horace Sharp on high alert." Patrick waved his phone in the air. "What am I telling him?"

Hutch shot a quick glance at Ryan. "I assume your cell phone monitoring system is working?"

"System working," Yoda reported. "No calls made or received."

Hutch acknowledged Yoda's status update with a nod. "I want to scare Suzanne Fisher into making a call to her husband. If I can do that, I'm counting on your cell phone interceptor to locate the place where Glen Fisher is taking the call."

"No problem," Ryan said.

"Good." Hutch turned back to Patrick. "Here's what you're telling Captain Sharp. He should deploy his SWAT team to Suzanne's building. We need him to send six SWAT members, a truck and a bunch of patrol cars. The scenario has to look pure Hollywood, right down to the flashing lights and squawking radios—the complete opposite of a real tactical SWAT deployment, where the element of surprise is crucial. In this case, we want the target to *know* they're coming for her."

"Got it." Patrick was already punching in the number.

"This has to work, Hutch." Ryan looked like death. "You know what Fisher will do to Claire and Casey."

"What I *know* is that we've got to stop him."

★ ★ ★

Suzanne was trying to focus on her future in Dubai when pandemonium erupted.

She heard the sirens as they approached. Minutes later, she saw the reflections of the red lights bouncing off her window shades. She froze. Heart pounding, she crept over to the window, knelt down and eased the shade aside so she could peer out.

The area was a beehive of law enforcement activity. Suzanne turned her head all the way to the left and then to the right. The entire street was blocked off to vehicular and pedestrian traffic at both ends. A dozen police cars with red lights flashing were screeching up the street, stopping right outside.

Panic surged through her as the commotion intensified. A large black truck cut through the bevy of patrol cars and parked in front of her building. Six NYPD officers jumped out, donning bulletproof vests. Three of them hurried across the street and entered the building directly across from Suzanne's. The other three ran behind her building to the courtyard.

Ten minutes later, laser beams aimed at and shot through every window of her apartment, sweeping the entire room as if looking for a target.

Suzanne sank to the floor. After another two minutes, she heard the sound of police radios emanating from the hallway just outside her door. She flattened herself on the floor and crawled into a corner like a terrified rat.

The scene commander's voice was loud as he yelled into his radio, "Green light! Green light! Acknowledge!"

"Alpha ready," came the radio response from her hallway.

"Stay down, you idiot," hissed one of the cops. "Didn't you hear the sniper say 'ready'? Captain Sharp just authorized a kill shot."

That was all Suzanne needed to hear.

Crawling frantically across the floor, she reached up and fumbled on the coffee table until she found her burn phone.

She punched in Glen's number.

One ring. Two.

Glen picked up on the third ring.

"Why the hell are you calling me?" He was clearly livid.

Hysterically, Suzanne blurted out everything that was taking place. "They're going to kill me, Glen! I heard them! Please, do something!"

"Calm down, you stupid bitch. They don't want you. They want me. Now hang up before they can trace this call."

Glen practically threw the phone across the room. "Fucking idiot."

He whipped around, his blazing stare finding Claire, who was lying in the same position she'd been in for hours, naked and bound.

She cringed as he approached her.

"Scared? Good." Glen squatted down and gripped her neck with his hand. He smiled when he felt the racing pulse at her throat. He squeezed—just enough to make her whimper in pain. Then he shoved her aside. "You're a good stress reliever. But the prize is on its way."

Ryan, Hutch, Patrick and Marc were gathered in Ryan's lair, tense and waiting to see if their ruse had worked.

Ryan nearly jumped out of his chair when Yoda announced, "Call traced. Do you wish to hear the recording?"

*"Now!"* Ryan screamed.

"Call from 917-555-3644 to 917-555-6802," Yoda dutifully responded. "Message as follows..." He then replayed the terse conversation between the Fishers.

Ryan ignored Suzanne's hysterical voice and Glen's volatile response. "That's it," he said in excitement. "That's Fisher's number." He turned to Patrick. "How long will an NYPD warrant take?"

"A couple of hours, if we're lucky," Patrick replied.

"On an expedited basis? With Casey's and Claire's lives on the line? You've got to be kidding me!"

"It's close to midnight, Ryan. We have to wake up some judge and get him to agree we have just cause. Or do I need to remind you that we obtained this information illegally?"

"Fuck that."

"'That' is an ambiguous term, Ryan," Yoda said. "What are we going to fuck?"

"Everyone, that's who," Ryan yelled. "I'm not sitting on my ass for some sleeping judge to wake up while Fisher's doing God knows what to Claire and Casey. It's time I ran this show."

He crossed over and grabbed some black clothes and his gear bag, which he began to stuff with items he selected from his work area.

"Yoda, check the network used by Glen's burn phone," he commanded.

A few seconds passed. "Call was received using Verizon Wireless network."

"Deploy Tracer on call destination," Ryan ordered. "Operational mode is Stealth. Resources Maximum. Target is Verizon Wireless."

Tracer was a hacking script of Ryan's that would penetrate a cell phone provider's massive network of towers and use its own computer systems to triangulate the location of a cell phone, given its phone number and approximate time the call was made. Stealth insured that no one could trace the illegal hack to Ryan and FI. Maximum resources would simultaneously launch a denial-of-service attack at Verizon's network, using a worldwide network of zombie computers at Ryan's disposal, set to divert all of Verizon's security systems and resources to repelling the fake assault, letting Tracer complete its urgent mission undetected.

"Tracer deployed," Yoda confirmed. "Mode is Stealth with Maximum resources. Target is Verizon Wireless."

"Good." Ryan turned back to the other men. "Hutch, you and Patrick can excuse yourselves. Marc and I will handle this."

"I'm in," Hutch insisted, refusing to leave. "I'll deal with the fallout later."

"I'm in, too." Patrick's features were taut. "I'm an FI team member, first and foremost. We protect our own."

"Okay." Ryan nodded. He didn't seem all that surprised. But he did seem a lot less pissed. "Then it's time to get ready. We move as soon as Yoda gives me my answer."

The four men prepped for an assault to rescue Casey and Claire. They all found and changed into dark clothing, checked their weapons and packed their tactical gear bags.

Yoda still hadn't come back with an answer.

Ryan glanced over at Hutch and decided to do the guy a favor. He faked a cell phone call, sending it from Glen Fisher's burn phone to Hutch's.

Five feet away, Hutch grabbed his phone when it rang. "Hutchinson."

"Now you just received a call from Glen Fisher telling you where you can find Casey's body," Ryan said. "Your ass is covered with the Bureau."

Hutch gave him a tight smile. "Thanks. But it wouldn't have mattered."

"I know. That's why I did it."

Yoda interrupted their conversation, supplying them with the critical information. "Tracer has found the phone. Location is

275 South 2nd Street, Brooklyn. Accuracy is within three hundred wavelengths, based on the cell phone frequency."

Ryan's head snapped up. "Yoda, I need distance, not wavelengths."

"Fifty meters, Ryan, as you requested."

"That's all I needed." Ryan grabbed his gear. "Yoda, delete all traces of what went on here this evening—down to every last communication."

"Deletion under way," Yoda responded.

Ryan turned to the other three men. "Come on. We're out of here."

# CHAPTER
## THIRTY-FIVE

Jack entered the warehouse through the back door, an unconscious Casey slung over his shoulder.

"Here. As promised."

"What took so long?" Glen demanded. "You were only driving a couple of miles. It's been over an hour."

"There was an accident. I couldn't get around it. No worries. I just gave Sleeping Beauty some more chloroform. She'll be out of it for a while."

"I want her awake."

"She will be. Hang in there." Jack bent down and dumped Casey's limp body unceremoniously on the concrete floor.

Glen gazed at her. He couldn't help smiling. Finally. Lying at his feet. At his mercy. She was all his. He leaned over and fingered a lock of her red hair. This was going to be every bit as satisfying as he'd expected.

"Hey," Jack said, watching his uncle's irked reaction turn into a pleased one. "Is it time for my reward?" He jerked his thumb in Claire's direction.

"Not yet." Glen waved him away. "Not until I've had my fill of Casey Woods. I've waited a hell of a lot longer than you have. Plus, I don't want the psychic screaming and distracting me, or ruining the mood I have in mind. You can have her later. Red can watch—and know that it's all her fault and there's not a damn thing she can do about it."

Jack rolled his eyes. More waiting. He wanted to punch his uncle in the gut. But he wasn't going to take him on—not at this point. It wasn't worth the hell that would ensue. He'd waited this long. He'd wait a little longer.

But not happily.

"Fine," he said in a voice that clearly sounded pissed. "I'm going out to Carmine's for a thin Sicilian." He paused to wink at Claire, who was staring at Casey. "I'll be back for my dessert—a blondie."

As soon as Jack left, Glen went to work. He began to yank off Casey's layers of clothes, which only took a few minutes. She was a petite woman, and it required very little juggling to get her as naked as he wanted her.

That done, he dragged her over to an area of support beams, and stretched her out on her back. Pulling her arms above her head, he anchored them around one of the beams. Grabbing some of the rope he had nearby, he bound her wrists tightly together.

Shifting his attention downward, he couldn't resist pausing to eye every inch of her body—especially the part that declared her a natural redhead. Then he got to work on her legs. He spread them wide, tying each ankle to a support beam, set about five feet apart.

He sat back on his haunches and admired his handiwork. It was so tempting to do something now—but there was no way he was sacrificing the fear factor for a quick lay. He wanted her awake—and utterly terrified.

Still…he couldn't resist touching her, just for a second.

He laid his palm on her stomach, let it glide downward.

Claire gave a sharp cry.

"Shut up!" Glen commanded, rising to his feet. The mood was broken.

It was that damned blonde bitch's fault.

Glen strode over to Claire, fists clenched at his sides, and glared down at her. She cringed with terror. He ignored it, kneeling down and locking his hands around her throat.

"Do you want to feel what's going to happen if you make another sound?" he asked.

He didn't wait for an answer.

His grip tightened, cutting off her air supply as he applied painful pressure to her neck. He held it that way for fifteen seconds, pleased when he felt Claire struggling to breathe and to free herself.

Abruptly, he released her.

"Now, shut your goddamned mouth. Worry about your own life, not hers."

Claire continued to gasp, heaving air into her lungs. Red welts in the shape of hand marks—some of which had already been visible on her delicate skin from his previous assault—intensified, and were now far more pronounced than they'd been before.

Glen scrutinized her and decided his tactics had had the desired effect.

He turned his back on her and walked over to Casey.

Pulling up a chair, he straddled it and stared at his prize.

She'd be waking up soon enough.

★ ★ ★

Marc pulled the van around to the front of the Forensic Instincts office and screeched up to the curb. Hutch and Patrick tossed their gear bags into the backseat and climbed in. Ryan hopped into the passenger seat with his.

"Two seventy-five South 2nd Street, Brooklyn, New York," he instructed the voice-activated GPS on the dashboard.

The GPS displayed the most direct route with a bright blue line.

Marc glanced at the screen, then floored the pedal and took off.

As they drove, Hutch took out his cell phone and called the New York field office. He reported his supposed anonymous tip. The Bureau agreed to dispatch a team ASAP, but there was no way they'd arrive in time to save Casey and Claire. Not given the immediacy of the crisis.

They gave Hutch the green light to go ahead.

Ryan was using his computer skills to zero in on a local map of the area. Hutch worked with him until they had the diagram they needed.

Marc stopped at a red light and analyzed the diagram. The back entrance to the warehouse was on South 1st Street. It was clearly more deserted, and had easier access, plus the element of surprise would be in their favor. The only thing separating them from the building was a barbed-wire fence. Medium height. Easily scaled.

That gave Marc enough info to lay out assault plans. He, Hutch and Ryan would enter the warehouse through the back entrance on South 1st Street. Patrick would drive around to the front of the building on South 2nd and keep watch, just in case Glen and Jack Fisher tried to escape via the main entrance.

Either way, the bastards weren't going anywhere.

★ ★ ★

Casey stirred, wincing at the dull pounding inside her head. She felt woozy, as if she'd had too much to drink. Her bed was hurting her back. It felt as hard as a brick. And she couldn't seem to make her body work. She wasn't sure why.

She was so tired. She should recall the reason, but whatever it was, it eluded her. Dazed, she felt her head droop to one side, and sleep began to take over again. All she needed was a little more rest. Then she'd pop a couple of aspirin for her headache and get back to work.

She felt troubled as she drifted off. There was something she should remember. She wished she knew what. It was important.

But it slipped away as she lost consciousness.

Glen noticed the minute Casey started to come to. He perked up, then scowled when she faded back into unconsciousness. Damn Jack for giving her the extra chloroform. Glen wanted her awake—*now.*

He wasn't going to wait much longer. He'd smack her awake if he had to, rape her until the pain brought her around.

The thought of it made him smile. He didn't have the chance to play out his fantasy.

He'd barely started getting aroused when Casey moved her head again, this time in a more pronounced manner.

Casey let out a low moan. Pounding. Her head was pounding. She tried to reach for her temples, to rub them, but her arms wouldn't move. They were stuck. And she was freezing. Where were her blankets? And why was there such a funny smell in her nose and a bad taste in her mouth?

Something was very wrong.

Slowly, she cracked her eyes open. She wasn't in her bedroom.

Where the hell was she?

She blinked once, twice, and realized there was a man sitting across from her, staring down at her. Painful or not, she gave her head a slight shake.

Her vision cleared.

The man was Glen Fisher.

The room was a warehouse.

"Finally," Fisher said, visibly irritated. "It's about time you woke up. I was about to help the process along."

Woke up?

Memory crashed through Casey's mind like an avalanche. The text message. The warehouse that was a decoy. The man in black. The handkerchief. That smell—it was chloroform. He'd knocked her out with it. She'd come to in a car. He'd dosed her with it again.

She was a captive.

She tried to move again, this time more vigorously, but with the same lack of success. She stopped, gazed down at herself and an icy chill shot up her spine.

Dear God. She was naked. Open. Exposed. Arms and legs bound. Totally at his mercy.

She shut her eyes against the image, gritted her teeth to bite back the cry of fear that lodged in her throat.

"Is it all coming back to you now?" Glen asked with a wry grin.

Casey's eyes opened. "Actually, yes." She was stunned at her own ability to feign control. Was that really her voice, steady and even? How was that possible when she'd never been so horrifyingly afraid in her life? So afraid that the whole situation felt out-of-body, surreal, like a nightmare she'd force herself to awaken from at any moment?

It must have been, because Glen gave an admiring grunt.

"Impressive. You're one strong, feisty bitch. I'm glad you also have a good memory. It'll mean less to explain."

"No explanation necessary. You pulled this off well. Congratulations."

He looked pleased, like he was enjoying their sparring match. "I appreciate the accolades. What's more, I deserve them. You've made this one hell of a challenge, Red."

"That was my goal." Casey twisted in her bonds, trying to see past Glen and to find her friend. "Where's Claire?"

"Right over there." Glen stepped out of Casey's line of sight.

Claire looked frail and exhausted. All her limbs were secured with ropes the same way Casey's were. And there were ugly red welts around her neck.

"Claire?" Casey called out. "Are you okay?"

Claire raised her head a little and managed to nod.

She was definitely *not* okay.

"You choked her," Casey said, staring at the bright red welts on Claire's neck. "What else have you done to her?"

"Your psychic friend has been a perfect outlet for anger release," Glen told Casey. "But she hasn't enjoyed the benefits of our hospitality yet."

"Does that mean you haven't raped her?" Casey couldn't help it. She blurted out her question before she could stop herself. It was stupid. Her fear for Claire was something Glen was going to feed on.

Sure enough, he smiled—a cruel, evil smile. "It means I'd rather have you awake to watch when I do. Mental torture for you will be an added bonus."

*Thank God,* Casey thought. *She'd bought Claire a short reprieve.*

This time she was careful to keep her sheer relief from showing.

"Where are we?" she asked instead.

"What difference does that make?"

"I want to know."

Glen shook his head, more amusement twisting his lips. "Still hoping for a rescue? Not going to happen. Your boyfriend and your team have no idea where we took you. End of the road, Red."

Casey readdressed the current most pressing issue. "Then why can't you let Claire go? She's served her purpose. She got me to you. I'm the real deal—a redhead and the woman you most hate. Pull one of those black sacks over her head, and drop her off somewhere."

Glen leaned forward menacingly. "You're in no position to negotiate."

"I'm not negotiating. I'm being practical. Once you're done with me, I'm sure you plan to leave the country. So why ruin your perfect track record? You haven't had a victim who wasn't a redhead since you were a novice, like with Jan and Holly."

"True." He considered that and shrugged. "You're playing me. It's not working. But the fact is I don't really care what happens to your psychic friend. When the time comes, I'll see who I'm feeling more amenable toward, Jack or her." He jerked his thumb in Claire's direction. "For whatever reason, my nephew wants her."

*You and your nephew can both go to hell,* Casey thought.

Glen began pacing around the room. "Where the hell is that asshole?" he muttered. He glanced at his watch. "I'm giving him five more minutes. That's it."

Casey knew what that meant. She had to keep Glen occupied. It was the only way to buy enough time for her team to orchestrate a rescue. On the other hand, she couldn't be too obvious. He'd recognize mind games. Glen Fisher was nothing if not smart.

"By the way, I understand why you only want redheads," Casey told him.

Fisher stopped pacing and turned around. "What are you talking about?"

"Colleen McCoy. Your redheaded teacher. I know about her."

Rage contorted Glen's features. "You don't know shit."

He stalked over and squatted down, grabbing Casey's face with one hand. His vice-grip felt as if it was going to snap her jaw. But she refused to cry out. Tears of pain filled her eyes, but she stared Fisher down, feverishly praying she hadn't pushed him over the edge.

There was a glazed, faraway look in his eyes, and Casey knew he was remembering.

"That perverted bitch," he said, lost in his memories.

He was a fucking kid. Fourteen years old. A horny adolescent who'd never had sex before. She was a twenty-eight-year-old woman with a body to die for and an appetite for students. It had been easy to seduce him.

She'd taken him to the grounds behind the baseball diamond and touched him everywhere—with her hands, her mouth. She'd gotten him so hot that he'd do anything to get laid. But she'd made him wait. Made him beg. Hold off until he was in agony. And when she'd finally straddled him, taken him inside her, she'd clamped her legs around him, held him in place like a prisoner. She'd controlled everything, riding him hard, taking his hands and wrapping them around her neck, making him squeeze until she was gasping for breath.

That was when she'd climaxed. He wasn't allowed to come until she had. If he did, she punished him, kept her body from him like some kind of treasured prize.

He was addicted. He did anything she wanted. Anything so he could have that incredible release.

He'd literally been her slave.

Never again.

In one harsh motion, Glen released Casey's face. He groped inside his jeans pocket, pulled out a knife and flipped open the blade.

"Just like the first time, Red," he said, referring to that night in Tompkins Square Park when he'd taken her at knifepoint. "Only this time I'm going to slit your fucking throat after I rape and choke you."

He reached for the front of his jeans, unbuttoning them and unzipping the fly. He used his knees to stretch her legs as far apart as the beams would allow them to go.

He was just groping inside his pants to free himself, when the front door opened.

"Pizza delivery," a man's voice called out.

"*Goddammit, not now!*" Glen yelled.

Casey's breath was coming in harsh, shallow pants, and her body was shaking with shock and fear. But she recognized the voice of the man who'd just walked in. She couldn't quite place it.

Whoever it was had saved her life.

She angled her head to see him.

"Robbie." Relief surged through her as she focused on the pizza delivery guy who'd found the bloodstains in Deirdre's dorm room. "Quick," she rasped. "Help us. This is what happened to Deirdre Grimes. Call the police. Hurry!"

Robbie set down the pizza box and studied her. He didn't seem horrified by what was going on, or terrified by Glen's outburst.

What the hell was the matter with him?

"Robbie? Did you hear me?" Casey asked frantically.

"I heard you," he replied. "I was just thinking that it was a lot different with Deirdre. Quicker. Less fanfare. Then again, less investment." He shrugged. "I brought you half a pie," he told Glen. "It would've been nice if you'd waited for me before you started the party."

Glen's head came up. The crazed look in his eyes was fading. "You were gone too long."

"Looks to me like I timed it pretty well. And what's with the knife?"

"Instant replay for me. But I've got one for you, too, okay?" Glen sat back on his haunches. "Grab a chair. You can watch round one."

"Watch?" Casey whispered in helpless incomprehension. She was still staring at Robbie. "You're part of this? I don't understand. You called in the other crime."

"That was just me being clever," Robbie responded with a smug grin. "I grabbed Deirdre's cell phone when I stuffed her in the duffel bag and took her. I used it to call in her order. Her number shows up at the pizza place three times a week, so everyone there knows it. Johnny took her order that night. He asked if she wanted the usual. I just said 'yup' in a high voice. That place is so noisy, you can't make out a thing, anyway. Johnny said the pie would be there in thirty minutes. Great timing. I snuck back, put Deirdre's cell phone on her desk and left. Johnny called me to pick up the delivery. I showed up with the pizza, knocked and—what do you know—I found the door ajar. I went in, saw the blood, called 9-1-1. Pretty smart, huh?" He pulled over the second chair and straddled it. "All set for the show."

"Oh, my God," Casey whispered, past fear and into hysteria. "You killed those women? Why? *Why?*"

Both men chuckled, and Glen gestured at the younger man. "Meet my nephew, Jack. He delivers a great pizza—and a great dead body. He's multitalented."

Casey stared. "Robbie…is Jack?"

"Yup," Jack confirmed. "A little time away, a little plastic surgery and a whole new identity. Kept me safe from the mob, and eventually I was able to help out my uncle Glen. Till you got him thrown in prison. Then I took over. I resented the hell out of you at first. But, in the long run, it gave me the chance of a lifetime."

"All along, it was you." Casey processed that as best she could. "The phone calls, the rapes, the murders. You knew all the victims from your pizza deliveries and you exploited that fact to…" She broke off, too far beyond overdrive to even speak.

That suited Jack fine.

"Enough conversation," he said, gesturing to his uncle. "Like I said, now that I'm here, let's get this show on the road. I can't wait to get my hands on these two." He shot Claire a lascivious look. "Especially you, Ms. Psychic. You're gonna be worth waiting for."

# CHAPTER
## THIRTY-SIX

The Forensic Instincts van pulled up on South 1st Street, behind the building where Casey and Claire were being held.

Everyone but Patrick hooked their gear bags over their shoulders and got out of the car. Patrick drove away, making two successive right turns until he could pull over and park diagonally across the street from the warehouse's front door.

He punched in Ryan's cell number. "Ready," he told his teammate.

"Then so are we." Ryan disconnected the call. "Patrick's in place," he informed Hutch and Marc. "Marc, lead the way."

Marc had already kicked into navy SEAL mode. He moved forward and scaled the barbed-wire fence, dropping down on the other side. Squatting low, he ran up to the building, glancing inside each of the windows and peering through the crack between the shade and the frame to assess the lay of the land.

After a thorough inspection, he waved to Hutch and Ryan to follow. They quickly scaled the fence and joined him.

"We're at an entrance that's next to a bathroom," Marc said. "The entrance and the bathroom are deserted. Then there's a short hallway, also deserted, with a bigger room at the other end. Fisher and his nephew are in that bigger room. One of them is sitting down. The other is crouched over Casey." A pause. "Shit. He's got a knife at her throat."

"Where's Claire?" Ryan demanded. "Can you see her?"

"Yeah. She's not far away from Casey. She's still in the same position she was in the text photo."

"Still tied up?"

Marc nodded.

"Shit."

"No time for freaking out," Hutch told him. "We've got a job to do."

"I'll pick the door lock," Marc said. "We'll stay low and ease past the bathroom, then press ourselves flat against the interior wall and move partway down the hall. From there, I'll recon the big room and figure out the best assault vectors." Marc glanced at Hutch. "We'd better be prepared to storm the place if the door is alarmed."

"Understood," Hutch said. He knew that Fisher holding a knife at Casey's throat created exigent circumstances. Fortunately, that meant the FBI's deadly force policy and his heart were aligned. But the truth was that, with Casey's life on the line, it wouldn't have mattered.

"If all else fails, I have a backup plan." Ryan patted his gear bag.

Marc's lips twitched. "Of course you do."

Moving forward, Marc picked the lock and slowly opened the back door.

Silence. No alarm. Crisis one averted.

Relieved, the three men inched into the dark, narrow hallway. Flattening themselves against the wall, they edged along, trying to find a clear line of sight into the bigger room.

They found one a quarter of the way down. But what they saw stopped them from acting.

Jack had dragged Claire over until she was perpendicular to Casey. He clearly wanted her close by to witness Casey being violated. He was kneeling beside her, holding a knife at her throat and watching as Glen leaned over Casey.

"Dammit," Marc growled. He'd already reached for his holster. Now his hand paused on the handle of his pistol. "The four of them are too close together. We can't risk hitting one of the women."

Hutch agreed. These had to be kill shots. Marc could definitely make one. Hutch was a "probably." And probably wasn't good enough.

"They won't kill them until they've raped and tortured them," he said. "Which is about to happen. We've got to act now."

"It's time for my idea," Ryan said. "I can split them up. Fast. Trust me."

"As always," Marc stated simply, stepping back.

Silently, Ryan opened his gear bag and extracted a gray mechanical mouse. "Meet Jerry."

"Jerry." Hutch stared at him in disbelief. "Are you fucking kidding me?"

"Nope." Ryan placed Jerry on the floor. Using his iPhone, he drove the creature silently into the room where the Fishers were holding Casey and Claire. "I'll use Jerry to create a diversion." He gave Marc and Hutch a quick explanation of his intentions. "Just let me know when it's time."

If the situation hadn't been so dire, Marc and Hutch would

have burst out laughing. As it was, they huddled behind Ryan and discussed assignments. Hutch would take out Glen. Marc would take care of Jack. Ryan would put Jerry into action on Marc's signal.

Ever so cautiously, Marc and Hutch crept down the unlit hall, and stopped several steps from the narrow doorway to avoid detection. Hutch crouched down. Marc remained standing. This way, they were out of each other's lines of sight. Ryan stayed where he was, gripping his iPhone and watching Marc intently.

Marc turned and signaled Ryan with his tactical flashlight.

Nodding to himself, Ryan typed Send on the command line, selected the MP3 file in the window that popped up and depressed the OK button on his Jerry Mouse app. Seconds later, he received an acknowledgment in the status window that the MP3 file was received.

Using a flashlight app on his iPhone to illuminate himself, Ryan displayed a thumbs-up to Marc, indicating that Jerry was ready to cause a commotion. Signal received, Hutch and Marc drew their Glocks, turning on the pistols' laser sights. Hutch tapped Marc's leg to indicate that he was ready.

Again, Marc used his tactical flashlight to signal Ryan.

That was all Ryan needed to set Jerry in motion.

He typed Move=Big Figure 8 and Play @ Volume=10, and depressed the OK button to confirm. The mechanical creature zoomed into the center of the room and began making large figure eights. Simultaneously the "Scooby-Doo" theme song screeched from Jerry's tiny, embedded speaker.

Utter confusion ensued.

Glen and Jack gave starts of surprise, and then staggered to their feet. Focused on their impending sexual gratification, they were thrown completely off balance. They searched the area in

bewilderment, trying to find the cause of the unexpected car-
toon theme song.

At that exact moment, Marc and Hutch burst into the room,
pistols raised.

"FBI!" Hutch shouted.

For a split second, bewilderment gave way to terror in the
murderers' eyes. Laser pointers found their marks on each man's
forehead. Marc and Hutch fired in unison. The impact of the
.40 caliber bullets sent them reeling backward and away from
Casey and Claire.

Their switchblades clattered to the ground.

Glen and Jack were dead.

Hutch and Marc rushed forward, removing their jackets, and
covered up the two naked women.

"All clear," Marc called out.

"Yeah, and for the love of God, turn off that goddamned
thing," Hutch added. He was holding Casey's face between his
palms, letting her feel his warmth, pausing to kiss her and whisper that everything was going to be all right.

Ryan took the hint. Jerry fell silent and ceased his frenetic
dance.

Having scooped up the mechanical mouse, Ryan ran inside,
straight over to Claire, dropping to his knees beside her. "Hey,
Claire-voyant," he murmured, his voice unsteady. "I'll have you
out of here in a minute."

Claire nodded, tears trickling down her cheeks.

Marc took out his Buck tactical knife, flipped open the blade
and sliced the ropes tying each woman down, until they were
free. He then intercepted a gesture from Hutch and acted on it.

He whipped out handcuffs, went straight to Glen's and Jack's
lifeless bodies and cuffed their hands—standard FBI procedure
that he well-remembered and was happy to do for his friend.

"It's over, sweetheart." Hutch cradled Casey's quaking body in his arms. "We're going to call an ambulance and get you to the hospital right away."

Casey shook her head. "He didn't rape me," she managed to say. "He was about to. But you stopped him. And Claire—they choked and traumatized her. But I was slotted to go first. So we don't need the hospital, not unless Claire's injuries are worse than I think."

"No," Claire said adamantly from a foot away. Her voice broke and she started to cry again. "I'll need to talk to someone—a professional. I'm a mess. But no hospital—please."

"Okay, okay," Ryan agreed at once. "No hospital. We'll just get you home and into a warm bath—with your favorite lavender bath crystals. How's that?"

Claire smiled through her tears. "That would be perfect."

"I'm going out front," Marc announced, already in motion. He wanted to give the women time to dress and to pull themselves together. And he knew they were in the best of hands. "I'll do a sweep," he said over his shoulder. "Then I'll call Patrick and tell him all clear. I'll also intercept law enforcement, who'll be showing up any minute. Anything they need to know right away, they can hear from me. The rest of the interviews can come later."

"Thanks, Marc," Hutch said quietly.

"No problem." Marc turned around for a second. "By the way, nice shot. You would've made a great SEAL."

A corner of Hutch's mouth lifted. "And you would've made a great cop."

# CHAPTER
## THIRTY-SEVEN

*Two weeks later*

Mike's Tavern was a good, old-fashioned Tribeca bar. Family-owned, it had been around for decades. Its well-worn surroundings and reasonable prices kept loyal patrons coming back time and again.

Ryan and Marc had pushed two tables together to accommodate both of them, plus Patrick, Hutch and Captain Sharp. They'd all been there for a few beers, trying to unwind after weeks of questioning, debriefing and paperwork.

"It's getting late," Captain Sharp said, pushing back his chair and standing up. "My wife's holding dinner." He clapped Patrick on the shoulder, then indicated the entire group. "The tab's yours," he told them. "It's the least you can do. My butt's still sore from being ripped a new asshole about this escapade. No more cowboy operations in my city, gentlemen."

"Bullshit," Patrick countered. "You and your brass buddies were all smiles at that press conference. Even your frenemies at the FBI looked happy. I almost puked at the public display of ass-kissing."

The other men's jaws dropped, and four pairs of eyes stared at Patrick. His blunt outburst and colorful expletives were so uncharacteristic of the "by-the-book" guy—even with three beers in him—that it shocked the hell out of them.

Then they all burst out laughing.

"Shit, I wish I'd gotten that on video," Ryan said. "As it is, everyone's gonna think I either made it up or said it myself."

"I'll vouch for you," Marc assured him.

Ryan grunted. "A lot of good that'll do. Your rep is almost as sketchy as mine."

Horace Sharp shook his head, still laughing. "I'm outnumbered and outgunned. Time to leave with my dignity intact." He leaned over, picked up his beer to polish it off and headed out, waving as he left.

Marc turned to Hutch as soon as the four of them were alone. "How did your debriefing go?"

Hutch shrugged. "I survived. Even with exigent circumstances on my side, my boss pointed out the blatant gaps in my report. He lectured me about policy and procedures. Despite all that, he had to admit I didn't violate the Bureau's deadly force policy. So I'm okay. Still, I guess I'll never make ADIC."

Everyone chuckled at the double entendre. They all knew that the acronym stood for Assistant Director in Charge—pronounced "a dick"—a high rank in the FBI hierarchy. They also knew how Hutch meant it.

Hutch inclined his head in Marc's direction. "I take it you're okay with the law enforcement community?"

"As okay as I'll ever be." Marc was clearly fine with that.

"Cops couldn't argue that the kill shots were necessary. Glen and Jack were about to stab Casey and Claire with their switchblades. So we took them out. Period."

"They were damned lucky there was a former navy SEAL on the scene." Ryan jumped to Marc's defense. "Your strategy was perfect. So was your shot—and Hutch's. You made the headlines read a lot nicer for them than the alternative would have. They should be grateful."

"I doubt Forensic Instincts is ever going to be getting medals from the authorities," Hutch said, taking another healthy swallow of beer. "But don't kid yourself. Right now, the Feds and the NYPD are counting their blessings that you were there. Two minutes later..." He shuddered. "Let's not even go there. All that matters is that Glen and Jack Fisher are dead. Suzanne Fisher went to pieces once the cops broke the news to her. She's spilling her guts and filling in all the missing blanks. Enough said."

"Consider the subject closed." At that particular minute, Ryan didn't give a shit what the authorities thought of them. No matter how many boundaries were stretched, in this case the end more than justified the means.

His attention was drawn to the doorway as he spotted Casey and Claire walking into the bar. They were the important ones to consider right now. They'd been through hell. The case had taken its toll—big-time. Their recovery was all that mattered.

Ryan motioned for them to come over. They saw him, and made their way to where the guys were already seated.

It didn't take a genius to see that their eyes were red and puffy, and their cheeks were streaked with tears.

"How did it go?" Ryan asked, grasping Claire's hand.

"A lot of crying today," she responded, her voice watery. "The doctor says we're making progress, but recovery from this kind of trauma will take a long time." Her hand went to her neck, and she rubbed the area that was still sore from Glen's brutal choke holds.

Casey didn't look much better. Even with the relief of knowing both her tormenters were dead, she was perpetually jumpy and nervous, and her nightmares were bad. Hutch had used a chunk of his vacation time to stay up here in Manhattan with her. That was helping.

There was a long emotional road yet to travel, and both women knew it. But they also knew they'd reach the other end, never the same but able to move on.

"It's important that Claire and I do this in joint sessions," Casey said quietly. "The psychiatrist agrees. Claire and I went through the ordeal together, so together we can help each other heal."

"Yes, you can. And you will." Hutch sounded adamant. He reached up to caress Casey's cheek. "Just don't forget you've got a powerful support team."

"We know." She gave him a small smile. "That means everything, to Claire and to me." A pause. "Almost as much as the fact that you saved our lives."

Marc rose and pulled over another chair, which he wriggled in next to the one Captain Sharp had vacated. Everyone shifted to make room, and Casey and Claire sat down and joined their friends.

Before returning to his own seat, Marc signaled to Mike, the bar owner, who was tight with the entire Forensic Instincts team.

A few minutes later, he appeared at their table, personally delivering two mojitos, one of his signature drinks. "On the house," he announced, placing the glasses in front of the women.

Casey and Claire were delighted, as Mike's mojitos were everybody's favorites.

Hutch raised his glass, waiting for everyone else at the table to raise theirs and to join in the group toast. "To togetherness," he said simply.

A look of friendship and understanding passed through the group as they silently counted their blessings and found strength in one another.

"Togetherness," they echoed in chorus.

★ ★ ★ ★ ★

# ACKNOWLEDGMENTS

With deepest thanks to my very own "core four":

To my family—my emotional and creative rocks—without whom I wouldn't have survived the past months, much less written a novel to be proud of.

And to three incomparable professionals, whose input I always trust, and who work tirelessly with me, no matter how many questions I ask or scenarios I pose:

Angela Bell, Public Affairs Specialist, FBI Office of Public Affairs

Former SSA James McNamara, FBI Behavioral Analysis Unit 4

Detective Mike Oliver, retired NYPD

You three make every novel I write a learning experience, a challenge and a triumph.

Additional thanks to:

Linda Foglia, NYS Department of Corrections, who took me through the policies, procedures and descriptions I needed to give my prison scenes authenticity.

Sharman Stein, New York City Department of Corrections, who got me started on the path to the Department of Corrections and pointed me in the right direction.

Former SA Richard DiFilippo, who came through for me at the onset and again in the final countdown.

My literary agents, Andrea Cirillo and Christina Hogrebe, who guided me through the hardest months of my life and acted as my "front line" so I could find what it took to create *The Stranger You Know.*

My editor, Paula Eykelhof, who jumped in with both feet, great faith and much enthusiasm and compassion.

My former editor, Miranda Indrigo, who started the process with me, and handed it over with grace and continued commitment.